Medieval
LORDS & LADIES
COLLECTION

Blackmail &
Betrayal

Juliet Landon & Elizabeth Henshall

M&B

*M&B™ and M&B™ with the Rose Device
are trademarks of the publisher.
Harlequin Mills & Boon Limited, Eton House,
18-24 Paradise Road, Richmond, Surrey TW9 1SR*

MEDIEVAL LORDS & LADIES COLLECTION
© Harlequin Books S.A. 2007

The publisher acknowledges the copyright holders of the
individual works as follows:

A Knight in Waiting © Juliet Landon 1995
Betrayed Hearts © Elizabeth Henshall 1996

ISBN: 978 0 263 85882 2

53-0807

*Printed and bound in Spain
by Litografia Rosés S.A., Barcelona*

A Knight in Waiting

by

Juliet Landon

Juliet Landon lives in an ancient country village in the north of England with her retired scientist husband. Her keen interest in embroidery, art and history, together with a fertile imagination, make writing historical novels a favourite occupation. She finds the research particularly exciting, especially the early medieval period and the fascinating laws concerning women in particular, and their struggle for survival in a man's world.

Chapter One

In spite of the sun's brightness and the gently warming rays on her back, Aletta noted that the grass was still white with frost here on the edge of the woodland. Her mount breathed out clouds of glittering whiteness which hung suspended in the still air; its hooves crunched on the crispy spikes of grass. She eased the sleeves of her woollen gown further over her knuckles and readjusted the basket in front of her on the saddle, smiling in anticipation at the forthcoming delight of its recipient.

Milk for the little one, yesterday's trenchers soaked in gravy, apples, soft cheese, newly baked oat bread and a whole cooked chicken.

Looking ahead, she saw the smoke from the tiny cott rising vertically above the trees, confirming that her orders to provide Verity with constant fuel had been obeyed. Only another field to cross, and then she could warm her hands by a crackling log fire. She urged the horse into a trot, listening to the dull thud of the hooves.

The gentle rhythm suddenly changed as the great head tossed, ears swivelled and pricked at the clear melodic note of a hunting horn sounding from the woodland beside her. Aletta frowned and pulled up sharply, her fingers gripping the reins in anger, for the sound had come from her own demesne. Now shouts could be heard, dogs yelping and baying among the crashing of undergrowth nearby, then another blast of the horn. Her frown deepened, and a spasm of rage shook her as she growled through her teeth.

"No! No, by the saints! Not this time. No matter *who* it is! I won't have it!"

Kicking her heels hard into the grey gelding, she left the headland and plunged into the open field. At that same moment, a terrified doe broke cover from the darkness of the trees and bounded towards her. Momentarily blinded by the bright sunlight, it checked and almost cannoned into the horse, and Aletta caught the flash of its huge eyes as it swerved across her path, its delicate legs braced against the turf to avoid collision, its winter coated grey-brown body taut with fear and lean muscles.

The gelding lurched to one side, startled to see a doe so close beneath its nose, and sent the basket of food hurtling through the air to land with a bounce on the hard ground, its contents spilling and scattering everywhere.

"Go on!" she yelled at the frightened creature, struggling to control the horse at the same time. "Go on! Go!"

With a flash of its white rump, it sped away across the field, and now Aletta turned her mount's head towards the gap in the trees where four huntsmen on foot were being dragged bodily along by eight yelping greyhounds, mouths agape and tongues lolling between slavering jaws.

Though she knew the dogs were fierce, her seething anger left no room for fear in her mind. Taking advantage of their surprise at being confronted by a horse and rider, of their disorientation in the bright light, she rode at them, with whip flailing about her on both sides, halting their pursuit.

Frantically ducking beneath her blows and warding off the long lash of her whip, the four huntsmen attempted to pull the precious hounds clear of the horse's hooves as it pranced sideways into them, knowing only too well that any injury to the valuable creatures would have far more serious consequences than any to themselves. Eight hounds took years to breed; men were cheap by comparison.

"Stop! Stop, all of you! Let it go! Get back, damn you!"

Her whip came down hard across the shoulders of the nearest grey-liveried huntsman, whose face registered alarm as he recognised his antagonist, though his preoccupation at that moment was not so much with the danger from her blows but of the hounds being injured, tangled as they were into a writhing knot of leather thongs and snarling teeth, their excitement frustrated and difficult to check.

The whip was raised again, ready to strike, as she noted that one man had freed himself and his hounds and was already looking across the fields for a sign of their lost quarry.

"No!" she yelled at him. "Don't you dare follow it!" Her arm was poised to add emphasis to her words, but she found that a sudden restraint prevented her from completing the blow, and she turned in anger to discover the reason for her sudden immobility. Holding fast to the thong of her whip was a man's gloved hand.

A deep and commanding voice cut through the din from a point behind her. "What the devil do you think you're doing, woman? By all the saints, are you mad?"

Aletta pulled again at her whip, still intent on lashing out, but found that she was in danger of being unseated by the resistance. Turning round in the saddle to see who spoke with such rude authority, she was briefly disconcerted to see that she was dwarfed by a powerful figure on a huge chestnut horse whose rolling eyes and clouds of snorting breath were uncomfortably close.

The rider was in full view now, a deep-chested man, whose sun-bronzed face registered anger as blazing as her own, his eyes glaring unflinchingly at her while she sought to rein her gelding back and to ease the unwelcome tension on her arm. It was clear that he had no intention of relinquishing the end of her whip, and, though she manoeuvred round him in a circle, his grip was inflexible.

Her eyes, narrowed in fury, now locked with his. "Let go of my whip, sir! How dare you hunt on my land? Let go, I say!" She tugged again, but the thong was held as though in a vice as the stranger's eyes held hers, still hostile.

"Don't dare me, woman, if you value your hide! And don't ever use a whip on my men or my hounds again, or by God I'll—"

"You'll *what*, sir? This is my land, and you're trespassing. I do not allow hunting on my land. Not by anyone. And least of all by strangers. Now, let go!" She pulled sharply, but though his eyes widened slightly in surprise his hand on the thong was as firm as ever, and she could see that he had wrapped it round his wrist to keep it under tension so that she was forced to extend her arm uncomfortably or move nearer.

"Your land?" He turned sharply in the saddle to look enquiringly at one of the other two mounted men behind him. One of them moved closer, and Aletta recognised him as Robert le Hare, the bailiff from the neighbouring manor of Allerton.

Robert spoke respectfully, and with concern. "This *is* the Lady Aletta's land, sir. I beg your pardon. There are no marked boundaries in this woodland." He glanced at Aletta, knowing the reasons behind her refusal to enclose her deer. "So the huntsmen ran on too far. They're none too familiar with these parts. My apologies, m'lady."

As the bailiff explained the stranger on the chestnut horse turned to her, eyeing her openly now but still obviously puzzled. "Lady Aletta…?" He frowned in disbelief.

"I am Lady Aletta Markenfield. *Now* do you understand?" Thinking to take him off-guard, she tugged again at her whip, but he ignored the gesture as though he hadn't felt it.

Instead, he coiled the thong slowly around his wrist, and by degrees Aletta was obliged to extend her arm towards him. His eyes glittered in obvious amusement at the flash of panic in her own. Instantly she dropped the leather-bound handle, and sent its silver knob swinging beneath his horse's belly while she wheeled her mount well away from the group, feeling that she was in some danger.

He laughed, a deep, soft chuckle of amazement. "So! The Widow of Netherstone! Well, well!" His gaze travelled slowly over her from head to toe.

As she turned her head away, Aletta saw that the hounds were now making light work of the chicken and savoury bread scattered in the grass, and that the milk jar was now lying empty on its side. She gasped in annoyance. All Verity's food, wasted on this stupid incident.

"Robert!" She looked at the bailiff. "Who is this…this person?" She tossed her head dismissively towards the stranger.

"Sir Geraunt de Paine, m'lady. Newly come to take up residence at Allerton."

"And this person," the deep voice cut in, "wants his deer back."

"My deer!" flared Aletta, glaring at him. "You're trespassing on my land and the deer belong to me."

"You can tell the difference between Allerton deer and Netherstone deer, can you? Remarkable." The voice was sardonic.

"Yes, I can! If it bolts out of the Allerton side, it's yours. If it comes out of the Netherstone side, it's mine. Simple!" She turned again to the Allerton bailiff. "You'll have to explain it to him, Robert. Choose simple words or…"

From the corner of her eye she sensed a movement of Sir Geraunt's horse towards her, and her words dried in mid-stream as the look in the stranger's eyes now signalled imminent danger. Fortunately, the tense moment was eased as all ears picked up the sound of galloping hooves on the hard ground and, as they turned, a horseman pulled up alongside Aletta. She whispered a silent prayer of relief and thanksgiving. Roger. Thank the saints. Trust him to be on hand when he was most needed.

Aletta's bailliff, Roger Holland, greeted her courteously, as though unaware of the antagonism hanging heavily over the group. "M'lady, I see you've already met our new neighbours!"

He made a short bow from the saddle towards Sir Geraunt, then to the younger man who, until now, had remained quietly in the background, staring with open admiration at Aletta. "Sir Geraunt. Master Willan. G'day, Robert." He grinned at his Allerton counterpart, already taking in the atmosphere after his assessment of the situation.

His ride across the fields towards the group had given him plenty of time to see the problem, and now Aletta's angrily flushed cheeks and flashing dark eyes verified this. He moved closer to her side as he greeted them, giving Aletta the chance to see her new neighbours from a safer distance.

In spite of the stares, she had already noted the stranger's authoritative manner and noble bearing, though his dress was ordinary enough. But the handsome head and powerful figure were, she felt, far from being ordinary. The thick, close-fitting cap of dark hair made a glossy frame for well-defined cheekbones and a strong jawline. Hazel eyes glittered with a disconcerting boldness under straight dark brows, emphasising the set line of his mouth and elegant nose. He sat erect and easily on his great horse, completely relaxed but in control, his long muscular legs in close contact with the creature's sides.

Aletta forced herself to quell an inward shiver, and in return for his bold, amused stare she sent him a look of unconcealed disdain.

Roger was doing his best to be diplomatic, to smooth

over the troubles. "Easy to mistake the land, m'lady. It's difficult enough for those of us who know it!" He laughed, looking for an acceptance of his efforts to Sir Geraunt, who nodded.

But Aletta refused to concede. She needed no reasons, no explanations, no gestures of friendship, for she was sure that this new neighbour would not have treated her quite so insolently had she been a man instead of a mere woman.

"Then you and Robert had better point them in the right direction and explain to them the difference between a royal forest and a private chase. With a little more effort, you might get him to overshoot his own manor and lose him for good!" The last parting shot was directed at Sir Geraunt, who received it with a slight nod of approval and a barely concealed glint of amusement.

But Roger was taken aback at her display of uncharacteristic rudeness. Even though she had been angered by the pursuit of the deer on her land, something about which she had very strong feelings, surely, he thought, this was taking things a little too far.

Truth to tell, Aletta herself was surprised by her own outburst of venom, and wheeled her horse away to hide the confusion in her eyes, leaving Roger to catch up in his own time.

Standing at her horse's head was the younger man, and she was obliged to stop. Like his brother, he was tall and well-built, and came to her side with a friendly smile, holding the basket and the remains of its contents up to her.

"Lady Aletta, please forgive the blunder. I do hope we shall meet as friendly neighbours before long. Allow me to present myself. Willan de Paine, at your service, m'lady." He bowed gracefully.

Aletta accepted the basket with a murmur of thanks and settled it once more on her lap. It was impossible to ignore his attempt at friendship and she was glad of the chance to show the better side of her nature so soon after her shrewishness the moment before. She gave him a smile in acknowledgement, and their eyes met briefly. He was as fair as his brother was dark, neatly bearded as opposed to Sir Geraunt's clean-shaven style, blue-eyed and handsome with the glow of youth, and obviously wishing to impress her with his gallantry.

"Thank you, Master Willan. Please think no more about it." She moved away without another glance at the company, except to note that Sir Geraunt had made no similar move towards her, and it was with a vague and transitory pang of regret that Aletta was denied a chance to rebuff any attempt on his part to follow his brother's act of appeasement with one of his own.

Instead, she was forced to hear Sir Geraunt's parting shot directed at Roger, though she understood only too well that he was paying her back in her own coin.

"Make sure she has an escort next time she's allowed out, Bailiff. She could get into serious trouble one day... Might even be mistaken for a vixen!"

Before the hapless Roger could respond, Aletta whirled round, outrage written clearly on her face. "Take care of your words, sir! I need no lessons from you about my movements—"

A hearty bellow cut off the rest of her words. "I wouldn't be too sure of that, my lady, if I were you. Come on, lad, stop gawking and let's be off," he called to his brother, indicating that he should remount. "Let her go, boy. We've more important matters to deal with right now. Move them on, Robert. Let's go!"

He moved over sideways to Aletta's bailiff and nodded in the direction of her receding back. "I wonder you're not wearing a full suit if armour, man!" Then, laughing still, he turned and followed the men and hounds into the woods, twirling the heavy handle of the whip about his head and allowing the thong to wind around his wrist.

Roger was nothing if not completely loyal, and nothing

would have induced him to comment on the actions of his mistress to a stranger, though he understood only too well the look of mixed admiration and awe in Sir Geraunt's eyes and the implicit challenge in his words. What he was not quite so sure of was Aletta's overreaction to this man, their new neighbour.

Her usual reaction to men was to keep well out of their way as much as possible and to exhibit her boredom with them at most other times. He had never seen her anger and rudeness so flagrantly displayed at a first meeting. Was her patience wearing thin? he wondered. She had made constant efforts to make her wishes known to the late Sir Hubert's cronies, who still descended upon the place in droves whenever the fancy took them, hunting her woodland in spite of its unsuitability and her express wishes to the contrary.

Aletta heard the thud of Roger's horse's hooves as he caught up with her before she reached Verity's cott. ''I must take what's left of this, Roger,'' she said, without looking at him. ''Will you go on up to the manor? I'll see you there.''

''No, m'lady.''

''What?'' She turned to face him and searched his eyes reluctantly, knowing that this refusal must signify his concern at her earlier outburst. ''What do you mean, no?''

''I mean, I'll wait outside for you.''

''Oh Lord, Roger!'' she said in exasperation. ''Not you, too. For pity's sake, I'm not going to let that…that *person* dictate the way I do things. I don't need an escort in my own village. Go on home!''

''No, m'lady. I'm staying here.''

''Roger…?'' She tried to imply anger, a threat, but the twinkle in her eye responded to his expression of mulish unconcern at her protestations, and she shook her head in silent laughter. They drew up outside the tiny cottage, its low thatch decorated with tiny icicles along the lower edge, and for a moment they both sat in silence, looking at the place, a haven and a refuge steeped in memories.

Roger spoke. "Go on. I saw what happened to the chicken and things. Tell her I'll send some more down to her before nightfall. That's a promise. But hurry up, or there won't be time."

Aletta dismounted and went inside. She was glad that Roger was with her, here of all places, for he knew, better than many of the other villagers, of Verity's plight. Furthermore, after the recent events of the afternoon, she felt in need of his calm support. He was the only one of her servants who would dare to disobey her.

Roger tied up the horses and went to break the ice on the water-butt, thinking back to the time, just two years ago, when the first thing Aletta had done after her husband's sudden death was to find Verity, her young maid, whom the sixty-seven year old Sir Hubert had abused and eventually got with child. Naturally he had disclaimed all responsibility, and when the poor girl and her family had been unable to pay her leyrwite—the fine imposed by the lord on an unchaste serf—he had thrown her and her newly born child out of the village to fend for themselves as beggars.

Roger shuddered at the memory of the man, at the thought of his contact with Aletta—his well-known brutality to her, too. That he should have fined a fourteen-year-old lass for being the target of his own lust and then thrown her out of her own home like a worn out rag was beyond belief, but his had been a history of depravity, culminating in his marriage to Aletta when she was an innocent woman of some fifteen summers. The marriage had lasted seven and a half years, mercifully brought to an end by his death just over two years ago.

Roger had stayed with Sir Hubert's household as bailiff for ten years now, his unspoken love for Aletta, and his wish to serve and protect her taking precedence over his loathing for his abominable master.

He jabbed viciously at the thick ice with a stout pole. Aletta had cared for Verity since finding her an empty cott close to the village, taking her food and supplies, arranging for fuel to be cut for her, bread to be baked, clothes to be donated. Those who knew were happy to make her comfortable, aware that this was a balm to Aletta's bruised soul. Their charity to the young mother was an expression of their love and regard for their lady.

He filled two wooden pails with the ice-cold water and placed them by the door, along with a stack of wood, and untied the horses just as Aletta emerged. "If you'll take the reins, m'lady, I'll put these inside."

Soon they were heading back to the village, the dramatic events of the afternoon still uppermost in their minds. Roger waited for her to speak, knowing that he might have some explaining to do, for it had been clear that he'd known of the arrival of the de Paines before she had. However, it was not a question which began the conversation, but a revelation.

"Roger! He's taken my whip!"

"What?"

"My whip! He took it!"

"You mean, he took it off you?"

"Yes." Suddenly the voice was subdued.

Roger looked at her sideways, noting the stony face. "How did he do that?" His mouth twitched.

There was a silence while she tried to form the words to explain the undignified tussle to her bailiff. "Well, he caught the end of it and…there was a…kind of…tug-of-war. And he won," she finished lamely.

Their sideways looks met each other, igniting a grin from him, quickly followed by one from her too. "Yes, I can well imagine that," said Roger. "Are you going to go over and ask him to return it?" Aletta's look was so loaded with

contempt for the idea that he could not contain his already
bubbling mirth.

"Brute! You approve, don't you? Admit it!"

"Well, m'lady, it's a brave man who'll try to disarm *you*
in mid-rage. Approval? I don't know. But admiration, certainly." His eyes, grey and twinkling, looked straight
ahead, while he rubbed his nose with the back of a brown,
muscular hand.

"Huh! How did you come to know of their arrival?"

"Robert told me only the other day, and I told Oswald
yesterday. I'm surprised he didn't pass on the news to
you."

"Oswald's getting old and forgetful, Roger. I think in
future you'd better pass information on to me personally.
But remember to tell Oswald too," she added, "I don't
want him to think we can manage without him."

That was typical of her concern for her servants, thought
Roger, glancing at her lovely profile, at the dark brown
glossy hair piled in disarray on top of her head, her wimple
in a heap around her neck.

The old steward, Oswald Freeman, and he had been
largely responsible for ensuring the continuity of manorial
policy during Aletta's first two years as sole mistress—
policies which she had tried hard to improve on, both for
herself and the villagers alike. Oswald, a man of gentle
birth, able and efficient, was now old, and his duties were
falling more and more into Aletta's own hands, a none too
satisfactory state of affairs, since Aletta owned the nearby
village of Ellerby too, and all the surrounding lands. Far
too much responsibility for one young woman, Roger
thought.

"Why have we seen nothing of them until now, do you
think?"

"Well, Robert and his reeve had been looking after
things between them, with a reduced household. But the
last time the lord lived there was well before your time,

m'lady. Sir Geraunt's father wouldn't live there as a neigh-bour of Sir Hubert Markenfield—they quarrelled, you know.''

''Quarrelled? What about, Roger?''

''I don't know,'' he lied, hoping she'd move on to an-other topic.

Aletta looked at his honest, glowing face, tanned from the air and sun of the wild hillsides, and knew that he would never be able to lie to her successfully. He knew it too. ''You do know, don't you?'' she said.

''I know some of it.''

''Well?''

''It was about a wench, I believe. I don't know the de-tails. Honestly.''

She nodded in silence, deep in thought. She might have guessed. ''You mean, Sir Geraunt's father was like that too?''

''Oh, no. He most certainly was not. No, it was to do with some marriage negotiations. They kept it all very quiet, but the old man died round about the same time as Sir Hubert. Their old steward was about the same age as old Oswald, and he only got up here about once or twice a year. Their estates are much larger and more scattered than yours, m'lady, so he only did the yearly audit, and he didn't do that very efficiently either.''

''Yes, I knew he was inefficient.'' They exchanged looks, both of them knowing the significance attached to her words.

''But the bad news is—''

''Bad news? What?'' She looked at him sharply.

''The old steward's been replaced, and now there's a new one in his place. According to Robert, he's already turning the place inside out to make it profitable again.''

Aletta reined the grey gelding to a halt and looked pen-sively at the sun, now like a golden orange suspended over the tops of the trees. Roger stopped too, seeing the large, dark-lashed eyes grow troubled and wide with apprehension.

"You realise what that means, Roger?" she said.

"Yes. I thought you ought to know that things've changed."

They had reached the bottom of the hill which led up to the manor of Netherstone, perched high up on the crag overlooking the village and the surrounding countryside. It was from there that Roger had witnessed the doe's escape and the resulting fracas with the de Paines' huntsmen.

Aletta sat rigid in the saddle. Clearly she was uneasy at Roger's news. "Is he living there with them, Roger?"

"Who? The new steward? Yes, I believe so. Well, for the time being, anyway. Look," he said to her consolingly, "don't start worrying. They'll have plenty of other things to attend to before they start counting men, and by that time it probably won't matter, anyway."

"Won't matter? What do you mean?"

He smiled and jerked his head towards home. "Come on," he said, "Verity won't get her food tonight unless we hurry. It's going to be dark soon." He allowed her to go before him up the steep track, half regretting that he'd mentioned the de Paines' new steward. As though she didn't have enough to worry about, running things more or less single-handed, and so efficiently too.

Roger had known Robert le Hare for many years. Being bailiffs of adjoining estates, it was common enough for them to meet and exchange news regularly. Both were thirty-two years old, though Robert was married with a growing family, and over the years there had been many times when they had sought each other's co-operation over the management of their masters' estates. It was therefore not surprising that each should know a good deal about the other's affairs and should choose whether or not it was in their masters' interests that they should be told.

The late Sir Hubert Markenfield's unreasonable brutishness had, however, been common knowledge, for it had affected everyone with whom he came into contact to a greater or lesser degree. As a close member of the household, Roger had been more aware than most of the man's treatment of Aletta, aware and yet powerless to help as he watched her life being wasted and made miserable, day by day, month by month. Now, at last, she was mercifully free of him, and the load of despair and darkness had lifted from the household like sunshine after a violent storm.

To serve Aletta was Roger's sole purpose in life, though he took care to see that his devotion caused her no embarrassment. As a free man, of good birth and education, he was intelligent enough to understand that she regarded him only as a trusted friend and servant. But he was human enough to have been secretly relieved when the rejection of the many suitors to her hand—and to her property—was consistent and unrelenting. He had little doubt that this had much to do with her unfortunate experiences at the hands of Sir Hubert. Indeed, even her household thought so, though they all agreed that it was a waste, her being so beautiful and all.

As for Aletta, remarriage was a constantly recurring theme in her life, though only as a state to be avoided at all costs, in spite of the tremendous pressures which were brought to bear on widows—particularly those with youth, beauty, property and money. Her jointure and her dower, together with the inheritance from her deceased parents, had left her able to keep hold of her home and two villages, though she would have been even better off if her unbusinesslike late husband had managed his estate more efficiently.

In the last two years the door had seldom been free of unwelcome suitors, many of them the late Sir Hubert's aged and uncouth friends on the look-out for more land to add to their own. A beautiful widow with money and property was a rich prize indeed, even if she was so far up in the dales that any town seemed a lifetime's journey away. But, not unnaturally, Aletta was happy to remain free of the unbearable constraints of marriage. No tyranny, no more beatings or maulings, no more days of fear or loathing.

Two years of comparative peace, marred only by the thought that she would never hold her own babe in her arms, nor bury her face against an infant's downy head and smell its warm, sweet babyness. To be a childless widow was a price she'd chosen to pay for her freedom, though there'd been times, especially recently, when she'd felt that the price of freedom was exceptionally high.

As the young groom led away the horses, Aletta's two maids rushed down the outer stone steps from her solar, anxious to know the outcome of her earlier encounter on the edge of the woodland which by now, it seemed, was the talking-point of the manor.

''Bridie, have another basket made up for Verity, if you please, then let Roger have it. But hurry, the light's going already.''

''Another basket?'' The pretty young maid looked perplexed.

''Yes, I'll tell you why later. Go!''

With a quick peep at Roger from beneath her eyelashes, the maid scurried off towards the kitchen buildings, and Aletta entered the warm peace of her home. For some reason, the idea of recounting her adventure held an appeal which she couldn't explain.

Chapter Two

The news of the de Paines' determination to redress the inefficiencies of their previous steward and to attend more diligently to manorial matters had caused a flutter of alarm in Aletta's breast which refused to go away during the following days.

She would have preferred to push the hunting incident out of her mind altogether, for heaven knew there was enough to occupy every waking moment, and to ensure a sleep of exhaustion every night. Suddenly it seemed as though a dark cloud had appeared on the horizon of her hopes, bringing with it the threat of storms and possible damage unless she could either run for cover or pray that it would blow over.

''They'll have plenty of other things to attend to before they start counting men'' was what Roger had said, hoping to allay her fears, no doubt. But it hadn't. For Aletta knew as well as he that one of the first things a diligent steward would do would be to make a correct tally of all the men in his lord's villages—their ages, their possessions, land and dues, their sons and their tithings.

The tithings were groups of ten, to which every man over the age of twelve summers must belong. The bigger the village, the more tithings. Each man in the tithing was held to be responsible for the good behaviour of the other, and heavy fines were exacted by the lord if a man was found not to belong to such a group, or if any man went missing from one without permission.

The revolutionary changes which Aletta had made to her own two villages of Netherstone and Ellerby in the last two years had attracted the attention of villeins from surrounding areas, so much so that, one by one, they had crept into the empty dwellings left by those who'd died in the great pestilence several years ago. Quite unlawfully they had begun to work their newly acquired lands, paying rent to Aletta without question, working for payment when required, and secretly praying that no one would discover their whereabouts until it was too late to take action or until their lord lost interest in their cases.

Aletta's newly adopted system of rent-work was in direct opposition to other landowners in the area, who still tied their villeins to the land and made demands on their time and energies which they were learning to resent.

Naturally, some of those who had fled their village were Allerton men, belonging to the de Paines, and though Aletta had merely closed her eyes to settlers from other more remote villages, and asked no questions, those who had left Allerton without permission had presented a rather different case, in which Aletta's collusion had been requested.

This had all been simple enough, she reflected uneasily, when the steward had been so inept and the bailiff powerless without the direct intervention of his lord, but now, it seemed things were about to change.

The more she thought about it, the more entangled her fears became. Most of all, in the quiet emptiness of her large bed at night, a dark-framed face came to disrupt her sleep, a face she tried hard to replace with a fair and friendly one, but which insisted on returning to haunt her with fierce eyes.

* * *

"Can you spare a moment, m'lady?"

Roger intercepted Aletta on her way through the hall, her arms piled high with white linen sheets for her solar. Stalks of dried lavender had been placed on top, and she was attempting to keep them from rolling off with her chin. She laughed as Roger removed the sheets from her arms and laid them on one of the trestles.

"Yes, of course. You've been with Oswald and Jem?"

He nodded. "With Oswald, anyway. Jem hasn't appeared yet."

They sat on benches on each side of the trestle. The daily meetings were usually attended by bailiff, steward and reeve, and quite often by Aletta too, especially since Oswald's lessening abilities, but today she'd had other household duties.

"Have you had all the rents in now, Roger?"

He patted the accounts book before him. "Yes. Adam Beck and his family have just paid theirs, seven days late after Lady Day. But you did give him extra time, if you remember?"

"I do remember. Is his wife still ailing, after the birth?"

"No, she and the babe are well now, after the extra food you sent down." He smiled at her relief.

"Keep an eye on them, won't you, Roger?" She could tell that he had some news for her, for there was a knowing air about him this morning. "What is it? You know something, don't you?"

He gave a quick laugh of embarrassment and sat back from the trestle, wondering if he would ever be able to keep anything from her. Ever. "It's about Widow Margery."

"Margery atte Welle? Down at Middlestone? She hasn't…?"

"No, no, m'lady. She hasn't died. Much more interesting than *that*. She's moved out of the manor and into a smaller property on the estate."

"Moved out? You mean she's surrendered it?"

"Surrendered it, yes. More or less everything."

A hand flew to her breast as she felt a pang of sympathy for the recently widowed old lady, a dear soul of much wisdom and kindness. "Was it all too much for her?" she asked quietly.

"Well, I don't know about that, but apparently she's quite happy about the arrangement. She's being well provided for. Got everything she wants, according to Robert." He knew the name would rebound.

"Robert? You mean the Allerton bailiff? What does he know about it?" There was a pause, just long enough for her to deduce the answer to her own question. "No. Don't tell me. I can guess. It's *them,* isn't it? They've moved her out, haven't they? Did they put pressure on her?"

"Steady." Roger was almost laughing at her passionate reaction. He'd known she'd not be unaffected by the news, after her encounter with the two brothers recently. "They haven't got horns, you know!"

She brought her hand down emphatically on the pile of sheets, making the lavender stalks jump. "*Did* they, Roger?"

"No," he said, serious now, "apparently not. They didn't need to. They offered her everything she wanted to the end of her days, so Roberts says. And she's content that it's now back in the owner's hands again."

"Content!" Aletta spat the word out in disbelief, leaning back and swinging her long legs over to the other side of the bench.

With her back to him, Roger could not see the look on her face, but he had no need to. Instead he savoured the view of her shoulders as she leaned on one elbow.

"Do you believe that?" she said over her shoulder. "After all those years as lady of the manor?"

"Yes, I believe it. Things don't stay the same," he said to the back of her head. "People have different needs as they get older." She turned to look at him as he spoke gently. "You should know that as well as anyone."

There was a silence as their eyes met, and Aletta digested a piece of truth few would have been allowed to offer.

Her voice was more subdued now. "Who's there now? It's to be young Master Willan's, I suppose?"

"No. Not Master Willan. He's still a squire and hopes to be knighted before long. Then he'll do service for the King for a time. No, it's been rented to a newly married couple, friends of Sir Geraunt's, Sir Thomas Newman and his lady. They're to take over the whole of the Middlestone estate and farm it."

Aletta leaned forward now, her arms on the trestle-table, her body twisted along the bench. "Roger, you realise what this means, don't you?" Her look of deep concern could not fail to move him.

"I know what you think it means, but with respect, m'lady, I believe you're mistaken. There's no reason to suppose Sir Geraunt's got his eyes on every woman's property, just because he's resumed possession of his Middlestone estate."

"But you know what pressure one is under in this position. The very thought of a widow managing her own estate is more than most men can bear." She looked away angrily.

The memory of the streams of acquisitive suitors since her husband's death was uppermost in her mind, grasping, unintelligent, pathetic little creatures, all of them. Not one of them had known as much about running a manor successfully as she did, nor about how to woo a woman gallantly either, it had seemed. Well, if the de Paines had any grand ideas about her estate, they could forget them. She had no doubt that they would make enquiries about her efficiency, but let them. She'd already shown them what she was made of. Let that be a lesson!

"Jem!" Roger's voice took on a tone of authority which

made the hall servants cease their chatter as they prepared the hall for the meal.

Jem stood inside the screens opening and looked round for the direction of the voice, then, seeing Aletta and Roger, strode towards them. Jem the Reeve was a burly man, young, good-natured and popular, though his duties as overseer had been diminished since land and manorial duties had been reallocated in the last two years. Still, there were many advantages, and he'd been re-elected for the past five years now, and had even adopted his name of employment.

"Where've you been?" Roger asked him curtly.

"Beg pardon, Master Holland. M'lady." He touched his forelock and signalled to his lurcher to stay to heel. "Sorry I'm late. There were a problem down on t'road, and I didn't really 'ave no choice but to 'elp."

"What problem?" Roger signalled for him to sit down.

"Well, I were coming up from t' Middlestone end ert village, an' then on t'other road, coming down from Allerton, were this wagon wi' its cover come loose. Well, I felt I 'ad to go an' elp, sir. That's why I'm late." He looked at Aletta for understanding.

"This wagon… Whose was it? D'you know?" She tried to sound uninterested, but Roger was not deceived by the tone.

"No, m'lady. I never asked. But there were a lovely lady in it… Expectin' too, she was. An' 'er 'usband ridin' alongside."

"The man on the horse—what did he look like?" She couldn't help it, though she saw Roger watching her. But she had to know, and it was too late to withdraw the question now.

"He were dark, m'lady. Tall chap. Powerful, like."

So. It must have been him, going off somewhere with a lovely pregnant wife. Well, now she could stop thinking and put the whole thing out of her mind. A tiny sigh escaped her, and she turned away to avoid Roger's eyes.

But he didn't need to see her face to read her mind, for he had caught the drift of her innocent-sounding questions, as would any man in love. He also knew that whoever the lady in the wagon had been it had certainly not been Sir Geraunt's wife, for according to Robert he had no wife. Come to that, the man on the horse could have been anyone. Jem's description had been brief enough. But if Aletta wanted to clutch at straws for her temporary peace of mind, he would not reconstruct the picture for her.

She picked up the bundle of linen and stood, poised once more. Then she turned to Roger. "The new paling. Did you see to it, Roger?"

So, she did have them in mind, he thought. "Yes. Jem had it put up, didn't you, Jem?"

"Aye, sir. Right across the woodland, from one side to t'other. We spent three days at it. There's no deer'll get through *that*—nor nobody else, neither. Not wi' that owd ditch in front of it, an' all. Not now!"

"Good," said Aletta, turning to the staircase in the corner of the hall. "Good! Now there'll be no mistake."

The temptation to see for herself was overwhelming. It was almost as though she regretted having to erect a barrier and yet felt that it must be inspected for strength and reliability. It must be obvious to all who came across it that it was new, impregnable, and a symbol of intent. Aletta hoped that the de Paines would see it before too long, mark it, be warned by it. And yet, for the deer's sake, it was a pity, for it now restricted their freedom and made the hunting of them easier for everyone.

Strangely, there was almost a feeling of trespass now, since that ridiculous incident. Whereas at one time she had felt equally at ease, whether in her own territory or in Allerton's, now she was wary, checking the air for sounds that anyone was about. She resented her reaction, but curiosity to see what the boundary looked like drove her on.

In the clearings snowdrops clustered thickly under the gelding's hooves, and the tiny wood-anemones, primroses and lilies-of-the-valley fell in swathes through the thick undergrowth. Reaching the rough and rocky ground, she dismounted, and followed the pathway beaten down by the sleds which had drawn the stakes for the wattle fences. Even a week's growth had not yet covered it over.

Leading the grey by the reins, she moved deeper into the wood, the bright noon-day sun playing hide-and-seek with her through the tops of the larches, and at last the stakes of new wood, the palings, began to show clearly through the greenery.

She moved up carefully, listening every now and again for calls from men gathering wood, goosegirls, swineherds, shepherds, but all was still.

It had been well-made, deeply embedded, with stout timber and firmly-woven wattle lathes.

The gelding was now finding it impossible to follow her, for the ground was steep here, and he was slipping and slithering dangerously on the rocky surfaces. She tied his reins to a low tree and gave him a pat before moving along the fence. Only a little further along, however, a gap appeared, where stakes had been wrenched out of the ground and removed completely.

Aletta groaned inwardly and shook her head. Oh no, she thought, not already. Surely not. They only had to ask me for timber. But, to some, stealing was more fun than asking, a way of getting even with authority, and she wondered if Allerton villeins might be responsible, rather than those from Netherstone.

She passed through the gap to the other side, looking to see if any tracks led away through the new grass. But here the bank sloped downwards much more steeply, and the palings had been erected on top of the old established earthworks, now covered with primroses and vetch. In an instant her feet began to slip from under her, and she was obliged to choose whether to slide down it on her bottom or to run full-tilt and hope that she could stay upright.

Before she could decide, she was moving. She almost flew down the steep grassy bank, falling flat on to her face on the wide base of the ditch. Winded and annoyed by her fall, she rolled over on to her back and lay staring up at the sky dappled by leaves, waiting for a moment to recover. At last she flung out an arm to feel at the cool primroses and sat up slowly, brushing the bits from her woollen bodice and sleeves.

"Are you dead, or just resting?" The deep voice brought her bolt-upright in fright, her heart nearly leaping from her chest. Only a few paces away from her further along the ditch, and looking at her in amusement, was Sir Geraunt de Paine, hands on hips and feet apart.

For a moment she was speechless, disbelief and shock plainly written in her eyes. And then she moved. In a bound, she leapt to her feet and on to the steep bank in a frantic effort to reach the top and go through the gap, but in two strides of his long legs he had reached her, closed an iron grip around one ankle and slowly but firmly pulled her downwards on her front, until once again she came to rest at the bottom of the slope. She rolled, and kicked at him frantically, pulling with her imprisoned leg against his grip, but he laughingly refused to relax it for an instant, watching her fury as he sat on the bank in a bed of primroses.

"No, you don't, my lady! Now it's my turn! The doe can leap in, you see, but not out again. Effective, isn't it?" His laughter infuriated her.

"Let me go! Let me *go!*" She kicked again, panic now replacing her anger, for it was clear he was going to make full use of his superior strength.

"What was it you told me, Lady Aletta Markenfield of

Netherstone Manor? If the deer leap out of the Netherstone side, they're yours. If they bolt out of the Allerton side, they're mine. Simple, you said. Well, you see, I've understood. Now. What's all the fuss about?''

Aletta's heart was pounding with fright. Still lying on her front, she tried to pull herself along, using her hands and elbows, but he let her get so far and then pulled her back again, chuckling. Her head fell on to her hands, her hair now uncoiled and falling in glossy tendrils around her face as she turned to look at him over her shoulder.

He appeared to be taller than when she'd last seen him on horseback, broad-shouldered and powerfully muscular. He wore a short leather jerkin over a soft woollen chainse, the sleeves rolled up to his elbows in the warm spring sunshine. His long legs were encased in close-fitting chausses of russet-brown and soft leather riding-boots. But it was his face which held her attention, taunting and handsome, his eyes like two darkly glittering lines, watching for her next move.

''Are you going to let me go?'' She pulled again, but to no avail. ''Or are you going to keep me here forever?''

''Only until you've paid your forfeit. Then I'll reconsider.''

''Forfeit?'' She turned and rested on her elbows, searching his face. This was beginning to sound vaguely sinister. Did he mean to revenge himself for her scathing words to him on their first meeting? she wondered. ''Forfeit? What do you mean?'' she whispered, her eyes widening in alarm.

''Have you forgotten, Lady Aletta, that I forfeited my deer…?''

''*My* deer! It was mine, and you were on my land.'' She kicked against his knee viciously, but he moved before it made contact and continued as though she'd not spoken.

''I forfeited my deer when I trespassed accidentally on your land. Now *you're* trespassing, accidentally of course, on mine, and I'm waiting to hear what you intend to forfeit.''

His face was more serious now, and Aletta searched his eyes for the meaning behind his words. They held hers steadily, unwavering and unfathomable. This was beyond her control now, and frightening. A feeling all too familiar. Two years was barely long enough to blot out the memory of Sir Hubert's methods of revenge—the beatings, the fearsome abuse. Surely this could not happen to her again?

Exhausted and afraid, she flopped over on to her front and spoke into her hands. ''Let go of my foot, please. It's hurting.''

He picked up her other ankle and put down the one he'd been holding. ''Is that better?''

''No.''

''The forfeit,'' he reminded her.

There was a silence as she thought of the possibilities. If only she knew what his real intentions were, she could play the same game. She struck her right hand out, sideways. ''Well, you could chop off my right hand, I suppose. Or would you prefer my left?''

He shook his head solemnly at her as she peeped round over her shoulder. ''No, I think not.'' His mouth twitched as he controlled a smile.

''My horse? My favourite grey gelding?''

''No. I have one already.''

''For your wife, then?''

''Who?''

''Your wife.''

''I have no wife, thank heaven.''

''But I thought—''

''The forfeit! Stick to the point.''

Aletta growled, and pulled again at her captured foot, hoping to break his grasp in a moment of preoccupation, but he laughed and merely pulled her skirt down into place to hide her exposed legs. The tiny gesture gave her hope.

Such concern for her appearance, however small, could surely not imply dishonourable intentions. She wondered if an appeal to his honour might have some effect, though it went against the grain to appeal to him at all.

"Sir Geraunt?"

"I'm still waiting."

"Has this not gone far enough now? I don't know what it is you want. Though if it's revenge, you've surely had it now in good measure, have you not?"

The foot was gently lowered to the ground and the grip relaxed at last. Aletta turned quickly, ready to bound up and away before he could reconsider, but before she could rise he was closely above her, his arms on each side of her shoulders, pushing her backwards with his body. She gave a cry of fright and surprise, and lurched to one side, but he was quick, and though she heaved with all her strength against his shoulders, she was pinned beneath him, helplessly outmatched.

Her fury at her misinterpretation of the signs lent her courage, and she fought with every ounce of strength she could muster. But it was not enough; her hands were held easily away, and he was hard and lean, enjoying every moment of her struggle. Eventually she lay still, exhausted and trembling, hardly able to believe what was happening to her.

She saw his face above her, no more than a breath away, his eyes looking deeply into hers, hazel flecked with green and dark-lashed, not angry eyes, nor cruel, but amused.

"Now, m'lady. If you really don't know what it is I want, I shall have to explain. Simply."

She recognised his jibe. "No, please don't," she whispered, turning her head away.

"Why?" His mouth brushed against her chin. She could feel the firmness of his lips and see the dark hair above his ears as her eyes closed. "Why?" he insisted. "Because you're afraid? Is that it?'' He had recognised the fear in her dark eyes.

Yes, she was afraid, but she would not tell him so. ''No, I'm not afraid,'' she said against his ear, feeling the thick, crispy hair beneath her lips. It smelt cool and fresh, not sour with the odour of sweat she was used to associating with a man, and for one moment she allowed herself to experience the gentle weight of his thighs over hers, his shoulders on her breasts. This was not as she remembered it; frightening, it was, but not terrifying.

Now he released her hands and moved his warm fingers to her throat, turning her face towards him. Her throat constricted and he felt the spasm of fear under his hand as she waited and braced herself for the familiar assault, trembling and wide-eyed. Then, slowly, his lips moved teasingly along her jawline and across her mouth, surprising her with their tenderness, and as his hand moved up into her hair she lay motionless, captivated by the unexpected sensations flooding through her.

Expertly, his lips teased a response from hers, insisting on her participation, reminding her that she must give, just as he was taking. In all her years of marriage she had never been kissed like this, not once. Tenderly, and without a pause, his lips moved over hers, closing her eyes with skilful sweetness, pushing her resistance far out of reach, enclosing her in a cocoon of timeless perceptions.

At last he raised his head and looked at her, revelling briefly in her loveliness, her vulnerability beneath the former fury, her fear and innocence of the joys of lovemaking. She was obviously a stranger to tenderness, he thought, watching her eyes open to reveal the wonderment beneath.

He smiled at her. ''Now, Aletta Markenfield, I believe the score is almost equal.''

''Was that the forfeit? Am I free to go now?''

''That was half of the forfeit.'' He could not resist the temptation to make it last longer, for he felt that she'd only just made a personal discovery, and, for that matter, so had he.

"Please, I don't want this to happen."

He smiled again and she felt his shoulders bunch beneath her hands as his thumb brushed gently across her lips. "I think you do, m'lady. I think you do."

A hot surge of excitement flooded downwards into the depths of her body and on into her thighs as he lowered his head to hers again.

He felt her hands moving over his shoulders, clutching at him as he slipped one hand beneath her back to caress the long curve hollowing above the grass. He heard her cry of alarm beneath his lips, felt her body stiffen and then soften again as she lost herself once more to his demands.

The longings of her body, for so long suppressed, welled up into the kiss. All the years of desolation, despair and misuse, the aching, the bruising, the loneliness and the craving, all came together under the canopy of his firm body, the trees and the spring sunshine.

The kiss lasted an eternity, for he was not dismayed by her reaction. It merely verified what he'd already suspected. At the same time he did not press his advantage, knowing that this was neither the time nor the place for more than this.

Suddenly it was too much for her. Her moan became a soft whimper as she tore her mouth away and turned her face into the palm of his hand. Here she was, paying a forfeit to a stranger, a neighbouring enemy, at the bottom of a ditch, when she'd told herself over and over that she'd never want to know a man again. Never.

She shook her head violently, angrily, unwilling to allow her body to savour this new experience any longer, forcing herself to recall the picture of Sir Geraunt on his huge chestnut horse, pulling at the thong of her whip, goading her to rudeness and now taking his revenge, treating her like some country trollop for his pleasure.

His experience told him that she'd be angry, that though her body had responded to him as a woman hungry for loving, her common sense was already chastising her for this and urging her to retaliate as best she could. All the same, he would dictate the pace of its conclusion.

Aletta heaved against him, and spoke into his hand against her face. "Let me go now. I've paid your forfeit. Let me go!"

"When I'm ready."

"Please!" She turned to him more desperately now. "Please, they'll come looking for me if I'm not back soon. I *must* go. Sir Geraunt. Please!"

He took her chin in his hand and kissed her again, while she wondered if he was going to ignore her plea or free her. Then he lifted himself from her and stood in one smooth movement, holding out his hands. She was pulled upright, shaking now, confused and weak after her struggles, her legs aching and useless.

She strove to regain her composure as he held her, not daring to look at him, knowing that his eyes were upon her, and then she turned to brush the grass and debris from her gown, stumbling against him as she adjusted her fine leather boots. He caught her and held her as she bent, removing wisps of dried grass from her hair when she stood silently before him again.

"Do you subject all trespassers to this kind of treatment, sir?" she snarled.

"I settle all scores in the appropriate manner, whatever that happens to be."

"And you think that *that* was appropriate, do you?"

"Very!"

"Then you'd better make certain no one else falls down into your ditch, sir. Otherwise you might be tumbling the forester, the charcoal-burner, the swine—"

"Enough, vixen! It didn't take long for you to find your tongue, though, did it? I thought I'd silenced you once."

With a grin, he pulled her to him once more. "Come, let's try it again, and I'll see if I can manage it better."

"Stop! Let me go, damn you!" Aletta pushed at his chest, now coldly angry at his tone. "I'm not one of your house-wenches to be pawed at so, nor do I see this as a game in the way that you obviously do. Allow me to replace my wimple and leave me be, sir!"

The linen had fallen into folds and now lay knotted around her shoulders, and while he stood with hands on hips, watching her efforts to find the knot, she grew increasingly annoyed at her failure. She was surprised when her fingers, fumbling into the folds at the back of her neck, touched his warm ones and discovered that he'd taken it upon himself not only to untangle her, but to replace the wimple deftly and knowingly. When she would have taken it from him, he told her to stand still. And so she did, obediently.

Puzzled at his change of role, she watched his face as he arranged the folds of linen carefully around her neck once more and stood back to see its effect. She was even more puzzled when he took a clean kerchief from his leather pouch, bunched it up, licked it and took her chin in his free hand. She flinched away but he caught her arm.

"Stand still! You don't want to be seen with grass-stains on your face."

And, with her head held firmly in his grasp, she stood quietly as he wiped her cheeks, nose and forehead, feeling for all the world like a child with an irate parent.

"Well?" he said almost brusquely, releasing her.

"Thank you," she whispered, now totally perplexed.

He nodded at her. "You're learning, vixen. Now, come!" And he led her towards the steep bank.

Pulled to the top of the bank by his strong hands, she turned to indicate where the palings had been removed. "Sir Geraunt, I came here to see the new palings, but now look." She waved a hand at the holes where they'd been.

"Yes, I saw it too. You needn't have gone to this trouble. I know it's many years since there was a fence across here. My father didn't even bother to observe a Fence Month in midsummer. Nor did your late husband."

Aletta looked at him sharply. "You know? I thought you were a stranger to these parts."

"Stranger? I was born here, wench. You're the stranger."

"Born here? So you know the land…the woodland."

"Like the back of my hand. Better than you. Come, where's your horse?"

"I'll have the gap mended. Roger will—"

"No!" He interrupted. "Leave it! These woods have never been suitable for hunting, except on foot. Let the deer pass freely, as they've always done."

There seemed to be no more to say. There was no time to ask him about his reasons for pursuing deer on to her land, nor did she want to strike up polite conversation with him at this point, still smouldering as she was from his high-handed treatment of her.

He unhitched the gelding from the tree and signalled to her. "Come on, up in the saddle."

"No. I shall walk. I can see the rough ground more easily that way. It's very rocky further down. Oh—"

Without listening to her argument, he placed his hands around her waist and swung her up into the saddle as though she were a child. "You can be mistress when you get back to the manor, but when you're with me, you do as you're told. Now, hold on."

And he took the horse by its bridle and led them down through the woodland slopes, not by the way she'd come but by a much easier route, where the footing was less dangerous for a horse. It was obvious that he knew her land better than she did, avoiding the low-hanging branches and setting a much quicker pace than Aletta could possibly have done alone.

On the lower slopes below the rocks he halted, and placed his hands around her waist. "Move back here." He jerked his head towards the horse's rump. Obediently, she moved back out of the saddle while he climbed into it and took the stirrups. "Put your arms around my waist and hold on tightly. Ready?" He turned to look at her over his shoulder.

"Ready," she said.

For the rest of the journey, short though it was, they rode at a smart trot. Aletta felt deliciously helpless, like a young maid again, free even of the responsibility of finding her own way home. His back was broad and warm and his hair above her nose was crisp and wavy, and she found it difficult to sustain her resentment throughout this strange brew of roughness and tenderness, curtness and chivalry. She had never ridden pillion with a man before, never sat so close to one who rode so easily and gracefully, even though the gelding was somewhat small for him.

As they approached the pale green glow of common land he slowed to a halt and jumped to the ground. "Why did you not have an escort when you rode out?" he asked.

Aletta was taken aback, almost speechless. She was unused to having anyone question her movements in this way. "I...I never have an escort! Not on my own land. I like to be on my own!"

"Well, for pity's sake, woman, stop wandering round the countryside by yourself. Take at least two men with you."

She looked at him without moving, saying nothing.

"Do you hear me, Aletta Markenfield?"

"Yes, I hear you, sir! You may be sure I shall take at least six men with me whenever I go out from now on." Her expression was stony.

"*Six* men? I'm flattered. That should do the trick." The corners of his mouth twitched as he moved her back on to the saddle.

Waiting until her feet were once more in the stirrups, he

reached up to grasp her arm and the back of her head with a suddenness that nearly toppled her over, pulling her head down to his. This time his kiss was hard and anything but gentle.

"That's just to remind you," he said, setting her straight again. "Now go!" And he gave the horse a gentle slap on its rump.

Shaken by his fierce kiss, Aletta gathered the reins without a word and headed out into the open fields towards home. A few strides out, she turned to look back, but the edge of the woodland was dark and deserted, and it was only the tingle on her lips and the pounding of her heart that told her she'd not been dreaming.

Chapter Three

The remainder of Aletta's journey home reflected the dream-like quality of her thoughts. She noticed little on the way, greetings were returned with unusual absentmindedness, and it looked as though her day would end without the usual hunger-pangs of a healthy appetite. It was as though emotions and experiences hung suspended in time, to be reflected upon repeatedly but not understood. It was as well that the gelding knew the way home, for her directions were of the most cursory nature.

Her arrival in the solar was not unobserved by her maid, as Aletta had hoped it would be, for Bridie was just entering it from the hall stairway as her mistress came up the outer steps, and she needed no second glance to see that she had been involved in some kind of situation again. Aletta's manner was vacant, and her woollen bliaud bore the tell-tale signs of having been rolled in a ditch.

"M'lady! We were getting anxious about you! Are you all right?" Bridie looked more closely as Aletta showed no sign of answering. With her back pressed against the door, she stood, deep in thought. "Come," said the maid, gently leading her into the room. "What's happened to you? Did you have a fall?"

"No, Bridie. Nothing like that. I'm not hurt, only a few

scratches from a slither into the ditch. I went to see the new palings.''

Bridie knew perfectly well that this was not the whole of the story. ''I'll go and get a bite for you to eat, and a warm posset. You sit down here, pet.''

In the peace of her solar, Aletta struggled to find some explanation for the events of the last hour, while her fingers absently explored her lips, still tingling from his kisses. But his image blocked out all else. His hard body, his lips, hands, voice, the gentleness, the fierceness, all these were too strong in her mind to allow rationality even the smallest foothold.

The kisses he'd demanded in payment had turned her world upside-down, though neither love nor mere affection had had any part in it. His blatant hostility had been a far cry from the flattering and fawning attentions of her suitors over the last two years, all of them falling over themselves in their hurry to gain access to her bed and her property. But *his* demand he'd made sound like a request, though he'd left her no choice but to comply, and, while she'd had no intention of giving him anything, his skill had converted her passivity into participation.

Her half-serious question about his usual treatment of trespassers had provoked an answer about appropriateness, and she wondered why he thought it was appropriate to demand such an intimate forfeit in her case. She could only conclude that Sir Geraunt used women to slake an immediate appetite whenever the chance arose. But how strange that he should have been there at the very moment of her accidental trespass. So many questions, none of them answerable.

Bridie was soon clucking and tutting over the scratches to her hands and arms, knees and chin, and eventually Aletta satisfied her maid that, with hair rebraided, and dressed in a clean gown, she was back to normal, at least in outward appearances. As for the inner mistress, well, Bridie had come to her own conclusions about that, knowing that if her mistress had truly been distressed, she, as her closest confidante, would have been told the cause.

That night, with the two maids asleep on their pallets at the end of the solar, Aletta stood silent and immobile in the moonlight, staring out through the east window. Slowly her gaze travelled across the silver landscape to the left, where Allerton nestled into the vale of alder trees in the distance. At the soft pad of Bridie's bare feet on the newly polished floor, she turned, and felt the girl's soft arm steal around her shoulders.

"What's over in Allerton, then, m'lady?"

Aletta's hand crept unconsciously to her breast; she was unaware of how it crept downwards of its own accord and came to rest under her breasts over the thin linen shift.

But Bridie noticed. "Someone from Allerton? He was in the ditch too? And he kissed you?" Her voice was little more than a murmur.

Aletta gave a start of fear, and she looked over her shoulder to where Gerda lay sleeping. "Shh! For heaven's sake!" She placed a warning finger over her maid's lips and looked at her, wide-eyed in alarm. "Who told you? Was I seen?"

"Hush, love. No-one told me, I promise you." She smiled at Aletta's sigh of relief. "It doesn't take much to see what's happened to you. And you'd hardly lie about falling into a ditch, now, would you? I could see that much, anyway."

"But the rest," Aletta whispered, "how did you guess? Is it so obvious?"

"Only to me, love. I know that it was not unkindness that made you look the way you did when you came back after noon. And who was it put the primrose in your hair?"

"What?" Aletta's hand reached up to her head. "A primrose? What do you mean?" She was incredulous.

"It's here, look!" Bridie pointed to the carved chest beneath the window and picked up a drooping yellow flower, holding it up in the moonlit room. "It was tucked into your braids at the back, under your wimple. You didn't put it there, did you?"

Aletta's lovely face convulsed as she took the tiny flower from her maid's fingers. Through parted lips huge sobs rose up, and pushed past words in their intensity, overflowing into the silence of the room, and on Bridie's shoulder her body shook with a passion too deep to be explained.

Early April storms swept across the northern hills for several days, bringing down old and decayed branches to litter the tracks and scatter blossom like snow. The new foliage in plot and field changed to a luscious deep green and the doves performed their ablutions in the deep puddles, as though to make up for lost time.

In the shelter of the solar, Bridie and Gerda had decided that the remainder of last year's fleeces must be spun and woven up before the new clip appeared in midsummer. They were almost up to their knees in rolls of fleeces on the polished wooden floor as Aletta walked in from her morning meeting in the hall.

"Oh, girls!" she wailed, stopping on the threshold. "Did you have to do this up here? You know what a filthy mess it makes. And the smell!" She went over to the east window, which overlooked the outer staircase, and flung it open. "Whew! What a stink!"

The two maids smiled at each other, aware of Aletta's usual fuss about cleanliness, but they had prepared their answers. "Don't worry, m'lady. We're going to sort this lot through first, then we'll card it and put it ready in the baskets. We can begin spinning tomorrow. That way, we'll only make one lot of mess."

"But what about the mess *now?*" she asked, still aggrieved.

"M'lady," said Bridie, "I suggest you go and do what

you've got to do. Before you get back, this will all be cleared away, the floor cleaned, and everything smelling sweetly again.'' The maid's smile lit up her pretty face, helping to assure Aletta that the room which now looked like a stapler's warehouse would once again be transformed into her warm and pretty solar by suppertime.

Aletta demurred, but had to be content. The spinning had to be done. ''Roger's downstairs in the hall,'' she said softly.

This was to tease Bridie, as a way of getting her own back for the mess. Everyone knew that the maid was desperately in love with Roger—everyone, that was, except the bailiff himself. Bridie blushed but said nothing, though Aletta and Gerda exchanged glances.

''Well, then, as there's nowhere for me to put my feet, I'll leave you to it.'' And she went on down into the courtyard below.

It was her usual custom to spend part of each day looking around the manor within the great stone wall, seeing and being seen. She knew from experience how easy it was to ignore its daily activities and to leave everything entirely in the hands of the manor staff. ''Leave it to them... That's what they're here for...'' Sir Hubert had used to say, as he spent yet another day hawking or hunting. But his failure to take any interest in the servants had made them resentful, neglectful and cunning, and had made Roger's job even more difficult, sometimes impossible.

After Sir Hubert's death, Aletta had plunged into her new role with startling efficiency, as though to purge the place of all signs of him—changing conditions of tenure, freeing villeins from their bondage and making it clear to all her workers that she understood what they did, would pay them fairly and accept only high standards in return.

There had been surprisingly little opposition to this and, after the shock of having these changes implemented, and of discovering the obvious benefits to both them and her, everyone regarded her with respect, gave her their loyalty and even their love, for they had suffered under Sir Hubert's uninterest for too long.

For her part, Aletta insisted on the place being kept clean, well-tended and in good repair. She had already spent much of her inheritance refurbishing the buildings, inside and out, repairing ploughs and tools, laying in stores of food and replacing worn out and sickly animals with new, strong ones.

She had appointed new staff to replace many of Sir Hubert's inefficient people, and even allowed the villagers to grind their own flour if they preferred, instead of trekking with it to one of the manor mills, as they had previously been obliged to do. She suffered little from the loss of revenue, and neither did the miller appear to be too upset, for he was now stocking the mill-pond with much-needed eels and doing well from the proceeds, especially now, during Lent.

In the neat kitchen garden new leaves had sprung on almost every plant, even new cabbage leaves had begun to sprout from last year's stumps. Spinach and sorrel were advanced too. Dandelions and dock-leaves were ready, even the young nettles could be brought in, dripping, green and juicy. Aletta passed through into the kitchen, spoke with both butler and pantler, and then went on into the screens passage, almost colliding with a young gentleman.

He was being escorted by a relieved-looking Gerda. ''M'lady! There you are! We've searched everywhere. Master Willan de Paine's here to see you.'' She rolled her eyes heavenwards as she spoke, curtsied, and left Aletta to receive the young man's bow of greeting.

He was obviously delighted to have discovered her after being led on a search of the outer buildings, and made her laugh at his description of the pursuit, showing not a hint of embarrassment at their previous meeting.

Fully able to appreciate the difficulties of the search, Aletta laughed. "Ah, yes. I could have been more or less anywhere at this hour of the day. I have to be master and mistress at the same time, you see." She was happy, if somewhat surprised, that he should have made the effort to visit her.

"Obviously a very capable combination," Willan remarked gallantly. "I wonder how you are able to keep everywhere in such good order, single-handed."

They walked to the end of the great hall. "Well, I'm not entirely single-handed, you see," she replied. "I have a very able staff of servants and workers."

She indicated seats at the end of the high table where they could sit and talk. No man, save Oswald and Roger, had ever entered her solar since her husband's death, and she intended to make no exceptions.

She tried to shed some of the credit for her good management, but Willan was not taken in so easily. Indeed, Aletta would have thought him a fool if he had been, but they both knew how unseemly it would have been for a young woman to boast of her managerial achievements as men were wont to do, especially on a first acquaintance.

Gerda brought in a tray with wine and tiny sweetmeats of crushed almonds, then went to join Bridie again. Handing him a goblet of wine, Aletta couldn't help comparing Willan with his elder brother, seeing a similar bone-structure in the face, the strong nose and high brow, though Willan's fair hair and short beard were in direct contrast.

There was, she realised, something about Geraunt which was missing here, something she couldn't define. Willan was a merry and gentlemanly companion, serious when listening, interested and animated, but in spite of these delightful courtesies there was no spark to quicken the heart's rhythm or to bring a flush of excitement to the cheeks. There was little to provoke the curiosity, to make one wonder how his lips would feel, or his arms…

Aletta had no siblings with whom to compare herself,

being the only offspring of aged parents, so it was always a source of wonder to her how parents could produce such variety within the same family. "Does your brother approve of your visit to Netherstone, Master Willan?" Aletta wondered why even the question made the blood race in her veins.

"Oh, yes, indeed he does, m'lady. He said I should come to see how you did. I think he's quite curious to know how you manage sin—" He broke off, hesitating.

"Single-handed?" She finished the word for him, smiling at his caution.

"Yes. That's what I was about to say. He wasn't prying, you understand. It's simply that folks around here are obviously impressed by the way you've changed things in the last two years. We all want to know how you've done it. Most of the others are having difficulties, and Geraunt is turning his land over to sheep now."

Aletta was charmed by his honesty, though she wondered why, if Sir Geraunt was so interested, he had not come to see for himself. "Perhaps he doesn't approve of property-owning widows?" she murmured innocently.

"Oh, I wouldn't say that, Lady Aletta. He's seen much more of life than I have. After all, he's twelve years my senior."

"May I ask how old you are, Master Willan?"

"I'm twenty-one, m'lady, and soon to be knighted."

"But you're not from these parts, I've heard?"

"No, I was born on another of my late father's estates, in the south of England, near Oxford. I've been squire to Sir Thomas Newman for five years, brought up in his household."

"Sir Thomas Newman?" Aletta pretended to be puzzled. "Now, where have I heard that name…?"

"He's just come up to live at Middlestone with his new wife. He and my brother were squires together."

"Ah, yes, my other new neighbours at Middlestone. But

why did you all leave the warmer south to come this far north? It's usually the other way round, isn't it?''

"Well, it was Geraunt's decision. Allerton Manor has needed some attention for some years now, and Geraunt says he wants to add to the property up here. Perhaps he'll do an exchange for some in the south.''

Aletta's mind was racing ahead and she made no reply. Add to the property? Add whose property? Mine? Her expression betrayed her anxiety.

Willan looked at her over the top of his goblet. Had he said too much? He watched the slender fingers lightly stroking imaginary creases from the skirt of her bliaud; she was obviously deep in thought. He was entranced by her shapely figure and lovely face under the snowy-white wimple. He thought that the Widow of Netherstone, as his brother was pleased to call her, was utterly magnificent.

"Lady Aletta, I would like to visit you again, if I may. Would you allow me to?''

His face was so honest, his company so refreshing, that her reply came without hesitation. "I would not mind in the least if you came again, Master Willan. But all my visitors must take things as they find them here, knowing that I have a busy household to run…'' She hoped he'd understand.

"I understand perfectly, m'lady. Even with things running smoothly there's much to be done, and I'd always go away again if you felt it was not convenient.''

Aletta smiled at his courtesy and his obvious delight, thinking what fun she'd find in his company.

As he prepared to mount she noted the hands that took the reins from the groom, brown and workmanlike. Without a fair amount of strength and skill, she thought, he'd never have been able to control the nervous filly under him, for as the groom leapt aside, to avoid the delicate hooves tapping out a rapid staccato on the cobbles, foam flew from her mouth and the black mane and forelock were already wet with sweat, and barely concealed the whites of her eyes.

"It's Geraunt's bay filly," Willan called down to her, laughing at her concerned expression and gradually moving the glossy brown creature round to face her. "He said she needed some exercise and schooling... He's a bit tied up with things at the moment. Hope I get back in one piece." He laughed merrily and waved a hand as the horse bounded away under his tight control.

Aletta's heart was suddenly pounding as she fought to check the mixture of excitement, annoyance and laughter inside her. The message could not have been clearer if it had been written on parchment and delivered to her by hand. "Arrogant brute!" she growled. "So that's what the visit was all about. Exercise and schooling!"

Whirling round in a flurry of skirts, she found Bridie and Gerda standing just a pace behind her, staring in concern and amusement.

"Gerda said you were getting on well together." Bridie's face registered concern. "So who's the arrogant brute? *He's* not, is he?"

Aletta placed a cool hand on her burning cheeks and shook her head. "No, not him. He's charming."

"Then who, m'lady?"

"Shhh!" She placed one finger on her lips and smiled a secret smile. Once again her mind was racing backwards, to the laughing hazel eyes and the flash of white teeth, and the dark-haired man who disturbed her thoughts and plagued her nights.

Up in the solar, she picked up a spindle and fingered its pointed end savagely, toeing a basket of carded fleece into position with such force that the topmost rolags bounced on to the floor.

The concentration needed for spinning a fine thread was an excellent way of ridding her mind of other matters, and at last she managed to produce a thread which met with

Gerda's approval. When her aching arms could no longer hold up the spindle, she dropped it into her maid's lap and went downstairs.

Roger was in the hall below, and Aletta signalled to him as she entered. Two mastiffs had followed him in, searching for morsels to gulp, but, as usual, the floor was free of rushes and of debris after the morning meal. One of them began to lift its leg against the stone wall, but Aletta was watching, picked up a three-legged stool and hurled it with such ferocity that the terrified animal yelped in fright, though not hurt, and fled the hall, sending dark looks of outraged humiliation over its shoulder.

"Roger, I will not have dogs in here that can't tell the difference between the hall and the stable. That's something I will *not* put up with!" she yelled.

The bemused bailiff looked at her with a raised eyebrow and a slight smile, picking up the stool, pushing its leg back into the hole and setting it down. Aletta's fanaticism about cleanliness was legendary within the household—admired by the women, tolerated by the men. Looking at the other dog, Roger pointed to the doorway. "Out!" he said. It went at a smart trot, head down.

Aletta waited for him to reach her, her lips pressed together. "Don't look at me like that, wretch! I know what you're thinking, but I've had enough of dogs and hawks fouling my rooms, even my bed. Now I choose not to!" Roger lifted his hands, palms towards her in a gesture of peace, saying nothing except with his laughing eyes. "Come," said Aletta, "I need to talk to you."

Outside the stables, he watched as Aletta perched on the mounting-block in the hazy sunshine. He leaned against the wall, tucking his thumbs into his leather belt, thinking that he knew what was on her mind. "What is it, m'lady? I hear that young Master Willan was here."

"Yes. And I've a suspicion that they're after more land.

You don't think they'll attempt to get hold of Netherstone lands, do you?''

Roger raised his eyebrows and paused. ''Well, they could make an offer to exchange or lease, but that doesn't oblige you to accept. The worst that could happen is that they could make themselves so unpleasant that you'd be glad to give in to them, but I don't really see that happening, do you?''

Aletta was silent for so long that Roger turned his head to look at her, seeing the way she bit at her top lip in uncertainty.

''Well, do you?'' He pressed her for a reply.

''No, I suppose not.'' Her reply, when it came, held little conviction. ''But I got off to a bad start, didn't I?''

He gave a short bark of laughter. ''I'd call that a middlin' good start, m'lady. Let 'em know you're not to be disregarded. A man would've done the same.''

Aletta searched his face. ''You don't disapprove, then?''

''Disapprove?'' He smiled into the distance. As though speaking to himself, his reply was so quiet that only she could hear. ''I've never disapproved of anything you've done since I've known you.''

There was a silence between them in which words were unnecessary, each of them knowing the other's mind and aware of the special bond which had been forged through the ebb and flow of the shared years. Aletta knew, and Roger knew that she knew.

''Roger. I have something to ask you.''

''Ask, then. Anything.''

''You must tell me if it's impossible for you.''

''I'll tell you.'' Don't ask me to stop loving you, that's all, he said inside himself, and she heard as clearly as if he'd said it out loud.

''For my sake, will you begin to pay some attention to Bridie?''

His head turned very slowly to look at Aletta, his expression vacant, not understanding. "To Bridie?"

"Yes. To Bridie. If you were not so blind," she explained gently, "you'd see that she's very much in love with you."

There was no sound from him as he continued to stare, but now his expression had changed from blankness to one of sheer amazement.

Aletta smiled at him and nodded. "You hadn't noticed? Ever?"

Roger shook his head. "Nobody's ever been in love with me," he said in a flat voice.

"How would you know that, if you haven't seen how Bridie feels?"

He spread out his hands in a helpless boyish gesture, then folded his arms across his wide chest and pushed his shoulders away from the wall. "Wouldn't I know? Don't people know when someone's in love with them?"

"Not if they're looking in the wrong direction."

"Did she tell you?"

"She didn't need to *tell* anyone, simpleton. You're the only one who hasn't noticed. It's obvious."

"Is it? Obvious?"

"Yes. It's obvious once you start looking. You'll see."

The bailiff unfolded his arms, now clearly perplexed, and shook his head from side to side, unbelieving. In love? Bridie? With him? Surely, she was pretty, but he'd never even noticed the colour of her eyes. Perhaps he'd better.

"Will you, Roger?"

Again his eyes rested on her face, and for many moments the conversation continued in space without a word being spoken. His nod of agreement was almost imperceptible, but Aletta knew that it was merely the verification of what his eyes had already said.

She smiled a message of thanks. "I don't want you to be unhappy."

"Typical!" Roger's retort came out with a laugh. "When are you going to start thinking about your own happiness, m'lady?"

"Perhaps I already have."

His head went back in scorn. "You mean young Master Willan? Soon to be *Sir* Willan?" His voice was so loaded with contempt that Aletta turned to see his expression. "You're not serious, are you?" he asked.

"Shouldn't I be?"

"Serious? *No,* m'lady! You know as well as I do he's not meat enough for you. Try the other one!"

"The other one?" She knew full well his meaning but wanted him to say it, to drag her secret longings out into the daylight and shake them in front of her.

"Yes, the other one. He's more your match."

"How do you know that, Roger? You've only seen him once."

"So's *he* only seen *you* once. But it's obvious, isn't it?"

"Is it? Obvious?"

"Yes. Apparently it is. Once you start looking."

"*Touché!*" She smiled.

Chapter Four

It was clear to Aletta that Oswald was failing. Her old and faithful steward had fallen asleep at each of the morning meetings that week, a sign that the burden of the estates was too much for his tired mind and body.

With Easter only a short time away, there were outstanding accounts to attend to, yearly dues and rents, the manor court to preside over, provisions to discuss for the coming holiday period and estate policies to decide.

Oswald's young clerk took notes and messages, made records and generally kept Aletta notified of financial affairs, but he was slow and caused them no small concern. Meanwhile, the burden of Oswald's work fell mostly on Aletta, so when Gerda begged her for a private word after supper, she hoped desperately that this didn't herald yet another small crisis.

"M'lady, it's about me and Thomas." She smiled shyly.

"He's spoken to your mother at last, then?"

The young maid blushed slightly, and Aletta knew that it wouldn't be long before she was, at seventeen, married and bearing children. Even so, she hoped that it would be some time before she'd have to do without her, for she was by far the best spinner and weaver in the area.

"Yes, m'lady. Yesterday. We're to be betrothed at Easter."

Aletta hugged her in delight. "And have you decided whose house you'll live in?"

Gerda's face clouded for a moment as she looked away. "Well, that's the problem," she said. "Thomas wants to come and live here in Netherstone with me and my mother. There's enough room in our cott and there's hardly any room in his, with his father and brothers living there too. I couldn't go and live in Allerton, m'lady. Really, I couldn't."

"Allerton, Gerda?" Aletta frowned. "He lives there? I thought he was an Ellerby man. One of my own villagers."

"No, m'lady. That was the Thomas I had before. Last year. He was from Ellerby. This Thomas is Wat's son from Allerton. It was last May Day…"

"Oh, Gerda." Aletta's face reflected the seriousness of the problem for she knew, without giving it another thought, that Sir Geraunt de Paine would be most unlikely to agree to one of his strong young villeins moving away from his village when workers were so hard to come by nowadays. Not unless he could be persuaded to accept chevage, the fine for moving out of his fee. But, she pondered, he would no doubt fix that at some ridiculous sum which would take the man years to save, effectively tying him to Allerton for many more years.

"Do you think Sir Geraunt would let him go?"

Rather ask me if I think the moon will turn to cheese, Aletta thought, but was reluctant to dampen the girl's hopes too soon. "It's difficult to say what he'll do, Gerda." She put an arm around her shoulders. "Leave it to me. I'll try to think of something. Just give me a little time. Will you be seeing Thomas soon?"

"Yes, I'm sleeping at home this evening."

"So you are. Well, then, tell Thomas to ask Sir Geraunt

as soon as he can if he'll release him. Find out what his chevage will be and let me know.''

As the heavy door closed Aletta sunk her head in her hands and gave in to a deep sigh. This is a complication I can well do without, she thought to herself. Why on earth could she not have stayed with the Ellerby Thomas instead of the Allerton one? Smiling at her own unreason, she wondered how she'd be able to please everyone, fearing that hope and optimism were not going to be enough this time.

Thoughts of how and why and wherefore drove sleep far away that night, the concerns of management tangling with the remembered feeling of his hands and body on her, his kisses. And, in the darkness, these jumbled into fears that the episode in the forest might simply have been the prelude to something more sinister, that it might have been just another way of making inroads towards her property. She lay, tossing and restless, wondering how to resist it when her body was clearly of a mind to respond to his. She needed no man, and yet a part of her said otherwise, and it was not until dawn that sleep finally came, heavy, overpowering and dreamless.

The light of the day did nothing to rouse her. With the usual bustling noises of one whose duty it is to disturb another, Bridie prepared water for her bath and brought her back to an awareness of the day ahead, of its attendant problems and a strange sensation of not having slept at all.

Though Bridie was a mere two years older than her mistress, she adopted her motherly tone this morning. ''You'll look better if you put something pretty on,'' she said.

And so Aletta took time to wash her hair and to choose a favourite cream woollen bliaud and a new pale yellow cote-hardie, with such wide side-openings that the front and back bodice, as Bridie said, might as well not be there at all.

By the time all this had been achieved, food eaten, hair coiled into a pile on top of her head and her appearance

checked in the long steel mirror on the wall, Aletta realised
that Roger and Jem would think she'd decided not to appear
at the usual morning meeting.

With only the lightest of gossamer veils over her hair,
she left the solar and stood at the top of the hall stairway,
looking over the balcony to the scene below. She grasped
at the wooden rail for support and bit back an exclamation
of annoyance as she saw Roger at the far end, showing Sir
Geraunt through the screens. Her first impulse was to turn
back into her solar, to calm the loud hammering in her
chest, but it was too late, for they had both seen her and
stood watching as she descended, trying her best to appear
unaffected by his unwelcome visit.

Roger watched the apprehension grow in her dark and
unsmiling eyes as Sir Geraunt greeted her courteously.
Even from where he stood, he was sure that his first assessment of the situation had been correct, that in spite of
the unconcealed antagonism of their first meeting their mutual attraction was almost tangible.

He signalled to Bridie with his eyes and a slight movement of his head to follow him outside. She opened her
mouth in protest and frowned, but Roger took her arm and
marched her firmly away. "It's all right," he muttered into
her ear, "those two don't need a chaperon any more than
we do. Come, lass."

Bridie blushed, and complied as she felt his hand move
to her waist.

"Good morning, Sir Geraunt. Trespassing again?" Aletta addressed him coolly, holding out her hand as she was
obliged to do and aware of his firm fingers beneath hers,
the light brush of his lips as he bowed over them.

"Indeed I am, my lady. On your time and on your property." His eyes searched hers, glinting wickedly. "But I
would be happy to pay double the appropriate forfeit!"

"That will not be necessary, sir, I assure you." She made

a show of glancing behind him. "But where is your escort? How many men do *you* need to come all this way?"

"Sheath your sword, vixen," he replied in a low and deliberate voice, still smiling.

Aletta looked pointedly at his sword-belt, low-slung across his hips, but he wore only a short scabbard with a silver-mounted dagger showing, as Willan had done on his earlier visit.

"Perhaps we might talk in private, Lady Aletta?"

Aletta glanced around the hall, noticing that everyone had vanished except for three kitchen officials in conference at the dais end. Her hesitation clearly reflected her discomfort at his suggestion, for she *did* want their discussion to be in private, but was reluctant to invite him into her solar. She did not want him to be an exception, and yet he was, nevertheless.

"In your solar?" he insisted, indicating the upper door with a glance. Before she could respond, one way or the other, Sir Geraunt had taken her elbow lightly in his hand and turned her towards the stairs, steering her forward.

Aletta had reacted with a ferocious zeal in defence of her privacy once her husband had died, throwing out everything which the room had contained, including the hawks' perches and dogs' litters which had made it stink like a stable. Now, having entirely refurbished it, she was loth to share it with any except her two maids, to whom it was both day-and night-room.

She turned to face him, wrenching her elbow out of his grasp. "Sir Geraunt, my solar is kept for my private use! I never invite anyone into it. No one!"

"Lady Aletta," he replied gently, "I understand your reluctance to make an exception. But we have some private matters to discuss which I believe you would not want the rest of your household to overhear. Do you think...? Just this once...?"

Aletta had to concede that, just this once, it would be as

well to speak in private and in comfort, and so she led the way to her room without another word, her lips pressed tightly together with annoyance at having so easily yielded to his request.

Sir Geraunt held the door for her as she passed and closed it behind them, casting an appreciative glance at the pretty feminine colours, the flowers, the tapestried walls and brightly polished wood. His eyes returned to her face. "I can see that things must have changed here too. This is hardly Sir Hubert's kind of room, is it?"

The mention of her late husband's name brought a frown to her face. "You knew him, did you?"

He noticed the frown. "Knew him? Oh, yes, I knew him, quite well." He spoke almost as though to himself.

"How did you come to know him?"

He hesitated, obviously on the brink of an explanation, and then he smiled. "Remind me to tell you some other time. It's a long story, and we have some business to discuss, do we not?"

"Do we, sir? Will you sit?"

He had not moved since his entry into her private domain, for he understood that she was a creature of fiercely defended territories—her property and herself. Single-handed, and a widow, the disadvantages were stacked against her, and he would not take his boldness so far as to roam uninvited around the room as though on a tour of inspection.

As he accepted the high-backed carved chair, she noted that on this occasion he had apparently paid much attention to his dress, for he wore an elegant gown of rich brown, split up the sides for riding, and an under-tunic of deep blue which matched his clinging chausses and riding-boots of soft leather. A blue velvet cloak was carelessly thrown over one shoulder, fastened by a large silver clasp, and more silver glinted from leather belts where his scabbard, purse-clasp and buckle shone on his slim hips. His dark brown hair glinted in the early sunlight which caught his face, and she felt that the size of the room had been diminished by his presence.

"Is it about Gerda and Thomas that you've come, sir?" She prayed that he was not going to be difficult, but wondered how easy it was going to be to keep her mind away from his lips which had searched hers so thoroughly. She looked away from him quickly, in case he should catch her thoughts.

But his face was serious. "Partly, yes. Though there's little to say about it, really. You'll agree that the answer is quite straightforward."

"Straightforward?" Aletta's eyes lit up with hope at the word. "You mean, you'll agree to release him?"

"The maid can live in Allerton, surely?"

"No, indeed she can't, sir!" Was he now going to make objections, after telling her that it was quite straightforward? "For one thing, she has a mother for whom she must care. And Thomas has a father and two brothers. They would do all the week-work for you that he now does. And one can hardly blame Mistress Gerda for not wanting to leave her mother and move into a house with *four men!*"

The venom she spat into the last two words were enough to make him smile, but he hid it behind his hand and it was dismissed in a flash.

"Apart from that, she's my maid and I need her. She's the best spinner and weaver to be had around here. I could never part with her."

"Ah!" The sound was loaded with meaning.

Aletta was stung, and realised that perhaps she'd said too much. "No! It's not like that! You can see that there are better reasons why the lad should come to live here at Netherstone—"

"And I lose a strong worker? I think not."

Aletta was incredulous. "No?" she whispered.

"No."

This was not at all what she'd hoped, though perhaps, she thought bitterly, she should have expected it. Now she would have to plead for them. ''Can he not pay chevage for his release? Four shillings is a fair sum, I believe.''

''Not a chevage they could afford.''

''How much?''

''I would fix it at eighty shillings. I'm not willing to let Thomas go for less than that.''

''Eighty shillings?'' Aletta mouthed the words rather than spoke them. This was preposterous. He could not be serious. Surely this was a jest. But his expression bore no evidence of that.

Aletta bolted out of her chair and went to stand behind it, using it as both barrier and support, her knuckles showing white as they gripped its prettily carved finials. ''Eighty shillings! You know full well they could never pay that in a lifetime! Neither he nor his father and brothers between them could ever raise that kind of money!''

Sir Geraunt sat back at ease, catching the reflections of light from the window in her angry dark eyes.

''Ah, yes, I know what it is,'' she said, slowly moving away from the security of the chair to stand before him, menacingly rigid, all thoughts of fostering his goodwill melting beneath the heat of her fury at his unreason. ''I know what it is. You haven't finished paying me back yet, have you? You don't want to hear reasons, do you?''

''How like a woman to take it personally.'' He laughed, softly. ''Do you never stick to the facts?''

''Facts! The facts are that you don't even want to discuss it!'' She whirled across to the other oak table by the lower window and placed her hands on its cool surface, her anger held in abeyance as she caught the fragrance from the jug of spring flowers.

She heard a sound and turned to see him approach her, but she stepped aside, well out of his reach, seeing him smile as she put the distance of half the room between them. His movement brought her thoughts once more into total confusion, and for a while nothing was said.

"Well? Discuss, my lady."

She turned and glared at him. "I can hardly discuss alone!"

"I'm here."

"Yes, you're here. But you're not listening to me."

Almost languidly, he seated himself again. "Go on. I'm listening."

It was difficult for her to pick up the thread of the argument after the pause of the last few moments, and she had almost forgotten where it had truly finished. Then she thought of Gerda and Thomas, saw their disappointed faces in her mind.

"Don't you realise that you're dealing with people's lives?" she asked, shaking her head at him in question. "By restricting their freedom, you're affecting their happiness." She tried to make her voice sound calm, reasonable, philosophical.

"Lady Aletta." His voice was deep, but the tone remained as inflexible as before, and his fingers were pressed tightly together, making an arch with their tips. "I'm not in the business of making my villeins happy or otherwise. That's their concern. I'm more interested in their capacity to work and pay their dues. Workers are invariably lost by natural causes, but I don't regard a marriage between villeins as a natural cause. It's something they've decided for themselves. If they didn't have the sense to see the complications ahead of them, then they deserve to suffer the discomforts. That's all there is to it!"

Aletta stared at him in horror. "And you call that *discussing?* I call it inhuman, unfeeling, unreasonable and— Oh!" She flung away to the far side of the great curtained bed and stayed in the shadow of its white linen hangings, where she could blot him out of her sight. There was no point in pursuing this argument any longer; she realised that. He *was* an arrogant brute, unfeeling and without pity.

Something that Master Willan had said to her on the day of his visit entered her mind. Something about folks wanting to know how she'd managed alone, why her villeins, freemen and servants were all so happy, why she was so well-organised. Turning to look over her shoulder, she saw that he'd not moved.

"I have reason to believe, Sir Geraunt," she begun, her in most formal manner, "that my methods of concerning myself with my villagers' happiness are producing results better than most other landowners in these parts. Both my villages of Netherstone and Ellerby are efficiently managed and peaceful because I respect people's freedom as individuals, whoever they are. To disregard the welfare of one's workers, as you appear to do, and to take no interest in where or how they live is less than human." She turned her head away once more, so that she could forget the handsome creature while she fuelled her dislike of him.

There was a tense silence in the room when she thought that at last she'd made some impact on his inflexibility, that perhaps she'd penetrated his uninterest, given him something to think about. But she was not prepared for his reply, when it came.

He spoke quietly, politely. "I believe, Lady Aletta, you may be mistaken in thinking that I take no interest in where or how my villeins live. Indeed, in the last few weeks, I have made it my business to find out exactly where four of them live. Four grown, healthy male villeins by the names of Adam Beck, John Clough, John Wheelright and Peter Ghyll. Knowing this, you will now perhaps understand why I am so reluctant to part with yet another. At this rate, I shall have no one left in Allerton at all. They will all be in Netherstone."

At his words the breath halted in her lungs, and on her arms she felt the hairs prickle as they stood on end. So, the thunderbolt had struck, as she'd prayed it never would. Curiously, as the silence in the room deepened, her heart resounded deep in her chest like a drum, and a blackness swam before her, though her eyes remained open. As though from the far end of a dark tunnel, she felt her arms encircle the bedpost and the floor rock unsteadily beneath her feet like a boat on rough water.

So, he'd checked. He'd discovered they were missing. Less than a year, and now he'd want them back. Her innocent gesture of charity had misfired, as she'd been warned it might.

Shakily she went to her chair, and sat with a sudden thump, her knees still trembling. "You won't change your mind about Thomas?" she whispered.

He looked surprised. "No. I'm not going to change my mind. Is there any reason why I should?"

"Not even if the chevage is paid?" She made a last desperate effort to solve that one problem before letting go of it for good.

Sir Geraunt stood and carried his chair to place it directly in front of her, and sat leaning towards her with elbows on knees and hands dangling elegantly. His expression was as uncompromising as ever.

"I know what you have in mind, m'lady, but you can quickly dispel it. In theory, even if he or his family had eighty shillings, it would belong to me, since everything of theirs is mine. He would *have* to get someone else to pay it for him. But again, in theory, I don't have to agree to part with him." He leaned back and took a sip from his goblet, regarding her steadily. "I shall tell the lad he'll have to wait until it's more convenient. You will have to tell the maid that, too. The problem will no doubt be resolved in time."

There was nothing more she dared say on that subject now. The bright sunlight streaming through the east window beckoned and she wished she were anywhere else but here in this web of trouble. What was he going to do? she wondered. It was serious.

Had she known that the owner of Allerton Manor was to return after so many years, and make detailed checks on all his possessions, she supposed she would have thought longer and harder about the requests those eight young people had made of her on that happy May Day last year. They had all seemed so carefree then. Now she had put them, their families and their villages in danger of his retaliation. Herself, too. And this fiend knew it!

"I believe it's time you gave me an explanation of how my four men came to roost in your estates, Lady Aletta."

Under his penetrating gaze it was going to be difficult to explain her reasons for giving eight happy young people something she herself had never had—a chance to live with a loving partner with babies crawling around her feet.

Sir Geraunt leaned back in his chair and waited for her to begin, while she, in confusion, kept her eyes on the bright window, seeing the merry glance of love on that May Day.

Haltingly, she began. "Yes, I suppose I do owe you an explanation. It was May Day last year when they decided they wanted to stay with the girls they'd...they'd—" She stopped, not knowing how to continue. She looked at him for understanding.

"The girls they'd slept with the night before. Yes, go on, if you please..."

"Yes, they were girls from my villages. They all spent the night in the woods, bringing...bringing in the May..." Her voice was a whisper now, as her throat constricted with tears at the memory of such freedom.

He could see her lip being bitten to keep it still and he waited without speaking until the trembling passed, aware of her pain and the emotional loneliness of the past years.

Hurriedly she wiped a hand across her nose and cheek, but kept her eyes on the window. "And then the girls came to ask me...if...if the boys could rebuild the old cotts that had been left empty since the deaths...the pestilence..." Aletta glanced at him briefly, to check the effect of her words. He had not moved, but nodded slowly in understanding. "They asked me if they could take over the crofts and pay rent, and earn wages like the others." She looked at Sir Geraunt again to explain. "I have labourers, and pay them proper wages, you see, in money, not in kind."

He nodded. It was becoming more and more usual to put an end to the usual week-work and boon-work done by the villeins on the lord's estate, and to pay them good money for their labour, especially those who had little land of their own for growing on. But he knew that this was not to be done suddenly, and assumed that Aletta, like others he'd heard of, would have both villeins and labourers in her villages.

Aletta continued. "I think the girls were afraid they'd become pregnant. And three of them have had... babies...since..." Here Aletta's voice disappeared as she heaved herself blindly out of her chair and went to stand by the window with her back to him. Her shoulders shook as she fought to regain control, ragged gasps of desolation and longing poured to the surface, released by the words of her explanation.

Sir Geraunt did not intrude. This was a private and personal grief, which he'd obliged her to expose, and he didn't move or speak until the sobbing eased and she became calm again. For a brief moment she rested her head on the stone-cold wall, placed her hands on her cheeks, then continued the story.

"Now two of them live in Ellerby and two in Netherstone, as you've discovered. They're good workers, have never broken the law, not once. Not any of them. I promised them I would never tell where they were, and all the villagers have kept quiet about it. Until now, it seems."

She shot him a look, but there was no response. "You

must not blame your bailiff. He did what he could to persuade them to return, but once the four days were up there was nothing more he could do except tell the steward, but apparently he didn't seem too concerned. It was easy enough to fool your steward, when he was so inefficient and only visited the manor twice a year.''

''How often does Oswald visit?''

''Oswald? He *lives* here!'' Aletta pointed to the floor beneath them, indicating the rooms below. ''Under here. And Roger Holland, my bailiff, lives under there.'' She pointed to the far end of the room. ''I can see them both every day, if I need to. But Oswald's sick and can't do the job any more, so I've had to do it recently. And Roger, too.''

''*You've* had to do it? You can do accounts?''

''Of course,'' she replied quietly. ''How do you suppose I kept myself sane for seven and a half years? Oswald taught me.'' There was a bitter edge to her voice which did not escape her listener. Suddenly, as if to disown the words which might be construed as disloyalty, she walked across to the other window, looking into the courtyard while he watched with a glint of admiration in his eyes.

She turned at last. ''How did you find out?''

''I held a view of frank-pledge last week.''

''*You* did? You mean, the Sheriff did!''

''No, I did! I have the right, granted to my father by the King. I can review the tithings on my own land. I discovered that the four men have been missing since last May, and now the tithings to which they belonged will have to pay a heavy fine for their failure to bring them back. In fact, the whole village may be amerced and all their property seized for not finding and producing them.''

''*What?*''

''You knew it was a serious crime. No landlord can afford to lose four men all in one go. You must know that anyone who withdraws from my land without licence can be seized and brought back—''

"No! Not after four days!" It was a brave attempt to throw him off-course, hoping that he would be less informed than she was about the details of recapture and punishment. But he was adamant.

"Rubbish, Lady Aletta! You know full well that there's more to it than that! The four-day rule applies to their immediate arrest and return, to be tried in the manor court. All I have to do now is to apply to the Sheriff for writs for their arrest and then they'll have to prove their case in *his* court. They're villeins. Can they afford a court hearing? Can they afford to lose what little they have?"

Aletta was trembling uncontrollably, staring at him wide-eyed, shaking her head as the nightmare worsened. She reached for the goblet and gulped, not tasting anything, not feeling the drink in her mouth. Her knees lowered her into the chair opposite him, and she wondered what more was to come.

"My villagers are mostly free. Yes!" She responded quickly to his disbelieving look. "I offered freedom to anyone who wanted it, after…he…died, and it was written into the manor rolls. And most of them have charters of manumission to prove it! The girls those four men married are free…and that makes their marriage partners free too!" She sat back in her chair, trembling and triumphant.

"They married, did they?"

"Yes!"

"Then they married without my licence, and so I'm now deprived of their fines for that too. And they are *not* free, my lady, for you cannot free someone else's property, married or not! Those four belong to me, and their brats too. You cannot change that!"

Her eyes locked with his, defiant and full of hatred. "You cannot do this to them. You cannot take them back now, distrain their families, fine the Allerton villagers, seize their goods, tear them apart from their—'' She gripped the arms of her chair, raging inwardly at the knot as it tightened around her.

"Can I not, my lady?" His steady look told her that he certainly could.

"No. I mean, you *would* not."

"And do they belong to a tithing in *your* villages?"

"No. Free men have no need to. It isn't required—"

"But for villeins, it *is!*" he interrupted sharply. "And I could tell the Sheriff at the next court review that they don't belong, and he may then think fit to fine the tithings in *your* villages for *their* omission. Or do you have a better idea?"

There was nothing she could say to him. So far, he had countered everything with cold facts. She tried a last desperate bid. "Yes! I do! You could free them as I have done!"

For an answer, he threw back his head and his chest heaved with laughter. "Lady Aletta! That was a good effort, I suppose. But that wouldn't solve my problem. Only yours." His perfect teeth flashed in the sunlit room and Aletta wondered how she could have thought that he might understand. The man was a devil!

"You may find that the laws up here in the north are different from those elsewhere, Sir Geraunt. Forest laws, property laws—I would not be too sure of all your facts on these points, if I were you."

Aletta had nothing specific to go on, but she'd been advised that it was so, that these points of law were by no means cut and dried and varied greatly from one part of the country to another. Seeds of doubt could often be sown in this off-hand way, she knew. She went to stand behind her chair.

"And the law concerning theft? Is *that* any different, my lady?"

"Theft?" She glared at him, puzzled.

"Yes, theft."

"Who…? What…? What are you talking about? What theft?"

"Had you not realised that *you* could be arrested for theft of my property, and that your refusal to hand it—them—over could result in expensive court action, confiscation of your property until they're returned, fines—"

"Stop!" Aletta clamped her hands tightly over her ears, closed her eyes against his face, his words, his presence. She felt his movement as he carried his chair back to its former position, felt the vibrations on the wooden floor beneath her feet, felt the pounding of her heart too large for the cage of her ribs.

Now she knew that what she'd feared above all else was actually happening. He had no need to do all this. He simply wanted her property, was grabbing at any excuse, albeit a serious matter, to prise her away from her efficient manor, perhaps to put Willan in her place. His threats were all too real, and it was obvious that he knew precisely how to implement them. She'd find herself in a legal battle, perhaps lose her property, the men and their families…after all her promises to them…

She shook her head, and lowered her hands to look at him. "I can't believe it," was all she could say.

But she could believe it. One look at his face told her that she could. He could haul them back at any time he wanted to and he could ruin her any time he chose. She was speechless. Then, with a startling abruptness, she erupted with fury and despair.

"You fiend! You *fiend!*" The primrose yellow gown whirled as she flew across the room to hurl herself bodily at him.

But he had seen the look in her eyes even before she'd moved and he caught her in mid-flight, halfway across the room. Before her hands could make contact, they were imprisoned in a grip of steel close to his chest, while she fought to make some impact on the solid wall of his body.

Already exhausted by emotion and lack of sleep, she was helpless against him and could only sob and push at him with her arms, shaking with pent-up anger.

"Aletta! Listen to me!"

"No!" Her screech came out hoarse and ragged.

"*Listen* to me!"

"No! No! Don't speak to me! I don't want to hear any more. You've done your damage. Now go! Just go!"

"Aletta, you're going to hear me!"

"No, I'm not!" She was sobbing now, her wrists hurt in his grasp and her legs were buckling beneath her. "I've heard enough! Enough! Let me go! Tell the Sheriff! Do your damnedest. I'll fight you for everything I've got!" Her head came to rest on her hands against his chest, her hair now tumbling down in wild tendrils beneath the filmy veil. "You want to see me ruined, I know…"

"You're going to hear me, vixen, whether you want to or not," Sir Geraunt growled between his teeth, and, picking her up in his arms, he carried her struggling body over to the large white-curtained bed and held her on to it.

Where she found the strength to continue her fight she was afterwards never quite sure. Perhaps it surfaced as a vestige of the previous years, when being carried protesting to the bed meant only one thing, ending inevitably in pain and degradation. But, as she weakened against the restraint of his hands and arms, she began to understand that the familiar elements of brutality were missing and were being replaced by his calm voice, deep and reassuring.

Sir Geraunt was well aware of her late husband's methods in this field, and he needed little imagination to understand her fears. He had, after all, sampled them already, at their second meeting, and knew of its origins. By degrees, her wild struggles abated under his firmness, and she lay, still and exhausted, angry, but assured that she was in no physical danger.

"By heavens, wench! I was right about the suit of armour!" He smiled ruefully at her glaring eyes.

Aletta turned her head away, not understanding, but too breathless to enquire.

"Look at me, Aletta!"

"No! Leave my house!"

"Come on. Look at me. We're going to discuss terms."

That had the desired effect. "Terms!" she spat at him. "You're going to undo all the good work I've done since—"

"I've not said anything of the kind. I *could* do, and I would if I felt it was appropriate—"

"Oh, you're being appropriate again!" she snorted, writhing against his hands. But she was held back, easily. "You want me in your power, then, don't you? *Don't* you? Admit it! That's what you want, isn't it? Power?"

"Yes!"

As though she'd misheard, her struggles against his hands ceased. It was not what she had expected to hear. A denial would have allowed her to argue longer, to hurt him with words, perhaps. "What?" she whispered, frowning.

"Yes. I said yes."

Are we talking about the same thing? she wondered, forgetting to struggle. "Yes, *what?*"

"Yes, you fierce vixen. I *do* want you in my power. *Now* do you understand? And I shall certainly do everything to exercise my legal rights in this whole matter unless you place yourself in my power and do my bidding. Do you understand *that* too?" His eyes had narrowed to two dark and glittering slits above her, ominously harsh and forbidding, deadly serious.

"You're going to direct the manor and the estates through me?" she whispered, filled with dread. "Is that it? You're going to take over the running of my property or you'll ruin—"

"Aletta!" His voice was harsh. "You're not listening to

me! I do not intend to touch your manor or your estate, unless you ask me to. I said, I want *you* in my power!''

He had said it quite plainly. She could not pretend to misunderstand, and for some moments she could do no more than look up at him, totally speechless, while the implications of his words found a niche in her understanding, settling into place, comparing themselves against the alternatives.

Sir Geraunt released her hands and waited until she could find words.

''Me? You intend to take advantage of *me*, then?''

''Certainly!''

''Certainly,'' he'd said. As though it was the easiest thing in the world for her to accept. Did the man have any idea what he was suggesting? Did he really believe she was so desperate to have a man near her after all those years of hell that he could calmly walk into her room and demand this of her? What a price! No! He could go to hell first!

Chapter Five

"No! I cannot accept that!" Aletta rolled away in one huge leap, intent on putting some distance between them, but his long arm scooped her back to him, this time into his arms, and she was held across him, her reaction discounted.

"Do you have a choice, Aletta?"

She held herself rigidly against him, bracing her arms and pushing at his wide chest, still barely able to believe in the man's audacity. How she wished she'd taken the advice of her counsel when they'd warned her of the dangers of her actions, the consequences if the owner of Allerton Manor should ever return. She had overridden their fears and laughed, far too preoccupied with the happiness of eight young people to think seriously of the effect it might have on her own future. Now she was faced with alternative threats—one to them, the other to herself. Neither was acceptable.

"Yes! I *do* have a choice! Let me go!" She pushed violently against him, infuriated by his restrictions, but he would not allow her to escape him and she was pinned once more to the bed, glaring at him, straining and growling in her efforts to be free. "I do have a choice! I am the mistress of this estate and everything on it! I do not allow *anyone*

to take advantage of me in the way you demand. No one!
Not for any reason.''

''Not even for four families who rely on your charity?''

''That's unfair! No knight would take advantage of a
lady so—''

''Yes, he would! If he wants something badly enough, a
knight will do whatever it takes to get it. You know that
as well as I do! And what I'm demanding is not so very
terrible, you'll discover.''

''You came here with this…this scheme…already sewn
up, didn't you? All that argument about your four villeins,
it was already decided, wasn't it? In spite of anything I
could say in their favour? You wouldn't have accepted anything…would you…? Let me go! You're trespassing on
my… Let me *go!*''

''Listen to me, vixen! This arrangement need not last
forever—''

''It won't last at all! I want nothing to do with it.''

''Only until you ask me to marry you.''

''What?'' She lay rigidly still. ''What? Are you *mad?*''
she whispered. ''Until I ask *you* to marry *me?*''

''No, I'm not mad, Aletta. Think about it.''

''I don't need to think about it, Sir Geraunt. You need
not think your little game in the woodland has left me wanting for more. You've had your forfeit, now go. The time
will *never* come when I shall ask anyone to marry me. Nor
shall I ever accept anyone's offer. I have been married, if
you recall. And I didn't find it to my taste.'' She turned
away from him and heaved herself forward to roll off the
bed again. For her, there was nothing more to be said.

But, with a hand beneath her chin, Sir Geraunt pushed
her back again, and she landed on the coverlet with a soft
thud. He leaned towards her, his fingers holding her face
to his. ''And if *you* recall, Lady Aletta Markenfield, I believe you discovered something very much to your taste

out there in the forest, in spite of your saying that you want no more of it. Shall I remind you, m'lady?''

The memory of that incident had already begun to filter into her anger, to soften the edges of her obduracy, and now his words and the nearness of his lips overpowered all argument, as he had known they would. Unable to move or speak, Aletta could now only watch helplessly as he slid one arm beneath her waist, arching her towards him, slowly pulling her close against his body as though daring her to resist, giving her every chance to twist away, to cry out, knowing that she would not. His mouth hovered above hers unhurriedly, allowing her to watch his eyes and feel his warm breath on her face.

''Shall I?'' he repeated.

Her lashes drooped against his cool cheeks as she savoured the first touch of his lips on hers, her resistance curbed by an uncontrollable longing to taste him just once more, to feel his hands, his body over hers—experiences so different from her previous ones that it was as though she needed another chance to verify her recent discovery. Yes, she did recall. In spite of her violent protests during their quarrel, his kiss brought all the dreams of the past week back into focus and sought to transmute his unreasonable demand into a prospect so alluring, so beguiling, that her body cried out for her to say, yes, yes.

Gently, on a warm current of sensation, she was swept along and submerged, knowing that she should resist, push him away, maintain her outrage, but aware that her hands betrayed her participation, not pushing but holding him, not fighting but caressing.

''Now do you remember, my lady?''

Aletta turned her head away. He knew the answer to his question as well as she. But she would not say so.

''Look at me, Aletta,'' he demanded. ''We're going to reach an agreement on this…''

''In *your* favour, I suppose?'' she snapped, her eyes blazing once more. "One kiss and I'm supposed to fall in with your demands, am I? Well, I've done very—"

"Yes, vixen! In my favour, as you say! Unless, that is, you want to be held responsible for ruining the lives of a number of families?"

"Oh! How can you *dare* to say that?" She lurched away with such speed and fury that she was off the bed and across the other side of the room, like a tightly coiled spring suddenly loosed.

She saw nothing of the smile on her antagonist's face. It was true that his case had been thoroughly prepared, and from what he'd learned about the lady he knew that there was nothing which would have made a better weapon to dig her out of the set pattern of her existence. Already he had gained access to her where others had failed, and now it would need all his firmness, all his tenacity, and a neat bit of sword-play to take the contest to its conclusion.

Let her fume for a while, he thought, as he walked across to the door and leaned against it with folded arms. He glanced at the heavy outer door in the far corner, where stone steps led into the courtyard below, checking to see if its bolts were drawn. They were, but she'd have to get past him to reach it. Meanwhile, she stood with her back to him, rigid with anger.

"This arrangement will not be entirely one-sided, my lady. It will have advantages for you too."

"I don't want to listen to you!"

He ignored her remark, smiled, and continued, knowing that her words were merely a formality. "I'm not set to hurt or abuse you, in spite of the method of my proposal. This may seem to you like an act of brutality, but I have my reasons, and one day you will come to understand them."

Aletta turned at that, and Sir Geraunt was aware of her great dark and troubled eyes searching his. He wished that he could rub away all the years in which she'd been abused.

"Reasons? Hah!" she hissed. "I think I know enough about men to know what your reasons might be, Sir Geraunt. But there must be plenty of willing females who'd be glad to accommodate you!"

"Enough, vixen! I've told you, it's *you* I want."

"My property and my bed, sir. Why not be honest?"

"*You,* Aletta!"

She shook her head slowly, a frown flickering across her brows, and she came towards him, skirting the edges of his position like a fencer looking for a way under his guard. "Why?" she whispered. "If not my property, why me? You must know you'll find no joy here, sir. Let me be frank with you, since nothing else I can say appears to have any effect."

She placed herself beyond him, out of arm's reach. "You don't understand how it was with…with Sir Hubert…" The nightmares came flooding back and she hesitated to remember how it had been with him—the hurts, the humiliations, the appalling touch of his hands on her body, his mouth. She could not go through all that again. "He was…" She could not even say it, the loyalty of years was too deeply ingrained for her to change now. With hands spread helplessly wide, she shook her head and turned away to the window, her face burning with shame and disgust and her arms crossing her body tightly, as though to keep the demons of memory out. How could anyone ever understand? A man, at that?

But Sir Geraunt needed no detailed explanation. "Lady Aletta," he said, "I've already told you that I knew your husband."

"I didn't like it." Suddenly the words found a way out. "With him?"

"Yes. You think it will be all right. But it won't. You'll be angry with me because I won't be able to…to…" Her words fell out in gasps.

"To give yourself?" He noted that although she was

setting out her reasons to refuse him, she was talking as though it was a problem waiting to be solved.

"Yes," she whispered, distressed by the memory of those nightly obligations, which had so repulsed and hurt her. "You're expecting me to do…that… And I can't… Not any more… It hurt me… Please…" Her last word was engulfed in a sob of anguish, and she turned quickly to find a shadowy corner away from the light, away from him.

She was caught by his two strong arms and held against his wide chest, and, while soothing hands caressed her back, soft sounds of comfort were absorbed into her disordered hair. For many moments she was held close against him as she'd never been held before, soothed, softened, hushed into peace.

"Aletta," he said at last, turning her face up to his. "Listen to me. The way we'll do it will be nothing like that. I swear it."

"How can you know that?" she wailed.

"I do know. I shall never force you. Or do anything you don't want me to. You'll not be hurt. The time will come when you'll want it—"

"No! Never! I don't need a man…"

"Peace, vixen!" he laughed, stroking her hair, now free of its veil. "Tell me you haven't enjoyed my kisses, then. Come on. Tell me!" He waited, smiling down at her, knowing that she could not.

"No!" she said, pulling away from him.

"No, what? You haven't enjoyed them? You expect me—?"

"No, not that."

"What, then?"

"Sir Geraunt." Aletta focused her attention on the bowl of flowers, trying to shut him out of her thoughts as she concentrated on her argument. "This is ridiculous. You must know it cannot be. You're demanding that I become your mistress to save four of your villeins from prosecution and to save myself into the bargain. The situation is absurd. I cannot win, either way, but at least I shall know what fate has in store for me if I decide to fight you in the courts.''

''*You* might know, that's true. But what of them? You're willing to put them through all that, and risk losing, just because of your personal qualms?''

''Personal qualms? Is *that* how you see my objections?'' She whirled round to him, bristling with indignation. ''I was right! You don't understand!''

''I understand only too well, wench!'' He caught at her wrist as she tried to hold him away. ''I understand that you've broken the law and helped four of my villeins to break it too. I understand that you must have known what the consequences would be but you chose to ignore it. I understand that your body needs a man— No, wench, you'll hear what I have to say. Your body longs for loving, but your armour is buckled on so tightly that no one can get near you. Well, I've found a way in, my lady, and I'm going to get to you. Think on it!''

Though her head was turned away from him, she was held by one wrist, with no option but to hear him, hear words of such authority and potency that her legs felt weak with longing and dread. Everything he'd said was true, but his arrogance was insufferable. Yet his way with her, his commanding manner, his kisses, his combination of roughness and gentleness, these were exciting and infinitely preferable to months or even years of wrangling in court and a possibly disastrous result. He'd said there would be advantages for her; he'd said he'd not be unkind...

Slowly she turned and looked at him, at his powerful shoulders and strong jaw, his hazel eyes glinting at her in readiness for her answer. ''Are you going to be demanding?'' she whispered, knowing that her body had already sent out signals of capitulation.

''Certainly! Whenever necessary. But I shall not be unreasonable, if that's what you fear.'' He knew what she would ask next.

''And the four families? They can stay? You won't pursue them?''

He smiled and released her wrist. ''Little champion of all defenceless creatures.'' He laughed, looking down at her. ''Yes, they can stay. As long as you accept my terms I will not pursue them, their families or their tithings. But I will have no more pilfering of my villeins. Is that understood, my lady?''

She nodded. Yes, she understood, and at that moment hoped that he would let the matter rest there, without pressing the agreement any further. But she was not to be let off so lightly.

''Come here, Aletta.''

A moment's hesitation, and she came to him, unwillingly.

His arm went around her waist and a hand held her chin. ''Now, vixen. Tell me that you've accepted my terms.''

She tried to jerk her chin away but he would not let her and her eyes sparked into his, adding fuel to what she saw as an unnecessary confirmation of the future state of things. She'd not wanted it to sound like a formal contract, more like an understanding of sorts.

''Come on. I want to hear it from you. Simply!''

His use of the last word was deliberate provocation, she knew, and the dangerous flash of anger in her eyes was fully matched by his. She was outstared. ''I don't have any choice, do I? As you've already made clear.''

''No, my lady. You don't have any choice. None at all.''

''Then I have to accept your terms, sir. Reluctantly.''

''Reluctantly or otherwise, Aletta. It makes no difference.'' His arm tightened about her waist and his hand moved to cradle her head as his lips closed on hers, demanding, as he'd assured her he would be.

She felt the difference in his kiss this time, intense, powerful and deep, sweeping her into his life like the strong currents of the river in spate. The gentle eddies and swirls of the previous times were now engulfed in a new torrent and she could only cling to his shoulders like one drowning in the depths of his will. This was a demonstration of his power. He had got what he came for.

Leaning over towards the jug of flowers on the table, Sir Geraunt removed a tiny primrose and tucked it into the coils of her glossy brown hair. And that was where Bridie found it some time later when she entered the solar.

For all the cook's efforts, Aletta might as well have been eating cattle-fodder, for she tasted nothing. The attractive dishes were presented and served with the usual grace and style but her mind was not on the food, nor even on the gentle humour at the high table. It was on the guest at her side and their conversation of that morning.

The main meal of the day in mid-morning was always a pleasant affair, and all those present knew how important it was for them to maintain a certain standard of etiquette as long as she was there. For this reason, she made a point of being present every day, when it would often have been more convenient for her to have eaten alone. But they looked to her as master and mistress combined, and formality was rarely dispensed with.

No more noisy howling, yelling, brawling or bawdiness, which had been the normal pattern of behaviour in former times, but a place of ease, comfort and laughter, polite conversation, debate and good manners. Though the great hall was used as dining-room, bedroom, court-room, parlour, office and general meeting-place, it was kept spotlessly clean, sweet-smelling and free of rushes on the floor, a peculiarity of their mistress which strangers did not understand but those who knew her did.

Sir Geraunt's presence by her side was now, she realised, something she'd have to adapt to, though his reasons for choosing to be there remained an enigma to her. If this was simply another variation on the theme of a way into her bed and her property, then she had to admit that it was more effective than anything else which had so far been tried, including many bold suggestions and an attempt, a year ago, at physical coercion.

Even Bridie had admitted, on finding the second primrose in her hair, that she'd have shed no tears to have been kissed, in a ditch or elsewhere, by a man like that. It was the first time that Bridie had seen the cause of Aletta's previous anguish, and while she had replaced the tiny flower in her mistress's newly-arranged wimple she had also noticed the reddened nose and eyelids, and knew that it was far from being a simple love-match. But she had asked no questions, nor had Aletta enlarged upon their morning's encounter, except to say that Sir Geraunt had agreed to allow the four Allerton men to stay, that he'd refused to release Gerda's Thomas and yes, he had kissed her again. But which of these had caused the tears Bridie had not deduced.

While she had been restoring her mistress's face and hair, Sir Geraunt had been taken by Roger to see the stables. Now, at the close of the meal, while Aletta sat back in her chair and toyed with a piece of apple spiced with cinnamon, she was able to observe him as he leaned forward across her to talk to Roger about the horses.

Had things been different, she might not have been so reluctant to accept him as her lover, she thought, but things were not different. She was not such a fool that she could not recognise a property-seeker when she saw one, and if he pretended now that his interests did not lie in that direction, she, for one, was not convinced.

"Until you ask me to marry you…" he'd said. Marry him? Ask him? She could think of no reason why she should ever do that. Maybe in time he'd realise that it was an impossibility and give up. But another peep at his strong jaw-line reminded her of his fierceness and of the others who'd run off, almost yelping with fright at her own fierce attitude towards them. He had not been put off, it seemed, but had actually challenged her. And, so far, he had been the victor on all three occasions.

She noted his neat ears, flat against his head, surrounded by dark, crisp hair, and she longed to touch them with her fingertips, surprising herself by the almost irresistible temptation. Madness, she told herself. Madness. There can be no joy in this ridiculous alliance. For one thing, how was she going to account for his frequent presence at the manor? Was she to pass him off as just a friend, and how long would it be before everyone realised he was more than that?

Again, her eyes searched him as he continued in conversation, noting his long, elegant hands, strong enough to fight, for he'd been trained as a knight, and she had felt their strength. Gently she eased a long pointed sleeve-end away from her wrist to look. Yes, there were bruises plainly etched in pale blue and red along the line of her thumb. Clasping her hands to her, she looked up to find that Roger had turned away and that Sir Geraunt was watching the investigation with an unmistakable twinkle in his eyes.

"Bruises, m'lady?"

"Yes, sir," she answered, darting a resentful glance at him, aware that this was a perfect opportunity to emphasise her vulnerability. "Bruises, all over again."

The twinkle in his eyes grew and he shook his head slowly at her. "Oh, no, Aletta. My sympathy can't be bought so cheaply. You know full well there are other ways to get bruises than with outright violence. I look forward to teaching you to fall without getting hurt."

His voice was low enough to escape the hearing of any but herself and she shot a withering glance at his laughing face, aware that her bid for compassion had misfired. "Shall we go, sir? You said you'd like to see Oswald."

"Gladly, m'lady. May I congratulate you on a superb meal? You obviously know how to get the best from your servants. You deserve much credit."

They left the table and walked through the centre of the hall until they reached the screens passage. Turning along its dark length towards the inner courtyard, Aletta stopped to peep into the kitchen, called out an order to the pantler and closed the door again, thoughtfully turning to her guest. "The credit you speak of has cost me much," she said seriously. "My two years' freedom was dearly bought. Now I've lost it again."

He leaned against the wall, noting her defiant expression, and wondered how much she would try to fight against his control. She would certainly try everything she knew to break it, he was sure of that. "Was your act of charity to four families dearly bought too, Aletta?" he asked.

The freedom which she had lost was now his; she had to make some show of rebellion to make him earn his adopted role of keeper. "I believe it was a price which need never have been demanded. I've noticed that you're inclined to ask payment of a strange nature, but I don't pretend to understand it. Why should anyone wish to have power over anyone else? Is it something I should know about?"

He chose not to answer directly. "I believe you will not find it too unpleasant, Aletta. You may even grow to enjoy it!"

"Never!" she flashed angrily, her eyes blazing fire in the reflected light from the doorway.

The quick retort brought a wide grin to his handsome face as they approached the busy inner courtyard, enclosed by buildings on all sides. He stood with her for a moment on the threshold. "Don't be tempted to lay a wager on that, vixen, for you'll surely lose... Now, which is Oswald's door?" And he had turned before she could make a suitable reply.

* * *

"Oswald Freeman. Well, well. A treat indeed." Sir Geraunt's words were quietly spoken, but Aletta's sharp ears picked them up as he bent his head under the low beams of the room. The old man was awake, pale grey eyes wide and searching, finally coming to rest on Aletta with the warmth of recognition.

"Someone's here who wishes to see you, Oswald."

The skeletal face registered a frown as Sir Geraunt's large frame blocked out the light for a moment, and the voice was faint. "Who is it?"

"A neighbour from Allerton Manor, Oswald. Sir Geraunt de Paine."

A wildly uncertain look clouded his eyes. "De Paine? Geraunt de Paine? Geraunt?"

Two strong hands on her shoulders moved Aletta to the side, and she watched in surprise as Sir Geraunt knelt down by the bedside and took the old man's hand between his own. Perplexed by this sudden intimacy, Aletta watched in astonishment as Oswald's free hand came to rest as lightly as a feather on the dark glossy head, then, without another word, she and old Edwise withdrew, rather than intrude upon a private moment.

"They know each other?" Aletta asked Edwise.

Together, they sat on the wooden bench against the wall, watching the activities within the courtyard. Edwise was old, and leaned her head back wearily.

"Aye. Fancy him coming to live up here, though."

"How, Edwise? How did they come to know each other?"

"Oh, lass. I don't know, for sure. Oswald knows scores of people, and I remember Geraunt went with his father to live down on one of their other estates when they quarrelled with Sir Hubert. I heard he'd gone abroad, but don't ask me why or what. My memory's going now, lass." She rubbed her forehead with a gnarled hand and yawned. "It was before he was knighted they knew each other. Aye,

that'd be it. He was a squire, I believe, a young squ…''
The yawn overflowed into her words and slowed them to
a halt.

''Can't you remember any more? Not just a little bit?''
Aletta coaxed, noting the already closed eyes.

''No, lass.'' The frail voice tailed off, and it seemed that
she'd fallen asleep in mid-sentence.

There was much to be learnt about Sir Geraunt's con-
nections in the area, that much was clear, for he was no
stranger here, as she'd at first thought. He had shown, in
part at least, that he was aware of her own experiences at
Sir Hubert's hands and had known of Oswald too. And yet,
she realised, it must often happen that years passed before
people met once more those they had known in earlier days.

She could only assume that the circumstances would
emerge in due course, so she would ask no questions and
hope that he would tell her in his own good time. It was
not in her scheme of things to give him the impression that
she was curious about him; she would much rather he believed that she thought about him rarely, if ever.

The truth was, she thought, listening to Edwise's snore
at her side, that her life had suddenly grown complicated—
too many contradictions, complexities, fears and doubts,
mixed up with past experiences. Too much to explain; too
much to understand. But this much she knew: while her
physical attraction was almost too strong to bear, those
things which she'd learnt to hold most dear and inviolate,
her body, her privacy and, most of all, her freedom, were
being threatened. After years of mishandling, her emotions
were as though balanced on a knife-edge, teetering and uncertain, and in spite of her so far successful efforts to keep
her fortress intact, this overbearing and dominant creature
had engineered a way—wilfully, not accidentally—of removing her control and replacing it with his own. A complete stranger, at that.

Only one good thing had been achieved so far, the fact

that, as long as she appeared to go along with his wishes, the four May Day families would be safe. They would never know the cost to her personal happiness, nor would anyone else, but that was a problem she would have to learn to live with.

The subject of her musings appeared in the doorway, blinking at the midday sun, then, without saying a word, he held out his hand to Aletta and she took it obediently, glancing sideways at old Edwise as she slept in the warmth, and he led her back into the cool, dark passageway of the manor.

The pantler approached them from the great hall. "Beg pardon, m'lady. I've done as you ordered, but who's to be almoner today?"

Aletta halted. "Alms? Hykke took them yesterday, didn't he? So I think it's time Tebb did it, don't you? But keep an eye on things, because you know he'll eat the lot before they get it if you're not watchful!" They laughed.

He touched his forehead in respect and went on into the kitchen.

Aletta turned to Sir Geraunt, her hand still enclosed firmly in his. "Tebb's a dear man. One of the indoor servants, but in all his fifty-odd summers he hasn't yet learned how to stop eating. So we don't let him do alms duty too often. I prefer not to have an almoner. It's something I think they should all take a turn at."

Sir Geraunt looked down at her almost tenderly. "Remarkable!" he said.

"Remarkable? It's not *so* remarkable, is it?"

"You. You are."

Aletta lowered her eyes to cover the sudden glow of confusion at his unaccustomed tenderness. "I think you should release my hand, Sir Geraunt. My servants will be thinking things…"

"What things, Aletta? What will they be thinking?" His voice was teasing, but he kept her hand in his.

Aletta bit her bottom lip, refusing to look at him. "Go home," she said urgently. "Go home and repent on your day's work and regret your sins. Then you can come back tomorrow and tell me it was all a jest, or a dream."

He moved her back against the cool, white-washed wall of the passageway and placed a hand on it alongside her head. Despite the comings and goings of her household, she was aware only of his closeness, intense and exciting.

"I shall go home now, indeed, m'lady, taking back with me exactly what I came for. As for repenting and regretting, I do neither of those things. They're dangerous habits. I'd not hoped you would invite me so soon. I *will* come back tomorrow, but don't expect me to tell you that our conversation this morning was a jest or a dream, for I was never so serious about anything in my life. Is that clear, Aletta?"

Unwillingly, her eyes were drawn up to his, and she saw the strength of his words in the deep, green-flecked hazel of them. She nodded, wordless and enthralled, and whether she trembled from the coolness of the wall at her back or from his confirmation of intent, she did not know. He answered her nod with a slight one of his own and straightened up away from her. With a hand resting lightly on her waist, he escorted her to the wide open door at the front of the house.

"Ready to go!" he called to a grey-liveried groom in the front courtyard. Instantly the young lad brought his conversation to an end and dashed like a rabbit through the passageway, his feet echoing on the stone-flagged floor and his voice reverberating in the distance.

"Ready to go! Master's ready to go…"

"What? How many grooms did you bring, for heaven's sakes?" Aletta asked, half laughing in surprise.

"Five!" he said nonchalantly, trying not to smile.

"Five? I thought you'd come alone this morning. That's why I asked you where they were."

"I know. I knew you'd ask me!"

"But why five, sir?"

"Because you told me you'd have an escort of six, and I had to let you win something, didn't I?"

She lowered her head to hide her grin. "And what of my whip, sir? Have you returned it?"

"No. It belongs to me now. Spoils of war."

Aletta felt another surge of excitement as he stood before her, four-square and undaunted by anything she could throw at him. This man, she thought, is going to be difficult to budge. Again, she tried to hide her smile as he mounted and rode away, thinking that time was going to weigh heavily until he reappeared on the morrow.

"What are we going to do, m'lady?" Gerda had whispered, forlorn and distraught after hearing the news of Sir Geraunt's refusal.

"Wait, Gerda." Those had been his words, unfeeling and brutal, and were all that Aletta had had to offer at that moment. Further words from the maid had been quelled by a glance and a frown from Bridie, who could see that her mistress was preoccupied, and there the matter had to be left, for the time being unresolved. As a way of softening the blow, Aletta had told Gerda that she could sleep at home each night instead of at the manor, giving her more chances to meet her Thomas whenever he was free to visit.

Now from the comfort of her bed, Aletta watched the steady flame of the cresset-lamp providing a point of focus for her meditations on the day's events. The afternoon had been busy enough for her to hold the morning's confabulations at bay while she examined stores for the coming Easter week—checking the stocks of fish, beef, bacon and poultry, beans, butter, last year's honey from the hives, eggs, cheese and lard, enough malt for the ale, and bread baked enough to leave the oven free for the villagers who wished to use it. Many of them still preferred to use the huge manor oven rather than risk a fire by baking at home.

Tomorrow there would still be plenty left to do, but somehow she would have to put aside some time for her guest.

In the silence of the night, she reflected on the happenings of the day, for with the coming of darkness it was as though another page of her life had been written, resolving some problems and causing others. She recalled her question to Sir Geraunt, "You intend to take advantage of *me* then...?" and his prompt reply, "Certainly!" without a moment's hesitation. She squirmed deeper into the bed, still excited and angry at the indelicacy of his reply. Had she really expected him to give her anything but the truth of his intentions?

Nevertheless, the situation was a delicate one, and ambiguous too. As lady of the manor, she felt it would be unseemly for her to bestow special favours of friendship on their new neighbour so soon, especially in view of her well-known antipathy to property-seeking suitors, and she wished desperately that she could be more sure of the outcome of this liaison, with its overtones of friendship and its undercurrents of enmity.

Was this to be worse than having a husband, then? A lover? After just two years of freedom, another man, a stranger who'd not be shaken off as the others had been, who'd expect her to be available for his pleasure? No! The very idea was absurd. She'd told him so already, but he had brushed aside her arguments, determined to involve her in his plan. How could she convince him that it was impossible? Totally unacceptable.

She would have to explain to him tomorrow what problems it would create, tell him that although she knew that many noblewomen who had lost their husbands did take lovers, for her it was unthinkable. She had tried to set an example of good behaviour in every respect—he'd even noticed that during his visit—so how could she now justify the presence of a lover?

But the night was no place for viewing such problems.

In the darkness, the only place she could set them out before her was inside her head, out of context, and here they jostled and overlapped, vying for dominance. No space, no light, no time between tossing and turning, no respite from his voice, his eyes, his hands. No kindly sleep to rescue her. And, for the second night, the sounds of the dawn chorus lured her into slumber.

Chapter Six

Lady Aletta was not unused to nights of broken sleep, for until recently it had been the usual way of things. So she had adopted the habit of going about her daily business as far as possible and perhaps catching up on sleep at intervals during the day, between bouts of activity.

After making her presence felt in the hall, giving her ladies and esquires their duties for the day, speaking with the officers of the household, visiting Oswald and Edwise, organising Holy Day work with Roger and Jem, and giving instructions for the coming celebrations, she heaved a mental sigh of relief and headed for the garden, alone at last.

The loud clatter of hooves gave her warning of Sir Geraunt's arrival, but Aletta did not turn to look as she entered the large walled garden, expecting that it would take him quite some time to find her since she'd told no one of her intentions. Round to the left of the heavy wooden garden door, a pathway ran along the sunny wall, where cherry-trees were already sending out new shoots, and in the herb-plots on the other side the mint was knee-high and the woody stems of the rosemary were covered in pale new growth.

Caressing them as she went, Aletta headed towards the tunnel-shaped arbour, hoping that even the bare structure

would help to conceal her presence, though the eglantine
roses had not yet begun their journeys, nor had the honeysuckle grown thick enough to make a screen. Even so, a
wren had begun to house-hunt in the densest parts, and
Aletta stopped some distance away to watch the lightning-
swift darts of the tiny bird, quite oblivious of the figure
who approached her, silently over the soft ground.

It was the wren's reaction which alerted her to his presence and she whirled round to face him, her expression far
from welcoming. "You!" she frowned.

"Me. Another few weeks and you'd have been quite
hidden." He remained at a standstill several paces away,
totally at ease, finely dressed in dull blue, grey and silver,
his long divided bliaud hanging to calf-length and edged
with delicately woven braid. A blue velvet cloak hung over
one shoulder, trailing to the ground.

Aletta swept a glance from top to bottom and back up
again, then turned, with lips pressed tightly against any
courteous greeting. She would get this over and done with,
before he could think up new arguments. "Sir Geraunt—"
she turned halfway to him, touching the new leaves on the
arbour-frame "—I have reconsidered. Your suggestion of
yesterday—"

"It was not a suggestion."

Aletta heaved a sigh of annoyance at his contradiction
and tightened the muscles of her cheeks, her words now
clipped for accuracy. "Your *demands* of yesterday…" she
glanced at him and noted his nod at the new word "…are
not acceptable. I cannot go along with your…your…"

"Plan?" he volunteered.

"Your *despicable* plan!" she snapped, thoroughly net-
tled by his unwanted assistance.

"Despicable?" he asked mildly.

"Yes! Despicable!" She waited for his response but he
made no sound. His lack of reaction made her uneasy, and
her well-prepared sentences dried. "I think…think…you

may have forgotten that I must set a good example of behaviour here…''

''No, I hadn't forgotten.''

''Will you please stop interrupting me?''

He smiled, and folded his arms across his chest, waiting.

Aletta continued. ''I must set a good example. I cannot let it be seen…or even suspected…that I have a…''

She could not say the word, and now, when she would have welcomed his verbal support, he remained silent, smiling at her confusion.

''You have said that you will pursue your claim to your villeins, even after a whole year, and you're entitled to do that, if you think it's worth it, but I've decided to take the risk. After all, I was warned about the effect of my actions and I chose to ignore the warnings. I shall have to suffer the consequences. But I'm not going to get involved in any furtive comings and goings into my solar when the whole household knows how I feel about such matters. They would know it to be a lie and I would lose any credibility with them when I came to advising them about such matters. There it is.'' She looked at him at last. ''Now you know.''

She braced herself for the protests, the arguments, further demands, but nothing came. No sound except soft gasps of laughter.

''You're laughing!'' she said indignantly. ''This is no jest, I assure you!''

''No, vixen. No jest.'' He shook his head at her.

''What, then?''

''Predictable!''

''Predictable? What d'you mean, predictable?''

''You, vixen. All it takes is one sleepless night, then we're back again, thinking up reasons why you can't keep your word. I knew it would happen.''

''You knew?''

''Yes. Of course I knew.''

"And you're going to release me?" She knew the question was a futile one, for his folded arms indicated his resolution; his narrowed eyes and gently shaking head confirmed it. "Sir Geraunt, you *must* try to understand… I'm in a difficult position here. A man may do what he pleases and no one will think anything of it… But a woman cannot behave…behave in the same way. Please!"

Sir Geraunt unfolded his arms and moved towards her at last, his face serious now, and softening at her despair. She could smell his coolness as he stood before her; the air of the pines clung to his clothes.

"Let me ask you something, my lady. And give me an honest answer, if you please. What did you do for protection during the last two years when you had visits from unwanted guests—friends of your late husband, I believe—when your household were unable to keep them out and prevent them creating havoc night after night, eating your stores, making demands upon you and your ladies? What did you do then?"

Aletta was taken completely unawares. It was true. Sir Hubert's friends had arrived more than once to take up what they believed was an offer of everlasting hospitality, pressing their attentions upon Aletta and her ladies, drinking and eating everything in the manor, and galloping over her land in pursuit of anything that moved. Not only had they forced her houndsmen down in the village to loose her hounds, but had then encouraged them to rampage all over the place and do untold damage wherever they'd roamed.

On each visit, they had stayed for twelve or more days, bringing with them retinues of servants and friends, all of whom had had to be housed and fed, after which Aletta's supply of food and drink had all but disappeared. It had been with the utmost difficulty that she had managed to keep them out of her solar, for they had been used to carousing in there while Sir Hubert was alive, and so the rest of the household had had to suffer the verbal and physical abuse, the rowdiness and fighting long into each night as the guests had revelled in the great hall. The memories made her shudder.

"How did you know about all that?" she asked, frowning.

"Heavens! It's no secret. Everyone for miles around knows what happened. How many times? Two? Three? Four?"

"Three," she whispered.

"After Easter? During the summer months?"

"Oh, yes. They wouldn't come all this way during the winter."

"So, how did you protect yourself?"

Aletta turned her head away, knowing that he was already aware of the answer. She had had little protection, for they had been guests, and her own household had been outnumbered since she had dismissed so many of her late husband's yeomen and squires, knights-at-arms and pages after his death, most of whom had been hand-picked by him. Since then, she had managed with far less than the usual number of personal servants and esquires, being little concerned with the show of power now that she was free.

"Well?" he insisted.

"If you already know so much, you will also know the answer to your question, Sir Geraunt. You do not need me to tell you."

"But I do, Aletta. Do you not remember what I said yesterday about there being advantages for you in our agreement? Did you not think that this might extend to protection against a repetition of such visits?"

"I cannot for the life of me see that having a…a *lover*—" she spat the word out, as though it had burned her tongue "—could protect me from the attentions of other property-seekers!" She turned quickly.

"Then think, vixen!" He took her by the shoulders before she flounced away and pulled her back to face him. "You're intelligent enough! Think!"

"Think?" she snarled. "Think what? That they'll see I'm not inviolate, as they were told. That I *can* be bought if the price is high enough? What is it that you want me to think? That I said no to them, and yes to you? Is that it?"

"No, vixen. Calm down." He held the hands which pushed at his chest. "You're on the wrong track. The problem can be dealt with quite easily, so that it need never bother you again. Look…" He pulled a soft leather pouch over his hip to the front of his belt and brought out something small in his closed fist. "This thing in my hand, Aletta, will stop all idle speculation before it even begins, all suppositions, all chatter about what you call the furtive comings and goings into your solar, and it will be the ultimate answer when uninvited guests come to call in the future." He opened his hand and revealed a gold ring.

Instantly, without a second glance, Aletta turned and would have strode away. "No!" she barked, her face set and closed. "I know what—"

"No, you don't, vixen!" Sir Geraunt had anticipated her flight and caught her back by one arm. "Come back here. You haven't seen—"

"A ring, Sir Geraunt? A wedding-ring? I don't need to see!"

"Look again, Aletta!"

Sharply she looked again; the tone of his voice had implied that she was mistaken.

"Look at it!" He held it up before her eyes into the sunlight which poured through the frame of the arbour. "Not a wedding-ring."

"A betrothal ring. That's just as bad, sir."

The ring was small, gold, quite new. Two hands clasped each other in the familiar design of betrothal rings. And he held it to her for her protection, her safety.

"Listen to me. Come over here and let me explain."

"I know what you're going to say, and I don't want to hear it."

"No, you don't know." He pulled her down against him on the bench just inside the entrance and kept one hand over her wrist. "Now, listen to me. This is not a formal betrothal ceremony. It's merely a device, a way of keeping unwanted suitors and guests at bay, and a way of explaining my presence here with you from time to time. At the first hint of an unwanted visit, I'll be over here with my men before you can blink. Willan too, if he's at home. And there's Thomas and his men, if we need any more. We help each other. But wearing this, Aletta, will put it all on a different level—not lover and mistress, but betrothed. If you like, we can tell our closest friends that it's not for real, but simply for your protection. I'm sure they'll accept it, in the light of all the incidents in the last two years. And it will spare your blushes when I come to visit you, which you will find far more acceptable than me taking you to court." His hand slipped around the back of her neck, and when he kissed her all her carefully thought out reasons for resistance dissipated into the air like so much thistledown.

Moments later, and now totally disarmed, she looked down at the ring lying in his hand and floundered for words, knowing that she had already lost precious ground. "Is there more to this than meets the eye, Sir Geraunt?"

"More?" he queried.

"Yes. The ring?"

"No. The choice is yours. You've heard the reasons. It's simply a device—no more, no less. I'm not asking you to make any vows."

"Is that because you don't want to make any either?" she whispered, looking down at his strong hands over hers.

"Lady Aletta." He turned her by the shoulders to face him again, his face deadly serious. "If I thought there was even the slightest chance that you would exchange betrothal vows with me at this moment, I would ask you to. But I'm realistic enough to know that there isn't, is there?''

''No.''

''Because of your previous experiences, Aletta—'' he spoke gently, noting how she bit her lip and looked away ''—and because you feel, for some reason, that your property may be more alluring than you are. So, until you've resolved those problems in your own mind, I shall not waste my time by asking you, knowing what your answer will be.''

''And the bond? What's the real purpose of that, Sir Geraunt?'' She would take advantage of his honesty.

''To gain access to you and to prevent you shaking me off until you've had a chance to make some discoveries.''

''Discoveries?'' This was honesty with a vengeance, she thought, knowing what he referred to, but wanting to hear him.

''Yes, vixen. About yourself. Which I believe you've already begun to.''

''No!'' she countered, fencing at the words she had provoked him to say. ''That's nonsense.''

''Is it, Aletta? Then compare your response to my kiss just now to the first one, when you hardly knew what to do…''

''That's unfair! That's not what I—''

''Not what you expected to hear, I know. But it's true! And I shall show you much more that you've never known…''

''No!'' Suddenly she was in deep water again, fully aware that out there in the depths lurked something not even he appeared to be mindful of, something she'd longed for within marriage, but dreaded outside it. ''If you were a woman, Sir Geraunt, you'd not regard this charade as a game for your delight. Has it not occurred to you that one of the…discoveries…you have in mind might well lead to my disgrace?'' She had no real grounds for expecting this, for her marriage to Sir Hubert had not resulted in even a hint of conception. But, even so, the idea could be used as a barb to prick his complacency.

"You think this is a game, Aletta?" His voice was incredulous, and far from jesting. "Truly, I could have sworn that yesterday I told you I was never more serious. You surely cannot believe that I hadn't thought of the consequences? Or that I would put you in such a position without making some provisions beforehand."

He waited for some response from her, but she believed his questions were rhetorical and so she turned her head to him, to assure him that she was listening, and waited.

"Do you remember, yesterday, when I told you how long this bond would last?"

"Yes."

"Then you will understand that that's what I had in mind. If what you believe might happen *does* happen, you can remember that and ask me to marry you. And I will. Immediately. I swear it. Does that ease your mind, Aletta?"

It was as though certain thoughts were linked by a cord to her womb like harp-strings, which, when they were plucked, were set quivering and singing and crying all at the same time. Her arms and legs trembled, and for a brief moment her deepest inner parts came alive as he spoke. There were no words for her just then—as there are not at such times—but instead she allowed herself to cling to him and gasp huge ragged sighs of relief and longing that came in sobs into his chest, half laughing, half crying.

His hands caressed her back slowly and skilfully, easing away the tensions of the previous moments. So he *had* thought of the outcome, even though her childlessness was obvious to everyone, and he had offered her a solution to all the doubts which had kept sleep at bay for so many hours. News that she was betrothed would soon reach Sir Hubert's old cronies, and many other would-be parasites, and even though it was not genuine, the very thought would keep them away. She knew, of course, that this would be to their mutual advantage, since their land adjoined on one side and there had been little to stop the encroachment of her unruly guests on to Sir Geraunt's property in the last two years.

Aletta moved apart from him, brushed a stray tear from her cheek and looked once more at the ring in his open palm.

"Well, Lady Aletta? Have you decided what to do?" he asked.

"It isn't binding without the vows, is it?"

He sensed the wariness in her question. "No. It is not legally binding without the vows. As I've said, it's to protect your reputation and your safety. That's all. You can take it off any time you want to. It should give your villagers some sense of security, too. They must have suffered."

"Yes."

"Then you'll wear it?"

She nodded her assent and allowed him to slip it on to her right hand. "For my protection, you say," she whispered, watching his long brown fingers ease it over her knuckle. "But how do I protect myself from you? Tell me that."

"You can't, Aletta. It's too late. I've already found chinks in your armour and I mean to prise you out of it, piece by piece, until you capitulate. I shall have your surrender, m'lady, however long it takes."

The hair on her arms and at the back of her neck bristled at the merciless words and at the tone of his voice, and as she turned to look at him the fear in her eyes must have shown, reflecting the unhappy years of her marriage.

He spoke more gently. "I know what you fear, but you need not. I shall have it without resorting to unkindness, and I've told you that I'll teach you how to fall without being hurt. We'll have to have that lesson soon, methinks."

"That won't be necessary, sir!" she retorted fiercely. "I do not intend to fall!"

Sir Geraunt smiled at that, pleased to see that the fearful expression had already been replaced by the more familiar spark of defiance. But it was not his way to allow her the last word in an argument and he slipped his hand into the pit of her arm against her breast and pulled her up against him, hard. "We'll see, vixen. We'll see," he said, with his lips already on her mouth.

Once again, fear of his mastery over her and anger with herself fought for first place, and then joined forces in a struggle against the restriction of his arms, the authority of his lips. She pushed hard, twisting, arching away, but his mouth moved over her knowingly, brushing her resistance to one side, and she was swept along once more, helplessly, like a leaf downstream.

His kiss left no doubt in her mind that he would be her master, promising battles where there'd be no winners or losers, and bruises which could be treasured like trophies. And, though her head warned her to keep hold of her old wounds and nurture them, her body had already forgotten the pain as it floated upon new sensations.

Aletta's hands moved upwards over the soft fabric of his cloak into his hair, and now she found how soft and thick it was between her fingers. His neat ears, which she'd wanted to touch since yesterday, were cool, his cheek and jaw firm under her thumbs. Slipping her hand round to the back of his neck, her fingers moved against his skin, exploring, caressing.

"Good, wench! That's good," he murmured, moving his lips just far enough away to allow the words room to escape.

She opened her eyes and found that his twinkling hazel ones were looking deeply into hers, and for a moment she was puzzled. "What is?" she asked.

"You've started to explore. That's a good sign." He

laughed softly at her look of dismay and brought her hand round from the back of his neck to place a kiss over the ring.

"I shall not take kindly to this, I warn you, sir." Aletta drew away. "I've grown used to the idea of being my own master."

"Then you'd better start getting used to the idea of a new one. For I warn *you*, wench, that's what I intend to be." With one large knuckle, he moved her chin round to face him again and let his eyes roam idly over her, gently lifted a strand of hair from her forehead and replaced it on top.

It was not the new master which would take most getting used to, she thought, but the lover. The tender gestures— like the lifting of a strand of hair, the kiss to her palm, the caress of his eyes—these were things totally unfamiliar to her, shaking the firm ground beneath her feet every bit as much as his words or his bond.

He led her out of the garden by the hand.

"How did you know I'd had a sleepless night, Sir Geraunt?" she asked.

"How did I know? You're not the kind of woman to sleep in tranquillity after a day like yesterday. I can see that, wench. And I knew you'd need another bout of persuasion today, just to clear up certain points. I was right, wasn't I?" He held the gate open for her to pass through.

Aletta brushed past him, piqued by his sureness. "Your arrogance never ceases to amaze me, sir, and—"

"And your beauty never ceases to amaze me, my lady…"

"And you can put any further bouts of persuasion back into your purse, where they belong."

"A pity to keep them hidden all this time…"

Aletta stopped, and glared. "What? Keep what hidden?"

"My further bouts of persuasion, wench. What else?"

His bellow of laughter brought a flush of colour to her

cheeks, for she knew that he'd intended his innocent remark to apply to both elements of the conflicting banter, and she marvelled at his quick wit while secretly delighting in the earthiness of his thoughts.

Walking through the busy courtyard, now bustling with his grooms as well as hers, they agreed that certain people closest to them must be made aware of the pretend betrothal. Her maids, Roger and Willan, of course, and Mistress Margery, Aletta suggested. She was sure the old lady would understand and be supportive. Sir Geraunt smiled at that and agreed that she must certainly be told, if that was what Aletta wanted.

Later, in the privacy of her solar, Aletta searched her jewel-box for her father's ring and placed it before Sir Geraunt, suggesting that he ought to be wearing one too. At that, he opened her hand and placed it on her palm, asking her if she would not rather do it for him, as he'd done for her. And so she did, half suspecting that herein lay some trick, until he read the hesitation in her eyes and reminded her that it was not valid, only a device for her comfort.

"Comfort?" Bridie said, later still, in the glow of the lamp. "They're funny creatures, aren't they? It's as if I'd just arrived in the place instead of being here for years. Roger said he'd been looking in the wrong direction. Can you believe it?"

"Yes, Bridie, love. I think I can." Aletta smiled.

Predictably, Bridie and Roger had shown understanding when she'd told them of the deception, agreeing that it would certainly allay the fears of the household and the villagers too, who had begun to anticipate with dread another enforced invasion by uncontrollable guests. It was, they had said, a chivalrous act by Sir Geraunt to offer his protection by letting the news get about that Aletta was now spoken for, once and for all.

Though in the snug warmth of her bed, Aletta wondered what they would have said about it if they'd known of the bond too, and of her protection against gossip. It would not take them long, she thought, to note the frequency of Sir Geraunt's visits, or his admission to her private place. But that was for another day.

The peace of Good Friday came as a relief to Aletta after the eventful days of the previous week. Churchgoing and simple food helped to calm her thoughts and ease the tensions in her body, allowing her a chance to be alone, to recuperate, to salve the bruises.

In the past, the conflicts she'd learnt to deal with had been of a physical nature—even the verbal abuse had been delivered to this end. But those generated by her new neighbour were more difficult to recognise or counter by any methods she knew. The net he'd thrown had enmeshed her, tightened around her, and though she could still see the light of day, and feel the world beneath her feet, the freedom which at one time had stretched ahead far into the unknown now appeared to have shrunk.

His overwhelming self-confidence made her afraid, for he seemed certain to carry her with him along a track of his own choosing, whether she willed it or no. Worse than that, she could no longer count on the support of her own body to reinforce her protests, for it was already learning to respond to his skilful persuasions, melting beneath his hands like beeswax in the heat of the sun. If her body could not be relied on to do her bidding, what chance did she have against an early surrender?

The thought of passing her property into someone else's hands, the hands of a stranger to her, was almost too awful to think about. And yet her body demanded to be heard in the argument. She would be passing herself into his hands too, and would *that* be such a terrible thing, it asked her?

Down in the tiny village church, the rambling sermon of Easter Day was punctuated by more of Aletta's thoughts, despite the hushed but friendly chatter of the villagers who crowded in, sitting in groups on the floor or lounging against the stone pillars and the brightly decorated walls. There had been more congratulations and expressions of delight, especially that her betrothed was a local lord, familiar with themselves and the area.

Now the day was their own; the villagers were free to revel and take advantage of their lady's hospitality in the big manor-house. All were welcome—labourers and freemen, millers and alewives, shepherds and ploughmen, women and children, old and crippled. Those who could not find a bench inside the hall sat around the outer courtyard and along the sides, where the grass led into the orchard and round to the stewpond.

Even the freemen had insisted on bringing her the usual gift of eggs, like those of their friends who were still villeins, and now the trestle-tables at the bottom of the steps up to her solar were piled high with baskets full of them.

Everyone was fed, and given small loaves of bread marked with a cross, and every mouth was crammed with meat for the first time since the beginning of Lent, the idea of touching another morsel of fish as far from their minds as work was.

The grassy slopes outside the manor were the ideal place to roll the pace-eggs, and, once the stomachs could contain no more, eggs were handed to the children to roll down the banks, accompanied by shrieks of encouragement and laughter, both children and eggs rolling over and over to finish in tangled and sticky heaps, the winners hotly disputed.

Aletta slipped away through the screens and back into the great hall, laughing still at the antics outside and anxious that the hall servants should not feel they were being neglected. "Let them go as soon as this is cleared, Daw," she called to the house-steward's assistant, dodging aside as a pair of screaming youngsters flew past her legs.

The inner door to Oswald's room was tucked conveniently in the corner at one side of the dais where the high table stood. Having two doors meant that he could come and go into both the hall and the inner courtyard. It was the same for Roger at the other side. She knocked.

Edwise was relieved to see her. "Come, in lass, do," she said in a whisper, and pulled forward a stool. "Here, sit ye down. You look as though you could do with a rest. All this preparation." She took what Aletta offered her with thanks—a cooked chicken and a specially spiced stuffing, some tiny tartlets and the crossed bread-buns.

Every day Aletta had brought food, and every day had noticed how Oswald was getting weaker, sleeping more than waking. "How is he, Edwise?"

The old lady shook her head and looked across. The light from the window reflected on his taut white skin and shone through his snowy beard and hair like a halo. The gnarled yet slender hands lay relaxed and beautiful on the fur covering of the bed and Aletta wished with all her heart that he would not slip away from her like this, but stay to be the trusted friend and wise comforter he'd always been to her.

"He's hardly woken up today, m'lady."

As though to contradict her, Oswald's hand flapped gently and his voice broke through the reverent hush. "Is that Lady Aletta?"

Aletta went to him and knelt, taking hold of his hand. "It's me, yes, Oswald. Happy Easter. You'll join us for the games tomorrow, won't you? I'm having the litters prepared for both of you. You'll be treated like royalty." She smiled, and though his half-closed eyes did not focus, her smile reached him even so.

"Royalty!" His chest moved slightly, and she knew he was laughing inside. "Royalty. You're the only one, apart from my Edwise, who's ever treated me like that, Lady Aletta." His elegant hand closed round hers on the bed and he fell silent; the effort of his words had exhausted him.

Aletta wondered if he'd fallen asleep again, whether she should withdraw. Her late husband had treated Oswald harshly, despite the fact that he was his own half-brother as well as his steward. The refined good looks of Oswald's peasant mother had surfaced in direct contrast to those of the elder son born in wedlock, and, although their father had insisted on bringing them both up in the same household, Oswald had never been given the same advantages as Hubert, nor had he trained for knighthood. Instead, he had become learned, bright and businesslike enough for Sir Hubert to employ him as steward of his estates.

But gradually, as debt after debt had overtaken him, and he had been forced to surrender his cluster of manors, Sir Hubert had come down hard on his half-brother, accusing him of inefficiency, even embezzlement, and threw him out of office, out of his home, out of his life. But Sir Hubert's death had intervened only a few months later and Aletta had had Oswald and Edwise brought back within days and installed in the manor once more.

Her own debt to Oswald was immense, for his kindness and spiritual help had kept her sane during the unbearable years of marriage. He had taught her to account and reckon, and to manage the affairs of the manor, at a time when she had needed the solace of some aim in life.

After Sir Hubert's death, Oswald's good management, his reliability and his fairness too, at last had a chance to take effect, and so, with Roger's help and Aletta's enthusiasm for change, her two remaining villages had become models for other less caring landowners in the dales.

A slight squeeze of his fingers on hers told Aletta that he was not asleep. "What is it, Oswald?"

"There are some books—ledgers, rolls—up there." With his eyes he indicated the shelf at the end of the bed where the accounts were stacked in piles and bundles. "You should take them, Lady Aletta."

She knew what he was saying, but couldn't do it. Though

she knew they'd have to be returned to her eventually, this was not the time to reach over and carry them off. It would be like admitting that his role was finished. "No, not now. We'll go through them together when you're stronger. Sleep now, Oswald."

"Remind Edwise."

"Yes, dear one. I'll remind her."

"What's this?" His hand rubbed lightly over the ring on her finger. Sleep had suddenly been held away by the recognition that something needed an explanation. "A ring? Betrothed?"

"Yes," she whispered. What else could she say? The real reasons for wearing it were suddenly so complex that it was outside her ability to make it easy for him to understand. "Yes. Betrothed. Sir Geraunt."

To her amazement, he smiled. "Good," he whispered.

"You approve, Oswald?"

He patted her hand. It was like a kiss. "You couldn't have done better, my lady." His eyes closed, and sleep came to collect him.

Chapter Seven

So many fair days at this time of the year was remarkable, for it could quite easily have been a period of torrential rain, cold, violent gales or even snow. Last year, Aletta remembered, the Easter Monday games had had to be postponed in favour of rescuing some of the cattle from the flooded meadowland, and some of the people too. The hall had been overflowing that night with damp villagers washed out of their homes, and the rest of the week had been spent trying to fix up new ones on higher ground away from the river. Games indeed, she smiled.

She lay for a few moments longer, watching the shafts of light fall across the room and penetrate the curtains at the end of the bed. Bridie's shadow rippled across it, then Gerda's, bustling quietly, like ghosts. Idly twisting the ring on her finger, she felt a surge of excitement as thoughts of Sir Geraunt crept back into her mind, followed immediately by more wayward sensations of defiance and rebellion.

What an extraordinary state of affairs this was! Betrothed and yet not betrothed, free and yet not free, hating and yet… The ring slid up and down on her finger as she recited the conflicting states of her emotions, finally slipping off altogether to be examined more closely. Strangely, she'd barely looked at it since he'd given it to her, and now she held it up in the first rays of daylight.

It was new and quite unworn, deep gold, the two hands clasped together delicately and beautifully figured. Turning it over and over, she noticed that it was inscribed on the inside, and without making a sound on the wooden floor she slipped across to the east window and held it to the light, frowning to make out the words. *Je tiens les miens*— I hold what is mine.

A curious dull thud kept up a steady rhythm in her breast as she looked across to the distant Allerton, still covered with a night-blanket of heavy mist. I hold what is mine? Hardly a loving betrothal message, she thought. More like a statement of war! Was it his family motto, perhaps?

The ring glinted in the new light and her attention was caught by a slight change in the colour of the gold, dark and richly orange for the main part, but with an inset of slightly paler gold where the ring fitted into the underside of the finger. And yet it seemed as though the words continued through the darker and paler golds, as though they had been inscribed after an extra piece had been let in to make it larger. But if it was new and unworn, as it so obviously was, why had it been necessary to enlarge it? And to make a new inscription? Had it previously been intended for someone else?

For some inexplicable reason, the thought made her angry, and she bolted back into bed, drawing the covers up around her neck. The ring hurt her hand, so tightly did she clutch it. I hold what is mine! Well, she thought militantly, so do I! She had done her best to make that understood.

Angrily, she shoved it back on her finger again, muttering to herself that she would not even tell him that she'd bothered to look at it. All the same, it irked her not to know for whom it had originally been intended—someone who had not worn it—and the thought of wearing a ring made for someone else did not appeal to her at all.

He'd said he would be over to see her this morning, not as a request, but as a statement of fact. Well, then, he could hardly expect that she'd be available at whatever hour he chose to appear, could he? And with some good fortune, and a little more good management, they could both spend quite some time avoiding each other. After that, maybe, he'd be more careful to request a time when it would be convenient.

"Ready for your bath, m'lady? And some food? Will you have it now, or afterwards?"

"I've got an idea!" She sprang out of bed. "Let him wait!"

"What? Pardon, m'lady?" Gerda stood with the tray of food balanced in her hands, puzzled by the brevity of Aletta's instructions.

"Pack the food in that cloth, Gerda. I'm going to bathe up at the pool. Now, there's an old linen chainse, somewhere... That'll do."

A smile flitted across her face as she recalled Gerda's remonstrances. Too cold at this time of the year. Not enough time—How did *she* know?—should they tell him? No, indeed they should not! On pain of death!

Aletta grinned and climbed upwards through the budding hawthorns and over the mossy rocks. No one had seen her take the almost invisible path alongside the stewpond, following the beck that tumbled into it from the crag behind the manor. Almost at once, as the ground rose steeply upwards, she was beneath an awning of dense trees, hawthorn, ash and elder, quite hidden from sight, the tumbling water rolling darkly down at her side in a deep channel. In a few breathless moments she was through the gap where the water poured over the edge of the rocks, her feet planted firmly on the flat limestone shelf. Before her, the huge pool of water shimmered brown, blue, green, rippling with blue-white rings from the water that fed into the far end from the high rocks above. This was her secret place.

It was completely secluded, enclosed on all four sides by trees and rocks, covered over only by an extension of the tree canopy. Layers of bare rocks shelved the way down to the basin of water, easily warmed by the sun before tumbling over the edge and through the hillside down to the stewpond below. Aletta's private bath-house was where she climbed in the mornings, whenever it was not flooded at the entrance, and she'd used it for her personal cleansing ritual after a night of lying in the sweat of Sir Hubert, his hounds' and hawks' droppings, even the dogs' afterbirths, on more than one occasion.

She could never use lye to wash herself here, for it would have appeared in the fish-pond below and she would have been discovered, but it was one of the few places she could come without fear of being disturbed. Only her closest allies knew of its whereabouts, but only she went there.

The waterfall which supplied it was now only a trickle. Steady rain of just a few days could make it impossible for her to squeeze through the gap at the lower end, for it would be a raging torrent by then. Now, however, it was a haven, a sanctuary where she could bare both body and soul, cry, laugh, scream, howl, meditate. The large flat slabs of limestone made perfect steps up one side, and it was here that Aletta left her clothes and food and prepared to slide into the water below.

Gerda had been mistaken; it was not too cold except in the deepest parts and where the water from above splashed on to the surface. Working her way round the edges, she groped for the familiar boulders with her feet, noting the new growth of ferns lining the sides. The cascade bounced off her head and shoulders, then on to her upturned face before she moved on, rolling over and over on the shallow, moss-covered slabs where the water was warmed by the early sun.

Her long hair, now black with wet, spread out around her like a fan, and as she plunged it streamed behind so that she could gather it again as she came up. She sat on the flat rock to wring her hair and hold it on top of her head, and as the water's surface became still once more a glimmer of white rippled its way towards her. She gazed at it, mystified, and watched it become still, feeling her skin tingle as though plunged into ice.

Her arms now shielded her body as her hair fell again, and her eyes widened in horror as she looked up towards the high ledges of rock where her clothes had been left. Sitting at his ease by the side of them was Sir Geraunt, intently watching her, neither moving nor speaking. He had seen her, naked. For how long? Fiend, she raged inwardly. You *fiend!* She couldn't move. How could she move with him sitting there by the side of her clothes? The devil!

"Go away! Get out!" She had no need to shout for the enclosed space made the sound roll around and bounce back. He heard, but said nothing. Only the merest shake of the head told her that he had no intention of moving.

Aletta shivered and looked at the water, knowing that any movement of hers would reveal her nakedness, and regardless of the fact that he'd obviously seen it already, for heaven only knew how long he'd been sitting there, she could not bring herself to pretend that it didn't matter. So she sat, huddled and shivering with cold, fright and anger, wondering how he could possibly have found his way here without using the route up the beck from the stewpond. Her private place was no longer.

"Come on!" he said quietly. Like her, he must have known that he'd no need to raise his voice.

Aletta glared at him and looked away. "I shall stay here until you go! Forever, if need be!"

"That's a long time. And you're getting cold. Come!"

"No! *No!*" And she turned her back on him.

"Aletta! We have a bond. Remember?"

"To hell with your bond!" She was goaded beyond caution, beyond anything. "To hell with you! I'm not moving from here…" Her last words were choked by rage and fright. She would die here on this rock rather than parade up there before him. Her teeth were chattering with cold now, her hair still dripping icy rivulets down her back and arms.

She didn't hear his step behind her, but the old linen chainse which she'd left on the nearby ledge of rock was placed over her shoulders and held across her front by his hand. "Now, stand up! Come!" He lifted her to her feet. "Turn round!"

Her chattering teeth would not unclench fast enough to voice her refusal, but she was given no further chance to argue, for he lifted her up in his arms like a parcel and carried her up the flat rocky ledges where her clothes and food had been left. He lowered her down on to the slab of rock and sat behind her, holding her shoulders as he spread his legs on each side, cushioning her back against his chest. She felt his warmth as she sat, confused and angry, quite helpless to move for fear the linen should fall away from her.

"I hate you!" she growled, stuttering with cold and clutching the old garment tightly in her fists. "You're a fiend!"

She heard his soft laugh as he picked up the loose-hanging sleeves of the chainse and began to rub her hair, steadying her head with one hand while he rubbed with the other. No man had ever dried her hair before. Bewildered, she turned to look over her shoulder at him, but he gently pushed her face round to the front with the sleeve and continued, then moved to her back, rubbing vigorously until a warm glow began to pervade her skin at last.

Without a word, he unclenched her fists and removed the tightly held fabric, held up one wrist in his hand, and dried her arm. She managed to keep herself covered with her free hand, but when he picked that one up to be dried the linen fell away. Calmly and silently, he picked up the dropped fabric and continued drying, holding her wrists up high to reach under her arms. She knew he must have seen her breasts. Aletta was too mortified to speak, knowing that to leap up and away from him would be even worse than staying where she was.

At last he spoke. "Dry your legs while I unwrap your food."

Food? She could have eaten a horse! Draping the chainse over her shoulders again, and folding her arms inside it, he pulled her back against him with one arm. Aletta saw that the sleeves of his white woollen chainse were again rolled up to his elbows, as they had been on that fateful day by the palings, showing his forearms, thick and muscular, covered with fine dark hair. A hand came round under her chin, holding a piece of buttered bread to her mouth and, like a bird, she opened it while he popped it inside.

"That's better, wench. Are you warmer now?"

She nodded, chewing ravenously.

And so they sat silently, back to front, watching the waterfall and the rippling pool and listening to the sounds of the water and trees and the clatter of birds above, Aletta having small chunks of breakfast fed to her from his fingers, her hair tumbling untidily about her shoulders and his arm warming her ribs. Occasionally he ate a piece himself, and they shared the soft, juicy pear between them.

Aletta was now thawing enough to speak without venom. "How did you get in here?"

He turned to glance behind him. "Up there. There's a way in."

She turned to follow his direction, frowning. "How did you find it?"

"I told you before. I know this place like the back of my hand."

"This place, too? All of it?"

"Yes. All of it."

His tone was quite serious, but she turned her head to read his eyes, bringing her nose close to his. For a long moment she looked at his mouth, almost revelling in its nearness to hers, and slowly her eyes moved upwards to find herself locked in hazel pools of dancing light. He made no move towards her and finally her shoulders relaxed and she turned away, wondering.

"Is this thing what you're going to wear today?"

"This? No, this is my drying thing. I always use it. My old kirtle and bliaud are there in that heap."

"Then you'd better get dressed. Come on." He reached over and placed them on her lap.

"Are you going to turn your back?"

"No, I'm staying where I am. And so are you."

She brought her head round to her shoulder. "Please go," she pleaded.

"No."

"Well, close your eyes, then."

He smiled behind her. "Get dressed, wench."

There was nothing to do but to obey; she would have to get on with it as best she could and hope that he'd be courteous enough not to look. But there was no guarantee of this, and she wondered if his forbearance so far was an indication of the day ahead, or a deceit.

Her heart beat furiously as she eased her arms away from the linen and searched for the armholes in her kirtle, aware that the old garment was now slipping from her. As it fell, her hands found the holes; at that very moment his arm slid across her once more, and she felt her head being eased gently backwards on to his shoulder by a hand under her chin. Before she could cry out, his mouth was on hers.

In a daze, she realised what was happening, but his searching lips and his warm hand on her neck claimed all her attention. Weakly, she pushed against him, knowing that this was a useless move in the wrong direction. He allowed her no chance to collect her thoughts and so she was barely aware that his hand had closed over her breast, only that something gentle moved over her skin like the kiss of a butterfly's wings. Then it came to rest, and she knew.

From somewhere deep inside her a frantic demon surfaced, with all the black terror of a nightmare, and, tearing her mouth away, she let out a hoarse wail of dread against his cheek. Her body twisted and strained to escape the touch of his hand on her, struggling frantically against his restraining arms.

"No! No! Please don't!" The old fear of pain was still close to the surface of her memories, still able to break through at the first reminder.

But Geraunt had half expected a reaction of this nature and held her tightly against him, murmuring into her ear until the sound of his voice broke through her panic. "Aletta, hush, sweet thing. You're quite safe. Open your eyes and look at me. Look. It's me. You're safe."

Her eyes flickered open as the struggles abated and she saw who held her, though she was white-faced and trembling still at the memory of other hands on her, brutal and rough.

Again he soothed her with his voice and strong arms. "I shall not hurt you. Hush, you're safe now. Look at me. Watch me, Aletta, and feel the touch of my hand. You know I won't hurt you. Just feel it…" And as he spoke he eased his hand so tenderly on to her breast that she hardly knew he moved. "See," he whispered into her ear, "that's good, isn't it? It doesn't hurt."

The sound of his deep voice reassured her while his eyes held hers, watching the fear subside. As though in a trance, her eyes closed again as he caressed her throat and turned her lips towards him. She felt his warm hand move over her, cupping the fullness of her breast in his hand, and she arched, gasping with the sweetness that flooded into her where before there had only been the ache of emptiness and bruises and fear.

A soft moan escaped her as his kiss carried her away, and now his hands carried her too, into lands she'd never been before, had never known existed. Distantly, she heard the sound of her moans under his lips like a faraway call, aware that her breasts were being gently lifted and stroked, tenderly and slowly, leaving her gasping against him.

"You're still safe." His lips nibbled at hers to rouse her while his hands moved away, and she blinked and turned her face into his neck, feeling the slow rocking of his body as she nestled into him, shaken and speechless. She was thankful for his silence and warm strength, touched by the way he reached for the kirtle with one hand and shook it out to discover the neck opening for her.

As she dressed, her mind still dazed with an intensity of feeling, he sat apart and watched her without speaking, knowing that her words would flow again as soon as she'd recovered. He knew by the furtive looks she shot in his direction that he'd not have long to wait, so he took her shoes in his hand and pointed to a shelf of rock.

"Come on! Foot up!" He held out a hand for her foot.

Aletta obeyed, darting a reproachful glance. "Why did you do that?" she whispered.

"It was irresistible!"

"It was unfair!"

"It was delicious!"

"You took advantage of me!"

"I told you I would."

"Here in my private place!"

"Perfect. No interruptions. No distractions."

"You're impossible!" she growled as he tied the leather thong.

He placed his hands under her arms, laughing, and pulled her up to face him. "And you, wench, were trying to avoid me. Don't bother denying it, and don't try it again! I'm ahead of you in any game you care to play.'' And, taking her hand, he led her upwards to a gap in the rocks.

Conflicting emotions still fought within her, but his challenging words brought her resentment to the surface while others simmered below. ''I don't go this way! I go down there!'' She pointed to the gap below, where the water left the pool, and pulled hard against his hand.

But he held her firmly. ''This way's quicker and easier,'' he said, taking no notice.

''Is your horse there?'' She nodded towards the pathway above them. How did he know it was quicker, anyway?

''No, he's at the manor. Yours too, waiting for us.''

''Mine too?'' Aletta didn't understand. ''Waiting?''

He was leading her now at an unchivalrous pace down towards the manor, her small feet obliged to trot to keep up with him.

''Yes, we're going on a visit.''

She was stung by his tone, unaccustomed to being ordered on her own land, being told what she was going to do, being marched at this unseemly pace. Pulling away abruptly, she stopped in her tracks. ''I am *not* going on any visit with you! You'll have to go alone. I must attend to the tug-o'-war; it's important!''

Sir Geraunt walked back to her, rubbing his nose to hide the grin at her sudden waywardness. He had caught her off-balance earlier and now she was trying, quite naturally, to reassert herself. ''Then there is no problem. The tug-o'-war doesn't begin until just before supper and we'll be back in good time. Come!'' He held out his hand to her.

Damn him! How does he know that? she thought. Her face was rebellious and tight-lipped. She wished she'd thought of another reason. ''I must change! I cannot be seen like this! My hair…!'' That was it, she rejoiced, her unbraided hair would take quite some time to dress.

''Yes, I know, Gerda's waiting for you. Hurry!''

''You ordered my maid to wait on me?'' She was outraged by this presumption. How dared he order her servants?

"No, I *requested* her to wait on you, knowing that you'd need her. I could attend on you myself, if you—"

"No! I must speak with Roger! We have business…" She ignored his outstretched hands.

"I've already told him where we're going."

That was the last straw. "No! I'm not going *anywhere*, I tell you. I'm too busy! I've got other plans… No… *No!*"

She dodged sideways as his arm went round her waist, but before she could say another word she was being hoisted high into the air and flung over his shoulder like a sack of corn. Her hair fell down his back and she beat upon him with her fists, but to no avail. With her legs pinned tightly to his chest, she was carried on his shoulder at a smart pace down the hillside, sobbing with rage and humiliation, squirming in an effort to free herself.

"Put me down, you fiend. Put me down! I can't be seen like this by everyone! Put me down…*please!*" she yelled at him.

At the last word, he stopped. "What was the last word you said?"

There was a pause while she thought. "Please," she snarled through her teeth. "I said please, you brute!"

"Say it louder, vixen!"

"Please!" she yelled angrily at the top of her voice, beating again.

"Now say it politely. A request, not an order!" His voice was maddeningly calm as she was held, dangling helplessly upside-down.

"You're ordering *me!* Why should I not—?"

Without another word, he set off once again down the hill.

"Please, Geraunt! Please? Geraunt?" Her voice rose in panic, pleading. His grip slackened and he stood, waiting again. "Geraunt. Please will you put me down? I'll go with you.'' She was carefully lowered to the ground and placed before him, subdued and breathless, her hair all awry.

"Now, my lady—'' he kept hold of her wrist "—are we agreed that you do my bidding? Or have you any further objections?''

She clung to him for support while the ground settled to a standstill beneath her feet, aware of the dangerous look in his eyes as he waited for the answer they both knew would come. An arrogant, domineering, unrelenting look. Was she really going to have to suffer this ordering of her life as well as of her emotions? Was his "bidding" to be at his beck and call, to be fondled whenever he wished, to come and go when *he* pleased? To have her servants told what she was going to do? Could she take this interference, or would he eventually grow tired of the game and seek some other helpless widow to harass?

In the silence, the air hung heavy with her impotent fury. Half-afraid of him, as she'd been on their first meeting, yet drawn to his strength, his voice, his touch, she knew that even the conflicts like this were binding her to him every bit as effectively as his lovemaking. Through her still damp and tumbling hair, she peeped up at his stern face, but found that his eyes were twinkling with laughter, and she nodded in silent assent.

He saw a wild and stormy creature, vulnerable and tender-hearted, confused, hurt, passionate and yet frightened and defensive. But as they walked back to the manor, hand in hand, he could not help feeling that one more piece of her armour had been removed.

Sir Geraunt looked down from the height of his powerful chestnut stallion, hardly able to keep his eyes from her as she now sat demurely on her favourite grey. All in the space of half a morning she had changed roles from water-sprite to waif, passionate woman to furious child, then cool and poised lady of the manor. What else was to come? he wondered.

With hair now neatly braided and coiled over a circlet of gold set low on her forehead, a neat white wimple swathed around her neck and face, she looked angelic. The long and flowing dagged tippets streamed from the elbows of her sleeves in the soft breeze, showing the rose-pink silk linings like slashes of colour against the cream woollen bliaud and gilded leather girdle. She'd brought her blue woollen cloak with her too, for the journey back might well be cooler. Sir Geraunt had insisted upon it, as he'd insisted that Gerda came too.

The young maid, still somewhat in awe of this huge, fierce-looking man, had looked thunderstruck when Aletta had told her that she was to ride with them to Middlestone. But her trepidation at the thought of riding so far with only Sir Geraunt's two young squires for company had vanished like the morning mists when she saw her own Thomas alongside the Allerton men, liveried in the now familiar grey doublet and sitting astride a good-looking bay.

For a moment, she'd hardly recognised him, so well-groomed and newly-polished, but once she'd discovered that Thomas went too, the length of the journey, though only a matter of five or six miles, seemed suddenly to be of no consequence. Thomas, a brawny lad and a wonder with horses, had been singled out to be one of Sir Geraunt's grooms only the previous day and he'd already distinguished himself by dealing promptly with a case of colic before anyone else had noticed it.

"It was kind of you to employ Thomas in your household," Aletta said, having taken a peep behind her. "It certainly changed Gerda's enthusiasms this morning, and no mistake."

Sir Geraunt smiled at her. "It was not mere kindness, I assure you. I wouldn't think of employing him unless he was good. And he is. Very!"

"But now you'll be even more reluctant to let him go."

"Nothing's changed, m'lady." He grinned at her as she looked disdainfully at him and then beyond to the plough-team in the field across the track.

Aletta's face lit up as she recognised the two men returning their wave. "They're ploughing up the fallow field now, even on Easter Monday. I expect they'll finish by midday and then join in the games."

"You know both of them?"

"Yes." Aletta grinned at him and then back at the men. "One of them's Peter Ghyll and the other's John Clough. Two former Allerton men." She wondered if he would react to the information, and he did, by pulling up so smartly that the chattering quartet behind nearly ran into them. He watched the men, intent on the job even as they approached.

"Keep those alaunts well away, Tom," Sir Geraunt called over his shoulder. "I don't want those two getting underfoot." They were huge, sleek dogs with powerful bodies, long curling tails and sharply pointed ears, specially bred for the boar-hunt.

Aletta wondered if he was being especially careful for her sake, but he'd never once shown surprise that she had no kennels or mews within the manor precincts. "Those are my kennels, over there." She pointed to a low thatched hut as they passed through the outskirts of the village. "I don't have a mews, but I keep a few pairs of greyhounds, just for hunting."

Sir Geraunt looked at her, puzzled. "I thought you disapproved of hunting, Aletta."

She cast a glance at him, remembering how she had made her views felt on that day of their first meeting. "You know how unsuitable this woodland area is, far too steep and treacherous for horses. Rocks everywhere. I can't tell you how many poor horses were killed when..." She didn't finish the sentence, but bit her lips and looked away. "But

I don't stop the men going out when we need venison. We *have* to have that…and they know where to go."

Sir Geraunt knew that the unsuitability of the terrain was not the only reason why she didn't allow the sport on her land. His bailiff had explained to him after the incident in the forest when they'd over-shot the boundaries in their excitement. And, of course, it made sense, he had to admit. Anyone who'd lived for seven or more years with Sir Hubert Markenfield's lust for killing would, he felt, be entitled to revolt against the whole business of hunting, just for the hell of it. At the same time, Robert le Hare had told him that apparently it had been almost impossible to distinguish Lady Aletta's solar from the kennels while Markenfield lived.

He glanced at the lovely sensitive creature by his side, riding so gracefully and coolly poised, trying hard not to see her in the arms of that vicious swine, crying and begging him not to hurt her as she had done that very morning, when the nightmare had returned to haunt her. No wonder that her armour was so firmly buckled. "You don't mind my alaunts, I take it, then?" he said.

"I don't dislike any animal, Sir Geraunt. On the contrary, it's usually their owners I don't like!"

They laughed, and he teased her a little. "Does that go for me, too, Aletta?"

She hesitated just long enough to make him look sharply a second time. "No," she smiled. "Not at the moment."

"But this morning you said something different."

"That was this morning."

"You've changed your mind since this morning?"

"No, sir. You've changed! Then, you were horrid. Now, you're not so."

"Was I? Was it all horrid, Aletta?"

She gulped, trying not to respond to his merry eyes, and peeping over her shoulder to see if Gerda and Thomas were close enough to hear. She need not have been concerned for they were busily chattering to the two squires, Gerda making the most of three pairs of male eyes.

"Well, Aletta? Was it?"

"You delight in embarrassing me," she said, keeping her voice low. "You know I cannot answer you. If you insist, I shall have to say yes!"

"But that would be untruthful, wouldn't it, wench?"

"Yes, it would! And it would be untruthful if I said you were not horrid now. You *are!*"

His husky laugh sent shivers through her, ruffling her feathers as his teasing had done. She glanced at his strong hand on the reins, remembering how he'd held her and caressed her so boldly and so skilfully that morning, catching her off-guard, asking no permission, recognising no refusals. And at that moment, she wished she could have been back there alone with him at the side of the pool, feeling his hands on her again.

Looking up, she saw that he had caught her glance and had interpreted her thoughts, for he leaned forward and took her hand in his, kissing her knuckles lightly and holding on to it as they rode in silence for some moments. Aletta knew that they were both thinking about the same thing.

Breaking the silence, she asked who they were to visit. "Is it Sir Thomas and Lady Newman, your friends?"

"No, my lady. Someone else I think you know rather well."

Her eyebrows shot upwards in surprise; there was only one other person she could think of. "Mistress Margery? It's not, is it? Really?" She saw by his smile that it was.

"Mistress Margery atte Welle," he said, looking down at her pleased expression. "You like the idea?"

"If you'd told me sooner, I'd have hurried," she said, not realising until the words were out that she had just revealed her contrivance.

"I could say, if you'd have done my bidding sooner, I

would have told you. But I won't," he answered, laughing at her shamefaced glance. "I don't want you to be cross when we arrive. Do you know her well?"

"Yes, I do now. But only over the last two years."

"I see." He realised that her relationship with neighbours had been discouraged during her married years and that few of them had been courageous enough to risk getting too close to Sir Hubert. Poor young lass. "Someone else will be there, too. Someone you know."

"Tell me?"

"Willan."

Chapter Eight

The manor of Middlestone lay some six miles south of Netherstone, downriver from the high fells where Aletta's estates lay within an encircling arm of waterfalls, rocky crags and rough woodland. In earlier times, Middlestone had been one of three manors established by the men from the north, raiders who had crossed the sea and swept inland further than most others of their kind, looking for an isolation closer to their own experience.

The settlements of Southstone, Middlestone and Netherstone lay strung out along the banks of the fast-flowing river like beads on a necklace, while the de Paine estates touched them from one side like a tentative finger reaching towards the Netherstone demesne. It had not escaped Aletta's notice that Sir Geraunt's repossession of Mistress Margery's estate at Middlestone had now effectively enclosed her own between two portions of his, and she could not help wondering, once again, whether this was sheer coincidence or whether it was part of some long-term plan involving herself. Even Ellerby, her other village, lying close to the north of her, up-river, was within the same greedy grasp.

Middlestone Lodge, lying within the demesne and some half-mile away from the manor house, was a stone-built hall of no mean proportions, the roof securely covered with moss and lichen-crusted stone slabs. It had been built to accommodate the late Master atte Welle's hawking guests, a rowdy bunch who needed their own space.

In a flurry of grey and white, her veil flying behind her in spite of the still air, Mistress Margery rushed out to meet them as soon as the clopping hooves on the stone bridge signalled their approach. Whether the geese waddled quickly away and the hens flapped in alarm at her approach or at theirs, Aletta was unsure, but it was clear that the old lady's delight was unfeigned.

Aletta had assumed that Mistress Margery and Sir Geraunt were no more than neighbours, landowner and tenant, but soon saw that there was more to it than that as the widow, after hugging her warmly, hugged Geraunt even more so, and that her hug was returned.

"Truly, I never thought to see you two together. And don't you make the handsomest pair I've ever seen?" Her enthusiasm for the friendship made Aletta blush and Geraunt laugh. "Willan's there, in the stables," she twinkled at them, "so he'll be up to join us, now he knows that you've arrived. And now I shall show you round. Oh, I've never been so cosy in all my born days. Not having a big house to manage is such a release now, I can't begin to tell you…" But she *did* tell them, in great detail, how much she was enjoying her freedom from the responsibilities of managing the estate single-handed.

Geraunt made his escape and went down to join Willan in the stables and, when she found a chance at last, Aletta was able to tell her old friend about the Easter feasts and about Oswald too.

The news of his gradual weakening distressed Mistress Margery, for she'd known the old steward and his wife since they'd all been neighbours together, sharing a deep concern for Aletta when, as a lass of fifteen, she'd been brought by Sir Hubert to live at Netherstone. When he had thrown his half-brother and wife out of his home, it had been to the atte Welles' that they'd turned, knowing that Margery would shelter them, and it was here in this very lodge that they had made their home until Aletta had called them back to live with her again.

"What'll happen to Edwise, then, when Oswald goes? Would you not think it a good thing if she were to come back and live here with me?" Mistress Margery's kind and motherly face beamed at Aletta and she settled her plump arms across her body as though there was nothing more to discuss.

Edwise would have to be consulted, of course, when the time came, but this sounded like an ideal solution to a problem which had been occupying Aletta's thoughts for some days.

As soon as the chance arose, Aletta told her about the pretend betrothal and showed her the new ring.

"Yes," said Mistress Margery, "Willan told me something of it, which is why I didn't ask straight away." She patted Aletta's hand reassuringly. "It seems like a sensible precaution, but wouldn't you like to make it perm—?"

Instantly, Aletta knew what the question was to be, and hastily forestalled it. There were things about the de Paines she wanted to know first.

"Heavens, child! Of course they didn't compel me to move! Can you imagine anyone compelling me to do something I don't want to do? Not even Master atte Welle could do that!"

Aletta was bound to admit that she could not imagine it for one moment, and the answer to her question ended in a gale of laughter. The widow continued, "To be truthful, they've been more than fair. Done everything they could to make things easy. All legally drawn up, too. No loopholes, even though Geraunt is my godson."

"Your godson?" Aletta was astounded. Why on earth had he not told her?

"Yes, lass. He's my godson, and Willan too. Old Richard de Paine lived up here at Allerton until he heard that Sir Hubert was coming back to live at Netherstone with his new wife—you! But that's all water under the bridge, lassie, and not worth dwelling on. None of your doing, love, but none of us envied a young lass like you living with *him*, I can tell you. Can't think what your parents were thinking of, to let you go…"

"What any other aged parents of an only daughter think of, I suppose," Aletta said philosophically. "Money, property, position."

"They must have been blind not to see…"

"They were! They didn't want to see. Nor hear. And I didn't even see the man until our betrothal, and even then he must have been on his good behaviour!" She laughed bitterly. "Ah, well!"

"But Geraunt's caught up with you now, and Willan's taken a fancy to you, I can see that, if his chatter's anything to go by. Which one is it to be?" She leaned towards Aletta and waited for the revelation.

But Aletta said nothing.

"Can you not choose between them, love? Is that it?"

Aletta shook her head. "There's no question of a choice. Neither one nor the other. I don't ever want to get married again."

The old lady sat back in her chair and said nothing. Then she nodded. "I know what it is. It's what we've just been talking about, isn't it? Sir Hubert. It's *him* that's put you off, isn't it?"

Wondering how much her friend could see of the situation, or feel, or understand, Aletta looked out of the window. "Mistress Margery. I'm free for the first time in years. I'm enjoying my freedom and I'm determined not to be swallowed up again. They're good company, but they're not for me. Neither of them."

Again the older woman was silent for a time, and when

she spoke at last, her voice was quiet and gentle. "Aletta, it would be a mistake to push marriage out of your life just because your experience of it has been painful. There's no reason for it to be like that a second time, and I've just seen you with someone who's as desperate for you as you are for him." She held a hand up as Aletta turned sharply, ready to reject the notion. "Oh, yes, it's true. My eyes may be old, but I can recognise love when I see it…"

This time, Aletta *did* interrupt her. "Love? Mistress Margery, are you sure it was not just plain lust you saw? Desire? A young and wealthy widow to gobble up with her lands for dessert? Isn't that what you saw?"

"Aletta!" Mistress Margery heaved herself out of her chair and went to stand before her, taking her hands between her own. "Has he told you he's interested in your property?"

"No." She shook her head. "But then, he wouldn't say as much…"

"But he's told you he's interested in you personally?"

Aletta hesitated. He'd been more personal than any man had a right to be who was not actually her husband. Oh, yes, he'd made it abundantly clear that he was interested in her personally. She nodded, her eyes downcast, wishing she could explain more fully.

"From what I know of the de Paine family, which is more than many, and of Geraunt in particular, there is not a shred of deceit or knavishness to be found in them. Do you think I would have been foolish enough to do business with them if I'd not been totally sure of their honesty? Or their sincerity? You've seen how much they're caring, even when they don't have to be."

Aletta glanced up at the kindly and serious face and gave the fingers a squeeze.

The widow continued, "And as for lust and desire, Aletta, well, there's not a lot wrong with either of those when they go hand in hand with love. Lust and desire are perfectly normal feelings for both them and us, and sometimes it shows, pure and simple. The problem is, my dear, that you're trying to conceal it from him and from yourself too. And when you get to my age, you can see what a dreadful waste of time that can be.'' Her voice faded on the last few words and became husky with emotion and memories.

Aletta enfolded the old lady in her arms and silently they held each other deep in thoughts of the past and of the future. Gradually, she withdrew and went to stand by the window.

''But why should men have it all their own way? This is the first and only time I've ever been able to assert myself and make my own decisions. To control my life. And now—'' she waved her arm wide into the air ''—some great handsome creature stalks in and expects to take me over—my emotions, my body, my property, my life…everything! I've only just got them together, in one piece!'' She was now shaking Mistress Margery gently by the shoulders in a fervour of resentment, tears choking her words. ''I was all right until he came. Now he's spoiling it all!'' She could say no more for the hard and painful lump in her throat.

An old gnarled hand smoothed the hot brow and brushed away angry tears. ''Hush, lassie. Hush! I know how you must feel. I can understand. Anyone who knew Sir Hubert would understand your feelings, but there are few men who would know how to deal with them. That's why you've given them all short shrift until now, isn't it?''

A burst of laughter rose inside Aletta at the apt description of her own directness in dealing with the fortune-seekers, providing a relief from the anger of the previous moment. It was true; none of them had known how to handle a wounded, passionate but independent woman. They had all beat a hasty retreat to find someone more submissive, easier to dominate. She nodded her agreement. ''Pathetic little…'' She groped for a suitable epithet but failed to find one, and laughed.

"And yet,'' Mistress Margery continued, "when one of a different breed appears, a real man who can be all things to you, you balk and fight. Well, that's understandable. But think, Aletta. You want babies, I know. Isn't this man someone you'd want to make babies with? Isn't he?''

Aletta's head went back, eyes closed, and she leaned against a patch of sunlight on the wall, hands pressed over her womb, feeling an ache there which took her breath away. She let out a shuddering sigh which needed no words of affirmation, and Mistress Margery knew that she'd read the situation correctly. Seven years of marriage, and yet no children.

"How do you know this, Mistress Margery?''

"Years, my child. Just years. Keep your heart open, Aletta. Don't close it. You won't learn anything about life by keeping your heart under lock and key. You've met someone who's found the key but you won't let him get near the lock. Fight him, by all means, if you find it fun. But don't fight so hard that you break the lock in the process!''

The metaphors were so picturesque, so very close to the truth. The fighting was fun, she had to admit it, but the only way she could inflict any real damage to his authority was likely to hurt her too. Just the same, she thought, as the flame of rebellion leapt briefly in her breast, there was still no reason why she should make it too easy for him, even though it looked as though the outcome was less remote than it had been before. Locks, keys, armour… She laughed and pushed away from the wall, wiping a stray tear from her cheek. This was more the talk of the blacksmith than of lovers.

They felt the tiny vibrations of the wooden floor and turned to the door as the two brothers entered, laughing and disruptive, breaking the former tranquillity of the room like a sharp gust of wind. Aletta noticed how handsome Geraunt looked when he laughed, head thrown back to reveal a brown neck, muscular and set straight on to wide shoulders. His teeth were white and even, his eyes dark and bright with intelligence.

Willan came forward to greet her, hand outstretched, beaming with delight. "Lady Aletta! Geraunt promised me he'd bring you, so's we could ride back together." He bent to kiss her hand, and over the top of his head two pairs of eyes parried like rapiers.

"Did he, indeed? That was…thoughtful…of him! I shall enjoy riding back with you, Willan." She could feel Geraunt's eyes on her, laughing merrily, as she greeted the young man. "What do you think of the stable?"

"Well, we're not sure that you've got what you need there, mistress," he said, eagerly turning to his godmother. "At least two of those old nags could be fed to the dogs now, you know."

"No!" Aletta grabbed at Willan's arm. "No, if you please, mistress, I'll have them. I need two ordinary affers for carting work, and I can swap them for two of my own, two that I've no use for…" She shook his arm gently, looking at Mistress Margery for her agreement. She did not see the puzzled expression Willan sent to his brother, nor the brief nod in reply. "Please, let me take them with me," she begged.

Willan looked at Mistress Margery for approval. "Well, of course, Lady Aletta, if that's agreeable… But I can't see why you should—" He caught the quick frown from his brother and his words were overtaken.

"We'll take them back to Netherstone now. I've several suitable replacements up at Allerton," said Geraunt, "we'll see you get something soon. The rest can be changed gradually." He noted Aletta's relieved face and wondered what had passed between the two widows to provoke tears. It could hardly be a mutual sadness at the loss of husbands, he knew that much, so could it be the relief of having sympathetic ears to hear and the joy of being able to talk freely? "What do you think of our pretend betrothal, God-mother?" he asked.

"It's a very sensible precaution, m'dear. The quicker the word gets around, the less chance of being invaded by those dreadful creatures Sir Hubert used to entertain. I can't tell you the damage they've done in the past, and I don't know how poor Aletta—"

"Hush, please, mistress," Aletta interrupted, laughing as she hugged the old lady. "I've never had so much protection in my life. I don't think I'll ever get used to it."

"Yes, you will!"

She turned at the sound of the two softly spoken words and saw Geraunt watching her. To the two of them, his words implied a world of meaning which both understood. But they had reckoned without Mistress Margery's wisdom. She had both heard *and* understood, and that gave her great comfort.

The homeward-bound cavalcade had expanded from six horses to eleven; the two weary affers, newly acquired by Aletta, were led behind by Willan's grooms. The dust stirred up along the track was great enough to be seen for miles.

Though Aletta made a pretence of interest in the brothers' talk, her mind was preoccupied with her earlier conversation and the new experiences of the morning. She was especially interested to know of the esteem Mistress Margery had for her godson, swearing that she could tell he was in love with her. She had even been astute enough to recognise Aletta's mixed emotions, though heaven knew Aletta thought she'd concealed them right well. She smiled to herself, remembering how she'd told Roger how obvious it all was, and here *she* was, caught in the same blinkered trap, except that her blinkers were self-imposed.

They reached Netherstone in good time for the tug-o'-war and the merry feast which followed. Frail Oswald and his Edwise had been borne down to the green on litters, ministered to and cherished as Aletta had promised. They all felt that it might be his last Easter games, and so the love and kindness showered on the old couple spilled over on to Aletta too.

As darkness drew near Sir Geraunt and Willan made their farewells, and departed without another opportunity to talk amid the bustle of happy people, the shouts of laughter and merry ribaldry. The clatter of hooves alone was enough to drown out deeper thoughts and confused emotions, and it seemed that, for now, these would have to wait for attention.

After giving instructions to the house-steward for tomorrow, Aletta made her way through the hall, hoping for the peace of her solar at last, but Roger was leaving Oswald's door in the corner and was glad to see her.

"Oswald?" said Aletta. "He's worse?"

He nodded and sighed. "He's looking ghastly, and he's having trouble with his breathing."

"Oh, Roger! Perhaps we shouldn't have borne him down to the games. Was it too much for him, do you think?"

Roger shook his head. "No, m'lady. His end's been near for some time now, we've all known that, and he's had a wonderful day—everyone making such a fuss of them both." His words were comforting.

"Shall I send for the priest? What does Edwise think?"

"Yes, I don't think we should delay. She agrees with me and Bridie."

"Bridie's in there with her?" They exchanged smiles, but this was no time for explanations; they could come later.

"Bridie's in there, yes. I'll go and find someone to get the priest straight away."

Aletta's faithful steward, friend and comforter died during the early hours of the next morning while Edwise napped, exhausted, in the chair by the dying fire. It was as though Oswald and the fire and the night had made a pact to fade together, just as the first rays of light filtered into the eastern sky.

Earlier, the village priest had anointed him and administered communion, for Oswald had been unable to speak by then. After the priest's departure, Roger and Bridie had insisted that Aletta should retire for the night, saying they would stay with the old couple and wake her, if need be.

She had been reluctant to argue for, though the setting was unorthodox, it would at least give the two of them a chance to talk in some privacy. So she had given in, secretly relieved to deliver herself to solitude at last.

At dawn, Bridie tiptoed into the solar to wake her mistress with the news, and no matter that it had been expected, she was saddened nevertheless. It was as though the ground had suddenly shifted beneath her, a loved and friendly face slipped away out of sight, never to be seen again.

"He's gone, Bridie? Really gone?"

"Yes, love. He's gone."

"Oh, Bridie. I should have been there! Why didn't—?"

"He went so softly, love. Don't be upset. He slipped away so quietly. We didn't even realise he'd gone until he'd gone. He just slept himself away. It couldn't have been better for him."

Aletta's eyes filled with hot tears, remembering the kind and gentle man who had nurtured her through the pain of her early years as his half-brother's wife. "He was so kind to me, Bridie. I don't think I could have managed without him. Such a dear man. Edwise?"

"She's all right. She seems stunned."

There was a silence between them in which thoughts of the past, present and future flew backwards and forwards, until the early streaks of dawn drew them resolutely towards the day ahead, compelling them to make decisions.

"Where's Roger?"

"In his room."

"Have you slept, Bridie?"

"I dozed a little, not much." She smiled.

"Then you'd better climb in here, lass, while I go and see to things."

"No, m'lady, I can't do that…!"

But Aletta gave her a gentle shove on to the big bed, removed her shoes and pulled the covers over the maid, who was almost asleep before she'd finished. Pulling a warm woollen rug around her shoulders, she crossed to the alcove in the thickness of the wall where he prie-dieu was curtained off. She knelt and lay her head on her arms while the memories of Oswald's words and kindnesses rushed into the sudden void left by his departure.

She would never understand how two men as closely related as Oswald Freeman and her late husband could be as unlike in every respect. It was enough to make one believe in changelings, she thought. She prayed for the salvation of his soul, gave thanks for his life here on earth, especially with her, and asked comfort for Edwise for the rest of her days. Then she pulled on a warm gown against the chill of the early morning, tied her hair in a bundle and went down to Oswald's widow. I must remember to go and tell the bees, she thought, tying a knot in her long, hanging sleeve.

The day of the funeral was an ordeal for Aletta. The long spell of fine weather had broken at last and the sky steadfastly refused to indicate any difference between morn, noon or eve. The same dark blanket hung over the whole day. The rain chilled her as the damp procession crowded into the church, and the choking stench of the tallow candles and the torches inside the tiny building made her head swim and her eyes water. Finally she could bear it no longer and ordered the carpenter to remove two of the windows to let in some air, preferring to be chilled rather than choked.

The worst part was as Oswald's wooden coffin was low-ered slowly through the gaping floor of the chancel into the dark tomb below, so cold and dark, so far away now, so inaccessible. She did not believe that he would have ap-preciated a place at the side of Sir Hubert and so had de-creed that he should be placed to one side, so that when the time came she could take up her position between them, as go-between, so to speak.

Sir Geraunt took her tightly clenched hand in his as they stood, side by side, at the edge of the tomb, and Aletta was grateful for his strength as she watched her friend and men-tor disappear. Geraunt understood how her thoughts must also have been drawn to the time, two years ago, when she had stood here alone, watching a similar scene, too shocked and worn to appreciate the first signals of freedom. He looked down at the lovely pale face by his side and noticed a tear fall along her cheek and down her chin and wondered if the time would ever come when he would be able to explain to her the part that Oswald had played in his own life.

Afterwards they escorted the poor numb Edwise back up to the manor, and instead of insisting on her taking part in the feast had her put to bed, shivering and spent. Two of Aletta's younger chambermaids tended her, glad to have an important role to play on this most dismal of days.

As she changed her sodden garments for dry ones, Aletta reflected that it was at times like this that one appreciated how efficient the household had become, for the feast in the hall below had been anticipated for days in advance, and nothing had been spared to give the old steward a friendly and dignified farewell.

She glanced at the pile of ledgers and account rolls on the floor. That morning, Edwise had been most insistent that Aletta delay no longer in removing them to her safe keeping, and so they had been brought up here to favour the old lady in her anxiety. Strange, Aletta mused as she pulled on her dry shoes, what people regard as top priorities at such times. She was remembering how she had felt the burning need to strip her bedframe of everything—curtains, covers and mattress—on the day of Sir Hubert's funeral.

It appeared, from the damp and steaming crowd in the hall below, that Oswald had been by no means as unpopular a steward as many others of his occupation. People had come many miles to pay their last respects and to meet Lady Aletta, glad of the chance to make her acquaintance now that the hostile and churlish husband was not to be part of the occasion. Despite the dampness of their clothes, the company found relief in the bright warmth of the hall, the good food and the friendly faces of neighbours rarely glimpsed since last year.

"Such a pity we have to lose someone before we can all get together like this," remarked Mistress Margery in a loud whisper to Aletta. "Don't you think so?"

Aletta felt a firm hand on her elbow, and knew without looking whose it was.

"Mistress Margery, I think it's time we introduced our new neighbour to Lady Aletta, don't you? Are you prepared for the shock, m'lady?" asked Sir Geraunt.

Aletta was quick to recognise the thread of banter in the voice, having already caught a glimpse of Sir Thomas and Lady Newman among the congregation at the church. Sir Thomas was tall and dark, his burly frame filling his brocade and velvet gown handsomely as he stood very erect, one hand protectively around his young wife's shoulder. His voice was deep and booming.

"Lady Aletta! I'm delighted and honoured to meet you at last, despite being so poorly introduced by this ungentle oaf!" He bent over the hand extended to him and touched it lightly with his lips. "May I congratulate you on your betrothal, my lady, and wish you every happiness?"

For the briefest moment, perhaps because of her preoccupation with events, his words made no sense to her, until a tiny nudge in the small of her back prompted her to respond. "Thank you, Sir Thomas. Your oafish friend hardly needs to tell me your name—" her glance did no more than flicker towards Geraunt "—but I was not going to allow you to leave without a word. Please introduce me to your lady."

Lady Cecily curtsied, smiling prettily, a happy-faced woman, plump and already heavily pregnant. "We've been looking forward to meeting you, Lady Aletta. I hope you'll allow us to be your friends. We know no one up here, yet."

Aletta felt her warmth, and responded, "Of course we shall be friends. I'd like nothing better. Are you settling into life at Middlestone, or is the north too cold for you?"

Lady Cecily and Sir Thomas laughed together, as though Aletta's question were already a cause for amusement between them.

"Thomas and I have both agreed to lay on a layer of fat before next winter, but neither of us realised it would be so much easier for me than for him!" Lady Cecily patted her extended stomach and laughed again, an enchanting ring of sound.

Her happiness was so apparent, so unassuming, so poignant, and if it had not been for the tightened grip on her elbow at that point Aletta might have been able to bypass the words and retain the smile on her face at the gentle jest. But the grip on her arm, intended as support, had the opposite effect, reminding her that she might read into it more than was meant. Her smile was poised on the brink of faltering when the next jest unhorsed her completely.

"Don't gloat, woman." Sir Thomas hugged his wife good-naturedly. "The Lady Aletta will no doubt be preparing for winter, too, this time next year. But see—" he noted Aletta's apparent discomfiture, her fading smile and lack of words ''—we've embarrassed our hostess. My apologies, my lady.''

He smilingly turned to his friend for reassurance that he'd not truly stepped outside the bounds of good manners on their first meeting, but the smile he expected to find had disappeared.

Geraunt was obliged to give way as Aletta hastily excused herself and moved away. ''If you had *three* feet, man, maybe you'd jump in with all of them instead of two,'' he hissed in Thomas's ear. ''You know she's been childless for years! Where's your tact, you great clod?'' He turned to follow Aletta but she had slipped quickly away. ''Where's she gone, dammit?''

Aletta found that her arms and legs were trembling, that the smile she was doing her best to retain was hurting her face, that a hard, hot ball of pain was making it difficult to breathe. Words, she said to herself, only words. Forget, greet your guests, for Oswald's sake. Forget.

A familiar voice sounded at her side and she closed her eyes to pretend that she was invisible. ''Lady Aletta! I've found you at last! Here, you look as if you need one of these!'' Willan snatched two goblets of wine from a passing tray and held the dripping vessel towards her. Her hand shook as she took it but she could neither thank him nor drink it.

''You're upset, m'lady. Is it Oswald?''

She nodded, relieved that he'd misconstrued the reason for her distress.

''He was more than a steward, wasn't he? Dear old chap, I'm sure you'll miss him. But look at this…all these people to send him off. I shall be very pleased if so many people come to my funeral feast.''

The absurdity of Willan's sentiment dispelled the tightness in her chest as nothing else could have done, and she noted his head bent to hers in an effort to console, his expression full of eagerness and open admiration. He eased the bottom of her goblet upwards towards her mouth and she drank with a little sob of relief.

"Yes," she said, trying to smile with her eyes too, "the day has been something of a strain. I think Edwise is in the best place."

Over the top of her goblet, she saw the dark thatch of Geraunt's hair above the group around him, and saw his head swing towards her, eyes searching. With a sideways step she placed Willan directly between them, knowing that it would take only a few words of explanation from him to bring tears gushing forth uncontrollably.

The sight of Lady Cecily's radiant face, her precious bulge so lovingly patted, her merry laugh and happy talk had touched a raw nerve in Aletta, which she felt might have remained unexposed had not Geraunt himself been at hand. She did not want their embarrassment, but neither could she, at that moment, pretend an unconcern she was far from feeling. This mock betrothal was already taking her into waters too deep for comfort, and she twisted the new gold ring on her finger irritably.

"If it were not pouring with rain," whispered Willan to her, "and if you were not the hostess, I would ask you to walk with me in your pleasance so that we could talk undisturbed. As it is, with all these eyes upon us, I can only request that we sit down here for a moment and pretend that we're too old to stand any longer."

"Do you think they'll fall for it?"

"Oh, yes, sure to!" he said, keeping his face straight. "Come!" He took her elbow, led her towards a bench, and sat beside her. "Now, are you feeling a little stronger?"

"For an old lady too weak to stand, I feel much better. As a not so old old lady…"

"As a very beautiful not so old lady…" he corrected her.

"Are you flirting with me, Willan?"

He declined to answer her question, but barely glanced

at her, looking instead into the throng of people. "How serious is this so-called betrothal between you and my brother?" His head was tilted to catch her reply.

The gentle question was delivered in such an offhand way, and was so unexpectedly candid, that she was too taken aback to reply until she could think how the situation was supposed to read from Willan's angle. He had been in at the conception of the plan, had been made one of the few who knew the true reason for its perpetuation. What was it that he ought *not* to know? The bond. Ah, yes, the bond. "I told you why we were keeping up the pretence, Willan. So that word will get around that I'm not free, and then I shan't have to put up with invasions... Oh, that sounds so immodest! You know what I mean..."

"Yes, I do know what you mean. But you haven't quite answered my question, Aletta." She noticed that he had dropped her title for the first time. "How serious are you? Are you truly pretending, or is there something more to it?"

"I can only answer for myself, Willan, not for your brother. As far as I'm concerned, it's a pretence for precisely the reasons you were told. No more than that." What else could she say? That this deceit was unbearable?

"Good, then I know exactly where I stand." He smiled.

"Willan, I have to mingle with my guests." She stood up to go. "Will you tell Geraunt that he must not take his own horses to exchange for the old affers that I brought from Mistress Margery's? The exchange was not his to make, it was mine, but he seems not to want to listen to my argument. *You* tell him, please."

"It won't do any good, Aletta, I'm afraid," he replied, amused by his new role of messenger. "I've already had my instructions."

"Instructions? What do you mean?" She caught a glimpse of two hazel eyes watching her from a group of people across the room, but Willan's words were enough to hold her attention at that moment. ''Tell me!''

''He said you couldn't afford to lose two good horses for those old nags and that I'd better get down there quick with two of his, otherwise you'd be soft enough to exchange the whole damn stable before he could stop you.''

''He said *that?*''

''That was the gist of what he said, yes. That you only wanted them to save them from being fed to the hounds. They're all like that, Aletta. We saw them. They're only good for dog-meat, the lot of 'em!''

Her eyes moved across from Willan to Geraunt, still watching her and she knew that he was assessing the damage as clearly as if he'd heard every word. ''Excuse me, Willan, there's something I must attend to…''

She swung away like an arrow from a bow to evade Geraunt's approach and darted nimbly through the throng towards the screens. Already some guests were preparing to leave, to make their homeward journeys in the last hours of daylight. No one would want to linger on a night like this, except for a few old friends of Oswald's who would talk and sleep the night away in the great hall and depart on the morrow.

''Where's she gone?''

''Across there, look!'' nodded Willan. ''Saying farewell to her guests.''

''She's angry! What've you been telling her to make her so mad?''

''She asked me to tell you that the exchange of the horses was hers, and that you were not to take yours to Middlestone.''

''I said, what have *you* been telling *her?*''

''Well, only what you said to me, that she was soft enough to—'' He stopped, recognising the cold, murderous look, the look that froze words in one's mouth.

''Christ's wounds! I don't believe it! You told her what

I'd said to you, fool? And you couldn't even get *that* right?''

"Isn't that what you said…?"

"Willan! When you grow up, you'll learn that it can only take one word, or one *missing* word, even, for someone to misunderstand a complete sentence. I pray to God that you grow up soon. For your own sake, if not mine!'' He strode off towards the screens, the sound of his scathing words ringing in Willan's bewildered head.

Determined not to let her out of his sight for one moment, Geraunt stood behind Aletta as she made her farewells, occasionally joining in as he recognised friends. Sir Thomas and Lady Cecily moved forward with Mistress Margery, the latter's boisterous presence and remarks about the possibility of them all being drowned before they reached home making them all laugh, allowing Aletta to summon a happy smile especially for the trio.

Aletta was conscious that her previous hasty departure from the group must have made her guests uncomfortable, to say the least, and she was truly sorry for that, but hoped that they would put it down to the tenseness of the occasion and her own tiredness. She held out her hands to Lady Cecily and kissed her lightly on both cheeks. ''You know, you're more than welcome to stay overnight, all of you, if you'd rather wait until the weather clears. I can make you very comfortable.''

Lady Cecily beamed shyly, clearly delighted by Aletta's warmth and recovery. ''Perhaps not this time, Lady Aletta, but you must come and see us at Middlestone as soon as you can. Will you? Please?''

''Certainly I will, as soon as the weather clears, I promise. And don't overdo the fattening-up process.'' She turned to Sir Thomas, smiling. ''It won't look nearly as attractive on you as it does on Lady Cecily.''

He took her hand and kissed it gallantly, his eyes twinkling. It was clear to them that she'd rallied from her previous unsteadiness; he'd heard how close she and Oswald had been, and knew what a blow the old man's death must be to her.

An arm stole around Aletta's shoulders and she felt Geraunt's hand lightly squeezing her arm, but she refused to soften towards him, edging away to hug Mistress Margery as they trooped off, enveloped in cloaks.

"Aletta, we have to talk."

"*Do* we, sir? Isn't it time you were leaving?"

"Yes! That's why we have to talk now." He kept his voice light, but Aletta still seethed with anger at his words about her to Willan.

"I shall be too busy, I'm afraid," she answered coolly, turning quickly towards the hall.

But he reached out and caught her arm beneath the shoulder, bringing her to an abrupt halt. "Now, Aletta. If you please."

Her eyes flashed fire, with sparks that would have kindled the damp thatches outside, pools of blackness in a face white with anger. Pointedly, she looked down at the hand on her arm, then up into his eyes once more. His hand dropped, and he waited to see the anger brought under control, then walked beside her up the stairs to the solar.

Aletta called to Bridie with purpose in her voice. "Tell Roger I shall want to speak to him shortly. And Master Nicholas too." And she passed through the open door and across to the far side of the room.

Chapter Nine

Aletta stood with her back to him, trembling with cold and rigid with resentment, longing for him to leave.

"This has been an ordeal for you, wench."

She heard his words but gave no answer. The final departure of Oswald, her overreaction to Lady Cecily's pregnancy, the unfortunate words of Sir Thomas and then, to crown it all, the revelation that Geraunt thought her a fool. If only he would say it, then go away and leave her alone, never to appear again. She heard him throw logs on to the fire and push them into life again; there was a pause, and then his soft approach.

Her attempt to evade him was mistimed, for as she whirled away one of the woollen blankets from the chest was thrown around her shoulders and crossed over her before she could fight a way out of it. His arms were tight beneath her knees and back, lifting her towards a chair by the crackling fire, placing her firmly on his lap and tucking her into the crook of his arm.

Held by the blanket, she could only turn her face into his shoulder and pant with the effort of resistance while he calmly removed her deep satin-covered fillet and the gold caul which held the bundle of dark brown hair. It fell in a tumbled mass over him as he shook it free, pushing it away from her face.

"Now, vixen! Enough of this ice and fire! Let's have some explanations, shall we?" He sat back with her into the chair, holding her closely in his arms, and Aletta fleetingly wondered if it was worthwhile trying to sustain her anger in the comforting surroundings of his closeness. He nuzzled her forehead with his lips.

"Come on. Tell me about it."

"You've loosed my hair," she growled.

"That's one of the advantages of being betrothed."

"I don't want to be betrothed."

"Why, Aletta?"

"It's uncomfortable."

"The new ring?" He knew this was not her meaning.

"No, not the ring. People expecting…saying…"

"Like Thomas, you mean?"

She nodded silently and he touched her forehead with his lips, seeing again the hurt in her eyes, the pain of being childless in a society which depended on the breeding ability of the wife to keep the family possessions intact.

"I'm not trying to excuse his tactlessness, Aletta, but he didn't simply blurt that out without thinking."

"What do you mean, he didn't say it without thinking?" Aletta was furious at his attempt to cover up his friend's blunder. "He must know, as you do, that if I haven't produced a child in over seven years of marriage I'm not going to start now, am I? In spite of what I said about being disgraced—" She turned her face into his breast, a sob of anguish cutting off further words.

"Hush, wench, hush and listen to me! He and I knew Sir Hubert Markenfield long before you did, and it was a well-known fact that he'd never sired a brat, not once. Though God knows he tried hard enough!" he added under his breath.

Aletta's body suddenly went rigid; she struggled to sit upright on his knee and face him. "Yes, he did! Verity!"

"Verity?"

"Yes. One of my little chambermaids. She was fourteen when he seduced her. He threw her out when she became pregnant because her family couldn't pay the leyrwite. That was just before he died."

Geraunt looked astonished and faintly amused. He shook his head at her in disbelief. "Well, my lady, all I can say is that that was either his swan-song or you'd better take a look at the colour of the brat's eyes and hair again. Did he admit that it was his?"

"No, of course not!"

"No, of course he didn't! Do you think he'd have been so eager to throw the lass out if he'd believed it was his? Wouldn't he have been rather proud of his achievement after all that time? Don't you think he would have used it against you as proof that it was not his fault that you were childless?"

"What are you saying?"

"I'm saying, my fair champion of the tender heart, that he was as impotent as that grey gelding you ride so beautifully, and that Thomas was very near the mark when he assumed you'd probably be nicely fattened up by next winter!" He took advantage of her mixture of astonishment and outrage at his coarseness by kissing her soundly until she was breathless and limp in his arms.

Impotent? Hubert Markenfield impotent? Was that why he had been so desperate to acquire a young, healthy wife, why he had no previous heirs to leave his property to, not even close relations? Had that been the underlying cause of his anger, his frustration, his cruelty? But the thought of being nicely fattened up for winter was like discussing a breeding sow. What arrogance! Sir Geraunt obviously thought that he was going to be responsible for that event.

But he was laughing as he pushed her long hair over her

head and held it in his fist. "Now, my lady. Does that make you feel any better?"

"I hardly dare to believe you! Could it really be true? That Verity's child is not his, but someone else's? And that he knew it?"

"I wouldn't jest about something that means so much to you, Aletta. Truly I would not. Nor would I allow anyone else to in my hearing. What I am telling you was common knowledge. About your Verity, I don't know. Maybe you'd better ask a few more searching questions. I believe you may have been misled."

"It won't make any difference to my helping her, but I'll find out."

"Yes, you'd still help her, I can believe that. But now there's something else I want to explain."

"About being fattened up, as you so coarsely describe it?" She pressed her lips into a straight line, trying hard to prevent them from curling up at the corners.

He laughed, a husky masculine bellow that sent a surge of hot blood into her cheeks. "No, my lady, I'll explain that in the utmost detail at the appropriate time."

She squirmed on his lap at his delighted smile, struggling against his arms and the restraining blanket. "Let me out of this damn thing! This is unfair! Let me go!"

"No! You're my prisoner! It's one way of making sure you listen to me."

"I've heard enough! It's time you went home, sir!"

"You don't want to know what it was I said to Willan?"

"I heard what you said to him. He told me. You obviously think I'm soft in the head. That's what you said, isn't it?"

"*Will* you shut up, vixen? Or shall I have to stuff a gag in your mouth?"

She was silent under his fierce stare, and for a moment, while the firelight danced on his cheekbones and brow, she saw the man on the huge chestnut stallion bellowing at her as he held on to her whip. Her eyes locked with his, just as they had done then, but she could not hold his gaze any longer. Suddenly overwhelmed with a desire to sleep, she fell against his shoulder and snuggled softly into his arms, feeling them tighten around her protectively.

"I appear to be making a habit today of apologising for the blunders of my family and friends. I hope they confine their remarks only to funerals," he said, his chin resting on top of her head. "Willan is still not familiar with the way words are used differently up here in the north, so when he said you were soft enough to exchange the whole damn stable, implying that you were stupid enough, what he should have said is that you were soft-hearted enough. Which is what I said to him." He pushed a gentle knuckle beneath her chin and drew her sleepy eyes to his. "Do you understand, Aletta? Not daft, but soft-hearted."

"Yes, I do understand. Forgive me. I was overwrought and looking for slights where there were none. I needed an excuse to let off steam and fight someone after today's events. As you said, it's not been an easy day."

"You've done magnificently, Aletta. And you can fight with me any time you choose, day or night! Now. Have you decided to stay betrothed for a bit longer?"

"Just a bit longer," she whispered.

"Good. I'm relieved to hear it. Did Willan flirt with you?"

His question took her by surprise and she turned her head up to see his expression. Did he care? Or was this a superficial interest? "He seemed interested to know whether our betrothal was merely pretence or whether there was perhaps more to it."

"He asked you outright?"

She nodded.

"And what did you tell him?"

"What could I tell him? Nothing. That there was nothing more to it."

He was silent for a while, twisting a long strand of her hair around his wrist. She felt his deep chest rise and fall and wondered what it would be like to…

"I think I shall warn him off you."

Sitting up, she looked into his eyes closely, seeing the flecks of green in the glow of the fire. They were serious, intent, darkening with each passing moment. "Why?" she asked.

"Because, my girl, if he falls in love with you any deeper, he's going to get hurt. And that can be avoided."

"In love? What nonsense!" She shook her hair back. "He's not in love. Only playing."

"Wrong! He's in love. I can tell. And I don't want him to get hurt. Neither do I want him getting under my feet!"

"Oh! You're being particularly crude today!"

"Yes, well, when a man has a woman like you in his arms, with her hair falling about all over him, he begins to feel more than a little crude, my lady. In fact, it's just as well for you that you're wrapped up like this, or my crudity might not be kept under such control!"

She bit her lips tightly together to prevent an explosion of laughter bursting out from between them, but her rapidly heaving chest gave her away and she was forced to hide her face in his neck. She took deep breaths to recover and straightened her face. "You're not going to tell him of…of the bond?"

"No, of course I'm not! That's only between ourselves."

"Won't you release me, Geraunt?"

"No."

"You didn't even consider before you answered." She frowned. Why was the man so stubborn? she wondered.

"I don't need to consider. The answer will always be no."

"You wouldn't really carry out your threats, would you?"

"Have I ever threatened you, Aletta?"

"Well, you told me what you were legally entitled to do. Would you?"

"Certainly. Never doubt it."

She sat back with a sigh and watched the fire for a moment. "You're hard, Geraunt," she said.

His answering smile was one of pure mischief. "You've noticed! Better and better, wench!" His eyes glinted so wickedly into hers that Aletta was speechless with confusion.

"You know what I'm talking about…" she expostulated, not daring to meet his eyes but aware of a thrill of excitement trembling in her thighs.

"Yes, I know what you're talking about. And you know what I'm talking about, too." He pulled her backwards into his arms and slid his hand into her hair, turning her face to his. His kiss was like all the dreams she'd ever wanted to dream, warm, tender, hard and passionate, searching and deliberate, sending wave upon wave of tingling warmth flooding into her body. Her hands still wrapped against her, she was powerless to move, her hair held in his grip, her mouth beseige and stormed so sweetly.

"If Willan wasn't with me, I'd stay the night," he growled deeply, lifting his mouth to look at her.

"Willan? Oh, Geraunt! Let me up…please!" She struggled to release herself, remembering that she must see Roger, Master Nicholas and Bridie. "My hair! Will you call for Bridie? I can't be seen like this! Please, Geraunt, don't just stand there laughing! Unwrap me!"

"What if I refuse?"

"That would be unfair! They're waiting for my instructions. Please!"

Chuckling at her dilemma, he unwrapped the blanket and gathered her hair into his hand, holding her head and tilting her face under his. She thought he was going to kiss her again and began to remonstrate at his lack of understanding, but he spoke against her lips instead. "Flirt with Willan, if you wish, gently. But if he ever gets within an arm's length of a kiss like that, you'll both feel the full force of my anger.'' His eyes showed that the laughter had gone and that it had been replaced by a deadly seriousness.

Turning, he went to the door and called for Bridie.

Aletta lay in the snug warmth of the great bed, listening to the rival claims to territory of the farmyard cockerels answering each other as regularly as the hours and smiling at the thought that their instinctive behaviour was no more or less predictable than that of the human species. Territory, possessions, procreation. Was that really all they thought about, these males?

Stifling her laughter into the pillow, so as not to waken Bridie, her thoughts turned to the events of the previous day and a sigh of relief drifted into a yawn at the realisation that Oswald's funeral was now over and done with after so many days of preparation. She remembered her over-sensitivity, her shrewishness at the end of the day and how Sir Geraunt had reacted with understanding and firmness, how he had appeared to take control of every situation without the slightest resort to fluster or fuss. She could have suggested they stay overnight, several of Oswald's old friends had done so, but the rain had eventually ceased and five miles was no great distance to travel at dusk. And she had not wanted them to sleep in the hall with the others, nor had she wanted them in her room.

But now there was work to be done and the question of Verity's child to be answered, and Bridie was astir.

''Are you awake, m'lady?''

''Yes, Bridie.''

''I'll bring your bath up, then. Stay there where it's warm.'' Quietly she bustled away.

The few extra moments in bed while her half-tub was being filled with steaming buckets of water from the kitchen gave Aletta time to think of this new development, time that she'd not had last night before sleep overtook her.

It was strange, she reflected, that although the word "impotent" had startled her, it was not entirely such an unexpected revelation as it might have been. For one thing, for all Sir Hubert's sexual activities—and there had been as many infidelities on his part as anyone could manage in seven years—no one had ever mentioned a pregnancy or a hidden child to be maintained, or even denied. There had been no previous heirs by his first wife of over twenty years; she had died from a fall downstairs on one of their other manors, not from childbirth, as might have been expected.

Aletta had no good reason to suppose that she herself was infertile, for her woman's parts appeared to be in working order, though she had no other evidence to go on. All the same, it would be at once both a joy and a complication to know that the problem had been her late husband's and not hers. The doubts of all these years would be put aside at last, especially in view of the assurance that his impotence was open knowledge among those who knew him. But what of her own future?

That was something she would have to decide very soon, if her hopes were justified, for her body was leaving her in no doubt of its message. Worse still, it was leaving *him* in no doubt either, for now he must be assuming that his bid for power over her was almost won, with barely a struggle. To her shame, it looked as though he had almost gained the upper hand already, for, while she could still make things difficult for him, she was not to know the point beyond which he would assert his right to prosecute her. And that was a threat too awful to be taken lightly. What price her precious estates then? "I hold what is mine" suddenly seemed to have a hollow ring to it.

As usual, the bath was fragrant and comforting. The carpenter had made it for Aletta from a large wine-barrel, the top rim he'd covered over with leather, and the little wooden stool was curved to fit against the side. She'd had a round padded cushion made for the bottom, so that her feet would not slither on the bare wood, and rope handles were fixed into holes high up on the sides so that it could be carried away by two strong lads afterwards.

She ate her breakfast slowly, chatting to Bridie and Gerda as they tidied the room.

Gerda indicated Oswald's accounts, stacked up on the floor. "These rolls, m'lady. Do you want them left?"

"Yes, I have to look through them one day soon. Maybe today, if I get the chance. Just push them to one side. Edwise wanted them out of the way."

"Is she staying there, now Oswald's gone?"

"No, in a day or two she's to go to Mistress atte Welle, in Middlestone. But we have to sort Oswald's affairs out first. I want you and some of the girls to help her clear up, Gerda. She needs help. And today I want to get those furs outside."

Soon there was a stream of maids carrying armfuls of furs and blankets, mattresses and covers from solar to garden, where they were hung in the air and spread over bushes, beaten, shaken and brushed amid squeals of laughter. The furs were first dampened by rolling them in the wet grass, then sprinkled with wine, dusted with best white flour and allowed to dry over the rope lines. Later they were brushed out, shining and clean once more.

With her hair coiled around her head and an old linen scarf tied round, Aletta sat in the hall with Master Nicholas, learning how much the Easter week had cost and discussing requirements for the coming weeks. "There'll be at least ten extra ploughmen in for meals this week, don't forget," she said.

"Every day, m'lady?"

"Heaven forbid, no! About four days, I think. You'll

have to ask Roger which days, but they'll need all meals, extra ale—extra bread too.''

''Right. Then there's the accounts for Master Oswald's funeral. Do you want to see them, m'lady?''

''No, I know what we used. I don't need to check any further. But I want you to buy in some more barley, Master Nicholas. Have them make some of the ale with barley, this time, instead of the usual oats.''

''I can do that, m'lady, but you know I'll have to send for it. And it doesn't come cheap round here, you know.''

''Just enough to make a few barrels?'' She smiled at his worried frown.

He relented, nodding and writing as the grin grew broader. ''It wouldn't be anything to do with the two gentlemen, would it, m'lady?''

''Master Nicholas! If you're going to harbour such thoughts, I may as well come straight out with it and tell you I want fresh supplies of dates, raisins, olive oil, rice and almonds. They've been missing from the menu for some time.''

''We used up our supplies over the winter. I thought—''

''Well, re-order, if you please. Are there enough hands in the kitchen? I had to press some of the outside hands into service yesterday.''

''No, m'lady, there are never enough hands in the kitchen. The dairymaid's going off to have her bairn soon, and we'll need someone to take her place. Do you think you should come and have a look? Then you can decide what to do?''

Aletta suppressed a smile. It was quite an achievement to get Master Nicholas to spend money, so tight a rein did he keep on the household accounts. And as for taking on new staff, she often felt he would rather do the work himself than pay more servants to do it.

The tour of the kitchen, pantry, buttery and dairy took some time as stores were examined, plans were drawn up for the coming weeks, foodstuffs and other supplies were listed, counted and re-ordered. Grain and flour stores were checked, meat supplies noted and, now that the cows had begun to yield again after calving, menus were discussed. Even the stewpond was examined for fish stocks and the slaughter-house briefly peeped into, though Aletta didn't linger there. They walked through the gardens too, where the rain of the previous day still glistened on the green-blue cabbages and the frothy new shoots of parsley. The pathways were awash with mud.

"Why is there no straw down on these paths?" she asked the gardener across on the other pathway. "Where are the under-gardeners?"

"They're up at t'ives, m'lady."

"Why? Where's the beeward?" She frowned.

He looked sheepish, fumbling with the straw twine in his hand. "Ee, A doan't rightly know weer 'e is at this moment, m'lady. Honest."

Aletta turned to Master Nicholas, her voice low and angry. She would not tolerate inefficiency. "What's going on around here, I'd like to know? Is anyone doing anything in the right place?"

"I believe there was a help-ale over at Ellerby last night, m'lady, after the funeral. Maybe Henry Beward overstayed his welcome," Master Nicholas offered by way of explanation, making a mental note to speak harshly to the man when eventually he appeared.

"He'll certainly overstay his welcome here, too, if he leaves my bees to attend to themselves," she snapped. "Who was the help-ale for?"

"One of the Ellerby villagers has just had a bairn and gone down with milk-fever and her husband has just broken his arm falling down the mill steps with two bags of flour on top of him. The others thought they could do with a bit of help, since neither of them can work too well at the moment."

"Why was I not told of this sooner?" Aletta demanded, turning on the muddy pathway to face him so suddenly that Master Nicholas nearly fell over into the sodden foliage. "Why?"

"Well, m'lady—" he flung out a hand to balance himself "—you've been a bit elusive lately, if I may say so. Maybe no one wanted to bother you."

"Bother me? Sweet Jesu, Nicholas! I've *been* here, and well you know it! Since when did I stop wanting to know what's happening to my own villagers?" She slithered on ahead of him and away towards the orchard and the beehives, leaving the house-steward to straddle a puddle, half-shamed, half-perplexed.

He turned and met the amused gaze of the gardener across the cabbage patch, aware that he'd heard every word. "Get on with your work, man!" he snarled. "And get these paths strawed over!"

Had she been elusive? Or was that merely an excuse to cover someone's forgetfulness? she wondered. The help-ale was typical of the way these people pulled together when help was needed. Even the gardener's loyalty to the beeward was part of the same code of mutual support.

She knew full well that his words had been no more than the truth. He surely did not know where he was at that precise moment, but she knew also that a help-ale was a happy way of raising money for those in need, that the home-brewed ale was sold to all comers at a higher price than usual so that the proceeds of the night would be of comfort to everyone. Of course, everyone took advantage, rarely did anyone not attend, and just as rarely did anyone stay sober. No doubt the rain had persuaded Henry Beward that both he and the bees were better off indoors for a day or two. He was not to have known that the sun would set the straw hives humming the day after.

The row of straw bee-skeps nestled in specially built alcoves in the huge south-facing wall of the orchard, sheltered from wind and rain, positioned to soak up the sun and to be within Aletta's reach too, for she was as able a beeward as Henry himself.

As she let herself in through the wooden door of the orchard and strode up the stone-slabbed pathway through the heavily budded apple trees, the sound of laughter and shrieks did little to alleviate her annoyance. The three lads and a young maid didn't hear her soft approach over their own rowdy guffaws, and the only one of the three lads to notice her arrival was too late and too surprised to stop the hand of another one of them plunging down the maid's bodice as the others held her against the tree.

Aletta stopped dead, waiting until one by one they realised her presence, watching the grins slowly disappear and the eyes widen in horror. The maid, taking her cue from the sudden silence of the lads, turned and pulled up the neckline of her bodice, her face flushed and flustered, though it was clear she'd been enjoying the game every bit as much as they had.

"It was a bee, m'lady," she whispered. "Down me bodice."

"We were 'elpin 'er get it out, m'lady," said the lad apologetically, though his eyes continued to dance with merriment.

"I believe you three are needed in the garden, *now!*" Aletta scolded.

"Yes, m'lady." They ran, sending her looks of gratitude that they'd escaped a lengthy reproach.

"And you? Where are *you* supposed to be this morning?"

The maid was buxom and cheeky-faced but apparently had the good sense to keep her eyes lowered rather than reveal the remains of her laughter. "I'm supposed to be 'elpin Mistress Bridie, m'lady," she said.

"I can't see that getting a bee and three pairs of hands

down your front is going to be of much help to Mistress Bridie, can you, Mabe?''

The lass nearly exploded, and held a hand to her mouth to keep herself in check. Her eyes opened wide to meet Aletta's, and found not the fearsome anger she'd been half-expecting but more of an understanding between women, an exchange of experiences.

"I shall fine you if this happens again, Mabe. I'm not paying you to cavort round the orchard. Understand?'' She tried to sound stern.

The maid nodded, sober now. "Yes, m'lady. Thank you.''

"Now, if you haven't frightened the poor creature to death, will you show it the way home—'' she nodded towards the bee-skeps ''—and then get on with what you're supposed to be about?''

With a glance towards the bee-skeps, and another at Aletta, the maid bit her lips, bobbed a curtsy and fled up the pathway to the gate without another word.

Aletta watched her departure with laughter welling up inside her like a fountain. How could she scold, remonstrate, blame them? Had she not known the same excitement only recently at a man's touch, the same inexplicable animal arousal? Sunshine, springtime, bees, blossom, growing things, urges of the body; surely it was the same for all of them?

In a sudden daze of longing, her hands moved upwards towards her breasts and held them without moving, feeling once again the brush of his fingers on her skin. Her sigh became a moan at the memory, her eyes blurred, unseeing, her legs shaking. Sweet Jesu, how long will I be able to hold him away? she wondered as she moved towards the loud hum of the hives.

A row of jugs, dishes and bottles stood to attention before her on the stone slab by the buttery window. Nearby, a cauldron of water simmered, straight from the great fire in the kitchen next door, letting out a cloud of steam into which Aletta dropped new borage leaves. She mumbled contentedly to herself.

Hinting that her mistress might be getting carried away by her own enthusiasm, Bridie nudged her elbow. "Do you know what you're about, love?"

"No, Bridie. Put two spoonfuls of honey into that jug of wine and stir it up. Now, when the leaves have infused in this it has to go in there with that." She set aside a bottle for the concoction. "Pass me a label, if you please."

Bridie cast an eye towards the old stained recipe book propped before her, set out with ailments and their appropriate remedies, at the parchment labels already inscribed with the names of the potions and the twine ready-cut to tie them on.

"Now," Aletta was saying, "for her milk she drinks this one at morn, noon and evening. And for the inflammation she must take this one." She brought forward an earthenware jug and stirred it thoughtfully, then sniffed at it. She held it to Bridie to sniff, a questioning look in her eyes.

"Mmm! Thyme?"

"Thyme and ground ivy. She can make compresses of this too, if she wants to. There's plenty of thyme. Good thing she had her bairn in spring, otherwise it would have been difficult." She tied a label to the glass container and filled it with the clear liquid. "Here you are." She passed Bridie a piece of twine and a square of waxed fabric. "Tie this over the top in a bow. This last one is goose-grease with a drop of rose essence. It's for her sore nipples, poor lass. She shall have more, if she needs it. Now, what else?"

"Food?"

"Got that. It's over there." She nodded towards a large wicker hamper by the door.

"Heavens above! Is it for the whole village?"

''No, daft! There are clothes and blankets in there too. Nothing much.''

Bridie smiled. Nothing much, indeed. She knew that Aletta would have given the clothes off her own back if she'd thought they needed them, bless her.

''Shout for those lads, Bridie. They can start loading this lot now. Then get a groom to saddle the horses. We've a little visit to make.''

Chapter Ten

It had been Bridie's suggestion that Roger should accompany Aletta to Verity's cott. "After all," she'd said, "he knows more about the business than I do, and she's more likely to give you the truth when Roger's there than me. I'd believe anything she said."

So Aletta had a basket of food prepared and set off with Roger across the common land and along the headland towards the column of blue wood-smoke showing against the deep green of the larches. They rode in silence for much of the way, Aletta deep in thought, Roger aware of the change this discovery could make to her life.

Even if the child turned out to be Sir Hubert's after all, it hardly proved him to be as virile as he would no doubt have liked to be. One brat out of all *his* attempts was no great cause for satisfaction. And yet, for Aletta, this could solve the mystery one way or the other, he thought. Perhaps it would help her to make up her mind what to do about Sir Geraunt, for it was clear he'd made up *his* mind what to do about *her*. He smiled to himself; only a few weeks back he'd have been sick with envy. Now he was content that it should be so, for his attention had been directed towards a wonderful creature he ought to have noticed years ago.

"What am I going to say to her, Roger?"

He looked across at Aletta without speaking, the squeak of leather and the clink of iron sounding loud as she waited for his answer. "My own philosophy at times like this, m'lady, is not to prepare any questions but to say whatever comes, quite naturally. Let's wait till we get there, then we'll know what to say." He smiled at her reassuringly.

"You think so?"

"Yes. You'll see. It's no good trying to anticipate her reaction beforehand."

Aletta nodded, thankful for his advice, and shaded her eyes against the sun. "Who's that outside the cott? Look he's holding the babe."

Roger frowned, straining his eyes. "No one I recognise."

The man saw their approach and stood quietly waiting as they pulled up and dismounted, the young child in his arms holding on to the laces of his shirt with one hand and stuffing the other into a wet little mouth.

"G'day, m'lady. Sir." He nodded at them both without moving.

Why Aletta had never noticed before, she could never have said—neither then nor at any time later. The child's dark hair, dripping over into his great brown eyes, the apple cheeks, the golden skin like that of a ripe fruit—none of these features tallied with Sir Hubert's Nordic sandstone colouring, nor with Verity's silky blondeness. And yet Aletta had never questioned Verity's account of the child's parentage, not for one moment.

She held out her arms to the child, who leaned towards her eagerly, clearly recognising an old friend and a favourite source of cuddles. "May I?" she asked the man. "You're his father?" She knew the answer already.

The man nodded, allowing the child to slip easily from his arms into hers. "Aye. I knew it'd only be a matter of time before you discovered. Will you come on in?"

They were as alike as two peas in a pod, father and son. Same dark hair, overflowing into dark brown wide eyes, openly candid, honest as the day. Same rosy cheeks and brawny arms, short sturdy legs, as southern in appearance as Verity was northern.

"We realised someone else was keeping an eye on her too," said Aletta, following him inside, "but we didn't know who. This is Master Holland, my bailiff."

She greeted Verity and gave her the basket of food, looking anew at the longish face and willowy body, frail and waif-like against the robust roundness of the other two.

"Don't blame 'im for sayin' nuthin', m'lady," Verity said. "It were me mam an' dad that told 'im to shut up and stay out ert way."

"Why, Verity?" Aletta whispered. They squatted on stools on the rush-strewn earthern floor while the babe scampered off, alternately crawling and staggering drunkenly from one knee to the next, steadied by outstretched arms. "Why didn't you say?"

"Me mam and dad were that ashamed of me and what I'd…we'd…done that they wouldn't pay t' leyrwite. They said I 'ad ter fend fer miself. But they knew you'd think that the bab were 'is—Sir Hubert's—and that you'd see me all right."

"They thought that? That they'd rather see you turned out than pay the fine for you? Could they not pay it, Verity?"

"Aye, m'lady. Course they could. But they wouldn't. They knew you'd look after me, sooner or later. An' they knew e'd no business to be fining me anyway, not after what e'd done too. That made 'em mad."

"So they thought…hoped… I'd find you somewhere to live. But what if Sir Hubert had not died when he did? Did they not care?"

"No. Thiv got a family of another eleven, besides me. An' anyway, they knew Jack wouldn't leave me to starve.

They just wanted you to think it were your 'usband's brat, not 'is, so they told 'im to say nowt. They thought you'd send me back to 'em if you found out.''

"But Verity," Roger interrupted gently, "you must have known that Lady Aletta wouldn't have done that. How could you go on deceiving her like this for two whole years?"

Verity was stuck for words, and turned to Jack to help her out.

"She wasn't in no fit state to argue with her mam and dad at the time," he said, squeezing her hand. "Then, once you've begun deceiving someone, it's hard to stop, isn't it? She's been so comfortable here, everybody looking after her. I think that Verity thought it was all too good, and that if she blinked it would disappear. And I went along with it because it was what she wanted. But it was never what I wanted. Living with the story that my brat was fathered by somebody else is not what I like. And I'm glad you know now, m'lady.''

Aletta was trembling, and looked at Roger, willing him to take over.

"You were certain the bairn was not Sir Hubert's, then? Right from the start?" Roger asked, knowing that this would have been Aletta's next question.

Verity smiled secretly, and looked at Aletta as though *she* had asked. "Oh, yes. I was always quite sure. I'm sorry, truly I am, that I told you it was his. But I knew it wasn't. You can tell, can't you? You know. It wasn't like with Jack." She looked at him and smiled. "Sir Hubert was only trying to prove something, m'lady. That's why 'e 'ad everybody 'e could lay 'ands on. It was sad, really. It didn't mean nuthin'.''

Aletta realised that Verity was as sure of Sir Hubert's impotence as Sir Geraunt was.

"You're not from one of our villages, are you?" Roger said to Jack. "Where are you from?"

"Allerton. I'm a carpenter."

The look exchanged between Aletta and Roger said everything.

"Then it looks as though you'll have to get used to living apart, unless you build a new home for the three of you in Allerton," said Aletta quietly. "Because it's not in the least likely that you'll be allowed to move away from there, Jack."

"You don't think Sir Geraunt would—"

"No, I don't. Not a chance!"

"Are you sure, m'lady?" asked Roger, looking intently at her.

"As sure as I'm sitting here talking to you," she said flatly.

"One problem at a time," said Jack. "I take it you have no objection if we let if be known that I'm the father of Verity's child, m'lady?"

Aletta smiled at him, and at Verity. "It would make me as happy as it makes you. Now you can come and go openly, no more secrecy."

"And you won't mind me staying here?" Verity asked.

"Not in the slightest. You're free to do whatever you wish. Come to the manor court next…?" She looked enquiringly at Roger.

"Monday," he said.

"Next Monday, that's in three days' time. We'll make it all official."

"You were right, Roger. Whatever we'd decided to say to her beforehand would never have prepared us for what we found, would it?"

He smiled. "Funny, isn't it? Neither of us had ever seen the fellow before, and yet I had a feeling someone was about. And I think I would have known it was a carpenter."

"You mean the stools and the table?"

"Yes. But why are you so sure he won't be allowed to leave Allerton, m'lady?"

Aletta was thoughtful, her eyes fixed ahead on the view between the gelding's ears. She spoke without looking at him. "Because Sir Geraunt's already lost more than he can spare, and he's anxious not to lose any more. That's why he won't release Gerda's Thomas. I don't believe there's any point in asking him."

"I see. He's uncompromising, then?"

"On issues like that, totally."

"Well, at least you now have the truth. Are you relieved?"

This time she was silent for so long that he wondered if she'd heard him. He looked at her sharply, surprised at her delay in answering. "Aren't you?" he asked softly.

As though trying to shake her thoughts into place, she shook her head slightly. "It's difficult. I've lived with an image of a man for so long, been so sure of my facts, everything so black and white, right or wrong. Now I see that I must have been very naïve. Those people..." She turned to look back across the field. "I tried to help when they were in trouble, and they all deceived me. The lot of them. What a soft fool they must have thought me. I get the impression that's how everybody sees me."

She was getting close to self-pity, and Roger saw that as a bad sign. "Not those who've seen you hurl a stool across the hall or been on the wrong end of one of your famous rages, m'lady. You're confusing foolishness with compassion. Most people can tell the difference between the two, and those who take advantage of what's on offer when they're in a fix are not necessarily knaves, you know. Given a choice, most people would've done what those two did. Probably you would too, if it meant the difference between bringing your bairn up in a crowd of thirteen others and two oxen, and being alone in a place like that. Don't you think so?"

"I understand what you say, Roger." They turned into the gateway and reined in, just inside. "But it might have saved me much heartache if I'd known how things were before."

"Well, m'lady, forgive my bluntness, but if that means you'd have thought more seriously about marrying one of those other toad-heads who came skulking round the place in the last two years, I'm glad you *didn't* know how things were before. If you want to know what I think, I think the timing couldn't have been more perfect."

"Thank you, Roger. I *do* want to know what you think, but…"

"But?"

"I'm afraid," she whispered, so softly that he saw the words rather than heard them. The grooms came running and the rest of their conversation was delayed until they had dismounted and were walking round the side of the building towards the dovecote.

The dovecote was a stone tower housing hundreds of white doves. Several men were busy, inside and out, shovelling the soft droppings into a cart ready to spread on to the fields of the demesne.

"That reminds me, Roger," Aletta said, watching the men for a moment as they paused, "it seems that you took my advice seriously."

"The doves reminded you, or the muck-cart?"

"Doves, of course, idiot! Bridie's never been so happy. What about you?"

"Me, too. I wish I'd noticed before."

"Will it be a permanent state of affairs, do you think?"

"If I've anything to do with it, it will. We've talked. It looks good."

"I'm glad. Truly, I'm delighted."

They walked on round to the back of the manor, looking into the stewpond, agreeing that it would have to be cleaned up and restocked with some pike and perhaps some carp now that Lent was past, and on through the back entrance to the inner courtyard. Roger pointed out where repairs were needed to the stable roof, a new pigsty, a shelter for the wood-pile. They watched the blacksmith at work, explaining to his new apprentice how the iron must be heated, beaten, shaped and cooled, then together they went towards Edwise's room, where Oswald's presence still hung like a shadow around the doorway.

"You know Edwise will be going to Middlestone in a few days, Roger?" Aletta asked. He nodded. "Well, this room will be free. I have plans to have a hole knocked in the centre wall to connect it with yours. Do you think you could do with two rooms, instead of one?"

"Two?" His face shone with delight. "Two? I think we could manage very well in two rooms. Very well, indeed."

"Well, then, have a word with one of the builders, and get the carpenter to measure up for a door and frame. And perhaps a bigger window, d'you think? After she's gone, of course. I don't want her to think…" She knocked and went in, closing the door on him with a smile.

Although still shocked by Oswald's death, Edwise was happy to be going to Middlestone and she'd already begun packing and getting rid of the accumulation of Oswald's possessions of which she had no need—quill pens, inks, his abacus, rolls of parchment and books, old souvenirs. When Aletta had visited her the maids had almost finished, leaving only a few bits for Edwise to dispose of before she left on the morrow.

Now, as Aletta took her ease in the solar, she thought of her earlier visit and smiled at the way the gentle old lady had pressed something into her hand, trembling with emotion at parting with the pieces of her husband's life.

"I found this, Lady Aletta." She'd seemed to swing from formality to the most familiar in her form of address, to Aletta's amusement, and then she was being formal. "He said, just before he died, that you ought to have this. He actually chuckled as he said it, lass, as though it was a jest. But, I don't know. Here…take it. He said you'd like it.''

It had been a little parchment bundle, just large enough to fit into the palm of her hand, and she'd taken it upstairs to examine later. Now, wrapped snugly in a fur-lined gown, she held it again while she sipped one of her concoctions of dandelion root, young nettle leaves, primroses and elder shoots sweetened with honey—one of her favourite spring-time drinks for cleansing the blood.

''What is it, m'lady? A gift from an admirer?'' Gerda asked, combing the ends of Aletta's plaits tenderly, enjoying the silkiness and rich colour, and the way the hair curled around her fingers at the ends.

''It's something Edwise wanted me to have.'' She unwrapped the stiffened parchment, now creased with time into firm folds and unwilling to reveal its contents. But, held flat to the table, the parchment revealed a small golden buckle, beautifully engraved with tiny vine leaves. Or were they ivy leaves? she wondered. ''A buckle! That's odd! Is it from a purse or a belt, do you think?''

Bridie frowned over the tiny thing, then laughed. ''Have you seen? There's something written on the underside. Can you see what it says?''

Aletta frowned. ''Don't suppose so, in this light. Bring the lamp, Gerda, and let's see. It'll be 'love conquers all,' I expect. That's the usual thing.''

The words *were* familiar, though not what she had thought. They were the same as those on the inside of her betrothal ring. '''I hold what is mine,''' she whispered, and sat back in her chair, dazed and speechless with surprise.

What could this possibly mean? Could it belong to Geraunt? How had it come into Oswald's possession? Had Edwise been confused when she'd said that Aletta was to have it? Had she meant Geraunt? But why? More questions to add to those already stacking up in her mind like the logs just brought in from the woodpile. If only someone would provide some answers once in a while, she thought.

"I think you're right, it must be a purse buckle. Look, here's a piece of leather still fastened to the bar, as though it's been cut off."

She could not tell Gerda why the words were familiar to her. She would ask the same questions she herself was asking, be just as puzzled as she was. Best not to tell her. The buckle was left on the table before them. She would decide what to do with it on the morrow.

"Before you go, Gerda, bring me that pile of rolls up here, if you please."

"Isn't it a bit late for all that, m'lady? Won't it do tomorrow?" Gerda could see how tired Aletta was; a good night's sleep would be more sensible.

"I'm only going to glance at them, that's all." Aletta patted the table. "Come on, they can't stay up here forever. Now, it's time you were going home."

The flame of the lamp had burned out and been replaced several times by new cressets before Aletta finally sat back in the great chair and shook her head. A faint glow was breaking over the eastern hills and Bridie had long since given up trying to persuade her to go to bed, but instead had placed a folded blanket beneath her feet and another over her knees, then she'd fallen on to her pallet and slept.

At first, Aletta had merely glanced through the manorial accounts in curiosity, knowing full well what the recent ones contained, but wishing only to congratulate herself on their exactness, their completeness, their declaration of affluence and good management. Little by little, the fascinating recital of comforting facts and figures had demanded that she work backwards, make little comparisons here and there into previous years.

And then a curious sickly lurch, deep in her stomach, had acted almost as a stimulant, a masochistic urge to search for more of the same—more errors, more alterations, more mismatching of figures. Her unbelief turned to a feverish hunt, as if to verify her horror, to punch home the truth of her discoveries.

The rolls of parchment, only a little wider than her outstretched hand from thumbtip to fingertip, were close-covered with lists of receipts and expenses. Roll upon roll was sewn together where the accounts were continued, and bundles of receipts sewn to the edges to prove the various transactions. Rents from mills, houses and cotts, assarts and fishing rights, receipts from sales of oats and corn, grain, stock, poultry, leather, fleeces, fells and foodstuffs at the fairs and markets, animal sales and purchases. Every possible detail showed how Aletta had built up sales in areas which were more productive and cut down on non-essentials which had previously lain rotting in warehouses and store-rooms.

And yet... And yet during the years Sir Hubert had left all this to Oswald, and rarely bothered to cast an eye on the records, Aletta found that a total of five hundred pounds was missing over a period of two years just before her marriage. Almost two years' profit, at that time, though now *her* figures had risen remarkably.

She reached for the jug of wine but found it was empty, and her shaking hand, now numb with cold, sent her goblet flying off the table in an uncontrollable jerk. The thumping of her heart reached her upper arms, making them shake, making her sickness sink like a stone into her bowels. What on earth had been going on?

"What is it, pet? What in heaven's name is so important you have to sit here all night?" Bridie noted Aletta's ghastly face and trembling hands. "The accounts?"

"Look, Bridie! Look! You shouldn't be seeing these. But look! Figures scratched out... Can you see? Alterations everywhere for these two years."

"Well, I can't really understand—figures are not my

strong point, you know—but aren't alterations usual in these things?''

''Oh, yes, there are always alterations by the clerk of the accounts...small ones...or by the steward himself, or even the auditor, but never on this scale. Some of these have been changed since they were passed as true accounts. There's got to be an explanation, Bridie. There's got to be!''

''You remember when Sir Hubert said he'd lost some money, m'lady? Said the manor was in debt? When he sent Oswald away?''

''Yes,'' Aletta said softly, looking at her maid in the flow of the early light. ''He discovered it only a bit before he died, didn't he?''

''And nobody believed Oswald could make a mess of the accounts. Not Oswald. He was far too careful. Everybody thought it must have been Sir Hubert who'd needed money for something. But five hundred pounds! Are you sure?''

Aletta nodded. ''Yes, yes, I am, Bridie. I've gone over and over the figures and that's what it amounts to. It's just disappeared. Weeded out of every sale. Bit by bit.'' The two looked at each other in silence. ''Go and get Roger up here, Bridie. I want to see what he has to say about it.''

''Are you sure you wouldn't like to sleep a bit, love? Do it later?''

''No! Now, Bridie!''

The maid sighed in resignation. There was no point in arguing when her mistress was using that voice.

Aletta fond it comforting to have Roger's presence in the room, as though things would suddenly cease to be troublesome and frightening. He entered, tucking his chainse into his braies and running his hand through a tangled mop of hair. He gave Aletta a sleepy grin as he approached the table, and she explained what she'd found, carefully and without letting the sound of worry creep into her voice.

He sat in the chair that she'd occupied and set to work, following the entries from the early years of Aletta's marriage backwards, to where the discrepancies first began, while she was manoeuvred unwillingly towards the bed by her maid. In moments she was asleep, the white curtains drawn about her in a fruitless attempt to forestall the light of a new day.

"You'll have to wake her, honey." Roger reached up to Bridie and pulled her head down for a kiss. "She told me we have to make an early start for Middlestone with the old lady and I've got to talk to her about this before we go."

"You think I'm going to leave you here with her in bed while I get some breakfast?" she whispered in his ear, pretending distrust and pouting.

"Yes, I do, wench! Now, go on, or I'll have to beat you!" He slapped her bottom playfully.

"Promise?"

"Promise," he laughed, and kissed her again.

Over a brief breakfast in the solar, Aletta discussed the discoveries of the night with Roger, though neither of them could form any opinion about the reason for the enormous discrepancies over the accounts so far back. Neither could they quite believe that Oswald's hand was responsible, and yet both of them had clearly recognised his neat, spidery script. It was unmistakable.

They also agreed that, for some reason, roughly five hundred pounds had disappeared at about the time of Aletta's marriage, and though one might have thought that Sir Hubert would have extra expenses at that time nothing appeared under household expenses to show what they could have been. And yet it seemed that all this had not been discovered by Sir Hubert until many years later, if Oswald's dismissal was anything to go by. He had never denied any involvement, because no one except Sir Hubert had ever challenged him, and that had been in private. Certainly Aletta never had, even later.

"I shall go and talk to Mistress Margery." Aletta spoke through a mouthful of pear, the juice running down her chin. Bridie passed her a napkin.

"Well, she's about the only person who'll know anything, though there's no guarantee that he discussed it with her, is there? And old Edwise can't remember a thing at the moment." Roger bit into a piece of cheese and considered the muslin rind that he pulled from between his lips with a look of surprise. "We're going over there with Edwise this morning. Why don't you come, too?"

Aletta pushed her chair back. "Right. I will. Come on!"

"D'you mind if I finish my breakfast?" asked Roger lazily. "Or are you going to hustle me out of this too?"

"Roger?" Bridie was amazed by Roger's familiar tone, but caught the look between bailiff and mistress and smiled.

"Oh, eat your breakfast, then, dammit! Call those lads to bring my bath up, Bridie, will you? I'll be ready in about an hour, Master Holland, if that's not too inconvenient for you?" She winked at Bridie.

"Perfect, m'lady. But don't keep me waiting, if you please!" He ducked, and reached for the jug of ale as though nothing had happened as a small cushion flew past his head.

"We'll take a couple of spare horses, too, Roger. I owe her some."

"I think we may have to leave that for another time, m'lady."

"Why?" Aletta looked at him sharply. He was obviously not jesting now.

"They're all out, down in the far field. It'll take ages to get them."

"All of them? Every single one?"

"All except Magnus and your grey, and ours for this morning, and the ones for—"

"Oh, all right! Don't go on! But I'm not fooled! Not for one moment. I know perfectly well who's put *that* idea into your head! Don't deny it!"

Roger strode towards the door and held it open as two lads brought in the bath-tub, followed by two more with pails of hot water hanging from yokes across their shoulders. "I wasn't going to, m'lady. I'll be ready in an hour." And he went out, grinning.

"Damn the interfering…!" she growled between her teeth, glancing out of the north window. "Damn him!"

Mistress Margery was clearly in her element at the thought of having someone to care for again. "She's tired after the journey, but she'll be all right once she's had time to rest and find her feet." She bustled across the room and placed her large, motherly figure down beside Aletta on the cushioned window-seat, her face glowing and happy, her blue eyes twinkling. "You've always looked after them both so well, Aletta, and they adored you. Especially Oswald."

"I owe them both a lot," Aletta said, placing her hand over the older woman's. "Oswald taught me to account, and I can't tell you how valuable that's been to me, in the circumstances. I shall have to find another steward now."

"Why don't you let Geraunt help you?"

"I suppose because it wouldn't be right to let anyone else know too much about my affairs. I prefer to keep things to myself. Roger will find someone, no doubt."

"Well, my dear, at least you have a very capable bailiff. But you look worn, my dear girl. Have you not been sleeping well? You're not worrying still, are you?"

Aletta removed her hand, wondering how to begin, then replaced it again. "There's something I need to know," she said.

"About Geraunt?"

"No, as a matter of fact, it isn't. It's about Oswald."

"Oswald? Well, you knew he was Sir Hubert's half-brother, didn't you? His mother was a lovely woman, so they say."

"Yes, I knew that, mistress. It's not that."

"What, then?"

"Edwise passed all the old manorial accounts over to me when she cleared out a few days ago. She wanted them all out of the way. Last night I looked through them, just casually at first, and then the further I went back the more I noticed that there were discrepancies."

"Discrepancies? In the stock, or the money?"

"Money! Five hundred pounds, or thereabouts, missing over a period of two years."

Mistress Margery was silent as Aletta continued.

"It seems to have been pared away from the profits at about the time of my marriage."

There was still no reaction from her friend.

"You remember, just before Sir Hubert died, that he accused Oswald of misappropriating money from the accounts, of putting him into debt? He'd had to let some manors go, apparently, though I never saw them. It seems he'd just discovered something he should have seen years ago. But anyway, he sent Oswald and Edwise packing, didn't he? And they came here to you."

At last, Mistress Margery squeezed her hand and smiled, remembering the unhappy couple. Aletta went on.

"Well, I can't understand how Oswald could *not* have been involved. He was in charge of the money so he must have known something about it."

The old lady still kept silent, dreading the next question, and wondering how she was going to break the news.

"Did he say anything to you about it? What is it all about?"

"Oh, my goodness!" The motherly figure rose from the window-seat, ran her hands over the surface of the polished table and then pushed both hands inside her wide sleeves, facing Aletta with a shake of her head. "There was so much bad blood between Sir Hubert and Oswald. They were both so incredibly unlike. Nothing at all in common."

"But Oswald couldn't be dishonest, could he? Surely not!"

"No. Not in the generally accepted sense. But, you see, Oswald could never go along with what Sir Hubert had done, and he felt he had a right to—" She broke off, frowning.

"Had a right to what, mistress? A right to take money?"

But Mistress Margery's eyes had strayed to the window which overlooked the approach to the lodge, her mind now clearly elsewhere.

"What was it he felt he had a right to do?" Aletta insisted, trying desperately to refocus her friend's wandering attention.

But the competition was too strong, for the clamour outside could now clearly be heard in the room and the widow was already crossing to the window in curiosity. She turned back to Aletta in a flurry, beaming with delight. "Geraunt's here! Must have come looking for you. I certainly didn't expect to see him again so soon."

"Geraunt? So soon? What do you mean by that?"

"He and Willan were here yesterday with some horses for me. Willan had to return to Sir Thomas after the Easter celebrations—he's still his squire, you know." It was clear that she'd now dismissed their earlier conversation completely.

Aletta could barely disguise her annoyance. Much as she would normally have been happy to know that Geraunt had come in search of her, this particular moment, when she was about to hear an explanation of a night-long enigma, was the most inconvenient he could have devised.

"But…you were just about to tell me…about Oswald," she whispered, as steps sounded on the stairs outside the door. She groaned inwardly and leapt up to take the widow's arm. "Don't tell him, please! This is my affair...he mustn't know..."

They turned together, arm in arm, towards the door, taken by surprise at his speed.

Chapter Eleven

"Women's secrets?" Geraunt enquired innocently.

Involuntarily Aletta's arm tightened, but her companion patted her hand reassuringly, noting her confusion and what looked suspiciously like irritation.

"Geraunt! I can't believe you've come to see me on two days together. Admit it—" she giggled, kissing him on both cheeks "—you came to find Aletta, didn't you?" She held his hands and shook them gently.

Geraunt took hers between his own and held them to his lips, sending a look of conspiracy across to Aletta. "Alas, I am discovered, Godmother. You're too wise by half, woman." He moved towards Aletta. "Was it such bad timing, vixen? After scouring the countryside for you, am I not to be rewarded with a smile?"

As Mistress Margery left the room Aletta looked forlornly at the carved oak panels of the door, as though hoping that time would take pity on her and run backwards a little and allow her to make a slight readjustment.

"It was indeed poorly timed, sir. I can't deny it." She tried to place her hands behind her back and turn away from him, but he'd anticipated her move, and now she found that her hands were locked between his warm ones and held against the soft russet velvet of his hip-length tunic.

The rich fabric glowed in the morning sunshine where it fell in soft folds round the hood over his wide shoulders and nestled up to his ears. The elbow-length sleeves extended into long pointed tippets in the latest fashion, showing close-fitting under-sleeves of blue-green figured brocade with a long row of tiny decorative buttons from pointed cuff to elbow. A gold-studded belt was slung low over his hips, a sword-belt with short scabbard below that, and Aletta's eyes then travelled downwards towards the close-fitting blue-green velvet chausses, which accentuated the bulge of the muscles in his powerful legs. Leather boots of some soft green skin extended to neat points at the toes, and now her slow perusal of him was quite unconcealed as she tilted her head to one side to peer at them. Her eyebrows were still raised in approval as she met his laughing eyes with her own serious ones.

"So, if the timing was poor, what points do I score for appearance, then? Do I pass scrutiny?"

She would not tell him that he would have passed dressed as a peasant, even, for although she didn't believe that he had any personal vanity to speak of, and though he was indeed the handsomest man she'd ever seen, even dreamed of, she knew that any advantages which she'd begun with were fast being lost to him. It would not do to hand him any more on a plate, and her approval of his appearance could be seen as one of those.

"I cannot fault your appearance, sir, but I cannot believe that you have scoured the countryside looking for me." She tried to pull away, but he kept hold of her hands.

"It seems that I am not to be believed by either of you, though I've not strayed too far from the truth." He laughed, but she did not join him. His face grew serious; he was aware that something was amiss. "I called at Netherstone especially to see you, vixen. They told me where you were and you know the rest. That's all. Simple!'' He expected that the use of the last word would provoke some reaction.

But Aletta stood still, unsmiling and unsettled, angry that the reason for her visit was now quite eroded by his sudden appearance. Now she would have to abandon her attempt to talk in private about Oswald and wait for another time; a whole day wasted and the mystery no nearer being solved.

All at once she felt stifled and irritated, unable to conceal her disappointment, for in spite of Geraunt's fine appearance, and his efforts to reach her, the affairs of Oswald and the accounts were uppermost in her mind and would not be dismissed. With a perfunctory kiss of greeting, she released herself just as Roger, Bridie and Mistress Margery returned, sparing her any further intimacies, and she went to stand over by the window, wondering how soon she'd be able to make her escape.

The voices in the room faded into a soft buzz of sound, the bright light made her head swim and a wave of sickness washed over her, hot and cold both at the same time. Numbly her fingers closed over the goblet of wine that was being held out to her, but she felt nothing, and the top-heavy vessel tipped over to one side as her arm shook uncontrollably. As she turned to clutch at something firm, a chair pressed into the back of her knees and she sat down with a hard bump as her knees buckled under her. The goblet clattered to the floor. She stared at her fingers, dripping with wine, wondering vaguely whose they were.

''What is it, Aletta?'' Geraunt squatted on his haunches at the side of her, his face full of concern. He had been puzzled by her lack of response to him, her preoccupied air, bordering on apathy, her terseness, and he'd wondered if the previous days had been too much for her, especially with the stress of his demands too. ''What is it?'' he asked again, taking her hand in his.

''Nothing,'' she whispered. ''Nothing, truly.''

"Nothing? This is not nothing, Aletta." Geraunt placed a cool hand on her cheek and turned her to face him.

"Just tired." She closed her eyes, not wanting to see the concerned faces. She didn't want to be here. Why was she here, of all places? "Just tired, that's all. I'm so sorry about the wine…"

"She didn't sleep last night, Sir Geraunt," said Bridie, wiping Aletta's hand and sleeve, "and what with the last few weeks, I think she's exhausted. Nothing that a good rest won't put right, sir."

"I'm going to take you home, Aletta. Just a sip of wine, and then we go. Come on…"

She drank obediently as he held the goblet to her lips, stood against him as Bridie placed her cloak around her, and closed her eyes once more as Geraunt lifted her into his arms and held her securely against his chest.

"Take this thing off her head, Bridie, if you please," she heard him say, and felt the deep satin-covered fillet being removed. "That's better."

It was. Now she could nestle herself closely into his shoulder, smile a sleepy farewell to Mistress Margery and experience the euphoric sensation of being carried easily downstairs to the waiting horses.

He would not allow her to ride, but instead held her in front of him on the sheepskin saddle-cover while Roger and Bridie followed behind with her gelding between them. The great chestnut horse must have sensed his extra burden, for he adjusted his usual frisky prance to a sedate walk, the gentle rhythm lulling Aletta into a state of physical calm, her cheek resting on the soft russet velvet of Geraunt's tunic. From time to time, he looked down at her, smiling to himself but wondering if Bridie had meant it literally when she said that Aletta had not slept.

For the short time it took them to cover the six miles to Netherstone Aletta longed for sleep, but her thoughts were less amenable to her will and refused to be subdued. Why had he come to visit her today, dressed so finely? She was in no mood to be entertaining. How would she get rid of him? What of Oswald's doings? Could she return to Middlestone tomorrow, perhaps? The manor court on Monday, and Verity's case. Impotent. She was being lifted again, passed down to Roger, back to Geraunt.

"Bridie? Where's Bridie?" she whispered.

Geraunt looked around the solar as Bridie attended to her mistress, noting the old manor rolls now neatly stacked in a huge bundle on the table. He saw the cresset-lamp alongside and the small unfolded parchment, with a tiny buckle lying half-revealed inside it. He looked up as Roger entered and nodded towards the table. "Is this the reason for no sleep, Roger?" he whispered, his back to Aletta and the bed.

Roger's glance flickered over to where Aletta and Bridie talked together. "Yes, sir. The old manor rolls. They're interesting. Oswald taught her…"

"Yes, I know." Geraunt frowned impatiently. "She was reading them all night?"

"Yes, all night."

Geraunt's eyes strayed to the window. So, it was all becoming clear. The trip to Mistress Margery, in haste and unplanned, most likely. Well, his invitation could not have come at a better time. "Could you and Bridie manage things between you for a few days? Alone?" he asked.

He didn't need to explain, for Roger knew what he was intending. "Of course. We can manage perfectly. But she won't like the idea, sir." He kept his voice low. "Will you need some help?"

Geraunt met his eyes thoughtfully for a few moments. He would not say anything to put the man's loyalty to his mistress at risk and he was well aware, as any man would be, of Roger's feelings for Aletta. He could easily see how their relationship had grown and strengthened throughout her unhappy years, without going beyond that deemed acceptable by most people's standards. And for that reason Geraunt felt a kinship to this remarkable bailiff which allowed him to accept his assistance. He felt, too, that Roger approved of him; his offer of help was too precious to refuse.

"Help?" he whispered, and they grinned in conspiracy. "Just buckle me in tight, man. And don't go too far away."

He went to Aletta and sat beside her on the bed, taking her hand in his. She looked pale and drawn and very vulnerable. "Now, m'lady. Do you want to know the reason for my visit today?"

She looked at his hands, saying nothing.

"I came with an invitation to stay away from home for a few days."

"Away from home? Where?"

"Allerton Manor. A certain gentleman…"

"No!" She struggled to sit up, then, realising how uncompromising her reply had sounded, dropped her voice so that Bridie and Roger, talking at the far end of the room, should not hear. "No, I'm sorry. I cannot. There's far too much to be done!" How would she be able to visit Mistress Margery if she was at Allerton under his eye? But there was another nagging fear, one which she'd not allow to take shape but which was there, even so, lurking in the shadows.

"I'm sure there's nothing to be done that can't be done by Roger and Mistress Bridie. You need a rest, Aletta, you're exhausted. You were nearly out stone-cold at Mistress Margery's."

"No, that's nonsense! I just didn't sleep too well, that's all. And I have a manor court on Monday, and no steward to supervise, so I have to be there."

"How long since your last manor court, Aletta?"

"Three weeks, just before Easter."

"Then surely there's nothing so urgent that it can't wait another three weeks, is there?"

"Yes, there is. Verity!"

"Verity? You saw her?"

"Yes, she lives down by the woodland in a little cott. I was taking food to her that day when you hunted on my land and…" Her voice tailed off; she was too tired to explain.

"Ah, *that* day! The basket!" He couldn't resist a smile at the memory, and ran a brown finger beneath her chin to make her look at him.

"I discovered what I wanted to know," she said.

"I see." He realised that the discovery might also have something to do with her refusal even to think about visiting him at Allerton. At least here she was partly in control of the situation. It began to look as though he would have to insist. "But Aletta, presumably the world will not draw to a close if Verity's case is not brought to court on Monday. She's not going to notice any change in the next three weeks, is she?"

"No, but…"

"And she'd no doubt agree that you need a rest from all this business of Oswald's funeral, Easter, and all the work, wouldn't she?"

She was losing already, and too tired to think of all the reasons. She snapped, "I don't know what she'd think! I only know that I promised… Roger!" He would help her out, she knew. He'd been there. "Roger, I promised Verity that I'd have her child's paternity openly declared in court, didn't I? On Monday."

"With respect, m'lady," said Roger, approaching with Bridie, "you just told her to be there. I don't remember you making a promise. Why, is there a problem?" He tried to sound unconcerned.

Aletta was astounded. "Roger!" She jumped to her feet,

her eyes angry and accusing. She had relied on him for support and he was not backing her excuse.

Geraunt stood, towering over her and sensing her desperation. "I'm taking you to Allerton, Aletta. Now, this day!" he said calmly. "Will you require Mistress Bridie to prepare your things, or shall I?"

"No!" She whirled on him. "No to everything! There are things that won't wait! You can't interfere in my life this way! You're being totally unreasonable!"

Sir Geraunt strode past her to the door, preventing her from making the exit she'd intended a moment ago, and looked directly at Bridie. "Prepare the Lady Aletta's things, if you please, Mistress Bridie. We leave within the hour."

"No!" The outraged yell stopped Bridie before she could move. But Roger caught Sir Geraunt's eye and gave Bridie a nod of approval, and the poor maid was obliged to give way under such pressure. "Roger! I will never forgive you if you collaborate in this!" Aletta glared at her bailiff, fuming as his long legs reached the outer door before she could change direction. Unable to believe that he would actually prevent her leaving her own room, she faced him, indicating her wish. But he remained with his back to the door, his arms folded, his face a picture of concern.

"Listen to me, m'lady—" he began.

"Roger! Move!"

"Listen to me!" he yelled. His shout took them both by surprise. Aletta had never heard it turned in her direction before and stared at him, thunderstruck.

Before she could recover, he had taken advantage of her silence. "Listen to me, m'lady. *Please. Listen.*" He held out a hand to her, his fingertips falling just short of her arm. "You've taken my advice before, haven't you?" he asked in a low voice. "Haven't you, m'lady?"

"Roger…"

"On many occasions."

"Yes."

"Then take it again, now. Look. Hold my hand. As a friend."

Their years together as mistress and beloved servant gave him the right to speak to her in this way, and obediently she placed her hand in his, feeling a calmness and strength in the pressure of his fingers. "Roger—" she began, about to explain her reasons.

"No, hear me, just this once. You know I would not allow a hair of your head to be harmed. Don't you?"

She was reluctant to answer, knowing the gist of his question. Hesitantly, she whispered, "Yes."

"And you know that if you were not here, I would run this place as if you were?"

"Yes."

"Then go with Sir Geraunt. Remember what we said before Easter? Outside the stables? You know…"

"Yes."

"Then, I took *your* advice. Now it's your turn to take mine. Start looking in the right direction and have courage. You don't usually lack courage…"

"Roger!" she flared indignantly.

"You know what I mean," he replied, almost sharply.

Her attempt to misunderstand fell flat, and she nodded. He had never spoken to her this way before and there was no time for pretended ignorance.

"So, stop thinking of others for a few days. Think of yourself and what *you* want. The manor won't come to a standstill if you're not here, you know." There was a hint of laughter in his voice at the last phrase which made her look up at him quickly.

"Roger…" she still hesitated, but felt the squeeze of his fingers again.

"Go on. Don't be afraid," he whispered. "Just go."

But there was no need for her to cross the room, for as she turned Sir Geraunt was already coming towards her, his arms outstretched.

Roger had spoken too softly for either Sir Geraunt or Bridie to hear what he'd said, but it was clear from Aletta's stillness and from his expression that, on this occasion, her role as sole mistress of herself and of the household was being relinquished, for the time being. He turned, and went out down the steps and into the courtyard below.

Aletta rested her head on Geraunt's chest and felt his hands gently stroking her back. "He puts up with rather a lot from me. He'll be glad to get rid of me for a day or two."

"Or three or four," Geraunt replied quietly.

"Three or four? No, I don't—"

"That's enough! I didn't go through all this performance just for a day or two, woman! You'll do my bidding now, without any more fuss, and I'll let you home when I'm ready. Do you understand?"

She stood pressed against him, listening to his voice rumble in his chest. "I understand only because I'm too tired to do otherwise. But when I feel stronger I shall *not* understand. I shall have forgotten."

"Then I shall have to teach you in a way you won't forget, vixen. So it's just as well you'll be at my home instead of yours."

"Geraunt?"

"Well, m'lady?" His mouth twitched, suppressing a smile.

"You realise that you've chosen a very inconvenient time, don't you?"

"You're telling me that there would have been a convenient one? I can hardly believe that!"

"No. But I do have much to attend to. This is a particularly busy time."

"Aletta, you will have me believe that you're indispensable, I know. But, if your servants are as well-disciplined as they appear to be, they'll relish the idea of you leaving them to get on with things by themselves. It's a way of showing your trust in them. They're not going to run riot while you're away. Roger will be here, and Bridie. We'll take Mistress Gerda with us, so that she can be with young Thomas, and you'll be doing everyone a favour. Including me.''

"Including you?" She wanted him to elaborate.

"Yes, of course me. Everything's prepared for you. Your own room, everything. I want to have you by my side at high table, to show you my house and my village.''

"Yes, Geraunt.''

He held her chin up to him and looked teasingly at her. "You really are feeling a little the worse for wear, aren't you, vixen?''

Geraunt was aware that it appeared inconsiderate to expect her to accept his invitation at a moment's notice, knew that she'd think of every reason why it was inconvenient. But how many other excuses would she have been able to summon up, given more time, he wondered? How many delays, obligations?

He watched her across the table during an impromptu and rather hurried meal. She ate little, drank little, and said even less, and he thought of carrying her on his saddle to Allerton instead of allowing her to ride, though he knew she would balk at that, especially as they had to pass through the staring eyes of both villages. But he suspected that her silence was as much due to apprehension as it was to tiredness. All the same, he didn't relish the thought of another argument in front of the grooms outside.

"Will you allow me to carry you, Aletta, as I did from Middlestone?" He leaned across the table to her.

Aletta looked up from her carved wooden platter, where her finger was playing over the motto round the edge. Her eyes were mildly surprised. "Allow you? Are you asking me? I thought you would give me no choice.''

Her voice was curiously resigned and it appeared to Geraunt that the subject did not even interest her, for she was watching Bridie and Gerda packing her clothes into wickerwork panniers, bustling and whispering together. He was puzzled by her apathy. "Yes, I'm asking you. I don't want to embarrass you, but I don't think you should ride any more today, do you? Shall I carry you?" he asked again.

"No," she whispered, "I'll ride." She bit her lip and looked away.

Covering her hand with his free one, he leaned closer to whisper in surprise, "What is it, sweet thing? Have I pushed you too far? Have I been a little unfair to you, demanding that you leave everything at a moment's notice? It was unreasonable, I know."

She stared beyond him into the sky, where a flock of white doves wheeled against the blue. "No," she whispered.

"Can you tell me? Is it Oswald?"

The pile of manor rolls had been cleared off the table and now lay in a heap on the floor. At his question, her eyes were drawn to them as if by a magnet.

Brief though it was, Geraunt saw the look and felt reasonably sure he knew the answer. "Oswald?" he repeated.

"Oswald... Verity..."

"Me too?"

"No. No, at least I know where I am with you... I think... I think you're being honest with me. I can forgive anyone if they're honest with me, even if I don't like it! But when I'm deceived, I... I..." She snatched her hand from his and leapt away from the table with a clatter, knocking the pile of parchment rolls across the floor as she swept across the room.

Though she could not tell him, her anger was directed not only at herself, for being so duped, but also at Verity, and at Oswald too. And now others were being deceived by her, all who trusted and loved and admired her. The pretend betrothal was a massive deceit, she saw that now. It had already generated problems which she had neither the experience to anticipate nor the guile to brazen her way out of. She should never have agreed. At Allerton she was to face a new crowd of people whom she was expected to deceive, and for what? For her? For them? Or for him?

Again, the warm hand caressed her back until some of the tensions had died away under his fingers. "We'll talk about this later," he said. "It'll wait. Come now. Bridie's waiting to make you ready. And you're going to ride on my saddle, like it or not."

She was wrapped snugly in her favourite blanket of brown-black wool and made only the lightest protest as Geraunt stooped to lift her into his arms.

"I can walk downstairs, surely?" she said, though secretly she was excited at the idea of being treated as a helpless and fragile creature for once. His arms were strong and he strode with her towards the door as though she weighed nothing.

"No, you can't wench. It's not often I get to carry a woman out of her own manor-house. You couldn't do a bit of kicking and screaming, could you? Just for effect? Give 'em something to talk about when we're gone?"

He kept up a stream of nonsensical chatter, much to her embarrassed amusement, as though he were St George and she the sacrificial maiden. And by the time he'd passed her to Roger, to hold while he mounted, Roger was not sure whether she was laughing or crying.

She tried to straighten her face. "Now, Roger, don't forget to tell—"

"Oh, good grief! Here, sir!" He passed her up to Geraunt, who leaned down from the chestnut. "Take her away before she thinks up something else I have to remember. What's going on over there…?" He dodged beneath the horse's neck.

Loud shouts of laughter came from the group behind, where Gerda's high wail of alarm rose above the others. Turning the horse so that they could see, they discovered that the poor lass had been lifted on to her horse by Thomas and placed back to front in the saddle.

"Oh, no!" Aletta yelped. "Thomas is leaving her like that! Make him help her, Geraunt! Oh, poor Gerda!"

The unfortunate maid sat helpless, with nothing to hold on to except the high cantle of the saddle and the leather crupper along the horse's back. "Thomas! You brute! Turn me round! Help me, someone!" she yelled, not daring to look behind her, where Thomas was idly chatting to one of the grooms, pretending not to hear.

"Thomas!" called Sir Geraunt. "Before you mount, man, I think someone's going the wrong way!"

Thomas turned to look, and let his eyes roll heavenwards. "It's that saucy wench, sir. Do we want her with us?"

"Yes, man! I shall get into serious trouble if she goes off in the wrong direction."

Thomas grinned and returned to Gerda, holding out his arms. "Come on, lass. The master doesn't want you going off to Middlestone." He turned her round and led her, red-faced and laughing, to ride by his side.

Geraunt's chest was heaving with laughter as he pulled Aletta closely in to him, noting the grinning faces of the grooms and squires. He looked down at her face, snuffling into his doublet. "Quite a lad, isn't he? Young Thomas?" he said as they moved off.

It was nearly as far to Allerton from Aletta's manor at Netherstone as it was to Middlestone in the opposite direction, but the track was less used, and more full of holes than a sponge, as Geraunt said. His carriage might have been an option, had he not lent it to Sir Thomas and Lady Cecily, but he doubted whether Aletta would have relished the thought of being tossed about on this riverbed of a track, even had she agreed to ride in it, which he doubted strongly.

She confirmed this. Nothing would have induced her to ride in a carriage; it was only this temporary lapse in her usual vigour that had made her agree to be carried in this way.

Aletta had never travelled towards Allerton before. There had never been any point, since the track led only to the large neighbouring village and thence on to remote hill farms and the outer granges belonging to Southstone Priory. Now, as Geraunt pointed out the various features of the countryside to her, he put her lack of curiosity down to her sleepiness and was content just to hold her close to him and to feel her softness. To have got this far with her was, he thought, quite an achievement.

For Aletta, her normal curiosity was being subordinated to her inner thoughts of what the next few days might hold. Curiosity in one sense, but more akin to apprehension and a tingling expectancy. She realised that it would have been pointless to argue about it any more, but had she not felt so dispirited, defeated, confused, she might have made more of a stand.

As it was, she could not even bring herself to argue about the mode of transport, and secretly suspected that if she had ridden the grey over this difficult terrain she might have made a fool of herself and had to be scooped up out of the new fronds of bracken. So she lay, warm and content, aware that, for the time being at least, no decisions she could make would have much effect on those that Geraunt had already made on her behalf.

Remembering what Roger had said only yesterday about not forming replies until the questions had been asked, it seemed only sensible to tackle any future problems when they arose, though it was increasingly difficult for her to pretend, over a distance of only five miles or so, that these problems were not uncomfortably close.

She stole a look upwards at the line of his jaw and the set of his mouth and wondered where his bedroom would be in relation to hers. Her glance was noted and held, his arm tightened, her head was brought nearer to his face.

"What are you thinking, wench?" He smiled as though he knew already.

Aletta felt that a small lie would not be out of order. "I'm just wondering if your arm is aching after all this carrying of ladies out of their manors."

The smile deepened, accompanied by an equally deep chuckle. "My arm? No, not my arm. There's another part of my anatomy which is much worse affected, though. Shall I tell you where it is?"

She might have guessed! So that was uppermost in *his* mind too. Should she pretend not to understand? To be coy, outraged, amused? How could she blame him for thinking what she was thinking too, and having the courage to say it? Was it bravery, or bravado?

Before she could answer, he'd taken pity on her disadvantage. "I beg your pardon, Aletta. Forget what I just said. You're in no mood for that, are you?"

Aletta was amazed. "Do you know, sir," she said primly, but smiling nevertheless, "that's the second time in one day you've apologised to me? Are you not feeling up to the mark either?"

"On the contrary, m'lady. I feel on top of the world. As high as that buzzard up there!"

Smiling then, she snuggled her face once more into his doublet, asking herself whether she would ever get accustomed to a man who made commands sound more like requests, who cared what she thought and could also bring himself to apologise to her for overriding her sensibilities. Flatterers and fawners she'd met by the cart-load, and could recognise them at a glance. But this man had told her what he wanted right from the start, and had insisted on staying close enough to her to see the benefits of his strategy. He had told her that she would come to want it too, had made plans for the time when his predictions came to pass, and had then set to work to establish them irrevocably in her mind, knowing how her body would be the first to respond. And already it had done.

Now she had left her own territory for the first time since her marriage, and she could not blame him for feeling pleased with himself.

She felt his arm tighten around her. "Look, Aletta," he was saying. "Look, this is Allerton. And there's the manor, up there."

Chapter Twelve

Allerton sat imposingly on a slope at the far end of the village above a forest of alders—the "allers' from which the village derived its name. Aletta was surprised at its size, for she had not realised how much larger it was than Netherstone, that the manor-house was so impressive with its crennelated battlements and gatehouse at the entrance to the walled courtyard.

They rode over a stone bridge spanning a dry moat, through the massive arch of the gatehouse and into a courtyard which could have swallowed up Netherstone Manor as a pike gulped at a minnow. The two young squires vied with each other to hold the great stallion's bridle before the flight of stone steps leading to the door, no doubt hoping that the Lady Aletta would be handed down to one of them until Sir Geraunt dismounted. They were disappointed, however, for she was held in place until she was down and then gently lowered backwards into his arms.

"I can walk, now, Geraunt. Please." She looked at his dubious expression.

"Are you strong enough?"

She had to laugh. "Heavens above, yes! I shall lose the use of my legs at this rate. Do let me walk."

So he put her down and led her up the stone steps into

the large, cool, stone-flagged entrance hall panelled with pale oak, obviously new and smelling of the carpenter's workshop.

Gerda followed close behind, patently overawed. "Is this the great hall?" she said to Aletta under her breath.

"This is the entrance hall," Geraunt said. "And over there in the corner—" he pointed "—are the stairs down to the kitchens. The great hall is on that side, through the screens, and our private rooms are over here to the left. Come, I shall introduce my house-steward to you, and my chaplain."

For a moment or two Aletta wondered whether she might not be in a castle rather than a manor, so vast did it seem. How could she have thought that her own insignificant place, built in much earlier times, would attract any attention from one who owned this enormous dwelling? Even the entrance hall was beautiful, wide and spacious.

Two men stood respectfully to one side, and as Geraunt spoke they stepped forward with friendly smiles. "My chaplain, Brother Spen. The Lady Aletta Markenfield, Brother."

"Welcome to Allerton, my lady. It's time this place was graced with a fair face." He grinned wickedly at Sir Geraunt. He bowed low over Aletta's outstretched hand, his face open and intelligent, full of kindness.

"And my trusty house-steward, Master Bartold, who can tell you anything you wish to know about anything at all," Geraunt said quite solemnly, though his face hinted at a private jest between the three of them.

Master Bartold bowed low. "My lady, you are more than welcome." He straightened, and glanced sideways at the chaplain. "I rarely agree with our learned friend, but on this occasion I do. It's high time Sir Geraunt's lady came to see for herself what she'll be taking on. We'll be on our best behaviour, I assure you."

His smile was warm and welcoming, but his words reminded Aletta once again that everyone here was under the impression that their betrothal was genuine. Only Gerda and Geraunt knew differently.

In the absence of a lady of the manor, Master Bertold had sole responsibility for organising the arrangement of the rooms as well as the ordering of the household, but clearly he was a man of great capabilities. Competently he took charge of the young pages who had brought in the first of Aletta's luggage, clipping one of them gently round the ear when the lad over-dramatised the weight of it.

The first sight of her room brought a gasp of astonishment, for Aletta had half expected a man's heavy imprint to be clearly visible. She had not expected to find a light, sunny room painted in primrose-yellow above the pale oak panelling, nor to see new gaily coloured tapestries hanging from the walls, nor a huge bed swathed in gold and white velvet, embroidered with flowers in green and pink.

Geraunt watched as her face broke into an astonished and radiant smile. "Do you think you could manage more than a day or two now, my lady?" he asked.

"What a perfectly beautiful room," she breathed.

Geraunt noticed that her first reaction was to check the windows, kneeling on the yellow velvet cushions of the window-seat to open them wide. The view stretched across the back of the house, where gardens, lawns and trees, orchards and walkways stretched into the distance.

Aletta turned to Master Bartold. "Thank you. I think this is the loveliest room I've ever been in. Flowers too. Someone must have told you..." She looked sideways at Geraunt, and then to the bowl of primroses and lilies-of-the-valley on the small table. Just like her own room. They had thought of everything for her comfort.

As Master Bertold and Gerda bustled about the room Geraunt took her hand and led her to one of the two large windows. "I'll take you down there later, before dark. The gardens are being redesigned. There's still much to be done outside and inside.''

Aletta looked over to the left, where scaffolding indicated building in progress. ''Building, too?''

''Yes, additions. I'll show you all that tomorrow, perhaps. But look, here's the garde-robe.'' He opened a small door in the thick stone wall to reveal a small room with a wooden seat against the outer wall. There were pegs on the wall too. ''For your furs and robes, if you wish. But there are chests…''

Yes, she had noted the large carved clothes chests, and the small cupboard, table, two chairs and the prie-dieu. She ran a hand over the chequered grey and white fur cover on the bed. Miniver and grey squirrel. What luxury, she thought. ''That door…'' She indicated the closed heavy oak door in the opposite corner of the room. ''Where does that lead?'' Unlike the main door, there were no bolts on it.

''Go and open it. You'll see.''

Beyond the door was another solar, as light and airy as hers, hanging with bright tapestries and a long narrow embroidery above the panelling on one wall. A huge bed stood over at the far side, with soft blue curtains of velvet looped up on to each of the four posts and an intricately carved headboard across the top end. Books lay about in piles, and rolls of parchment, there was a table with quills and inks, stringed instruments hung on one wall; there were signs of use everywhere. Aletta turned to him, knowing. ''Your room?''

''Yes, my lady. My room.'' He smiled with his eyes.

For some unaccountable reason, the breath in her chest remained trapped, and she parted her lips to loose it on a long sigh. Backing away, she allowed Geraunt to close the door behind them, the deep pounding of her heart rising into her throat, the question which had been uppermost in her mind now answered.

"Come," he said, taking her hand again, "you shall refresh yourself and then we'll eat. No—" he caught her look of concern "—no, not in the hall. You needn't suffer their curiosity until you feel rested. I've arranged for our food to be served in the parlour."

The parlour? A room for talking in? Aletta looked puzzled, and Geraunt laughed.

"Yes, there are enough rooms here for doing different things in. It's wonderful. So, I keep them separate, and I have a room where I can talk to people, entertain guests, see my officials, and we can eat there too, if we wish. Gerda has a room too."

"Gerda? Her own room? She's not with me?"

"No, Aletta," he said softly, making her blush by his tone. "I think she'll be pleased to have a room to herself, don't you? Especially if we make sure young Thomas knows of its whereabouts."

He led her out of her room, into the passageway overlooking the front courtyard and along to a door next to hers. This was Gerda's room, small, light and cosy. Two silver bells as big as goose-eggs hung on the end of a long cord by the side of her bed, the cord disappearing through a tiny hole in the wall by the angle of the ceiling.

"Bells for you to summon her," Geraunt explained. "When you go to your bed you'll see the other end of this cord, caught by a bar below a ring in the wall. When you pull your end of the cord these bells will jangle and she'll know that you need her."

Aletta laughed. She had to admit it; he *had* thought of everything. "I think I'm almost hungry now," she said, closing the door to Gerda's room.

They ate their meal quite alone, except for the pages who served them. Gerda had been taken to the hall by Thomas and Geraunt's two young squires, happy to be chaperoned by three young gallants and to have the attention of so many curious eyes. Aletta was relieved not to have been obliged to join them in the hall, for although the evening meal was not usually one of great ritual or ceremony, nor even of great formality, she would have felt it necessary to be sociable when she would rather have a chance to reflect. She was curious about Willan's disappearance. Was it really true that he'd had to return to Sir Thomas Newman's?

"Oh, yes, it's perfectly true, Aletta. He asked me to beg his pardon of you." Geraunt took her hand across the table and gave it a gentle squeeze. "He's Sir Thomas's squire until he receives his knighthood, you know."

"Yes, of course. I knew he'd have to return. But what did you say to him?"

Geraunt knew what she was referring to, and searched for a diplomatic way of telling her, one which would not make her angry at his interference in the young man's affairs of the heart. "I told him that I understood the way he felt."

"About…about me, you mean?"

"About you, yes. You'd told him that our pretend betrothal was only a matter of convenience, that's all. That it was just as we'd said at the beginning."

"But that's true. Isn't it?"

Geraunt held his head a little to one side, and regarded her quizzically. He squeezed her hand again. "You only spoke for yourself. You told him you couldn't speak for me, but apparently he'd hoped it was the same for both of us."

"And you told him it wasn't?" she whispered, alarmed.

"I told him that as far as I was concerned there was more to it than that."

"And that's why he couldn't come and bid me farewell personally? He thought I'd lied to him, did he…?" She pulled her hand away angrily, but he caught it again and held it fast.

"No, Aletta! Hear me! He knows you had no reason to

lie to him. But now he knows of my interest, which I believe he'd suspected anyway. He knows that I'm in a better position than he is—from every point of view.''

It was difficult for him to elaborate without offending her, but she knew what he referred to. The elder brother would always have the advantage over a younger one, especially when the elder was a landed knight with daily access to the object of his attentions. She didn't suppose that Geraunt had needed to spell it out too clearly to his brother.

''Was he hurt?'' The concern for Willan showed clearly in her eyes, and Geraunt found that he could not answer her question directly. Yes, he had been hurt.

''He was resigned. He'll get over it.'' His bluntness had a finality about it which went against the grain.

''And me? I get no choice in the matter, do I?'' It was academic and she knew it, as did he, but she had to make the point, just the same.

It occurred to Geraunt that her question was as much a form of self-flagellation as purely academic, that maybe she wanted to hear him affirm his power over her so that she could tell herself that, whatever happened, it was not by her choice, thus freeing her conscience of the charge of duplicity. So he denied her an answer. Let her play that game, if that's what she needs to do, he thought. It would make no difference to the outcome.

''Do you want to tell me about Verity, or shall we save her for another time?''

Aletta realised that he was not going to rise to her bait, but neither did she want to spend time dwelling on Verity's deception. That would wait. Her eyes were drawn to the slanting rays of the sun through the fine-cut glass of the goblets, casting a complex pattern of shadows on the white table-linen. ''Do you have a chapel here, too?'' she asked.

''Yes. It's Brother Spen's secret pride. Just redecorated.''

''Then I have a plan. You show me the garden before the sun goes down, then I go to confession… It's Sunday tomorrow, you know. Then I go to my room. I have some sleep to catch up on.'' She hoped that sounded final, businesslike, decisive.

Apparently he found favour in her plan, for he made no objection. The gardens were far too extensive to be seen in one go, and so their walk was confined to the part nearest the house, to the new fountain that spouted and cascaded into the carp-filled pond, the newly planted line of rose-bushes along the border and the trelliswork tunnel which was being erected down the middle. A group of gardeners were just packing up to go, their wheelbarrow piled high with tools and heavy gloves, empty pots and stakes.

As they walked back towards the house a chill breeze lifted the veil covering her wimple, and Aletta held it to her face. Geraunt placed an arm around her waist and drew her in to his side. ''Come on, m'lady. The sun's going down. The rest will have to wait.'' And he led her along the pathway and into the entrance, where the lamps were already being lit for the night.

In the short time between snuggling down into the soft bed and allowing sleep to claim her, Aletta searched her mind briefly for a more eventful day to compare with this one. Nothing sprang to mind. If her face had earlier reflected her concern about the adjoining door between their rooms, Geraunt had not commented on it. Indeed, she reflected, he had seemed as intent as she that they should have an unbroken night's sleep. He had simply checked the wooden shutters over the windows, reassured himself about her requirements, her comforts, answered all her queries and then bid her a courteous goodnight and left her to her maid.

At that point Aletta had not been too sure whether to feel relieved or somewhat disappointed. Had she hoped he might request her company for a little longer? Demand a lingering goodnight? Take advantage of her less than usual energy? She yawned. It was warm, the crisp linen sheets enveloped her, caressing her skin under the softly quilted fur cover, and she was asleep even before Gerda had closed the door.

Chapter Thirteen

"A whole day without plans. No decisions," she said.

"Only about whether to go out or stay in…"

"Just to wander about in. Talk. Eat."

"Several days. As many as you wish."

"I can hardly believe it."

"Well, just to spoil it all, here's a big decision for you, m'lady. Do you wish to go and see the rest of the gardens now, or wait until after dinner?"

Aletta knelt on the sunny yellow-cushioned window-seat and watched the waving trees over in the orchard, then the scudding grey clouds hanging low over the fells beyond, pushing grey patterns over the new green moorland. Suddenly, she knew how the lambs felt when they leapt their arching spring-loaded little bodies high into the air. An excess of energy and nowhere else to put it.

"Let's go out before it rains," she said. It was Sunday. She had received Holy Communion, she was rested, refreshed, bathed and breakfasted, and furthermore had the rest of the day to see new sights, to enjoy his company and to feast herself on the kind of conversation she'd been starved of for nearly ten long years.

As much as they dared, Geraunt's two squires insisted on accompanying them through the gardens. Richard of

Thame and Robin Oakwell, both of them sixteen, were sons of Oxfordshire noblemen, near neighbours of Geraunt before he'd moved up to Allerton. Thrust into the life of a new manor and household, their rivalry in all things, physical and spiritual, was a constant source of hilarity to everyone around, and now they almost fell over themselves to escort and protect Lady Aletta and her maid from all harm, even where none was remotely likely.

Thomas suffered their presence good-naturedly, knowing that he'd nothing to fear from their puppy-like diversions around Gerda, and Geraunt's mock harshness towards them made them feel that they could justifiably look upon him as an adversary without compunction, a game they alternately enjoyed and resented. They had just offered to give Lady Aletta a demonstration of their skills in the tilt-yard, but Sir Geraunt had intervened.

"On Sunday, Robin? Have some sense, lad!"

"But won't Lady Aletta and Mistress Gerda be going—?"

"Well, if I were them, I'd think seriously about packing my bags already, especially at the thought of having you two hanging on my heels. But no, you'll have a chance to show off in the tilt-yard tomorrow. Meanwhile, practise a little circumspection, if you please." He turned from them and winked at Aletta.

"Yes, sir." They looked blankly at each other, raised an eyebrow each and shrugged. But his meaning was clear, even if the word was unfamiliar to them. They knew better than to prolong an argument with him for he had a fiendish way of putting them in their place during fencing practice in front of their peers, and at staves, too.

Aletta peeped up at his stern expression as they walked towards the gardens. "You're very harsh with them, Geraunt."

"Only polishing their edges. They're still young pups...they need a firm hand."

His words released an impulse which had hovered over her since first she had bidden him good morning, and without another thought she slid her hand into his. Strange, she thought, he had not kissed her since yesterday's quick peck at Mistress Margery's house, neither last night nor this morning, and now, as she felt the warm pressure of his hand over hers, he did not look at her, but carried on telling her about the new developments.

"Is this to be the pleasance, Geraunt?" a voice called from behind them. Brother Spen came through a gap in the neatly clipped hedge, picking his way over planks set by the gardeners for their wheelbarrows.

"Yes," said Geraunt, waving his arm across the partitioned areas before them. "Arbours along the wall over there, covered with climbers... I don't know which ones..." He turned to Aletta.

"Honeysuckle, roses, sweet eglantine..." she ventured.

"Ah! It sounds as though we have an expert here," Brother Spen said in surprise. "Have you shown Lady Aletta your plans for the herb garden, too?"

As they talked, it became obvious to Aletta that although Geraunt had firm plans about the lay-out of his gardens he was less sure about which plants to grow so far north, for his childhood memories were more of cabbages, leeks, onions, beans and peas, his lady mother's simples, pot-herbs and very little else.

"Did your ideas for a complex garden come from the ones you have in Oxfordshire?" Aletta asked as they felt the first spots of rain.

"No, there's nothing very grand down there. I spent some time in France. There are some remarkable ones there and I'm trying to follow a similar design, but I know too little about plants. Plenty about building, though. We're going to get wet. Come! We'll see the rest tomorrow."

There was no sense of loss, for it was time for the main meal of the day, and Aletta knew that she had time enough to see before she had to return to Netherstone. "What was your reason for going to France, Geraunt?" she asked, watching Brother Spen lean towards Gerda, deep in conversation, as they led the way to the house. "Were you on the King's service?"

"Originally, yes. I went to represent the King's side at a tournament. I was to have returned within the month, but I stayed a bit longer."

"How much longer?"

"Two years!" he laughed softly, looking down at her.

"Two years?" Aletta exclaimed. "And that's where you saw the lovely gardens and wanted one of your own? To remind you?"

"To remind me, yes."

She could not quite make out whether the slightly ironic ring to his voice was intended, or whether it was merely that he was ducking his head as they entered the arched door of the house. The squires held the door and stood courteously to one side as they passed.

"It's time you two were getting ready to serve the meal," said Geraunt. "Go, quickly. Or you'll have Master Bartold to reckon with!" It was part of their training to wait upon their master and his guests at table, and they bowed and set off at a run. Geraunt's voice rang out. "Don't run in the hall! How many times do you have to be told? God's truth," he muttered, "I shall be grey before they learn some sense!"

He watched as the boys screeched to a halt, as though pulling at a horse's reins, then, as if at a signal, lifted their knees and high-stepped slowly forward, holding heads and imaginary reins up high in the air; horsemanship without horses.

The company came to a standstill and watched, grinning at the display. Then, as the two lads peeped over their shoulders at Geraunt's face, they broke into their normal gait and disappeared round the corner.

"Irrepressible little varmints," he laughed, and, holding Aletta's hand, he chuckled his way to prepare for the meal.

Aletta watched Geraunt's strong brown fingers hold the water between them, allow it to fall away into the bowl and then receive the towel for drying. The page moved the huge silver basin and ewer towards her and she repeated the ritual, glad to remove the stickiness of the sweetmeats from her hands at last. She was glowing and elated, for at the close of the meal Geraunt had proposed a toast to her, and the whole hall had responded with such gusto that she'd blushed with happiness at their warmth. As they watched the almoner receive the leftovers in his wide platter Geraunt turned to her with a questioning expression.

"You cannot escape the decisions, m'lady, after all. Shall we have our comfits in the parlour, in your room, or in mine?"

Gerda leaned towards her from the other side of the table while Thomas waited some way away, watching. "Do you need me, m'lady?"

"More decisions," Geraunt murmured, his voice holding a hint of laughter.

"You're going with Thomas, Gerda?"

"Yes, m'lady. He's free until tomorrow. He'd like me to go and meet his father and brothers. He'll bring me back safely before dark."

Aletta nodded. "You go, then. You're going to give them the good news?"

"About Thomas? Oh, yes, m'lady." Her face lit up with a happy smile as she went to join the young groom.

"So," said Geraunt, watching them go out hand in hand, "I shall have to combine my duties as host with those of maid until she returns. But did you decide? This young lad needs to know where to serve us."

"Shall we talk in the parlour? I suppose it's still raining?" Aletta replied.

"Pouring down. Parlour, lad." He placed a hand on her waist and steered her away from the busy hall, now clattering with the noise of servants clearing tables, whisking off cutlery and dishes, cloths and the remains of food after the Sunday feast.

There was now a fire in the parlour, crackling merrily in contrast to the grey, mist-laden day outside, and the occasional burst of wind and rain against the window-panes of greenish glass.

"Gerda's going to get soaked," Aletta said, looking at the heavy cloud which had descended over the fells, enclosing the sheep and their lambs in a white blanket.

"Come and sit by the fire. Thomas will keep her safe. Was she pleased about the news?" He poured out the sweet white wine spiced with mace and waited for Aletta to settle on the cushions of the L-shaped wooden box-seat.

She turned to receive the goblet from him. "She was overjoyed. She doesn't know how it will solve the problem of where to live, because Thomas is more than happy in his new position of groom. But it's a move forward, anyway." She realised that, after all, it had been no great sacrifice for Geraunt to free Thomas, since the possibility of the lad leaving Allerton was now quite remote after his promotion. All the same, she felt she had achieved something for them, and that pleased her.

"As you say, it's a move forward. And it made somebody happy, didn't it? Now," he said, sitting beside her and taking her free hand, "do you want to tell me about your visit to Mistress Verity?"

Aletta looked into her goblet and watched the shimmer of light on the surface without speaking. Then she turned and placed it on the table behind them.

Geraunt coaxed her to speak. "You were upset yesterday, when you mentioned it, and yet it seems that you discovered what you wanted to know," he said softly. "So why were you upset?"

It was difficult to begin. "It was not only that Verity and her family made use of my *naïveté*. They *could* have paid the leyrwite, but they knew that they could get a better deal if they refused. And they did. They kept up the pretence, even though the little lad's father claimed parentage at the time. So the family got rid of Verity, she got a free home, food…everything… And all by pretending that my husband was the father. And I didn't believe him when he denied it, even though I had no reason to suppose that he was! What kind of a fool does that make me look in people's eyes? I have to accept now what you said the other day, that it seems he was impotent. But how much anguish could have been spared me if I'd known that earlier, I wonder?"

"I see. So you know who the brat's father is?"

"He was there. We met him, Roger and I. There's no shadow of doubt."

"One of the villagers?"

"As a matter of fact, he's one of yours. Your carpenter."

"Not Jack Carpenter, surely? Small, sturdy chap?" He was incredulous.

"Yes, the same."

"God's wounds! He's the chap who's been doing all the oak panelling in the house. Marvellous workman."

"In the entrance hall and the solar?"

"Yes, he's been in my pay since I moved in here."

They were both silent for a time, while the logs fizzled and crackled in the fire. Then Geraunt spoke again. "Well, that certainly makes them look like first-rate deceivers, wench, but it doesn't make you look like a fool. Only a kind-hearted and caring woman, and no one will blame you for that. Now, what was the problem with Oswald?"

Aletta shook her head and looked across at the window where the rain beat now, and the wind gusted. "No, I shouldn't have said that yesterday. I was upset. I really can't talk about it. It concerns only me."

"Heavens above, wench! I didn't think we could get any

more private than Sir Hubert's impotence and your fears of childlessness. You were upset, and that concerns me too. And Oswald is no longer around to know he's being spoken of, so tell me how he deceived you, if you please.''

''Must I? I'm not even sure…''

''Yes, you must. Perhaps I could shed some light on it.''

''You?'' Aletta looked at him.

''Tell me!''

So she did, hesitantly at first, and then angrily, as her recital of the facts as she saw them seemed only to verify what she suspected—that Oswald had indeed been responsible for the disappearance of a great deal of money and had been eventually discovered just before Sir Hubert died. Her hurt was doubled as she remembered how she'd trusted him implicitly, relied on him, honoured him. And now it seemed that her trust had been misplaced.

When she'd finished, he made no move to comfort her as her voice faltered, though she'd half-expected him to hold her to him, to soothe her hurt in his arms. She sat, forlorn and unsure, while he strode over to the window.

''Aletta, I think you should put this incident out of your mind, at least for the time being… No! Hear me!'' He turned and went to her as she exclaimed, and sat on the other side of her, silhouetted against the window, his wide shoulders almost blocking out the light, his face glowing in the flames of the fire. ''Nothing can spoil the love and support you and Oswald gave to each other. No matter what you think he was responsible for, you were kind to each other when you both needed kindness, you relied on each other, you cared for each other, didn't you?''

Aletta nodded in agreement. It was true, but…

''Then leave things as they are. Leave the memory as it was before. Put the rolls and accounts away and wait for an explanation to turn up one day, as it surely will.''

''Explanation? You think it will just appear one day?'' She sounded sceptical.

"Yes, I do. Meanwhile, to dwell on a mystery like this can only make you unhappy, distrustful, cynical. Don't undo all those lovely memories of him. Let them lie intact. Please. Will you?"

Though she could understand his reasoning, his insistence was less easy to understand. Still, she would go along with his advice, since she could not better it. "Yes," she whispered, "if you think that's the best thing to do. Is that what you'd do, if you'd had an Oswald?"

"Yes. If I'd had an Oswald, I wouldn't let my good opinion of him be spoiled by something I couldn't understand. Let it lie, Aletta."

She sat back against the wooden seat and gave a sigh, and he took this as her assent.

"Is this what you were asking Mistress Margery about yesterday?"

She nodded.

"Then don't bother her with it. She won't know anything either."

"How can you be sure of that? She was about to—"

"Promise me you'll let it lie, Aletta!"

She frowned, puzzled by his insistent tone.

"Promise!"

"I promise," she whispered. "But you were going to tell me how you came to know Oswald and Sir Hubert. Do you remember?"

He hesitated just long enough for Aletta to glance towards him, but at her movement the words came—too nonchalantly, she thought.

"Well, I told you I was born here in this place, and we were neighbours. I roamed everywhere around here—forests, hills—fished in the river, swam in it, climbed, hunted, fought. Oswald was at Netherstone until the household moved on, so it was inevitable that we should know each other. We hadn't met for years until that day I came to see you."

"But you knew them in the south too?"

"Oh, yes. I was in a household down there, as page, then as squire, then was knighted, so Sir Hubert and I bumped into each other, you might say!" He laughed. "I think I still have the bruises to prove it."

"Was he good at fighting? My husband?" she asked.

"He was a fearsome fighter, Aletta. No one would choose to fight against him in a tournament. But let's not dwell on all that. It's so long ago…and you wanted to see the rest of the manor, didn't you?"

So, for the rest of the afternoon, Aletta was taken on a tour of the massive building, shown the many rooms where guests could stay without having to share, offices where members of the household worked, the store-rooms and weaponry on the ground floor, even the kitchens and its various departments. Brother Spen welcomed them into his parlour and was amazed to discover that Aletta could read, write and speak Latin as well as the usual Norman-French and the English dialect of the villagers. Her eyes opened wide at his collection of leather-bound books, not all of them religious, but many of Celtic literature, poems, sagas, romances, too.

"You should see Geraunt's collection. Has he shown you yet?"

"Not yet…that's next on the list," Geraunt said before she could answer, and she wondered whether the day was going to be spent this way or whether he had something else in mind.

But as they walked back through the great hall to the entrance she could barely dispel a curious resentment that he still had made no move to take her in his arms. It was true, she usually made some form of protest, tried to evade him, which he obviously enjoyed. But that was only possible if he made a move in that direction. And so far, he had not. He had held her hand, placed his hand gently on her waist, but no more than that, and now the bodily hungers that assailed her each night plagued her in the daytime too.

To have him so near her and yet so distant was a feeling so powerful that she could think of little else. Had she made it *so* abundantly clear to him that she was not interested that he'd decided to give up? Could she change her mind, at this stage? I'm the one, she thought angrily, who's supposed to be holding off. Not him! And she almost collided with the dripping wet figure of Gerda, with Thomas only one pace behind.

Chapter Fourteen

With the relentlessly driving rain and gale-force winds the night had descended early, and the shutters across the windows verified the situation. Gerda had been put to bed, protesting and shivering, with a warm posset of eggs, ale and milk, and Aletta had assured her that she could manage quite well on her own, for once.

The game of chess had not been a success, for she could not keep her mind on the complex moves of each piece. She was a beginner, and Geraunt's looks at her to see if she'd understood had had the opposite effect from the one he'd intended. For all she could understand, it seemed, was the nearness of him, his eyes and hands. Surely he would bring the evening to a close with a kiss this time?

His offers to summon a chambermaid to assist her un-accepted, she now stood alone, with the brush of his lips on her knuckles still lingering. Trembling and perplexed, she undressed before the dying fire, slipped on the big fur-lined robe and tied its leather cord around her waist, pulling at it so viciously that it snapped.

"Damn!" she cursed, undoing her braided hair impatiently. It fell over her face as she sat, cross-legged, watching the last flickering flames and listening to the howls of the wind, thinking that perhaps she should be back at Netherstone. Should she plead with him to allow her back for the manor court tomorrow?

Leaving the cresset-lamp burning for comfort, she threw off the gown and rolled into bed, lying face-down in the soft pillows, fists clenched, her body aching and rigid with anger. I shall go tomorrow, she told herself. I have to go. She turned her head on the pillow at a sound from the next room, then raised it higher, listening in wonder to the soft tones of a stringed instrument being played and a low voice singing. She sat bolt-up right. The sound was so low that she had to strain to hear it, holding her head on one side, turning this way and that to catch the vibrant notes.

Very slowly, so as to catch every sound, she crawled out of the sheets, down the bed, over the chest at the bottom and slipped into the fur robe, holding it across herself with a shiver, the hairs bristling on her head. She crept towards the door, listening as the magical sounds continued, entranced, magnetised, and, without thinking, lifted the latch and slowly pushed the door open. The dim light from a lamp made a fine line of light which broadened little by little as she pushed.

Geraunt sat at the table, facing the door, a gittern on his lap, his head bent as he plucked carefully at the strings, singing in a husky baritone voice. Aletta noticed his bare feet beneath his fur-lined robe. He showed no surprise to see Aletta in the doorway of his room, her huge dark eyes wide with astonishment, one hand on her breast holding the robe tightly to her. The song ended and his eyes held hers. The enchantment had worked. He laid the gittern carefully on the table and leaned to blow out the lamp, then moved across to the doorway and stood before her, his face serious.

"Well, my lady? Have we delayed long enough, do you think?" His voice was barely above a whisper, but he made no move to touch her.

Aletta knew he waited for her to speak, but there were no words. Only her eyes and her body spoke, and she could only pray that he'd be able to understand their message. Mutely, she nodded and reached for his hand, taking it in hers, drawing him step by step into her room.

As he pulled the door closed behind him his eyes scarcely left her face, only narrowing as she brought his hand to her body and slid it inside the top of her robe and on to her breast. Then, with all the willingness of a man released from prison, he scooped her towards him and covered her throat with his lips, burying his face in her perfumed hair, holding her breast gently and feeling her tremble like a captured bird.

"You didn't kiss me," she whispered against his ear as his mouth moved over her. "You had chances, but not one kiss. Why? Why didn't you?"

"To make you wait," he whispered. "To make you come to me."

"For two *days?*"

"Days, months, years I've waited for you, woman. Were two days too long for you? *Were* they?"

"Yes," she cried. "Two hours are too long to wait, Geraunt. Kiss me now. Please. I can't wait any longer."

She drank in his kiss, filling up the empty well of her senses, taking it in greedily, with an insatiable appetite, a desperate longing, trembling with her own ardour, breathless and unnerved by the responses of her own body.

"I'm going to take you to bed now, Aletta," he said.

"Yes... But, Geraunt... I'm... What if...?"

"I know. I know you're afraid. You're terrified that you're going to be hurt again, that you won't be able to give yourself. That's been something to do with the delay, hasn't it?" He felt her head nod slightly against his fur robe and he removed his hand from its warm hiding place to brush away her hair and lift her chin. "Well, you won't be hurt. That I promise you. And we'll go slowly." He kissed her eyelids. "We'll take all night, if that's what we need. I've waited long enough for this moment, and I'm not going to rush through it like a lad with his first lass. We've some exploring to do, first.'' He slipped out of his robe and pushed hers off her shoulders, dropping it into a pile on the floor. Then he lifted her against his naked body. ''Put your arms around my neck and don't let go,'' he whispered.

Lowered on to the soft bed, her arms still around him, she felt no sudden shock of cold air between them, no separation, for his hand was beneath her buttocks, warm and firm. After all the loveless years, the hardness of a man's naked body on hers was almost frightening, and for a moment she could only tremble until she became accustomed to his weight, his smell, the feel of his skin beneath her fingers. Then her hands moved while he lay quietly above her, waiting. She allowed them to roam over his neck and back, gliding over the taut muscles, the slender hips and strong hard thighs, all the way down and back again to his shoulders, chest and powerful arms.

She remembered the first time he'd kissed her in the forest, when he had laid on her, clothed. How angry she had been then, and how moved by his gentleness after the rough capture. Now she could run her fingers through his hair as she'd wanted to do so many times, feel its crispness, hold his cheek beneath her hand, finger his brows and fondle his ears.

He watched her eyes in the dim glow of the lamp. ''Now,'' he said, ''my turn.''

But she caught at his hand before it could begin and looked questioningly into his eyes. He saw that her fear was barely under control.

''I swore that I would never do this with any man, ever again,'' she said softly, watching his eyes to anticipate his reaction.

''Aletta, tell me, have you ever truly made love with a man before?''

"No, not love," she admitted. "It was always violent and painful."

"Then you won't be going back on your word, because this will all be new to you."

"Yes."

"So let go of my hand, wench, and let me show you how different it is from anything you've ever known. Let go, now."

Her fingers relaxed on his as he kissed her, long and sweetly, sweeping away her resistance to the path of his hand. Skilfully he began his search of her body, moving over to one side as he wandered downwards over her breasts, stomach and hips. Aletta could only gasp and moan, arching herself to meet the smoothing, the stroking, the gentling, and, as fear surfaced at the unexpected newness of his touch, his kisses reassured her again and again.

"Geraunt!" she whispered, breathless and dizzy.

He raised his head from her breast. "You like that?"

"Yes. It doesn't hurt the way you do it."

"It was never supposed to hurt, lass. A woman's body is a tender thing, and some bits are more tender than others, just like a man's. You have to find out just how far you can go before hurt becomes unpleasant."

"You mean hurt can be pleasant? How can that be?"

"Well—" he laughed "—that's something we'll go into another time. This time we're treading carefully."

"But I haven't done any of the giving so far, have I? Only the receiving. Am I not supposed to do something to give you pleasure too?"

He collapsed on top of her briefly, almost helpless with laughter. He raised his head, shaking it from side to side. "Ah, wench! I have the most beautiful creature in Christendom in my arms for a whole night and she's concerned that she's not doing anything to give me pleasure." He kissed her softly. "Your responses and your lovely body, your moans and cries are giving me pleasure, sweet thing.

The pressure of your firm pointed breasts and hard nipples on my chest and in my mouth are giving me pleasure. No…hear me, Aletta, don't be shamed by my words and turn away.''

"Geraunt, stop…''

"No. I'll say it, and you'll hear me. It's not shameful, it's good to say it and to hear it. You give me the greatest pleasure because I waited for you, and at last you came to me and put my hand there… And that made my heart sing sweeter that any minstrel before or since. And on this special night I'll take the lead and you can follow, because I know where we're going and you don't. Is that agreed?''

"Yes.''

"Every time will be different, Aletta. This time will never be the same again. There are so many other ways, too many for one night. This is your first time for real loving, and you're pleasuring me just by giving yourself to me.'' His words, his kisses and his hands drove her forward into new realms of experience and her skin came alive under his mouth. As he drew his fingertips softly and tantalisingly across her stomach, down her groin and into the softness between her legs it was as though they had pressed a secret catch.

Her thighs spread instantly as she gasped at the sweetness of his touch, and without hesitation he was there with his hand. Aletta quivered in fright at the immediacy of her response and clutched at his hand almost automatically, but he held it quite still, allowing her fear to subside.

"It's all right, sweet thing, this is me, remember. You can tell me to stop at any time you want me to,'' he whispered, "and I will.''

His hand was released and he began to caress, slowly, watching her, placing himself over her and at last entering her so carefully that a slight widening of her eyes and a deep shuddering sigh were the only signs he received, the signs that she welcomed him.

She heard her own breathing, ragged and rhythmic, in tune with his thrusts as though her lungs were also trembling in ecstasy. He had taken possession of her at last and now, as the heat grew, she was mewing with joy at the feel of his hardness inside her, her fingers digging into his back and shoulders. She had never thought that it could be like this, not in her wildest dreams, for this was what her body had hungered for, cried out for, ached for in the long nights at home.

Geraunt dropped his head to kiss her ear. "I'm not hurting you, am I? Tell me if I'm hurting."

"No, Geraunt," she panted, linking her arms around his neck, "don't ever stop. Don't stop."

He smiled above her and broke her grasp as he braced his arms on each side to lift himself away, now deepening each powerful goad. He listened to her gasps and sighs, saw her head toss from side to side in a frenzy but, for her sake, made it last until he felt her body push hard at him in a spasm of quivering energy. Then he let himself go, too. Following her climax, he was released immediately, all his waiting satisfied at last in an overwhelming groan of exultation.

Aletta held his head tenderly against her cheek, stroking his dark, damp hair and wiping his face with her own hair as it lay spread about them on the pillow like a black net. Breathless and vanquished, she couldn't speak, nor had any need to at that moment, for their bodies had said it all. She could only wonder at that part of herself which had remained hidden until now, that powerful and indescribable response to Geraunt's thrusts inside her which had taken possession of her body for those few moments and brought her to a climax of sensation she had never experienced before nor believed possible. Was that what he had felt too? Was this how it should always be?

Geraunt gave a huge sigh, kissed her throat and carefully withdrew from her, pulling the sheet and rug up to her chin and tucking her in as he enfolded her in his arms. "Are you all right, sweet thing? Not hurt?"

She smiled, thinking how different his tenderness was from her memories, and how she'd clung to Geraunt so tightly, not knowing quite what her fingers had been doing during those moments of sweet distraction. "No," she replied, "not hurt. But you…? I believe you may have suffered a little?"

His arms tightened as his nose snuffled into her hair with a gasp of laughter. "Yes, thank you! A man expects to have something to show for an encounter like that. Battle scars!"

"You're teasing me!"

"No, I'm not! We'll take a look in the morning and you'll see."

"You're going to stay here all night, Geraunt?"

"Certainly I am. Do you want me to?"

"Yes," she whispered into his neck. "Yes, I do."

"That's what I hoped you'd say."

"Do you know—?" She pulled away from him with a sudden jerk. "I've just had a dreadful thought…"

"What?" He turned to look at her.

"It's Sunday!"

"Yes, it's still Sunday. Is that so dreadful?"

"Bethrothed and married couples are not supposed to…you know…"

He grinned. "Well, we're in the happy position of being neither betrothed nor married, so it doesn't apply to us. But if it still bothers you, we'll make sure—" he turned, leaned across her and snuffed out the lamp with his fingers "—not to be seen. There, will that do?"

Aletta laughed and ran a hand over his chest under the covers. It was massive and deep, hairy down the centre and across the base of his throat. He lay quiet while her fingers moved about over him, caressing his chin and jaw, his ears and across to his mouth. "You're smiling! Why are you smiling?" she asked.

There was a pause. "Do you remember our first meeting? The very first?"

"How could I forget it, brute?"

"Do you remember how I smiled and you sent me a withering glance that nearly knocked me off my horse?"

She giggled and turned her head up to look at him in the darkness. "Yes, horrid man. That was what I intended."

"Well, this is what I was smiling at then."

"What is?"

"This."

"You mean...being here...in bed with me...?" She could hardly believe such a thing. Was this really what men thought of at times like that? Bed?

He leaned on one elbow above her and looked down into her face, and though she could scarcely see him she felt his warm breath. "Yes, you fierce vixen! I wanted you from that very moment. I wanted to feel your body writhing beneath me. I wanted you in my hands, like this—" he moved his hand up to cup her breast "—and I wanted to hold that dark, silky mass around my wrist."

She felt him lift a long strand of her hair, felt it tighten as he wound it round his wrist and enclosed her face with his hand.

"And I wanted to pin you down and kiss you until you were quiet and subdued." He kissed her with passion, stoking up her fires again by the graphic soldier's words, the vigorous description of his feelings for her on that day. "And now I'm smiling because I've got you, Lady Aletta, here in my bed. And because I've broken through your defences, and because I've made another discovery, just now."

There was barely a space beneath his lips to ask him. But he allowed her just two words. "And that...?"

"That you're the most desirable and exciting and beautiful creature any man could ever want and that you're worth waiting a thousand years for.''

She was not allowed to respond for some time, not until she was breathless again and could feel him hard against her thighs. Her body melted for him once more. ''Tell me…'' she whispered hoarsely against his mouth.

''What, wench?''

''Why were you so horrid to me in the forest?''

''To show you who has the upper hand.''

''Could you show me again, in more detail, please?''

''Certainly, m'lady. I can do it any way you please. Are you ready to take what's coming? Quickly,'' he whispered, ''answer me!''

She was laughing too much to answer. His mock fierceness excited her. ''Geraunt, please… I don't know… No… Yes…!''

''Are you ready? I'm coming to take you, willing or not!'' He slid his hand slowly downwards.

Inflamed by his growls in her ear, she parted her legs and lifted herself to him, hoping that his enthusiasm would be kept in check. But he had not forgotten; his fierceness was only slightly less gentle than before, still sensitive, still tenderly careful of her newness to the joys of loving. And so the fires were again fanned into a roaring furnace and they were lost in the flames, their cries drowned by the wind outside. Then, consumed and spent, they lay in each other's arms and slept until dawn.

Narrow lines of light between the wooden shutters told Aletta that it was dawn, and the quiet told her that the wind and rain had ceased at last. She was unused to having shutters block out the new light of each day and wondered whether to try to undo them, but Geraunt was lying on her hair. She took his jaw between her teeth and held it until he opened one eye.

"I'm dreaming," he said sleepily, "that I'm being eaten alive by a dark-haired witch. And I think I'm enjoying it."

"You're not dreaming it. It's actually happening to you. But if you'd let in some daylight she'd be able to see what she's about, and perhaps find some less bony bits."

"I can't wait! Stay there, witch. I'll be back!" He unfastened the shutters and folded them back, flooding the room with new light.

Aletta now saw him naked for the first time, saw how the muscles rippled under his golden skin and how the dark hair of his body ran almost like a stripe down his front. He was tall and beautiful and lithe, and she knew that she loved him.

Back in bed, he snuggled up against her. "Now, witch. About those more interesting parts. Less bony bits, you said. I have a suggestion or two that might just be the thing…" And he took her hand under the sheets, guiding it over his body and making her laugh until she tried to roll away from him. But he brought her back, and her resistance developed into a battle for supremacy, a battle which she'd no chance of winning.

"Are you going to gain the upper hand *every* time, Sir Geraunt?" she asked peevishly, squirming under his hold in feigned anger.

"Certainly, wench. Every time, except when it doesn't matter."

"In that case, I shall have to resort to foul play!"

"Just like a woman! You mean, you'd like to be on top, just once in a while?" And before she could reply he had rolled and pulled her on top of him, helplessly held around the waist, her hair cascading over him like a tent. "I think I like that!" His eyes caressed her breasts, just touching his chest as she strained to break away.

But for Aletta the innocent fun of the moment had gone too far over that sharply honed edge into realism, and the nightmare came perilously close again. Her wildly flailing arms and stiffening body were enough to show Geraunt that she was distressed.

"Oh, God! No! No!" she gasped, and as he released her she made a bolt out of bed, crashing into the door before she could open it.

He was after her in one bound, snatching at the fur-lined gown on the floor and throwing it over her shoulders, enclosing her inside it with his arms as he had done at Netherstone on the day of Oswald's funeral. On the bed, he held her securely and rocked her, listening to her dry, tearless sobs and feeling her violent shaking.

"I'm sorry…" she gasped. "Sorry… I didn't mean… Not your fault…just… I can't"

"Hush, sweet thing, hush! Don't say you're sorry. I'm an oaf. I should have remembered to go more carefully. Sweet thing, I'll be more careful, I promise. Hush now, and come back to bed and we'll lie and talk. Nothing else."

"No, no! I can't talk about it! Something he used to do…"

"We won't talk about that, no. Not now or ever, if you don't want to. Come on now, wench, you're quite safe."

They lay, enveloped and intertwined, warm and at peace once more, listening to the early-morning sounds and the clatter of Geraunt's squire drawing back the shutters. "Won't he wonder where you are?" Aletta asked.

Geraunt smiled and tightened his arm about her. "He knows if I'm not in there I'm in here."

Aletta's heart missed a beat. What was he saying? "Do you mean you've had other women in here?" She tried to sound casual, but he knew that she dreaded his answer. Please, Holy Virgin, let him tell me lies, not the truth, she prayed.

Geraunt leaned on his elbow above her and his hazel eyes looked openly into hers, reading her thoughts and knowing her anxieties. "Aletta, hear me. If I thought it was expedient to tell you lies for your comfort I would do, about such matters. But it isn't necessary. The truth will do perfectly well, as it happens. You know I've only been up here a short time, and you're the only woman I've wanted or had since I came here." He grinned at that and kissed the end of her nose. "No other woman has ever been in this bed except my mother. I only sleep in here when I've been working late in my room and my bed is piled so high with rolls and books and things that I can't get into it. So I come in here instead. Does that set your mind at rest?"

She nodded, relief sweeping over her at his words.

"As for other women, well that must be obvious. Of course I've had women. But only to satisfy a passing appetite, that's all. No loves."

"And the ring? Will you tell me its origin?" She slid it off her finger and held it up to remind him, turning it in the light.

"It was originally made for a young lady of thirteen summers when I was twenty-one and newly knighted." He lay back beside her and took it in his fingers, looking at it closely, remembering. "I was still landless, so I had little to offer, but her parents seemed willing enough at the prospect of an inheritance."

"Wasn't she willing?"

"I believe she knew nothing of her parents' plans for her."

"Then why did she never wear it?"

"Because we were never betrothed. I had to go to France, and while I was away her parents took the opportunity to marry her off to someone else."

"Is she still alive?"

"Oh, yes. She's still alive and well. You saw that it had been enlarged, then? I wondered it you'd notice." He slipped it back on her finger.

"Yes, I noticed. But the inscription—is it your family motto?"

"No, it's my own personal one. 'I hold what is mine.'

And that includes you, wench.'' He turned his head on the pillow to look at her, his nose almost touching hers, hazel eyes boring into deep brown ones, challenging her to defy him.

But Aletta knew that since last night the rules had shifted, that the bond she'd protested against so loudly had now become a sanctuary against so many things, not least of which were her own fears. She didn't want him to release her, to put her aside like a used whore after a night's sport, but neither did she know whether his tender, almost loving words were also much-used ones, to be brought out and aired whenever it was appropriate.

"Now *you're* smiling, wench. What is it?"

"Being appropriate. I wonder if it might not be appropriate to release me from the bond, now that you've had your way?'' She could not resist tugging at the chains to see if they were still in place.

"Aletta, I know enough about you to understand that you're simply testing my resolve. The casual question about other women. The bed. The origin of the ring, which you insist means nothing to you. Your question about the bond, couched as a plea, is really a fear. Don't deny it!'' He stopped her speaking as her eyes opened wide in contradiction at his perceptive reading of her mind. ''Since this night, the bond has not weakened but grown stronger. I cannot believe you haven't sensed that too. I've told you I'd wanted you since that episode with the deer, not just for a night, or even a week, but for always. And no matter how many times you ask me to release you, you'll get the same answer. I hold what is mine. And you're mine!'' His kiss was long, slow and deliberate, intended to dissolve her fears, put an end to her questions.

But one more question remained. "I have something you didn't manage to hold on to,'' she said, slipping out of his embrace and off the bed. She crossed to the small chest and retrieved the tiny parchment package which Edwise had insisted on her taking. Smiling, she passed it to Geraunt, not knowing that he'd already noted its appearance on her solar table two days ago. "Look," she said.

He opened it, knowing what to expect, his reponse well-prepared. "My buckle! He must have known you'd pass it back to me, the old fox!" Swinging his legs out of bed, he crossed the floor and disappeared into his own room. She heard him speaking to his squires, their replies, the sound of the door as they went out, then he returned, carrying a hip-purse in his hand. "Look here! This is where it belongs."

Aletta took the purse and buckle and matched the two together. It was quite clear they'd been cut apart; a piece of leather still clung to the bar of the buckle where it was stitched firmly round and the colour and pattern matched perfectly. Geraunt sat on the bed, still naked and at ease before her, while she leaned against the pillows with her knees and the linen sheet drawn up beneath her chin. "Yes, I see," she said slowly, "but how did it come into Oswald's possession?"

He had thought about this moment several times already. It would have been so easy to spin some tangled yarn about having lost it and found it again, but he knew that the truth would probably come out one day and that there would be better times than this to hear it. Times, perhaps, when she'd come to trust him completely. But, until he could take the risk, a half-truth would have to do.

"I sent it to him from France by a friend, to assure him that I was still alive and well," he said. "He'd expressed some concern that he'd heard no news of me from my father, and so when I heard that he'd been asking about me, I cut my purse buckle off and sent it to him in this parchment. Look, here's my hand on the inside." He opened the wrinkled skin wide open and smoothed it on his thigh, turning it for her to read.

She had not noticed the faded ink-marks before, and now

she read aloud, "'*Je reviens.* G.' I will return. And you did."

"As you see!" He grinned at her, opening his arms wide. Spoken out loud, he thought, his story had strayed very little from the truth, after all, and Aletta seemed to be content with the explanation.

There were bustling noises coming from the next room and Aletta looked at him in alarm. "They're not coming in here, are they? Quick! Pull the curtains round…please!"

Geraunt laughed at her expression of horror. "No, sweet thing. They're getting a bath ready for us. I thought we'd have it in there, rather than in here. Do you want to summon Gerda?"

"*We*? Do you mean…together? Geraunt… I…"

But he would listen to no protests, for as long as his household believed they were bethrothed there would be no remarks made. And as Mistress Gerda could be relied upon to do her mistress' bidding in all things, the only objection would be from Aletta herself, and since she was bound to do *his* bidding, the bath would be taken together.

There was no spare room in a tub made for one large male, but their closeness made it that much easier for them to wash each other, slowly and erotically, punctuated by kisses and caresses which were hard to distinguish from mutual ablutions. He laughingly told her that, as the host, he had a duty to bath his guest just as she would have done for him had the roles been reversed. And so he insisted on performing his obligations with meticulous care and thoroughness, making her blush and laugh at the same time. It was the most intimate and exciting bath Aletta had ever had.

Geraunt pretended to flinch in pain as Aletta reached over to soap his back, laughing in spite of himself. He twisted towards her and touched his shoulder. "Look, you can see my battle scars now."

And, indeed, she could see rows of fine red lines where

her nails had drawn across his skin, and she hid her face in his neck, not sure whether to look contrite or to laugh. "And you were so concerned about me being hurt," she gurgled, licking his ear. "I shall find some simples today, to put on them."

"You're staying then, wench?"

"Last night, before I came to your room, I was determined to go home…"

"Without my permission?" he mumbled into her hair.

"Be quiet, sir, if you please! I was going to plead with you to let me go…"

"I wouldn't have!" he whispered rebelliously.

"Quiet, I said! But now, well, I have to plan your herbgarden, learn to play chess, look at your library, your musical instruments, hear you sing…"

"Make love to me…"

"Quiet…"

His kisses put an end to more suggestions and the water was rapidly losing heat before they reluctantly climbed out and prepared to break their fast, for Aletta had discovered her appetite.

Chapter Fifteen

It was to be expected, Aletta supposed, with an inward shiver of excitement, that he would display a triumphant air, at least for the time being. As though to confirm his new possession of her he stayed close by her, kept hold of her hand, allowed her to feel his nearness and strength, and by this means assured her that his conquest and her capitulation marked only the beginning of events, not the end.

She was glad of this. For one thing, she needed to feel his closeness even more than before—even the brush of his sleeve on hers was one way of making up for the lost years and a way of hoarding against the days ahead when she'd be on her own again. She realised that emotionally the situation was unbalanced, for although he had been the hunter and she the hunted one, she was the one who loved. He had said nothing of that. So her air of quiet reflection was partly an attempt to still the overwhelming joy of her love for him, to keep it secret and in reserve against some time in the future when his interest in her would wane, and partly to rethink in detail the events of the night.

"Do I need to ask what you're thinking about, my lady?" he had said after their mid-morning meal in the great hall. "I swear Brother Spen spoke to you a dozen times before you heard him.'' He kept hold of her hand as he closed the door to her room behind them.

Aletta looked up into his laughing face. ''You don't think he knows, do you?''

''Well, if he does, he's probably envying me!''

''Geraunt! He wouldn't do any such thing. Not a cleric!''

''Cleric or no, wench, he's a man! And I'll wager there's not one here who doesn't wish he was me at this moment.'' He pulled her to him on the cushioned window-seat, her back on his chest, his arms like two tree-trunks across her.

''Sir Geraunt,'' she laughed into his sleeve, ''you look like the farm cat that's just stolen the cream. I suppose they'll guess from the gleam in your eye what's going on. That's if Richard and Robin haven't already yelped about it.''

''You need not fear on that score,'' he replied, ''they've been well-schooled there, if in nothing else, that a squire doesn't chatter about his master's personal doings, whatever they are. If they did, they'd have me to answer to, and they know it. And, anyway, I can be forgiven for looking a mite pleased with myself, can I not, sweet thing?'' He turned her head up to rest on his shoulder. ''In truth, I don't know how I'll keep my hands off you until tonight.''

He kissed her upturned mouth, lingering over her body with his hands and setting her instantly alight like dry tinder in a drought.

She strained backwards into him, her hands gripping his thighs, a sudden fire leaping downwards into her belly and groin like a sweet ache waiting for a hand to caress it. Her mouth searched his, her moans became cries as his hands passed under her gown and crept upwards over her nipples, teasing them to harden, fondling them as his lips fondled her mouth. She could bear it no longer. ''Geraunt... You must... Please...''

''Will you let me take you here, Aletta? You won't cry

out?'' He could feel her body trembling, eager for him, pulsing with readiness.

''Yes…yes, here, now, please… I won't cry out…. Please!''

He stood and lowered her back on to the cushions, untying his points in frantic haste, finally pulling them apart in desperation. Then he stood braced against the window-seat and held her buttocks to him. Aletta grasped at the cushions as he lifted her, parted her thighs and entered her immediately. There was no time for more than the first few hard thrusts; their release came at once, leaving them both shuddering with its impact and intensity, neither of them realising how close they'd been to the brink before plummeting over into the torrent.

Aletta had promised not to cry out, but her groan was a vibration which began and ended somewhere deep inside her, which she only felt but Geraunt heard above his own gasps. Her closed eyes, her deep sigh and limp body made him think that perhaps he'd let his previous self-restraint get out of control, shocked her, after all his efforts during the night to take things slowly and at her pace.

Carefully he removed himself from her, and pulled her upright, holding her to him, caressing her back and wondering what to say. ''Forgive me, sweet thing. That was rough, and crude. Did you mind…? I couldn't wait…couldn't hold it… Did I hurt you? God's wounds, woman, I've never felt like this before. I can't get enough of you! I can't even wait to get you on to the bed!'' He buried his face into the linen of her wimple, clearly shaken by the strength of his feelings.

Aletta couldn't speak. Breathlessness, laughter and exhilaration had lured all words away, especially at his last contrite words. Her muffled snort into his chest brought his head round sharply to look at her in disbelief, and he saw her lips parted in laughter, not anguish, her eyes dreamy with langour, not tears.

"You're laughing! You are, aren't you? Laughing!"

"Yes." She nodded, her breast heaving in gasps. "Yes, I am."

"I can't believe it! What a woman! You didn't mind, then?"

"Geraunt—" she kissed his nose, cheeks, eyes "—I seem to remember that I was in just as much of a hurry as you were." She looked down at the broken ends of the points tying his chausses to his shirt and laughed again, so much that she had to wait before she could continue. "And you *did* ask me! And that's a novel experience for me, to be asked." She returned his tightened hug and then eased herself away again. "Anyway, you see, dearest one, it's not the place that's so important, is it? It's how it's done, and whether it's shared, not inflicted."

His great arms enclosed her in a bear hug, sending the air out of her lungs in a whoosh which ended in a gurgle of laughter. In a moment he was looking into her face again. "Do you know what you just called me?"

Her eyes twinkled, and she nodded.

"Say it again. I want to hear it again from you. Say it!"

"Dearest one. Dearest one," she repeated, holding his ears between her hands and nibbling at his lips as she spoke. The huge handsome head bent to hers and he kissed her, while she held him and felt his crisp thatch of hair, the slant of his shoulders and neck beneath her arms. How far had they come, she thought, from that day when he'd pulled her down into a ditch. And she wondered at that moment who was being tamed—herself, or him.

"Before we go to the tilt-yard, to watch those two lads, do you think you'd better find some new points for your chausses? Or do you want to leave your household in no doubt whatsoever?" she asked.

Geraunt looked down at himself, a gleam of pure mischief in his eyes. "Oh, I think I'll just leave things as they are. They'll understand, I expect. Come on!'' He took her hand and moved towards the door.

''No, Geraunt! No! You can't go like that…!'' She pulled back in horror, her eyes drawn to his crotch, where his white linen chainse hung out between the torn laces and untied woollen chausses. Then his face told her that he was teasing, and his hearty bellow of laughter drowned her scolding.

For Aletta, so many new experiences crowded into those few days, so many new sensations and emotions, that she began to wonder if she ought to start life anew at this point, just before her twenty-fifth birthday, and begin counting again at one. She had set her heart on being at home for her special day, Friday, for it would not be fair to deny her dear ones at Netherstone the pleasure of greeting her in their own way, just as it would hardly be fair to spring the surprise on Geraunt.

Not only was it her birthday but also the eve of Beltane and of May Day. The first day of May which followed was always celebrated in the ancient manner, bringing in the may-blossom. It had been on this day last year when Aletta had given refuge to the four Allerton villeins as a special act of kindness after her birthday, for they had joined with her own people to decorate her hall.

So she set her deadline for Thursday morning, gave both Geraunt and Gerda due warning that this could not be extended, and then allowed herself to enjoy to the full what was left of the week. Gerda had been allowed free rein to make the best of Thomas's company whenever he was not required for duties, and Aletta couldn't help noticing that Geraunt freed him at every opportunity so that the two could be together.

He managed to disappoint his two squires at regular intervals, though, by keeping them so well-occupied with the master-at-arms that they were unable to accompany him on expeditions into the countryside to visit property and to see the high waterfalls after the storms. His daytime journeys with Aletta, like their night-times, were so punctuated by lovemaking that it was sometimes a wonder that they reached their destinations at all, and it was only when Aletta practised her habitual attempts at independence and insubordination, against some not very important restrictions imposed by Geraunt, that some of the old antagonism flared briefly.

On more that one occasion she suspected that he tried out her obedience to his bidding on purpose, just to see whether she had forgotten about the agreement. And, not to disappoint him, she rebelled, knowing what the outcome would be. Inevitably the conflicts were concluded to their mutual satisfaction—she allowing him to believe that he'd won the bout, and he knowing full well that the victory was only partly his.

Geraunt escorted her back to Netherstone early on Thursday morning. There had been times, during the night, when Aletta had almost asked him if his heart was involved in this affair, but had decided against it, especially since he had not asked her either. Sadly she concluded that he was not interested in that aspect of things, but supposed that that was one of the facts of life. She had to admit, though, that so far his predictions had come true. Though when he had teasingly reminded her of this she had hotly denied it, saying that she only allowed him to make love to her on sufferance, and then had immediately contradicted it by her passionate involvement.

The entire household was overjoyed by her return and all commented on the bloom in her cheeks and the happy glow in her eyes. She assured them that this was because she was glad to be home, but they could sense that the new radiance was more to do with love than with home. Accordingly they showered her with their own love, which had accumulated during her absence, making her glad that she had returned and helping to soften the moment when she would have to say her farewells to Geraunt.

He took his leave of her privately, in her solar.

"Come here, wench!" He stood in the centre of the room, watching her nervously pick things up and replace them, unsure of herself at this last moment.

She glanced at him, pulling herself erect and twitching her nose like a hare.

His eyes narrowed; his very stillness excited her. "Don't twitch your nose at me. Do as you're told and come here!" He waited, unsmiling. "Do I come and get you?"

"No," she whispered, not looking at him.

"Then, come. I have to go now, Aletta," he said as she went into his arms.

"Don't go."

"That's what I said to you this morning. Remember?"

"But I mean it."

"I meant it too."

"Not the way I do."

"Wench! Do you think I want to leave you? After the days and nights we've had together? I'm just about to face the longest five miles of my life. Don't make it any harder for me."

"Do you mean that?"

He kissed her, hard and long. "What do *you* think, vixen? D'you want me to throw you down on that bed and prove it again?"

He caught the gleam in her eyes. Suddenly he let her go and walked swiftly over to the doors, first the inner one and then the outer, and bolted them.

"What are you going to do?" she whispered, alarmed by the stern expression on his face.

"This…" With hardly a stoop, he picked her up and placed her on the bed before she was fully aware of his intentions, though her heart was thumping uncontrollably.

He had been right when he'd said it would never be the same twice. Quickly he unbuckled his sword-belt and threw it aside, knelt astride her and untied his front points, then lowered himself to her and kissed her again.

"Here's something for you to take to bed with you to-night, and for me to take to mine," he said.

In the dim last light of the solar, before they slept, Bridie gleaned what she could about Aletta's time at Allerton over the last few days. And wasn't it convenient, they agreed, that her visit had allowed Gerda to be with her Thomas, and Bridie to be with her Roger at the same time? Was she in love? Bridie wanted to know.

"Oh, Bridie! It's an ache, isn't it? It hurts. I don't want him to know because he's never mentioned love, so he obviously isn't. But he's certainly behaved more lovingly than ever Sir Hubert did. Yes—" she caught Bridie's word of query "—yes, nights too. Though we still managed to fight… Don't ask me why! I'm beginning to wonder if he waits for me to pick a fight, and if I don't, he picks one for me." They both laughed, understanding. "I haven't told him it's my birthday tomorrow."

"Why ever not?"

"I don't really know. May Day was the day last year when I pinched his four villeins. Perhaps that's something to do with it."

"Roger and I've been talking," Bridie said, after a pause.

"About your future?"

"About you, and Sir Geraunt."

"Oh? What?"

"Roger wonders whether you've done a kind of deal with him about his four villeins. He lets them stay with you if you let him…you know."

Aletta's silence confirmed that she was not far off the mark. "Why does Roger think that?" she asked.

"Well, because one minute you were all protests and angry, and the next you'd allowed a kind of mock betrothal that looks suspiciously like the real thing. And also," she added, "the fact that you're doing what he tells you to do. Which is a bit unusual, you have to admit, pet."

"Oh, Bridie!" Aletta laughed.

"Was Roger right, then?"

"Near enough."

"And now you're in love with him. So, it's no great penance, is it?"

"Not unless…"

"No," said Bridie. "That's right. I can see what happens next." Her voice was matter-of-fact.

"What if it does, Bridie? What then?"

"He's not mentioned marriage to you?"

"Yes, he has. I can't help feeling that that's what it's all about. Property."

"But he's got more property than anyone around here, hasn't he?"

"Yes. I've had chance to see just how wealthy he is."

"And yet you wouldn't want to marry him?"

"Oh, Bridie! I can't trust myself. It's only two years since…you know, and I'll be damned if I'm going to hand myself over to someone else so soon."

Bridie went to her mistress over in the big bed and sat on the covers. "Listen, pet. You can't have it all ways, can you? You'd be the first to tell me that, if it was the other way round. You love him. He's kind to you. He's wealthy. You want babies, I know. To hell with the property… It's happiness you're after, isn't it? And you certainly came back glowing with it today, didn't you?"

"Did it show, Bridie?"

They laughed together, knowing the answer.

The last day of April, Aletta's birthday, was fair and bright. Shafts of sunlight fell softly on the tapestries and the bowls of spring flowers, and for a moment she lay thinking of Geraunt and of the four nights spent in his arms. How long would it be before he came again? He had not said, except that it was to be his manor court in a week's time and that he would like her and Gerda to be there. How would she be able to wait so long?

Now Bridie was giving her the titbits of news she'd not passed on yesterday—how Edward the gander had lost his Phillipa to the fox last weekend and now was pining fit to break their hearts. How Roger had said they'd just have to eat him to stop him pining. How they'd cleaned and white-washed Edwise's room after the builders had finished making a doorway through, and windows too. How they were preparing the bonfire for Beltane, in spite of Aletta and the village priest's reservations about holding a pagan festival in a Christian country.

Bridie, Roger and Gerda, Master Nicholas and the priest, and all the senior members of the household came into her solar—some for the first time ever—to wish her a happy birthday and present her with little gifts of sweets, candied fruits, two black lambs, a tooled leather girdle and a bottle of mead reputed to be at least ten years old. Flowers by the armful poured in, brought by her villagers who knew of her passion for them, and she was told firmly that she was not to begin duties, today of all days, that they'd done very well without her and that one more day would make no difference. It was as Geraunt had said; they were flattered that she'd felt able to leave them.

While preparations for May Day continued Aletta was able to keep back thoughts of all else. But by late afternoon, when work was done, the air of excitement was almost tangible as the young people went off arm in arm or in groups, blowing noisily to each other on their borrowed cow-horns, and shouting jests into the still, warm air.

Forcing herself to smile and enact a gaiety she was far from feeling, she dismissed both Bridie and Gerda earlier than usual, insisting that she wanted to be alone, which was true. The unsettled and troubled thoughts in her mind clamoured for peace, for space to be reshuffled, re-ordered, even those as far back as last year when she'd given a new beginning to four young Allerton men.

Another birthday alone again, she thought, watching happy groups larking about across the fields towards the woodland, feeling an indescribable ache in her body as she pictured their pairing, their simple and uncomplicated freedom to give themselves willingly on this May Eve. Tomorrow they would all troop back at dawn, and spend the day merrily with those they loved.

It was now barely light as Aletta forsook the emptiness of her solar to climb upwards alongside the tumbling beck towards her pool. She had lain on her bed, reliving Geraunt's last passionate act of farewell, and now she longed to be reminded of another occasion, among the rocks and the reflected images of trees which would bring her closer to being one of those young people in the white-blossomed woods. The moon was already up as she climbed over the last shelf of rock and made her way to where they'd sat together on that day. The stone was still warm from the day's sun.

In the distance shouts could still be heard, horns too. Then all was still except for the splash of water hitting the pool from the high ledge above her, and the anxious squawk of a bird as it made its last dash homewards. She smiled, remembering his appearance on that day, sitting so still and sure of himself, saying, "Come on" and knowing that she'd have to, sooner or later.

"Aletta!" The word was barely a whisper. Was it in her mind? "Aletta!" The hairs prickled on her arms as a hand flew to her breast, and she whirled round to look.

He was ready for the impact of her body, using its momentum to swing her up into his arms and receive her mouth like a ravenous man while she clung to his neck, crying and laughing at the same time, whispering his name over and over between kisses.

"I'm dreaming. Tell me I'm not dreaming," she cried softly into his ear.

"You're not dreaming, wench! You can do that later, if there's time, though I think we might be a bit too busy for any of that." He turned and began to carry her up the last few shelves of rock towards the topmost clump of trees, white with blossom.

She laughed in breathless excitement. "Where are we going?" she asked.

"We're going to do what people do on May Eve." He stood with her in his arms before a bower covered completely with creamy-white may-blossom. It was a shelter made of sturdy branches growing from the soft layers of foliage beneath, its base thickly layered with bracken and blankets. Gently he lowered her feet to the ground.

"Geraunt! It's a may-bower! For us? Tonight?"

"For us. Tonight. On your birthday."

"You knew?" She turned to him in surprise.

He moved her forward under the green and white canopy and pushed her down on to the soft, crackling blanket-covered bracken. "'Course I knew, sweet thing."

Explanations would come later, but now it was too dark even to see his deft fingers unlacing her bodice and removing her bliaud and kirtle, unbraiding her plaited hair and spreading it over her shoulders. Soon he too was naked, his smooth skin glowing in the last light as he leaned to draw the blossom-covered wickerwork gate across the entrance.

Their hungry mouths sought each other and they became one with the sounds of the water and the creatures of the darkness, overtaken by night and the soft cries of love. They slept, loved again with slow tenderness, and slept again, Aletta weeping silently with joy that this was reality and no dream, and with sadness that it could not last. She was comforted and hushed to sleep again in Geraunt's arms while he lay for some time, thinking of the years they had missed.

At early dawn, as the first rays of light peeped through the blossom above them, they left their bower and climbed back down the water-course to the stew-pond and into the manor before anyone was yet awake. Up the outer solar steps and back into her room they crept, giggling like two runaways, into Aletta's big bed.

"Well, my lady. Now you'll be able to say you've brought in the may. Does that make you happy?" Geraunt leaned above her and looked down into her eyes like two deep brown pools of velvet.

"That was the most wonderful birthday present I've ever had. Perhaps if I'd known…"

"Yes, m'lady? Perhaps if you'd known it was going to be like this, you'd have pilfered the rest of my villeins, instead of the odd four. Is that it?"

She hid her face in his shoulder. "No," she mumbled. "That's not what I was about to say. If you're going to be horrid…"

"I'm never horrid. I'm about to suggest you look underneath your pillow."

She frowned into his arm, not understanding. Then she slid a hand under her head and drew out a long golden chain with a small gold and enamelled pendant hanging from it. "Geraunt! What is it?" It hung from her fingers, swinging slightly and catching the light, while her face broke into a radiant smile as she caught the shape of a tiny pale yellow primrose, no larger than the real thing. "Oh! Oh, this is so beautiful! The primrose. Oh, Geraunt. It's the one you put into my hair after…"

"The very same one. Turn it over and read the back."

"'*Je tiens les miens.*'"

"I hold what is mine," he repeated. "Now, let me put it on for you."

She allowed him to slip it over her head, easing her hair through the delicate chain and placing the primrose carefully between her breasts. "That's where I'd have liked to put the others." He smiled. "But I feared you might have bitten my hand off. Now I think you're learning to respond to gentle handling, are you not, wench? After all these years."

She loved the sound of his deep, husky laugh when he teased her like this, as though she were a wild thing and he her tamer. It was true. His kindness to her, his tender loving, had undermined her defences so skilfully. His harshness never ranged as far as brutality, his firmness forced her to see sense when sometimes she would have overlooked it, and, while she still could not understand his motives for involving himself in her life, it seemed that having him near her was not as unbearable as it might have been.

"It's all so new to me, Geraunt." Her eyes brimmed with tears. "Even our first kiss, down there in the ditch… That was new to me. You knew, didn't you?"

"Yes, I knew."

She drew a finger softly across his lips. "I still don't know what all this is about," she whispered, "but thank you for the most wonderful birthday I've ever had. For the bower. For the—" She stopped in confusion, wondering how to continue. "For the nights with you. And for this…" She touched the primrose pendant. "It's beautiful. It'll remind me of this day always…" Her tears overflowed.

"Sweet thing." He smiled at her tears. "You make it sound as though this is the end. And it's not, it's only the beginning."

"It can't last, can it? I know it can't. It's too much… Good things like this don't, do they?" She turned her face away.

"Stop it, wench." He laughed softly, kissing her wet face. "Who says good things don't last? A good campaigner doesn't involve the adversary and then quit the field just as things are getting interesting, lass. He stays to see the thing to its conclusion. Especially when he's winning…and enjoying it!'' He knew his reference to her submission so far would kindle her annoyance, and it was to jolt her out of this morbid vein that he made his words sting.

"Oh, you unfeeling brute! Winning? Who says you're winning?'' Her head whipped round to face him again, her eyes flashing with tears and defiance. She pushed hard at his shoulders and braced her legs to roll away, but he took her hands in one of his and held them easily above her head as she glared at him, unable to make any impression on his hold.

"I'm winning, vixen, and you know it! I'll take your final submission now, if you wish. To save time. It's no dishonour.''

His eyes unlocked the door into her soul, and just for one instant she knew how easy it would be to give in, to say yes, I'm yours, I'll marry you. But a lingering thread of uncertainty held her back like a chain and she could not break it. "No,'' she said against his lips.

"As you wish, my lady. But you'll tire before I do.''

She was not allowed to reply, for his hand was as skilful on her body as it was with sword and lance, and she knew that it was only a matter of time before she quit the field completely.

Geraunt chuckled softly to himself as he tucked his chainse into his chausses, watching Aletta pull on her soft leather shoes. She looked up, eyebrows raised, suspecting that she knew the reason for his mirth without asking. Her resentful look only prolonged his laughter until finally, as he balanced on one foot to pull on his boot, she hurled a pillow at his head. Seeing his attention held as he deflected the pillow and tried to keep his balance, she followed it up with a flying tackle to his body, hurling herself at his middle with her shoulders to knock him over, to wipe the smugness from his face.

Even so, his lightning reflexes allowed him to take advantage, and with a bellow of surprised laughter he held her to him as they hit the floor, rolling with her, pulling the sheet off the bed and coming to rest in a tangle with Aletta pinned beneath him. ''That's how to fall, wench!'' he grinned. ''On top of somebody!''

''Let me up, you big oaf! You don't know the rules! That was *my* point!''

''I do believe, vixen, that it's going to be a hard job convincing you that you're losing when your refusal to submit is as sweet as that—'' he indicated the bed with a nod of his head ''—and your rules are as unorthodox as this. But I'm not grumbling.'' His white teeth parted as he laughingly restrained her. ''My, but you're fierce today, wench! Perhaps I should tire you out a little more…''

''No! No more, Geraunt! Enough! Let me go, now.''

''Pax?''

''Yes, pax.''

''Shall I take you on a visit, then? Will you behave yourself?''

''Yes. Where to?''

''Sir Thomas and Lady Cecily.'' His head lifted and he looked beyond them towards the door. ''Come in, if you please, mistresses. We were just discussing today's plans.'' He grinned and helped Aletta to her feet, rising in an easy swing backwards on to his haunches.

Bridie and Gerda hesitated inside the open door, clearly enjoying the situation. Aletta smiled at them sheepishly. ''Happy May Day,'' she said.

As it turned out, their plans to visit the Newmans at Middlestone Manor had to be postponed until the next day for they had underestimated their own part in the celebration of May Day.

As soon as Aletta saw the happy villagers pouring into the great hall, pulling boughs of white hawthorn behind them, singing and laughing, she knew they expected her to be involved, to share her own happiness with them, to eat and drink and dance with them.

It didn't matter, Geraunt said, whether they went today or Sunday, as long as he was with her by nightfall. It was patently obvious what he had in mind, and the tremor which passed through her thighs as he looked into her eyes with such barefaced intent made her gasp.

"You're bold, sir!" she said, blushing but secretly overjoyed.

"Yes, m'lady. I wouldn't get far with you if I were not, would I?"

The hall was festooned with garlands of white blossom and birch boughs; the heavy candle-rings had been lowered from the ceiling and were being entwined with greenery. Outside, the bellowing of what appeared to be all the oxen in the village filled the air, the paired creatures bewildered by all the attention lavished on them, their horns tipped with pretty bunches of flowers and herbs and tied with ribbons. They had pulled the heavy maypole into place on the green, and there it waited for the dancing, later on.

The mid-morning meal for May Day included every green food that could be found, and what was not green to begin with was made so by colouring derived from parsley and spinach juice. Everyone who could wore green, and others wore sashes of green tied round or across them.

As neither Geraunt nor Roger was wearing the appropriate colour, Bridie tied strips of jade-green velvet across them from shoulder to hip, and gave some to Gerda for her Thomas.

Geraunt grinned at his young groom, standing with arms

akimbo to be adorned. "You see, lad, these Netherstone women certainly know how to tie you up!"

"They certainly do, sir!" Thomas replied, pinching Gerda's behind as she disappeared under his arm. He was soundly clouted for his impudence, the men's laughter bringing a flush of embarrassment to Gerda's face, for she was still a little afraid of Geraunt.

After the green meal the hall emptied as the revels began down on the village green. Aletta's guests that day included a dozen or so extra labourers, three lay brothers on their way down from the hill-folds after tending the sheep and lambs, and a half-starved old woman who'd been found in the woodland during the night. The strongest lads had carried her up the hill, too weak to protest.

Wrestling, mumming and dancing, archery and mock jousting were taken quite seriously by the young men and lasses, though not so seriously by everyone else. Geraunt was more or less obliged to appear serious, as he'd been asked to adjudicate, with Roger, the parish priest, Jem and Thomas. Aletta was delighted that he'd been included as one of them, relieved also that he appeared to be enjoying it, insisting that the jousters wear their ladies' favours on their arms, to the delight of the girls.

In the evening, the Beltane fire was lit, ale was produced once more and the happy chorus of laughter changed to murmuring duets as couples drifted away into the night and the older ones reminisced about their own youth and how times had flown so fast.

It was the happiest of days, one which Aletta would never forget. Later, in the privacy of her solar, she and Geraunt recalled the events which had made the day so memorable. He tied his green sash around her bedpost as they slowly undressed, Aletta enjoying the sight of his fluid movements, the arch of his back as he stretched, the bulges of muscle on shoulders and thigh. She wanted to run her hands over him, all of him, every part, not only those she'd been able to reach during their lovemaking, and an idea occurred to her.

Holding a small greenish glass bottle of almond oil in her hand, she motioned to the bed. "Lie down on your front, please."

Geraunt hesitated, glancing at her and then at the bottle. "Is this some new potion to make me disappear, wench?" he asked.

"Yes," she answered. "Lie down."

She removed the pillow from beneath his head and poured a puddle of the sweet, clear oil between his massive shoulder blades, then began to move it upwards and outwards with her palms, pushing and squeezing with firm strokes around his neck and shoulders, along his arms and down, slowly and thoroughly, to his wrists and fingers. Each tiny crevice was explored, manipulated, soothed and massaged.

Then down his back she moved, to probe and press, gently and firmly, feeling each knot and easing it away. Her fingers played along old scars, tenderly exploring them, wondering whose weapon and whose arm had caused them, pondering over his time in France and his unwillingness to elaborate on the details of his stay there. Slowly and erotically her hands moved over him, down to his strong loins and thighs, caressing and pressing, smoothing the oil into his skin, finding hidden valleys and mounds, revelling in the firmness, the tautness, the hardness of him.

"Turn over, please."

He turned, his eyes holding a question she could well anticipate but preferred not to answer. This was the part she had used to dread, knowing how it would only be moments before Sir Hubert would grab at her and hold her on top of him, laughing as she writhed in disgust and terror. But Geraunt was not like him in any respect. This man she loved and wanted to explore.

Even so, she held back.

"Aletta, what is it?"

For a moment she stood rigid, with the memory at the front of her mind, nervously fingering the enamelled primrose about her neck, struggling to bring herself back to the present. "Don't move, will you? Please? Not a finger, even. Promise?" Her mouth was dry as she watched his eyes and hands.

"I won't move, sweet thing. Not even a finger. I swear it." All at once, he knew the reason for her former panic and he was filled with anger and compassion. "It's all right, Aletta. I understand. I won't move a muscle." He closed his eyes, knowing that this would probably be one of the hardest vows he'd ever be asked to keep. Perhaps if he thought of something else...

Again, she massaged his beautiful body with love and tenderness, delighting in the perfectness of his structure, the spareness of flesh, the precise moulding over bones, the contours over muscle. She kept well clear of his tenderest parts, knowing full well what urges lay there and hardly expecting him to fulfill an oath for something which had a mind of its own.

Gradually, as her hands continued their task, she saw that she had no more to fear and forgot to watch his hands from the corner of her eye, so much so that she felt safe enough to bend to his firm stomach and touch it with her lips as a final caress.

"You can wake up now. You're back with me again."

"Aletta...?" He opened his eyes and smiled. She knew he was about to ask her some questions.

"No, don't ask me about it. Another time, perhaps. I wanted to say thank you for today, that's all." She turned away but saw that he was holding out a forefinger, inviting her to touch it, to contact him. Fingertip to fingertip, from two arm-lengths away, she moved towards him and slowly slid her hand into his.

"Come?" He moved aside to make room for her on the

bed, and with a great sigh of relief she lay beside him and was enclosed in his arms, the feel of his body still tingling on her hands. And so, for the first time in many nights, they slept before making love, waking near dawn to satisfy each other and then to sleep again.

Chapter Sixteen

Aletta had dressed with extra care for her visit to Middlestone after church. Her deep gold velvet surcoat was edged with gold embroidery and miniver, the soft white fur from the underbelly of the grey squirrel. The narrow centre panel of the surcoat was in the latest fashion, barely covering the firm curves of her breasts in the creamy-white silk bliaud. Her head was quite enclosed in a white wimple, a gold caul at the back holding most of her hair and the deep fillet of gold velvet accentuating the peach of her skin and the lustrous dark eyes. She knew she looked well and was quite aware of Geraunt's admiring glances as they rode, side by side, listening to the chatter of the four riders behind them.

She turned her head quickly and caught his gaze before he could withdraw it. "You promised to tell me how you managed to get into Netherstone without me knowing it, on my birthday," she said, "and how this got under my pillow." She indicated the pendant.

"One way of getting into the enemy camp without being seen is to recruit spies or accomplices. In my case," he said, trying hard to keep the bubble of mirth out of his voice, "I have agents at Netherstone who are sympathetic to my cause, m'lady." He grinned at her wide-eyed surprise.

"My own household? Who?"

"Mutual friends," he said mysteriously. "Richard and Rob and Thomas were told not to let you see them, which they tell me was quite difficult when you were wandering all over the place like a lost soul before you went out. And Roger too, of course."

"But how did you know I'd go up to the pool?"

"I didn't, only that it might be a possibility. But you appeared there before I could come down and collect you. I'd only just finished making the bower when you arrived. Good timing, eh?"

"And this?" She placed a hand over her breast.

"Bridie and Gerda. Very co-operative, your maids."

Aletta shook her head, her face dimpling with laughter. They had pretended to be surprised when she'd shown them the pendant that morning. No wonder they'd appeared a bit later than usual. Obviously, she thought, Bridie had taken it upon herself to tell him of her birthday; how else would he have known?

He was still chuckling as she rallied again. "Well, sir. If you've got agents in my camp, I've got at least one in yours!"

"Have you indeed, wench. Who?"

"Willan!"

He laughed silently, with a flash of white teeth that melted her heart and made her long for the feel of his lips again, so soon after last night. Does he know, she wondered, how deeply I'm under his spell? He seemed so sure of his victory.

"Ah! Willan. Well, he's not exactly in the right place, is he? But he'll be glad to see you today, no doubt. I wonder what kind of impression he's made on Lady Cecily's young sister."

"Her sister? She's there, staying with them?"

"Yes, she's living with them now. Young lass of about sixteen summers. Should keep his mind off you for a bit."

He glanced sideways at her. "You're silent. You don't like the idea?"

"On the contrary. I was merely thinking. I like the idea very much. Very much indeed."

After their first shaky start at Oswald's funeral, Aletta found that she could warm to Lady Cecily and Sir Thomas, Geraunt's friend since childhood. Their banter and brotherly accord was refreshing and full of fun, especially with Willan there, who was now coming to the end of his time as Sir Thomas's squire.

Lady Cecily's young sister, Maddie, was lively and pretty, and didn't care who knew that she thought Willan was a god. His teasing of her brought flushes of joy to her grey eyes, giving both Aletta and Geraunt hope that his wounds would heal and that he would concentrate on events within his grasp.

He had been glad to see Aletta, and Geraunt had sensitively kept well out of the way, taking young Maddie off to meet Richard and Robin, who were eager to be introduced to her, so that Aletta and Willan were able to talk in private as they had done before.

Aletta instantly felt at home and accepted as she was shown round the manor to see the changes which had taken place since Mistress Margery's occupation. Lady Cecily chattered comfortably without, as Aletta had secretly feared, dwelling too long on the forthcoming happy event, and by the time they were due to leave the two women were more like sisters than new friends.

Lady Cecily had accepted Aletta's reluctance to talk about her betrothal, thinking that perhaps the marriage was to be delayed until legal matters were sorted out. She mentioned this to her husband later in the evening. "There's something not quite right there, somewhere," she said.

"Nothing's wrong, sweetheart," Sir Thomas assured her with a kiss on the forehead. "Not wrong, but I'll admit that the situation is not quite as straightforward as it might be. Geraunt's being particularly vague about the details.''

''Is it something to do with France? When you had to go and pay all that money for his release? Is that part of it? He's never looked seriously at anyone until now, has he? And suddenly he's betrothed, just like that. And Aletta seems not to want to discuss it, though I do believe they're in love. You can almost feel it, can't you?''

''Hush, woman!'' he laughed. ''What a chatter! We'll find out, soon enough. I can see young Willan's in love with her too, just to complicate matters. The sooner he's knighted and put to some use, the better it'll be. Geraunt's told me it would be a good thing if Willan's attention was diverted, so it must mean that he wants the field to himself. We'll see!'' And he would not be drawn into further discussion.

Some weeks later, Aletta at last managed to hold her own manor court, at which Verity and Jack Carpenter made public the true parentage of their child. In its way this was cause enough for rejoicing, but a darker side appeared after the event, which Aletta could not have forseen.

The Netherstone villagers reacted sharply to the disclosure that Sir Hubert had not, after all, been responsible for throwing Verity out of her home, but her own parents, in a bid for Aletta's sympathy. They felt that this was disgraceful conduct, even from the parents of so large a family. They had deceived the Lady Aletta at a time when she had been most vulnerable, and had allowed her to continue in the belief that she had some kind of obligation to the mother and child.

There were many others in the village who'd been similarly used by Sir Hubert but who had never borne children as a result. They, too, would have been happy to be so comforted by their mistress, had they bothered her with the details. It was, after all, nothing new for the lord to use his villeins in this way, if he'd a mind to it, though most made some kind of recompense, if need be.

Verity and her family suddenly became very unpopular. The sympathy was all with Aletta.

Another problem came to light one morning shortly afterwards, when Gerda failed to appear in the solar at dawn. When eventually she appeared, well after the household had swung into motion, she was pale and shaky, saying she'd been sick. That much was obvious, thought Aletta.

Bridie and she looked at each other, their thoughts running along the same track. "Sit down, look," said Bridie, while Aletta stood watching, one thing only uppermost in her mind. "How many mornings have you been sick, pet?"

"Weeks," the maid answered.

"You know what it is, don't you?" Bridie said gently.

Gerda nodded. "Yes. My flux hasn't come. Three I've missed now."

"You've known since before Sir Geraunt took Thomas on as a groom, then?"

"Yes."

"That was a bit of a risk, wasn't it? With Thomas still bound to Allerton and you wanting to stay here with your mother?"

Gerda looked up at Aletta. "You know how it is, m'lady. It just happens, doesn't it?"

How could Aletta not understand? It just happens. Indeed it does, lass, she thought. But what's to do now? How could Thomas continue to be Geraunt's groom from five miles away in Netherstone? Or be a husband to Gerda while he was employed in Allerton? He was now tightly bound to his occupation, which, if Aletta knew anything, he'd want to hold on to. Would Geraunt help out with a home for the new family in Allerton?

Blessing or problem, it was to worsen. Later that same day, Aletta stood on a wooden stool spinning, using the occupation of her hands as a device to draw her mind away from the fears that crowded in from all sides. It was easier to step up on to something high so that the twist could run further down the fibres before she had to stop and wind it on to the spindle. She was so engrossed in her activity that she jumped in alarm as Geraunt's hands appeared round each side of her hips and held her tightly.

"Shall I lift you up on to the table, spinster?"

The spindle swung like a pendulum and stopped spinning, threatening to reverse and undo the twist already on the thread. "No! Catch it, if you please! Don't let it undo… Now, keep it taut while I wind the thread on."

"I don't often take second place to a spindle, but there's always a first time, I suppose." Geraunt took it and the rolag of fleece from her hands and lifted her down, quite unnecessarily. He kept her in his arms and kissed her. "This is more interesting than spinning, isn't it, wench?" His lips played with hers. "Wouldn't you rather come riding with me? You can bring Gerda, if you wish. Her Thomas is here too."

"She'd better not at the moment." She tried to keep her voice light as she cleared away the basket of carded fleece and removed her apron.

"Oh, is she not well? Well, we can still go—"

"She's pregnant," Aletta said, laying the apron aside and not looking at him.

"Oh, God's wounds! Pregnant?" His tone was so caustic that she was stopped in her tracks, and for some unaccountable reason was overcome by a feeling of dread. She had rarely, if ever, heard him use that tone before. "What in God's name has she done that for, *now?*"

Aletta stood stock-still, trembling and coldly angry. She would answer his stupid questions literally. "First, sir, she probably didn't do it in God's name at all. Second, she couldn't have managed it alone, I'm sure. And third, now is a good as time as any other, I would have thought!"

"Then she must have known of this before I took Thomas on as a groom?"

"Yes, I believe it just happened like that." She knew, as soon as the words were out, that it was foolish of her to expect him to understand that philosophy. That was a woman's way of seeing things, not a man's. Geraunt would not let that go unchallenged.

"Happened? Just happened? Christ, woman! It's the oldest trick in the book!"

She could hardly believe what she was hearing. A hot sickness filled her stomach and flowed down into her legs, like the time when he'd confronted her with his knowledge of the four runaways. "What do you mean?" she asked, frowning. "I don't understand why you're so angry. It was no trick! They're betrothed!"

"Betrothed or not, can't you see? She gets herself pregnant so as to force my hand. Just so I'll have to make a decision, in spite of my saying they'd have to wait. Now it looks as if I'll have to let my best groom go when he's nicely getting into the job. He can't be my groom from here, can he? And Mistress Gerda's not going to live in Allerton, because now Thomas has left home to live above the stables, like the others." He stood with his arms folded across his chest, looking out of the window. "Damnation!"

Aletta had rarely heard anything more unreasonable in her life. Did he seriously think that Gerda had let this happen on purpose? What of Thomas? Didn't he have some part in it too? What of the opportunities Geraunt had given them to be together? Was this really all about the loss of a groom?

"Do I *really* understand what you're saying? That you think Thomas is not responsible as much as Gerda is? That you never assumed they'd want to marry? Even though you knew they were betrothed? That you thought they'd wait for *you* to tell them when they could...?"

Her voice was now barely a whisper, the sounds forced

into a tiny space in her throat. "*You're* the one who's thrown them together in the past months. What did you think they were doing in Gerda's room while you were with me? Talking politely about the weather?" she said hoarsely.

Geraunt made a gesture of impatience. "It's not the lad's fault—"

"I see!" she interrupted, her voice suddenly like ice-cold steel. "It must be seen as a *fault*, of course. How stupid of me not to realise! And it has to be Gerda's. And it's not an event to be happy about. And it's all right as long as it doesn't inconvenience *you!* And there's no other way of looking at it! I see!"

"Yes!" He whirled round to confront her. "You've said that you see, Aletta! But clearly you don't see when you're being duped, do you? Verity pulled the same trick on you. And your lasses last May Day, remember? It only takes a pregnant woman to get you moving heaven and earth for them, doesn't it? Not to mention deer! And horses! And half the damned village! Meanwhile, where does that leave *you,* Aletta?"

A wall of ice built up inside her, hurting her lungs and holding her breath far back into her stomach. "I'll tell you where it leaves me," she said, pulling off the betrothal ring and slapping it down hard on the table, "it leaves me as far away from you as I can possibly get."

Despite the sounds of roaring inside her head, she picked up her woollen shawl and fled from the room.

"Where are you…?" she heard as she pulled the door behind her and locked it from the outside. In a red haze of sickness she ran through the hall and out into the courtyard, where Roger's horse stood waiting by the door to Oswald's room. Quickly she untied it, heaved herself into the saddle and dug her heels viciously into the startled creature's flanks. Across the cobbled courtyard she sped and out through the back entrance, sending up sparks from the horse's hooves, her wimple flying behind her. Her loosened veil drifted like an autumn leaf into the fish-pond.

Many times she'd fled along this path before, though not recently, and so she was able to guide the horse without thinking, along the deep limestone scar above the village, galloping like the wind at first, then having to slow to a trot and finally a walk as the boulders clustered thickly on the ground. Roger's mare flicked her ears back and forth as the sound of Aletta's sobs broke out in anguished gusts, robbing her arms and legs of her usual strength, blurring her eyes so much that she had to drop the reins and allow the horse to find its own way. Gradually it came to a stop and began to crop the grass, rattling the bit in its teeth as it did so, looking up occasionally to see what Aletta was doing.

Head in hands, she was sitting on a lichen-covered boulder, sobbing dry, racking gasps of sound, her heart torn by the unbelievable insensitivity of Geraunt's words. Her face and head were hot and swollen, and as soon as one bout of sobbing ended another took over. She prayed that no one would come looking for her; there was nothing she could say to any of them now. No one she could tell.

It had been over two months since that first night spent with Geraunt at Allerton and she knew that the times of her monthly flow had come and gone twice now. She'd never missed one in her life before, not once, and, though Bridie had not mentioned the fact, Aletta was certain that she knew, for Bridie kept a tally and knew when her flow was due to begin as well as Aletta did.

She sat staring into space, her eyes registering nothing, her mind dead to everything except his unkind words. In spite of all his previous assurances, she now knew how he felt—about pregnancy, about being duped, the inconvenience, everything. It had taken Gerda's dilemma to point it out to her.

The mare lifted her head and looked intently down into

the valley below, her ears pricked and eyes alert. Aletta wiped her tear-filled eyes with her wimple and looked, seeing two horsemen flying across the common towards Verity's cott, one of them on a huge chestnut. Well, at least they'd gone the wrong way. She watched for their return, and a little while later picked her way carefully down the hillside in the fading light towards the cott which she knew they'd already visited. There was no point in going home if he'd still be there.

She reached Verity's home just as darkness descended. Jack Carpenter was there, the baby asleep, and Verity preparing to settle down for the night. Neither of them were as astonished as they would have been if they had not already had a visit from Geraunt and Roger. As it was, they made her welcome, stabled the horse and fed it, offered her pottage hot from the cauldron and did everything they could to make her comfortable, asking no questions, guessing the answers. They were kind, simple people, no strangers to conflict, not curious, and neither blaming nor excusing.

Aletta's well-developed defence against hurt was to pull down an inner shutter and force herself to be so aware of the world about her that hurts were pushed behind it, obliged to take their place in the grand scheme of things, not to demand an importance greater than life itself. And in the past this had usually worked. But this was different, and no amount of telling herself that tomorrow would come and that she would still be here had any effect this time. For she didn't want tomorrow to come, nor did she want to be here when it did. She had known that things would have to end. But, Sweet Jesu, not so brutally as this.

"Please, dear God, I do not deserve to be hurt so hard," she whispered in the darkness while the pain in her heart kept her awake.

Jack saddled the mare for her at first light and she was off towards Middlestone, praying that no one would see her. It was quiet and misty and slightly eerie to be out quite so early, stared at by a lone fox across a ploughed field, flapped at by a startled pheasant, regarded sternly by a tawny owl in the larch above.

Fortunately, life was astir when she reached Mistress Margery's, though the widow herself was only just awake.

"Aletta! Dear God, child, whatever's the matter?"

The new bout of sobbing lasted some time. It was no use asking questions. Mistress Margery could only wait and order a warm bath to be prepared and a poultice of vervain and betony for her fevered head. She put Aletta in her own bed and sat by her side, holding her hand, the poultice across the hot brow easing some of the pain of distended blood vessels. Slowly, and with gentle patience, the old widow eased the facts from Aletta, ending with the most important one of all—that although Geraunt had implied that he was aware of the risk that she might become pregnant, it was clear from his words last evening that he would think it most inconsiderate and inconvenient if she did. And she was. She was quite sure of it.

"I can't tell him now, can I? It's obvious he doesn't want this to happen."

"He's asked you to marry him, though?"

"He knows I would not, because he knows I'm dead set against marriage. And I still can't be sure whether it's me he's interested in or my property. He sees me as a silly woman who's set on rescuing people from difficulties, all right for bed-sport but not for complicating matters with babies. I should never have trusted him!"

"Aletta, do you remember when you were here last, and we were talking about Oswald, and Geraunt interrupted us?"

Yes, she remembered. It had been the day she was taken up to Allerton to stay. She remembered it well. "Yes," she sniffed, adjusting the poultice on her forehead. "Yes, I remember. You were going to tell me something about the missing money, but Geraunt told me afterwards that I was not to ask you about it. And I promised that I would not.''

''I see.'' Mistress Margery thought for a moment, then said, ''Right, so I've thought of a way round that problem. There's somebody who knows even more than I do about it. And it's something you really ought to know about, in spite of that proud lad saying different.''

''Who knows more about it than you, mistress?''

''Sir Thomas Newman. Geraunt's closest friend. You know they were squires together, and before that they were brought up in the same household.''

''But what does Oswald have to do with Geraunt?''

''Quite a bit. I'm going to send a messenger to ask Thomas to come over. You make yourself presentable, now, and then come down. We'll get to the bottom of this. I think it's time you knew a few details.''

By the time Aletta had taken her warm milk and beaten egg, rebraided her hair, with the help of a deft young maid, and dressed in huge but clean borrowed clothes, she was ready to go downstairs. She had already heard the booming voice of Sir Thomas and knew that it had taken only a few moments for him to respond to the summons.

He greeted her with a kiss to both cheeks and to her hand, noting the red and swollen eyelids, nose and lips, and feeling a wave of deep concern for this lovely vulnerable creature. He had known that all was not well and suspected that Geraunt had not told Aletta his story, thinking, perhaps, that to do so might make it look like a bid for her sympathy and to gain a foothold in her favour. The proud oaf would want none of that... He'd always been too proud for his own good, even as a lad.

All the same, Thomas mused, watching the graceful and lovely woman before him, it was a pity that Geraunt had felt it necessary to withhold from her facts which so closely concerned her. Surely he could have done her the honour of allowing her to decide for herself whether to accept his attentions in spite of everything rather than in ignorance? Now *he* was being asked, he knew, to deal her some astounding news. Well, if Geraunt wouldn't, *he* would.

"Sir Thomas, I'm afraid this is an imposition," Aletta whispered, looking into the strong features.

"No, it isn't, Aletta. If I can help you, it's an honour. You're in trouble?"

She didn't answer directly. There was no need for him to know of the words, the fears, the night away from home. "There's some information I'd like to have, but I promised I wouldn't reopen the question with Mistress Margery, so I'm not doing. I'm asking you if you'll tell me what you know about the fact that Oswald appeared to have…made mistakes in the manor accounts during the years just before my marriage. I know it doesn't affect the financial affairs now, but it does affect my feelings for a man I would have trusted with my life. And now I understand it has something to do with Geraunt. Is that so? And if it's so, do you think I ought to be allowed to know?"

"I noticed you're not wearing your betrothal ring, lady. Is it *that* serious?"

"There was no betrothal, Sir Thomas. It was simply a device for keeping away some of the unwanted suitors who buzzed about last summer."

"An unconventional way of tackling the problem. Count on my help at any time, if you wish."

"Thank you. I'll remember your offer. Who knows…?"

So, he thought, the crafty dog had taken advantage of the mock betrothal to invite her up to Allerton and to stay overnight at Netherstone too, according to Willan. That was certainly putting the cart before the horse. All the more reason why she should be told how the land lay. "Aletta," he said, "I'll try to make this as brief as I can without missing anything out. If Geraunt turns up, I'm talking about the price of oats. Is that agreed?"

Aletta smiled sadly. "If he turns up, you'll be talking to Mistress Margery, not me. I'll have gone!"

They sat, all three together, Aletta tense and serious, her eyes scarcely leaving Thomas's face.

"You knew we were lads together, didn't you? Then squires." Aletta nodded and he continued. "Well, we both knew Sir Hubert Markenfield from that time. He had manors down in the south too, and served the King regularly. He liked it. He had quite a reputation… Well, we won't go into that. When Geraunt was knighted—we were both twenty-one at the time—he was requested by the King—commanded, you understand—to take Sir Hubert's place in a tournament in France. It was a return bout against the French which we'd lost the previous year, but Sir Hubert had injured his leg. Well, that was what he had the King believe. We now know that this was an excuse not to go, but to send Geraunt in his place. His personally recommended replacement, you see."

"But Sir Hubert was not a coward, whatever else he was," said Aletta. "So why did he pretend to have a leg injury?"

"To get Geraunt out of the way."

"Out of the way? Of what?" She frowned, wincing at the pain in her head.

Sir Thomas looked at Mistress Margery as though for support for the next part of the story. He caught her slight nod, so continued. "A gentlemanly knight and his lady, named Sir Melville Beaumont and Lady Maude—"

"My father and mother? What did they have to do with it?" Aletta's hands gripped her chair, her body tense with questions.

"Sir Melville and Lady Maude had been approached by Sir Richard de Paine to negotiate with him for the marriage of his son to their daughter Aletta, a young lady of thirteen summers."

Aletta had turned pale. Her hands had now left the chair

and were pressing beneath her breasts, as though to hold herself together. "Me? Geraunt?" she whispered, her voice almost soundless with incredulity. "I can't believe it. They didn't tell me. Why didn't they *tell* me?"

"Because things were still being discussed, I suppose. Dowry, jointures, settlements—there were all manner of things to decide before they thought fit to tell you. But they seemed to like the idea because a betrothal was spoken of."

"But I never saw him. Not once."

"No, but he saw you. Just once."

"The ring! That was the ring! Enlarged for me!"

"I beg your pardon?"

"No. Nothing. Please go on. Mistress Margery, did you know of this?"

"Yes, love. I knew. As his godmother, I knew all about it," she said.

Sir Thomas continued. "Unfortunately, Sir Hubert Markenfield had seen you too, and discovered that you were an only child. His wife had just died. He needed money and property. And an heir. And he—"

"He liked young girls. Yes, I know all about that! Then what?"

"Apparently he decided that if he could get young de Paine out of the way for long enough he could step in and take over negotiations with your parents for your hand. And so that's what he did."

"Sweet Jesu!" Aletta sat for some time, looking at her hands, shaking her head gently in disbelief. "France," she said. "France. He said he'd spent some time there…two years… Why did he have to stay for two years? A tournament doesn't take that long, does it?"

"No, Aletta, you're right. It doesn't. He never got to take part in the tournament because he was abducted and held prisoner in a castle, instead."

"In France? For two years? Who…?"

"Sir Hubert. He'd arranged it. Told no one where Geraunt was, so no one could rescue him. Your parents were told that he'd run off, that he was a coward who couldn't face the tournament nor the prospect of marriage to their daughter.''

"Sir Hubert told them *that?* And they believed him?"

"Yes, they believed him. He could be very persuasive at times, couldn't he, Aletta? And they were old, and easily impressed by his influence and reputation.''

"They obviously didn't hear *all* his reputation!" she retorted, glaring.

"No. Well, he took care that they only saw what he wanted them to see.''

"This is dreadful! Dreadful!" She covered her face with her hands, too stunned to say more.

"Anyway, when they understood that Sir Geraunt had disappeared they naturally broke off negotiations with Geraunt's father and started new ones with Hubert Markenfield. And eventually he married you, when you were fifteen.''

"And Geraunt was still a prisoner?"

"Still prisoner, except that Oswald Freeman, Sir Hubert's steward and half-brother, discovered where Geraunt was being held and Sir Hubert's treachery. And, when Sir Hubert and his new bride—you—came up here to live at Netherstone, old Sir Richard de Paine left Allerton and moved to his Oxfordshire estates. You can imagine the bad feeling there was for Markenfield, having stepped into Geraunt's shoes so neatly. Sir Richard wouldn't live anywhere near him.''

"I see now... Yes... I see. But how did Oswald discover...?"

"He found papers among Sir Hubert's things, quite by chance. He'd known Geraunt too, you see, having always been Sir Hubert's steward. And he realised what his half-brother had been up to. So he decided to accumulate money from the accounts to pay for Geraunt's release.''

"And that's why there's all that money—five hundred

pounds—missing from the accounts for those years. It wouldn't be too difficult to fool Sir Hubert, you know, because he didn't have much time for the money side of things. He only wanted to know if there was any or not!''

''I'm sure you're right, otherwise he would have seen what was happening straight away. Well, as Oswald could get about the country, on his manorial duties, he came to me and asked me if I'd go to France with the money he'd taken from Sir Hubert and offer it in return for Geraunt. So I did. Geraunt sent him a token that I'd arrived and that he was safe, and with a bit of persuasion his captors released him, took the money, and we came back together. You'd been married about six months by that time, Aletta.''

''Oh, my God,'' she breathed. ''And Geraunt didn't know? He hadn't heard?''

''No. Not a thing. He couldn't even speak to your parents, because they died that year, didn't they?''

''Yes,'' she whispered, ''the year I was married. What a year. Poor Geraunt.''

''Well, Oswald swore me to secrecy about where the money had come from. Only I knew, at the time. If Sir Hubert had found out, poor Oswald would have been thrown out.''

''He *was*,'' Aletta interrupted. ''He was! There was a terrible to-do when Sir Hubert discovered something was wrong, and he threw both Oswald and Edwise out, and they came here, to stay with you.'' She turned to Mistress Margery, her face pale and full of concern. ''Poor Oswald. What a brave man. Quite wonderful. He tried to put right the wrong with Sir Hubert's own money. But what a risk! He must have dreaded being discovered.''

''Yes, it was only after Sir Hubert's death that I was able to tell Geraunt who had arranged to have him abducted and who had paid for his release. If he'd known before, I'm quite sure he would have marched straight up here and killed Sir Hubert Markenfield with his bare hands. As it was, he was able to thank Oswald personally when he came to see you one day.''

Aletta went to stand by the window with her back to them, watching a new light dawn above the fells like an omen of new understanding.

They waited, without speaking, allowing her time to take in the appalling story of deceit and betrayal, intrigue and treachery.

At last, she turned and looked blankly at them both, feeling that for every question answered a new one had sprung up in its place. Why? Why? ''I can see now why he feels so strongly about gaining what he lost. He must have felt very bitter about losing to a man like Sir Hubert, and in such a cowardly fashion. I was wrong. He *was* a coward, wasn't he?''

''Aletta,'' said Sir Thomas gently, ''it matters not what Sir Hubert was, or was not, what does matter is that you should not believe that your property is the reason for Geraunt's interest in you. He's never been ambitious in that direction and he's got as much property as he can handle; he's told me that. He wouldn't have put me here to manage Middlestone Manor otherwise. He'd have managed it himself from Allerton. It's you he's in love with, m'lady. He told me that too.''

Aletta made a slight gesture with her hand, as though to fend off the words. ''He's never spoken of love to me. Not once. The nearest he ever got to it was when he said he'd wait for me forever, if need be. And that made me wonder…''

''He said he'd wait for you forever? Well, then, that confirms what I'm saying, Aletta, since it would benefit him nothing to wait forever for property, would it?''

''But Willan said he wanted to add to his property up here. He said it before I…before I got to know Geraunt.'' She remembered the feeling of dread as Willan had told her this, and her anger as she had mentioned it to Roger.

Sir Thomas laughed, and Aletta looked at him in dismay. "Young Willan hasn't yet learnt the art of subtle language, Aletta. You haven't discovered that yet? He's young. To him, property means land, farms, rentable things. I believe Geraunt had something else in mind." His look was unmistakable and his merry eyes danced, leaving her now in little doubt of his meaning, and of Geraunt's too.

Mistress Margery beckoned them both to the table. "Look here. All this talking, and it's still so early. I think we ought to eat, don't you, Thomas? A pickled herring—" she nodded to the page to leave them "—and some newly baked bread. Cheese, eggs… Help yourself… We'll be informal." She pushed the food forward, item by item, and patted Aletta's cold hand. "You're cold, lass. Here, put this over your shoulders."

Swathed in the soft woollen shawl, Aletta nibbled absently at a piece of cheese and watched Sir Thomas.

He returned her look openly. "You've had a shock, lady, but you must try not to think too hard of Geraunt. He could hardly have told you all this himself and expected you to agree to marry him on the strength of such a tale, could he? I'm sure he'd rather you went to him of your own accord. He's proud, you know. Stubbornly proud. He would hate you to feel sorry for him because of what happened."

Yes, she could see that this made sense, but what of the bond? They knew nothing of that, of Geraunt's hold over her. She felt sick, and put the cheese down on her platter, her hands visibly trembling.

"Did you find you'd lost some villeins when you came to live here?" she asked him. Since he'd been so informative, perhaps he'd know enough about the law to establish some of the facts in her mind, once and for all.

"Oh, yes," he replied, his mouth full of food. "Geraunt and I found that some had gone off to live further down, on Southstone Priory lands. They have more sheep there, you know. But there's nothing to be done about it now. Too late.'' He bit heartily into a boiled egg.

"Too late? Doesn't Geraunt want to pursue them, Thomas?''

"Oh, they've been gone well over a year, according to my information. Mistress Margery didn't feel like chasing them up, and Geraunt's old steward, who did Margery's business, knew about it but didn't feel inclined to pursue the matter, so that's the end of it.''

"Is it?'' asked Aletta, puzzled by his attitude. Was it really as simple as that?

"Well, nobody just leaves them where they are for so long and then suddenly decides to chase them up. It really has to be done as soon as it's occurred. No court of law would believe you were too serious about it otherwise, and it's for certain they'd come down on the side of the villein for being able to get away with it undetected. I just have to accept the fact that I've lost 'em!'' He reached casually for another slice of bread.

"So the Prior of Southstone couldn't be prosecuted for theft of Geraunt's property if he refused to hand them over now?'' She could hardly wait for his answer.

"Theft? Good grief, Aletta! Whatever put that idea into your head? Well—'' he laughed, putting down his knife and looking at her intently ''—I suppose that in theory he probably could, but I don't see Geraunt going to all that trouble. After all, he's turning his land over to sheep now, and he doesn't need men the way his father did a few years ago. No, my lady, a few less men here and there are not going to make any difference to either me or Geraunt.''

Aletta could hear the sound of her heart beating loud into her throat. If only she'd been sure of this before. What price the precious bond then? she wondered. ''Would they be free, then?'' she asked, trying to sound no more than politely interested.

"Oh, no, not necessarily. But I suppose that they could

request their manumission eventually. And once it was understood that the Abbot owned them—by acquisition, you understand—*he* could free them. But he wouldn't, of course. He's a wily old bird. Priors don't let their work force go so easily.'' He laughed at the joke. ''You ought to ask Geraunt about this kind of thing. He explained all this to me once, and he knows the ins and outs of it much better than I do.''

''Geraunt does?'' The breath almost fell out of her, as though she'd been winded, and her legs trembled beneath the table.

''Yes, did he never tell you? He made quite a study of property law. Are you having trouble with your villeins, Aletta? Trouble is, the whole thing's past history now, and not worth the time and expense of going to court. Probably cost more to hire a lawyer than we've lost in fines!'' And he laughed as he speared another hunk of bread with his knife and gently lifted a herring on to it. ''My God, Margery! Is she all right…?''

A cold numbness stole down Aletta's arms and the table faded into blackness. Slowly the room disappeared, and Thomas caught her as she slid towards the floor.

Chapter Seventeen

Thomas frowned. "I could swear she was more upset by what I said about the runaways than about Geraunt's imprisonment." He looked up at Mistress Margery as he rested on his haunches at Aletta's side. "I wish I knew what was going on!" He turned to coax another sip of wine into her pale lips.

"I'm cold…" Aletta whispered, so softly that he had to bend his head to hear her.

"Cold? She's cold," he repeated. "Pass me the rug, mistress, if you please."

"Thomas! Geraunt's here! What are we going to tell him?" She handed the rug and Thomas tucked it around Aletta before responding.

"Tell him everything! The fool!" he replied viciously. "He's handled this badly, if you ask me. I'll tell him if you don't want to, mistress. This lass knew nothing. Nothing!" He stood as Geraunt entered the room. "About bloody time, too! You call *me* clumsy, man! But, by God, you could teach me a thing or two! I hope you know how you're going to justify this…" He jerked his head towards Aletta, who, having now seen Geraunt's entry into the room, turned her head away with a cry.

The two friends glared at each other, their eyes accusing, questioning, helpless.

Then Geraunt went to her. "Thomas, is she…"

"No! She's not all right! She's just passed out," Thomas snapped.

"Aletta! Oh, my God! What's happened to her? Was it something you said to her?" Geraunt knelt by her side, his hands turning her face to him, stroking her hair, his lips on her brow, murmuring her name. He heard not a word of Thomas's reply.

"Yes. Something *you* should have said at the beginning, fool! Instead of leaving it to the end. Women are *people*, Geraunt! Remember?" Suddenly he felt desperately sorry for his friend, seeing the stricken look on his face, his desperate attempts to make contact with her. He put a hand on Geraunt's shoulder. "Come on, lad. Don't distress her any more. There are times when women don't want us around, and Mistress Bridie's here. Leave! We'll come back later."

He almost pulled Geraunt away bodily, out of the room, leaving Bridie to go to Aletta and touch her tenderly.

"What is it, pet?" Bridie asked, touching Aletta's lips gently with her forefinger. "What is it, then?"

The signal was understood and a huge sob rode on a wail of despair. The floodgates opened, the torrent poured out, and as she was scooped into Bridie's arms the jumbled words fell over each other, unintelligible, snatched by waves of unhappiness and dashed into fragments before they could form. Bridie let it go; there was no barrier effective against this tide, only the slow rocking, in time with the beat of her heart.

And, in time, as words and sobs wore out, the rocking and the tender arms were the only sensations left over, and so Aletta went with them, as a child did when the cause of its distress had been washed too far downstream to be caught. At intervals remnants of her passion tore out of her in rasping gulps, while Bridie wiped her forehead and pushed back the damp hair, hushing and cooing in the primitive language of mothering creatures, the soft sounds eventually penetrating the storm-clouds in Aletta's mind and quieting her.

Thomas nudged Geraunt brusquely into the small room across the passageway and closed the door firmly, noting Geraunt's haggard face in the dim morning light.

"Has she been here all night, Tom? We searched everywhere for her. We didn't think she'd get this far before dark."

"No, she came here very early this morning."

"What the hell's she being doing, then?"

"More to the point man, what the hell have *you* been doing? Why did she have to find out from *me* what you should have told her at the beginning?"

"About what?"

"About Oswald. And you! You even stopped her from asking Mistress Margery!" He pointed towards the door, and Geraunt followed with his eyes, understanding.

"Oh, God's wounds, Tom. You told her *all?*"

"Yes, I did, man! She had a right to know. We both…no, all three of us thought she had a right to know. She's not your property and you'd no right to keep it from her."

Geraunt looked stunned. "And then she passed out?"

"Strangely enough, I don't think it was *that* that did it. It was when she started asking me about runaways, and whether I could sue the Prior for theft of my villeins after so long…"

"And you explained the situation? Oh, God!" Geraunt turned to the window and stood gazing out silently, running his hand through his hair and holding his mouth.

"What is it, man?" Thomas asked sharply.

Geraunt didn't answer.

"What *is* it? Tell me, for pity's sake! You've done

enough damage keeping your damned schemes to yourself and playing at directing people's lives. Now, tell me what's going on!" Thomas had rarely felt so angry. "Come on!"

"I told her—" Geraunt stopped, and began again. "She'd given refuge to four of my villeins a year ago— Allerton lads, living with four of her lasses—and I told her that I could ruin them, and their tithings, and their relatives, and sue her for theft, if…" He couldn't bring himself to finish.

"If what? If she didn't co-operate with you? Is *that* it?"

Slowly Geraunt turned from the window to face his friend, meeting his eyes, showing the answer without the need for words.

"You *fool!*" Thomas said quietly. "You…great… stupid…oaf!" They remained staring into each other's eyes, reading the words, Thomas shaking his head in disbelief. "When a woman's been through all that she's been through with that…that *savage!* And then you discover her tender heart and threaten her with all that, allow her to believe you could remove her from everything she's built up single-handed, and hurt the people who've grown to trust her…just to revenge yourself?"

"No! No, Tom! It wasn't like that!" Geraunt shook his head. He spoke quietly, shaking with emotion. "I love the woman. I'm crazed about her. I would never have carried it through. I love her. I told you before."

"Love? *Love?*" Thomas spat out the words, whirling away to the other side of the room. "What in God's name do you know about love when you can deceive a woman so? Tell me, is this a new game you've devised to show a woman how much you love her? Is it? It wouldn't have been enough just to tell her? Was that too simple? So you had to invent something more interesting, some complicated ritual—?"

"Enough! Enough, Tom! It wouldn't have been any use telling her. She wouldn't have believed me. She was set on believing everyone was after her property and she wouldn't have let me near her. I told you what a disastrous start we had. I had to get to her somehow.''

''So you thought you could get to her by threats? Well, that's a new one on me!'' Thomas turned his back while his anger simmered. ''And you've never even got as far as telling her you love her.'' He said this not as a question but as a bald statement.

''Did she tell you that?'' Geraunt whispered.

''It's true, isn't it?'' Thomas whirled again, his eyes snapping.

''Yes. I was waiting for her to—''

''Sweet Jesu! Don't tell me! You were waiting for *her* to tell *you?*'' He pointed to the door, fury written in every line of his body. ''That's a woman in there, man! A *woman!* Not a bloody saint! Do you expect as much from yourself as you do from her? A tender, sensitive lass who's suffered absolute hell in her marriage without losing her wits or her dignity? Why in God's name *would* she let you near her? Or anyone else? You wouldn't either! You'd die rather than put yourself on somebody's altar all over again. Anybody would! You bloody great ham-fisted clod!''

Shaking, he poured a goblet of ale, drank deeply, poured again and handed it to Geraunt. ''And you've taken her to bed.'' He needed no confirmation. A flicker of Geraunt's eyes over the rim of the goblet was all he needed.

''It made her happy, Tom. It was good. I believe she's in love with me.'' He was not boasting; it was merely a softly spoken explanation.

Thomas growled. ''If her love can survive a massive deceit like you've just dished her it'll be well worth having, believe me. I've no doubt you've shown her a side of herself she's never seen before, but you're on shaky ground, lad, if you think you can build a future on that alone. It needs trust, Geraunt. Simple trust. Being honest with her, about everything. Anything less, with a woman like Aletta, is an insult. A bloody insult! And that's all I've got to say!''

He brushed past Geraunt on his way to the door, then stopped, remembering something. ''No, it isn't! There's one other thing! If you *must* play at fake betrothals, whether to suit your own ends or Aletta's, don't include *me* in your silly games! If I'd known you were not really betrothed I wouldn't have made that unfortunate remark about her being pregnant by winter. No wonder the lass was mortified. She didn't know where to put herself...and neither did I!''

''I'm sorry, Tom. It was to protect her from unwanted—''

''Hah! You expect me to believe that? It was to get you into her bed a bit faster, and you know it!'' Thomas's anger had placed him on the very edge of awareness and he knew, even before the words were finished, what Geraunt's reaction would be.

The blow from his fist missed Thomas's jaw by a whisker for, fast as it was, Thomas sidestepped as he saw Geraunt's eyes flicker open and narrow again. At the same time Thomas's big fist crashed into Geraunt's cheek, sending him staggering backwards over a stool and into the panelled wall beyond.

He picked himself up with the grace of a cat and brushed away the rushes clinging to his elbows. ''I deserve that,'' he said through his teeth.

The doorway was suddenly filled with Mistress Margery, alarm written clearly on her face. Before she could speak, Thomas took her arm. ''I humbly beg your pardon, mistress. I should have waited until we were outside, but we preferred not to have an audience.''

She squeezed his arm, hardly able to contain the twinkle in her eyes but knowing that a smile would be inappropriate. With a tiny lift of one eyebrow, she met her godson's level gaze. ''Geraunt?''

''Yes, Godmother.''

"I think it's time you took the Lady Aletta back to her own home now."

"Yes. Can I go to her?" he asked, wiping a hand over his reddened cheek.

The widow nodded. "Just one thing before you go, Geraunt. Don't assume that you know what she needs better than she does. A woman like Aletta is perfectly capable of holding her own reins until she chooses to hand them over of her own free will. Men and women don't all go along the same track and it's no good pretending that they do. They're different animals, my love. Will you try to remember that?"

"Yes, Godmother." He kissed her cheek. Then he turned to Thomas. "Tom, you're the only one…"

"Yes, man. I know I am." He took Geraunt's arm and urged him towards the door. "Now go and take that little angel home."

How Aletta ever reached Netherstone without passing out several times more was due only to her fight to stay in control of the waves of pain that gripped her hips like steel bands. Clutching at her lower stomach, unable to draw up her knees as she lay in Geraunt's arms across his saddle, she could only close her eyes and pant as the pains threatened to engulf her in blackness again.

By the time they reached the manor she could barely whisper to Bridie, "Quick…my cloths…my flow…Ah!"

"Sir Geraunt, you *must* go! Please! My lady needs some attention." Bridie spoke with such authority and with such weight of meaning that he left the room immediately. "I'll call you when she's able to see you, sir," she said over her shoulder as he hesitated at the door. He nodded and closed it.

"My flow, Bridie! It's come, after all… Oh God!" She curled up on the bed as another spasm gripped her, breathless and dizzy, gasping wide-eyed until it passed.

Not content with the emotional pain, now it seemed she was to know physical pain too. The implication of its ferocity forced her to understand that she was being emptied, drained in every way. She would have to start anew. Whatever it was she'd thought she had, this was to tell her that she did not. Nothing. Less than nothing.

Some hours later, wrapped up in bed, well padded and feet warmed with hot bricks from the kitchen, she was being spooned infusions of Lady's mantle and feverfew, too weak to protest that she felt sick.

"That'll pass, love. I know. It'll pass in a while. Just be still now and rest," soothed Bridie.

It did, and at last she lay in a void, as the pains subsided, pale, exhausted and numb of mind and spirit. Not angry but vacant. Hollow.

"Sir Geraunt's downstairs, waiting to see you. He say he won't go until he's seen you. Shall I let him in?"

Aletta turned her head away and couldn't answer, but Bridie saw a tear slowly trickle down on to her chin and understood that there was a response beneath the apparent uninterest. "I'll let him up for a bit, pet. But not for long so don't be distressed. There, now." She soothed the pale brow with her warm hand.

Geraunt had watched the progression of scurrying maids from solar to kitchen, carrying hot bricks bundled in blankets, steaming infusions and buckets of hot water. "What's going on, mistress?" he asked in a whisper as Bridie let him into the room. His anxious eyes searched the bed and frowned into the maid's. "Is she going to be all right?"

Bridie nodded and drew him away to the window. "Yes sir. She will be all right. Eventually."

"What is it, Bridie? Tell me, if you please."

"She was pregnant, sir. Until just now." Try as she might, Bridie could find in her heart no soft way to tell him, though she knew that her mistress would not wish him to be hurt by the news. She watched his eyes grow pale with shock, watched his hand slowly cover his forehead and stay there, saw him turn and look at Aletta. Her face was still turned away.

"A baby? She was expecting…? Oh, my God!" he whispered. "How long, Bridie?" He looked at the maid for some comfort, his eyes blank with dismay.

"Not long, sir. She missed two, that's all. But we were both sure." She didn't add that this was often the way of things first time round. That a false start was not unusual, that it was just as likely to be the vigorous riding as any emotional shock. These were things she couldn't say to him.

He let out a deep, long-drawn sigh and drew his hand down his face, and Bridie noticed again the reddened bruise now swelling on his cheek. Her heart softened. It was not in her to twist the dagger in his side. She put a hand on his arm. "Sir Geraunt, just a little while. Not too long. She's too upset to talk about anything. Give her a day or two, then perhaps…"

He nodded and went to the bed, and sat. "Aletta." Taking the one hand that was available, he held it against his cheek, pressing his lips into the palm, then holding it on to his lap. "I know you're tired, dearest heart, and very upset. And hurt. And I have a lot to answer for. But I love you, Aletta. I love you desperately. And I'm not going to let you go. I won't try to explain things now, but I shall come back every day to see you. And nothing will keep me away."

Her eyes had been turned away, but now there were tears rolling down her cheeks, and at his last words she turned her face to him. "Bridie's told you?" she whispered hoarsely.

"Yes, my darling, Bridie's told me. I'm sorry. I'm so terribly sorry."

Again she turned her head away and he waited, believing that there was more to come as she had left her hand in his. She turned back again almost immediately, with con-

cern in her eyes, and looked anxiously through her tears.
"What's that?"

"Just a bruise, sweetheart."

"A bruise? Who…?" She frowned, too tired to push the
tears away.

"Thomas. He's been trying to knock some sense into
me, that's all. No—" he forestalled the question she was
sure to ask "—no, we didn't have a fight. Not even a quarrel. He just landed me one, as he was perfectly entitled to
do. I deserve it! He should have done it sooner."

"Oh!" she breathed, turning her head away again. Then
she removed her hand from his, and Geraunt thought that
this signalled the end of her interest. But she turned once
more and placed her hand on the bruised cheek in the lightest possible caress.

Softly he covered it with his own, marvelling that this
lovely hurt creature could show anything but disgust for
him at this moment of all moments, when he had ridden
roughshod over everything she held sacred.

He replaced her hand on the covers and bent to lay a
kiss on her forehead as he saw the figure of Bridie from
the corner of his eye, approaching the bed. "Just remember
that I love you, and that I shall see you tomorrow. Now
sleep, sweet thing."

That night, as the soothing drinks gave her some ease
from her pains, Aletta slept soundly until early dawn. Her
last thoughts before sleep were of the assurance of his love.
He had not crept away shamefaced, nor tried to excuse
himself. He had still wanted to see her. "I have a lot to
answer for" and "I deserve it". The bruise on his cheek.
His look as he'd affirmed, "Yes, my darling. Bridie's told
me. I'm so terribly sorry."

Bridie had told her of the stricken expression on his face
as she'd delivered the news with little gentleness. "You
mustn't take it too hard, pet," the maid had told her as she
tucked her up for the night. "It's common enough for
things to start off like this and then get cracking properly

next time round. It might have happened like this anyway, even without your quarrel—'specially if the moon was on the wane.''

In reply to Aletta's puzzled frown Bridie had explained that it was always better to conceive at the rising of the moon rather than during its wane, just as seeds were sown in the soil at that time for best results, and just as the mares were put to the stallion then too. When the moon was on the downwards part of its cycle, she'd said, things stood less chance of being strong and vigorous, and perhaps that was what had happened with Aletta. And, with this comforting thought, Aletta had slept.

As the new light of day glimmered into the room Aletta, now rested, remembered that he would be with her again soon. She must try to marshal her thoughts into some kind of order. For the first time since he had propelled himself into her life she felt that she had the advantage, that the choice was now hers—whether to hold him off in a state of disgrace and penance, or whether to allow her love for him to override the words, the misunderstandings, the deceits.

She tried, in the warmth of her bed, to begin at the beginning and imagine his feelings on discovering that the girl he'd hoped to marry had been maliciously snatched away from under his nose in the most treacherous manner imaginable, robbing him not only of his prize but also of over two years of his life, his honour, his family and his career as a knight. How would anyone have felt at that? she wondered. Bitter? Resentful? Lusting for vengeance?

And yet he had shown no signs of those perfectly understandable reactions during their relationship. Dominance and high-handedness, certainly. But didn't she secretly enjoy that anyway? The deceit about the bond had made her wonder about his motives; it had certainly appeared to be an extreme and on the face of it a highly insensitive method of tying her to his will. But had he been insensitive in any other way? Had he been brutal? Unfeeling? Unkind?

She could think of no time when she'd been afraid of receiving physical violence from him, and she didn't believe he would ever have allowed her to be hurt. His forbearance had been remarkable, considering the limits to which she'd pushed him, just for the hell of it.

Not only that but his gentleness with her, his tenderness, his apology to her when he thought she might have been disgusted by his primitive urge on one occasion—all contradicted any ideas of vengeance or brutality. He had shown true concern for her well-being, had given her his protection, had tended her with true chivalry, had made his home available to her, had done everything for her comfort. How could she have equated this with the actions of a vengeful man, a deceiver, a dishonest property-grabber?

And then there was his lovemaking. He'd not made any secret of his intentions there, she, smiling to herself. On the contrary, he'd insisted from the beginning that once she'd discovered its true delights she'd come to enjoy it. And, in spite of being sure that she wouldn't, she had found that she was as desperate for him as he had appeared to be for her. In fact, she remembered, she had been the one to invite him to her bed, after all that. He had not forced her, but had waited patiently until she could hold off no longer.

And the bower. Suspecting how she's secretly longed to lie in the may-blossomed woodland with her lover on May Eve, he'd built a bower with his own hands on her birthday, and had taken her there. She fingered the primrose pendant around her neck. And who but a man in love, caring, thoughtful and romantic, would have thought of putting primroses in her hair or between her breasts?

Yes, even the pretend betrothal had been unorthodox. She remembered that the ring still lay on the table, where she had banged it down in anger, and she remembered the consummation of vows which had never been made.

Had this been the reason for Thomas's violent reaction,

perhaps? He probably disapproved of the apparently furtive methods to gain access to her, but naturally Thomas could not know that this side of things was of paramount importance to her, and that if Geraunt had not been determined to remedy her own fears and inhibitions his suit would have stood no chance of success—never in a thousand years.

Poor Geraunt, he wouldn't have had a chance to explain this, nor would he have felt it proper. Could this be the real reason why he had felt it so vital to get to her on a far more personal level, knowing how she must have suffered during her marriage, and how she must have been so set against any repetition? Not purely from selfish motives, but for her own sake? Because he loved her? She laughed. What an upside-down affair this appeared to be!

"You're awake, pet? And laughing too? That's good. Ready for some food now?"

And by the time she'd been bathed, changed and fed, put back into bed against the pillows and had heaps of flowers fresh from the garden brought in by Roger, Aletta was feeling more at peace, her thoughts clearer, her questions more reasonable, kinder, more answerable.

When Geraunt was admitted she did nothing to hide the smile in her eyes. How could she, when he'd made every effort to look his most handsome in a calf-length divided gown of violet and gold over a tunic of chestnut-brown? His pale tan gloves and boots, the deep violet fur-trimmed cloak thrown over his shoulder, the glitter of the golden buckles on his hips made a feast for her eyes as she surveyed him openly from top to toe with unconcealed curiosity, craning herself out of bed, almost, to see the gold spurs on his boots. She came up smiling.

He bowed, grinning at her amusement, and laid a bunch of dewy-fresh violet-coloured iris on her lap. "My lady," he said, "do I have your approval? Brother Spen advised me to make my peace with you and to ask your forgiveness as though I meant it. Am I welcome, sweet thing?"

Aletta held out a hand to him, laying the other tenderly over the flowers. "You are well come, sir. As always."

Flinging his gloves to the end of the bed, he sat facing her and drew her gently into his arms. "I don't deserve this, my darling. I don't even know where to begin to tell you how repentant I am. Truly, I don't know where to start."

At that moment Aletta didn't feel that it was important for him to begin at all, for what really mattered was being said here, in the protective circle of his arms. After all that had happened between them, how could she convince herself that it was meaningless? What would it achieve except unhappiness for both of them?

"Did you sleep, love? Are you feeling stronger now? No more pains?" His concern was genuine; she could see that. His warmth was so comforting, his arms so tender.

"I'm well… Oh, Geraunt…oh…" As though a dam had suddenly burst, a hot surge of tears spilled out and ran down the violet velvet of his gown, engulfing her in its flood. It didn't last. Like the last uncomfortable remnants of a bad dream, it subsided after the sobs and gulps had been rocked and soothed away, her hair smoothed back, her eyes patted dry. "Why didn't you tell me the whole story, dearest one? Were you afraid?" she whispered, tracing the embroidery round his neckline with one finger.

"Afraid? I was terrified that you'd think I wanted revenge, that's all, and not want to hear of my love for you."

"But you didn't give me a chance…" she pleaded.

"No, sweet love, I didn't. I dared not. I saw you only once, Aletta, when you were a lass of thirteen. And I thought you were the most beautiful creature I'd ever seen. I fell in love with you. I wanted you. I persuaded my father to make an offer for you, even though I was landless at the time. I was going to come back from France with laurels around my neck and present them to you. But fate took a hand in it…"

Aletta placed her palm on his cheek again, wordless, unable to say anything to alleviate the terrible shock of fate's interference.

He kissed her palm and continued. "And then, when I saw you again, I could hardly believe that you were even lovelier than my memory. I hadn't know what to expect after all those years, though I knew we'd have to meet sometime. But, on that day I hadn't thought to see you at all. And then this wonderful creature came hurling herself at my hounds like a demon, furious and proud, and I was smitten all over again—only worse!"

Aletta touched his chin, smiling. "You don't mean better, do you?" she said mischievously.

"Better...worse...it's all the same! But by that time you were firmly armoured against men, especially me after that episode. I couldn't have done worse to get into your bad books, could I? And I had to get at you somehow, so I attacked from all angles, sweet thing, fair play and foul. I had to have you this time. It was wrong of me. I've hurt you badly. I've wounded you..."

His voice was hoarse with grief. "God, Aletta, I've wounded you!" He held her tightly against him, his hands wandering over her back, his face buried deep in her flowing hair. "And my outburst yesterday... I'd give anything to take back those stupid words. I should never have said any of that. Whether you were pregnant or not, it was unreasonable, brutally unkind." He sat away from her and brushed the hair from her eyes, touching her lips with his fingers. "I'm so sorry, dear heart. Can you ever forgive me?"

"Were you very angry at Gerda, love?"

"It was anger at our own situation, rather than Gerda's," he said quietly, kissing her forehead. "But it burst to the surface at that moment, unfortunately. It seemed so ridiculous that ordinary villagers with simple lives were able to pair off and marry just like that—no fuss, no problems—while we were chasing ourselves round in circles and knots, wasting precious time. So I suppose I felt a wave of frus-

tration at that moment, that there was I, wanting you fo
my own so much that I could hardly think straight, and you
seemed more concerned with...others! Everybody excep
us.

"I don't mean that to sound like a criticism, love; it isn't
I have no right to expect you to do otherwise. I love you
for caring about others so tenderly. It's part of you. It's
endearing. But men see things differently. They're harder
more cynical and more selfish. Much more selfish. I want
you all to myself. All of you. I want to bind you to me so
that you never leave my side again, ever. Is that so very
bad, sweet thing? It's not an excuse, just an explanation
Perhaps I want to make up for lost time."

Lost time. Didn't they both have lost time to make up
Could they really afford to spend more time chasing each
other round in circles, tying themselves in complicated
knots when both of them knew exactly what they wanted

"The ring, Geraunt. It's still there, on the table."

He leaned her back against the pillows and went to col
lect it. To her horror, he placed it in the leather purse which
hung from his belt. A cold feeling of fear ran down her
spine. Had he withdrawn from the field? Surely not
"You're not going to let me wear it?" she whispered
dreading his reply.

"Sweetheart. Next time I place that on your finger
you're going to say the vows that go with it." He drew the
gold ring from his finger and put it in the same purse. "And
so am I." He looked at her stricken face. "It's not so much
a question of whether, sweetheart. Only of when!"

"Then get some witnesses here, Geraunt. Now. I'll be
damned if I'm going to let you take those rings back home
with you! They're both mine!" She was near to tears, panic
rising at the thought of a backward step.

"You mean it? After all you've learned about me? You
still want me?"

"Oh, Geraunt! How can you ask? How can you be
so...so *stupid?*"

"What?" He was totally nonplussed.

"I wouldn't have gone this far if I hadn't intended to stay with you. Wild horses wouldn't have dragged me into this tangle if I hadn't wanted to be with you every moment of every day. I love you, Geraunt. I want you. All of you. To be your wife. I want to make babies with you. I want to stay with you until we're old and crotchety. I don't want to live without you. And if you take my ring away now I'll go into a nunnery! I swear it!" Her last words were muffled against his violet gown, for he was holding her tightly in his arms, shaking with laughter and disbelief.

"Sweetheart! I don't deserve it. Are you sure…?"

"Yes. But one thing I'm not going to do is ask you to marry me, as you said I'd have to."

"What? Not marry me? Then what…?"

"It's the wrong way round, Geraunt. Ladies don't ask. They accept!" She held herself away from him in a simulation of maidenly modesty, but he could see the laughter bubbling beneath the surface.

"Of course. How very stupid of me," he said. "One moment." He slipped off the bed and knelt on the floor, taking her hands in both of his. "Sweetest and most beloved lady. My heart, my love and my life are yours, as they have been since I was twenty-one and you were a maid of thirteen. Will you now do me the honour of accepting my hand in marriage?"

"Yes, sir. I will."

Aletta brought his hands to her lips and kissed them, finding that they were barely a hair's breadth away from his mouth. Quite how her kiss moved from one to the other she was not quite sure, but it occurred to her that she'd not felt his lips on hers like this for one whole day. And that was far too long for either of them to wait.

* * * * *

Elizabeth Henshall is married with two young sons and lives in Cheshire. Following a degree in French and German, she had a variety of jobs before deciding to give up office life. A year in Germany teaching English convinced her that this was certainly more exhausting! She now teaches French and German at a local secondary school and finds her life is indeed very busy. Fascinated in particular by local history, Elizabeth enjoys writing and researching with wine at hand.

Betrayed Hearts

by

Elizabeth Henshall

Chapter One

The thin rope binding her wrists cut into her as Ghislaine struggled desperately to get free. The destrier beneath her snorted with what sounded alarmingly like disgust, and she hoped that the huge war-horse would not take her doomed movements amiss.

"If you do not have the wits to stay still, wench, then you will find my temper far less amenable than the horse's," growled her captor.

Ghislaine narrowed her eyes in fury and would have answered that threat with the contempt it deserved, but unfortunately her mouth had been gagged with a foul rag that smelled as if it had come from the midden.

Her guard's fingers pressed painfully into her arms as he pulled her back against his chest. The rivets of his protective leather hauberk gouged through her clothing. She was left with no option other than to remain where she was. If she tried to sit up without touching him, she risked being trapped tightly by two very muscular thighs. Opting for the lesser evil and pain Ghislaine sank reluctantly back against her foe.

The covering over her head was stifling and she

wondered honestly just how much longer she could endure being trussed up like a sack of grain, pummelled about on a horse and ripped to shreds by twine, without being sick. It seemed like hours since she had breathed fresh air.

The heartbeat of the man behind her thudded loudly in her ear and she whispered a desperate appeal to heaven to arrange for it to stop. Nothing terrible or messy, she suggested quickly. Just to have it stop. Father Thomas had warned her on many occasions of the dangers of malicious prayers but Ghislaine was convinced that, just once, God might grant her this small wish. After all, she had done nothing to deserve such treatment.

Well, she amended hastily, at least she had not deserved to be kidnapped by a bunch of marauding outlaws. Her crime was merely to have ventured further than she should from her manor. And, of course, had she heeded Edwin's warning in the first place, she would not be in this predicament at all.

The morning had been crisp and dry, promising to be the most clement day they had seen this February. Ghislaine, fed up with being inside the manor after a long, wet winter, had saddled her horse and set off, bow in hand, to see if she could shoot some game. The long-suffering Edwin had reluctantly followed his headstrong mistress, warning her repeatedly that outlaws had been spotted in the forest nearby.

She had, of course chosen to ignore him. Since she was hunting the Earl of Chester's game to give to the villagers, God, she was sure, would not interfere. After all, it had not been the villagers who had caused the murrain that had devastated the cattle herds. No one else, least of all the Earl, would provide them with other food.

It had not been until she reached the border that divided her land from the Earl's that Ghislaine had begun to feel uneasy. Even then, she had not heeded her own instincts. Disaster had struck whilst she had been patiently stalking a deer. Just as she had been about to loose an arrow, a large hand had clamped over her mouth and dragged her back towards the cover of the trees.

Instinctively she had bitten hard and kicked backwards, causing her assailant to curse loudly before yanking her up into the air and throwing something dark over her head. Within seconds her wrists and mouth had been bound and she had been dumped unceremoniously into the saddle of a large horse. Her captor had issued a few gruff orders and, since then, had barely uttered a word.

At first she had remained paralysed with fear, not daring to move in case she incurred the wrath of the man behind her. When she had realised that she was not going to die immediately, Ghislaine had come to the conclusion that she was being taken for some other purpose.

It was common enough in such a lawless county for young heiresses to be held captive and married for their lands, although Ghislaine found it hard to believe in her case. Aye, she had lands and a manor, but they were small compared to most. Nor did she look much like the lady of the manor. Mostly Ghislaine resembled one of the peasants, and her captor would have to be very shrewd to have known who she was.

It was a moment before she realised that the horse

had at last come to a halt. None too gently, Ghislaine was pulled down from the saddle and set on her feet. Her eyes blinked rapidly when the covering was yanked from her head.

"If you have any desire to survive the hour, girl, you will not utter a word," a deep voice growled in her ear. Swirling round unsteadily, Ghislaine stared at the man who towered above her. He was tall, very tall, and swathed in a filthy cloak and stained leather hauberk. His thick black hair hung around his shoulders and cold, ice-blue eyes impaled her. Danger seeped from the very depths of his black soul, and in an instant, Ghislaine knew that he was capable of murder.

Satisfied that his captive would not move, he pulled away the gag along with several clumps of her long hair. Her shriek of pain brought his hand over her mouth and she was pulled roughly into his chest once more.

"Hell's teeth, girl," he hissed furiously. "Do you want to die?"

Ghislaine toyed with the idea of biting his hand again but decided against it when she caught sight of the knife close to her throat. When she finally shook her head, he sent her sprawling to the ground.

Indignantly, Ghislaine rose as gracefully as her mud-covered cloak would allow and fixed him with a look of burning hatred.

"Have you always possessed such natural charm," she spat, her dark eyes flashing, "or are you merely practising on me?" Tossing her wild, red-gold hair over her shoulder, Ghislaine lifted her chin defiantly and waited for the death blow. If he was going to kill her, she would prefer it to be quick.

His eyes blazed, but instead of hurling the knife at her as she had expected, he turned to a blond-haired man standing a few yards away. "Are you sure it's her?" he ground out, the muscles in his jaw rigid with control.

When the blond man nodded, her captor rounded on her once more.

"So, Lady de Launay, you do not value your life overmuch?"

He knew her name so it was clear that this had been planned. Closing her eyes in fear, Ghislaine could not even begin to think why he had taken her.

"Oh, but I fear you have made a mistake," she began, her eyes widening. "I am Lady de Launay's maid. Effie."

His eyes narrowed as he assessed her appearance. "Effie is small, plump, blonde and," he added with grim conviction, "pretty. You are none of those."

The words were a deliberate attempt to upset her, but Ghislaine fixed him with a smile. "I am sure that…"

He advanced on her and grabbed her chin between his fingers interrupting her explanation most effectively.

"And I am sure that unless you co-operate, lady, your handsome companion over there will be meeting his maker earlier than he expected."

Ghislaine swivelled her eyes in the direction he nodded to and caught sight of Edwin, his long, thin frame bound and trussed between several armed men. Her eyes returned to her assailant. Pulling her chin from his fingers, Ghislaine glared at him. "Very well," she replied flatly. "What do you want?"

"I want you to behave like a lady, if that is possible." His stinging sarcasm caused her to raise no more than an auburn brow in response. "We travel on to Chester and my men and I wish to enter the city as unobtrusively as possible."

None of this made sense. "Why?" she demanded curiously.

"Because I have a desire to speak with the Earl of Chester, and by bringing him one of his wards I believe it may help him to view my cause in a more positive light."

So, she was to be a hostage. "And if I do not co-operate, you will kill Edwin," she concluded.

The dark-haired outlaw stared at her for a moment before nodding. "I hope you remember that, Lady de Launay," he warned ominously before turning back to the small army of men waiting some yards away.

Despite her brave words, Ghislaine was terrified. Edwin's life depended on her co-operation, but she was not at all sure that the Earl of Chester would look favourably on anyone using her as a hostage. Her tendency to poach his game had angered him greatly, and were it not for the fact that her father had been one of his most loyal and trustworthy vassals, Ghislaine did not doubt for a moment that she would have been confined to the abbey months ago.

Trapping her bottom lip between her teeth, she looked over at Edwin. Her father was no longer alive and their fate now depended on a greedy man who had never bothered to hide his dislike of her.

They reached the pink sandstone walls of Chester late in the afternoon and Ghislaine heaved a sigh tinged with relief and apprehension. Having had several hours to debate the matter, she fervently hoped that the Earl of Chester would save her from this ordeal, but remained uncertain. Nagging doubts crowded her mind. He was her guardian, despite their mutual dislike, but he was not averse to conniving with base outlaws if it meant filling his purse.

Her captor and his blond companion left the others with Edwin in the castle bailey, and accompanied her silently to the great hall. They stopped outside the heavy wooden door, and she barely had time to shake the dust from her dishevelled tunic before it was heaved open. The soft strumming of a lute and raucous laughter melted away as they entered the long, narrow hall which was lit by wall torches and a myriad hissing wax candles.

A huge fire blazed at the far end of the hall and around it clustered five or six of the Earl's favoured barons and some women Ghislaine had never seen before. From the tone of the laughter and the way the women were dressed Ghislaine suspected they were not ladies. The Earl was well-known for his lechery.

The sheer opulence of the place never failed to reduce Ghislaine to awestruck silence. Shadows caught in the candlelight danced on the crimson and gold wall-hangings, lending the room an air of otherworldliness that was far removed from her daily life. It also stank like the midden and Ghislaine held her breath as the stench hit her for the first time.

Anxious to put an end to this frightening ordeal, Ghislaine picked her way carefully through the filthy floor rushes towards the far end of the hall where the Earl was slouched in a large wooden chair, his huge bulk instantly recognisable. Indolently he scratched the ears of a hound sprawled at his feet.

Silence echoed around the tapestry-hung walls as Ghislaine and her two companions faced her guardian. His barons and their consorts whispered quietly and listened whilst she awaited her fate in the suffocating gloom.

The bleary blue eyes of Hugh d'Avranches, Earl of Chester, slid over the three newcomers and then returned once more to the tempting dishes awaiting his pleasure. His puffy white fingers trailed across two platters before his full lips twitched in almost salacious anticipation of the succulent viands.

To the Welsh, Hugh d'Avranches was Hugh the Fat, and to his own, he was Hugh Lupus, the wolf, but none underestimated the shrewd cunning that had set him above all others in the Conqueror's affections. He was King William's favourite nephew and the most powerful man in the north of England. Decisive, underhand and very brutal in his dealings with his vassals, the Earl wore the mantle of his success with arrogance. The county of Cheshire was firmly in his grip and he was determined to wring as many silver marks from the population as he could.

His appetite temporarily sated, Hugh dipped his fingers delicately in the scented hand-bowl and carefully wiped them with almost ritualistic obsession. Waving the food from view, he returned with a sigh to the task in hand.

"So, de Courcy, to what honour do I owe this visit?"

To Ghislaine's amazement, the question was addressed to her scowling captor in most familiar terms.

How on earth did the Earl of Chester know this stinking outlaw? It did occur to her, however, that Hugh Lupus was staring at them with little sign of pleasure.

''I have come to request protection under your law of advowry.'' The low, rich voice was almost a growl and used none of the fine words usually reserved for the Earl.

The Earl appeared to ignore the slight as he heaved himself to his feet before the men, his thumbs hooked into his jewelled belt. A smirk hovered on his grease-spattered lips.

''To what do I owe this happy occurrence?''

De Courcy just scowled more deeply. His smaller companion, however, returned the smile and bowed gracefully, his blond curls falling forward onto his handsome face. ''My name is Arnaud d'Everard, my lord. De Courcy is here to request an audience with you.''

Hugh d'Avranches surveyed them silently for a moment before merely nodding his assent.

D'Everard continued. ''De Courcy has been unjustly accused of a crime and wishes to reside in Cheshire under your protection until he is able to clear his name. As he has been of help to you in the past, he naturally hoped you would be willing to return the favour.'' The blond man's voice was soft and confident and he was clearly no base-born outlaw.

She looked nervously up at the tall man by her side, her brow wrinkling in disgust. The Earl was indeed famous for harbouring all manner of criminals within the county under the auspices of advowry. For a fee, Hugh d'Avranches was always willing to provide a safe haven in one of Cheshire's great forests for outlaws from other counties fleeing the consequences of their wrongdoing. His coffers might be full of silver marks, but the forests were crawling with dangerous outlaws.

Not even the King's men would attempt to cross the county borders to follow a criminal without having the King's seal first, and William was reluctant to interfere in the Earl's domain. No one was safe to ride abroad these days. It was suspected that her father and Peter Staveley had been attacked and killed a few months earlier by one such notorious band. Understandably, the Earl appeared reluctant to deal with criminals effectively since his treasure chests groaned with the fruits of such practices. Any criticism of his regime was dealt with harshly.

Ghislaine's mouth was as dry as dust and she gratefully picked up a goblet of wine offered to her by the page at the Earl's bidding. Her stomach, ever unaware of the sensitive situation, began to make loud gurgling noises. Her cheeks fired in embarrassment but, if anyone heard, nothing was said.

''And what is this crime?'' Hugh d'Avranches' voice held little of his customary boredom.

De Courcy's scowl deepened if that was possible. ''The murder of a noble woman. One Margaret Staveley.''

The harsh gruff voice echoed in Ghislaine's ears. Margaret was dead and the man accused of her murder was standing beside her.

Ghislaine stared at de Courcy in silence, horror and disbelief echoing in her mind. The healthy glow from her freckled face paled as she watched her friend's murderer demanding help from Hugh d'Avranches. No trace of remorse had softened his dark, stubbly face. She must have made some small noise, for once again, Ghislaine found those glittering eyes spear her for no more than a few seconds before returning to stare at the Earl.

"Margaret Staveley was the widow of Peter. She lived to the east of the Macclesfield Hundred, if I have the right of it?" The Earl's voice was slow and speculative "What business had you in that area?"

De Courcy's expression had not changed. "I had recently purchased a manor about half a day's ride from Staveley." The tone was weary and his irritation at the questioning was apparent to all.

"I had no knowledge of this," replied the Earl in such a way as to convince Ghislaine that he had indeed been privy to this fact. De Courcy's snort of disbelief earned him no more than a raised eyebrow from his questioner. Whoever this man was, thought Ghislaine, he had to be of some consequence, for Hugh d'Avranches was not normally so equable when faced with such appalling manners. He had shifted position slightly so that his arms were folded across his broad chest, and his strong legs planted wide apart. When he lifted his head a little, Ghislaine could see his blue eyes narrowed in anger.

The smaller man at de Courcy's side, clearly sensing his companion's unease, stepped into the breach.

"He purchased the manor last year from Bigot de Loges. My friend's services have been much in demand and he had a desire to settle. He took up residence a few weeks after Yuletide and my lord and I went to pay the lady a…courtesy visit a few days ago. When we left, she was in good health.

"However, it would seem that the lady and her people were killed in an unprovoked attack not long after our departure and we stand accused of her murder. No witnesses survived," he added quietly. "The lady's brother, Henry Dettingham, is demanding our execution. Dettingham managed to seize my lord's manor in our absence and has sworn revenge."

Light dawned in Ghislaine's mind. De Courcy was a mercenary. Cold seeped through her body. Margaret had been butchered by a mercenary. She scanned the harsh planes of his dark face, but found no trace of softness there. He would show no mercy to a woman, she was sure. What manner of man would kill someone as gentle and sweet as Margaret?

A vision of the pretty Margaret came to her mind. She had been married to Ghislaine's brother, Richard, for little more than a year. Whilst Richard was involved with the campaigns against the Welsh, Ghislaine and Margaret had struck up an unlikely friendship. Margaret was gentle and sweet, and often shocked at Ghislaine's tomboyish adventures with Edwin. But she had been loyal to her new family and had provided Ghislaine with the female companionship she needed.

The shock of Richard's death had forged an even closer friendship. Small and slender, her ash blonde hair and honest blue eyes had attracted many young suitors. That she had chosen a quiet, steady widower of middling years had surprised several of her friends except for Ghislaine. Peter Staveley had been a close companion of her father's and she had known him to be a gentle, wise and essentially lonely man who needed a young wife and family on whom to bestow his hidden well of affection and his wealth. And now they were both dead.

"And your men?" questioned the Earl, a thoughtful look on his face. Ghislaine was reminded of a hawk hovering over its prey. A very fat hawk.

"Twenty survived the subsequent attack by her brother on my manor and await my sign." De Courcy's toneless voice sent shivers down her back.

The Earl inhaled deeply through his nose and pushed back his silver-blond hair. "Pray explain the need for a sign, de Courcy." The blue eyes had narrowed as they scanned the back of the hall before returning to the men before him.

Before her captor could answer, Ghislaine turned to him. Propelled by fury and perhaps a surfeit of wine, she determined to find out about Margaret. "Why?" she demanded hoarsely. "Why did you kill her?"

All eyes in the hall turned now to her. Behind her, some of the women gasped at her effrontery. Women did not interfere in men's business. She could feel the whole hall hold its collective breath as they waited for the axe to fall.

Guy de Courcy turned once more to his hostage. Her dark eyes spat anger and condemnation, her whole body demanding that he respond to her question. Despite his tiredness and irritation, he had to admit to a small amount of admiration for the girl. Few men dared what she had.

"I committed no crime," he replied simply, his blue eyes boring into her.

His words only fuelled her ire. "Then why are you here?"

He gave her a hard, soul-searching stare. "My business is with the Earl of Chester.'' His cold words hung in the air between them until destroyed by the coarse laughter of Hugh d'Avranches.

''Aye. You have the right of it,'' he growled. ''I had not recognised you, my Lady de Launay.'' His cold eyes raked her dishevelled, dirty clothes and tangled hair. ''I had thought that you might have been one of de Courcy's camp followers.''

Such sarcasm only fired Ghislaine's cheeks and caused her chin to lift a little. From the corner of her eye, she saw Guy de Courcy's jaw tighten in anger. ''But since de Courcy seems to have the measure of you it brings to mind your purpose here.'' Although he was staring at Ghislaine, the words were clearly addressed to the mercenary.

''Lady de Launay is here to…persuade you to provide us with your protection.''

A slow smile formed on Hugh d'Avranches' generous lips. ''And what benefits would I receive in return for my protection?''

De Courcy frowned. ''I have my usual skills at your disposal for the forty days.''

''I believe your skills to be most unusual,'' came the Earl's reply. ''But I regret that forty days of knight's service is perhaps not quite what I had in mind.''

De Courcy's dark head shot up, but Arnaud d'Everard's arm stayed him. ''And what do you have in mind, my lord?''

The other man's softer, more co-operative tone seemed to please the Earl. ''The wars with the Welsh have drained many of my normal resources of late. I find that sixty days' service may be more acceptable.

In addition to one hundred marks of silver, should I accept.''

Hugh d'Avranches and Guy de Courcy eyed each other with dislike, tempered with something akin to respect. It would pay neither to underestimate the other.

De Courcy's brusque nod indicated his acceptance of the terms. ''I have a demand of my own.'' The words were received in silence.

''If I and my men are to provide sixty days' service in full combat, it will be necessary to accommodate us in better surroundings than Macclesfield forest. We need somewhere to live and train, preferably in a quiet area with few neighbours. The de Launay manor of Chapmonswiche is suitable for our needs. The one hundred marks will be forthcoming for as long as your full protection is required. When I clear my name, I shall quit the de Launay manor and return to my own.''

Hugh drew a deep breath as he pondered this latest demand. Ghislaine felt herself turn rigid. He could not turn her home over to this criminal.

''Which brings me back to Lady de Launay.'' Hugh's eyes slid once more over Ghislaine with barely concealed scorn. ''What role does she play in this?''

''She ensures your goodwill, my Lord. I am sure that you have no desire to see her come to harm.'' The blond eyebrows raised in question.

The Earl looked unimpressed by this latest threat. ''And if I do not agree to protect you from the King's men or Dettingham?''

''My men are scattered throughout the city awaiting

my signal should you decide against me, then they will set fire to key buildings.''

She was sure it was a lie, but the hand gripping her arm gave it a painful squeeze. Ghislaine did not need to be reminded about Edwin.

The Earl drew a deep breath as he pondered this proposition. His fingers stroked at his stubbly jowls. ''Let me think on the matter whilst you share bread and wine.'' He beckoned to the servants who hurried to do his bidding. There were no laggards in the castle of Chester.

Guy de Courcy, satisfied that the Earl would accede to his request in the end, relaxed his scowl and the grip on Ghislaine's arm. When they mounted the dais, Ghislaine found herself seated in between her captors. Was she now to sit by the man who had killed her friend and exchange pleasantries?

''Is it your custom to butcher innocent women?'' she began, a fire blazing within. She would not let Margaret die without a fight. Not for one moment did she believe his story of innocence. After all, only guilty men run.

The two eyed each other with intense dislike. Her words, de Courcy found, had destroyed any appetite he might have had. Taking a deep draught of the soft red wine, he glared at her with his customary frown. This was not the moment for a shrewish red-haired wench to start questioning him. Her dark eyes were smouldering with loathing.

''I take it, then, that as your father is no longer alive you did batter him to death with your tongue? My sympathies lie entirely with him.''

The sheer audacity of the man was breathtaking and

left her, for once, speechless. Ghislaine opened her mouth and then closed it quickly, realising what he was about.

"Your pretty speeches, sir, together with that natural charm you possess, will ensure your success in the court here. You will no doubt find yourself most at home." The silence about her should have been clear warning that she really was overstepping the mark, but Ghislaine could only think of Margaret.

"Murderers, thieves and outlaws inhabit the land in great numbers. I am sure that you will find a suitable stone to crawl under."

A large, tanned hand raked the black locks before slamming down onto the table. "Unless you are keen to join your father, wench, I suggest you hold your tongue."

Guy's head was throbbing and he was in dire need of sleep. Most girls usually cowered away from his scowls in terror. Why this one had to choose now to assault him with her tongue was beyond his reasoning. It was becoming clear to him that the dampness that abounded in this part of the country addled a body's wits. He took another gulp of the wine. At least that was palatable.

Help came from an unexpected source. "You must forgive the Lady de Launay, sir. She is clearly overset by the news of Margaret Staveley's death." A thin, grey-haired woman sitting to the far side of Hugh leaned forward to address him.

De Courcy's eyes glanced sideways, noting the curl of Ghislaine's lips at these words and gulped another goblet of wine down. His curt nod was the only indication that he had actually heard her.

"Perhaps," the woman continued smoothly, "if you were to explain the circumstances, it would be easier for us to understand?"

De Courcy suddenly jerked his head towards the unknown woman and stared at her. Ghislaine could not help feeling that her captor knew this woman, although he gave no clear sign of doing so. "I need explain myself to no woman," he growled, giving her a look of such distaste that even Ghislaine felt herself recoil.

The woman inclined her head in acceptance of his outburst, but did not seem at all surprised or even upset by the words. Ghislaine glared at him in outrage.

"There is, after all, little to explain." His voice was cold and irritable once more. "I am accused of the woman's murder. I know aught else save that I have been forced to forfeit my own manor and have lost ten of my men." He sank back into a scowl.

Hugh's eyes flickered carefully between the woman and de Courcy as he listened to this exchange. "It may be that we can come to an amicable agreement that would benefit both of us." His cold eyes rested on Ghislaine for a moment before returning to de Courcy.

De Courcy stared at the Earl, his distrust of the man barely concealed. Ghislaine rather thought for a moment that he wanted to throw the goblet of wine over him. D'Everard, however, seemed to have sensed that this was not the time to antagonise him.

"We are keen to hear your suggestions, my lord."

D'Avranches inclined his jowly face towards his ward, regarding her blandly with his calculating eyes. Ghislaine shivered a little under his assessing stare.

The man always got what he wanted, caring not a whit if it were by fair means or foul.

"I think," Hugh drawled lazily, "that we require more privacy for this discussion." His eyes turned to de Courcy, who inclined his dark head slightly in deference to the Earl's wishes.

"I believe, Helene, that my ward would benefit from a view of the river to restore her temper and clear her mind." He addressed the grey-haired woman who nodded silently.

As she rose from the bench, Ghislaine glanced at her dark foe. His head was lowered over his wine and his broad shoulders slumped forward as if in complete exhaustion. Suddenly, aware that her hostile eyes were on him, he looked up. For a fraction of a second, those summer-blue eyes compelled her to remain where she was, and then released her when he had taken his fill. Hatred flooded through her and she was glad that he was suffering. Her desire to exit with dignity however, was foiled by her foot catching in some rushes near the dais and she was forced to leave with a flush to her cheeks.

She had a bad feeling that Hugh d'Avranches was about to wreak his revenge on her.

Chapter Two

As they stood outside the wooden doors, Ghislaine turned to Helene. The words she would have spoken died in her mouth as she saw that a deathly pallor had enveloped the woman.

"Is there aught I can do?" Ghislaine took Helene by the shoulders as the lady closed her eyes. She shook her head silently while Ghislaine tried to loosen her kirtle a little. Her bones felt so thin and frail in her strong fingers that Ghislaine feared she would shatter if she held her much longer. "Some wine?" she whispered urgently.

"Nay. It will pass in a moment. Thank you, Ghislaine." Slowly the colour began to return to Helene's soft skin, and much to Ghislaine's relief, a smile touched her lips. "I think some air might help," she whispered, her hand clutching at Ghislaine's sleeve.

Nodding in agreement, Ghislaine gently steered Helene up the stone steps to the top of the keep.

"Do I know you?" she asked the woman curiously as they paused before the last few steps. Few strangers would have used her first name.

"No," came the breathless reply. "But I have followed your escapades about Cheshire with great interest," she added, eyeing the remaining steps with determination. Smiling, the woman turned the most expressive brown eyes on Ghislaine that she had ever seen. "My name is Helene du Beauregard. I have not met you before although I did know your mother." The doubtful look on Ghislaine's face caused her to shrug her thin shoulders delicately. "It was some time ago, but I am sorry for your loss. She was a most exceptional woman."

Ghislaine nodded curtly in acceptance, and breathed in the salty air as they passed through the door of the keep. The two guards who were lounging against the keep wall eyed them with half-interested curiosity before returning to their conversation. Ignoring them, Ghislaine and Helene turned to look at the view. From a vantage point normally monopolised by the soldiers, the women took deep gulps of the air blowing in from the Welsh border.

The last rays of the afternoon sun flitted across the countryside beyond the River Dee that meandered around the ancient city. As Ghislaine stared across the river towards Wales, night clouds gathered on the distant horizon. Thoughts of her brother, Richard, squeezed her heart. He had died fighting the Welsh little more than a year ago, and still she missed him. So many good men had died in those wild hills.

Ghislaine turned back to Helene. The woman was blue with the cold, for her fashionable tunic was made only for the warmth of the indoor fires. Draping her own cloak over Helene's thin shoulders, Ghislaine shivered a little. Her companion gripped her forearm once more and gave it a squeeze in gratitude.

"You are much like your mother in your attention of people," she said quietly, her eyes searching Ghislaine's freckled face.

Her words caused Ghislaine to look sharply at her. "I am nothing like her." Had her father not said as much for the last seven years? Had he not constantly said how much he regretted that she was not more like her mother?

Helene shook her head. "In looks and body, no. But she took care of people, no matter what others thought."

"How did you know her?" Ghislaine asked curiously

For a moment, Helene's eyes trailed over the palisade and beyond, staring almost sightlessly into the distance. Lost in her own thoughts, the older woman pulled the heavy cloak more tightly around her, as if it could somehow protect her from the memories.

"Did you know her well?" Ghislaine prompted, her interest stirred. Above all things her mother had loved people. She had often defied her father to take care of ailing peasants and servants, lavishing attention and her gentle spirits upon them. They had loved her in return. And yet her father had refused to remember that side of her. He had worshipped her memory, albeit a false one.

"Aye. She once attended me for an ailment that would not be cured. It took a long time and we learned much of each other then." She said no more, although Ghislaine waited for her to continue.

"My father did not like her to travel away from the

manor,'' she added, hoping that this would encourage Helene to continue.

"Nay," she said rather curtly. "He did not." Her lips closed tightly and it was clear that she would offer no more than that, at least for the time being. "Do you have her healing skills?"

Ghislaine shrugged her shoulders lightly. "Some, but I fear I have not inherited her gentleness." Her words were spoken with such feeling that Helene laughed gently.

"You have inherited her courage, though. And from what I have heard of you over these last few years, you have needed it to deal with that irksome father of yours."

Few people had spoken so truly of her father since his death that the irreverence of her statement caused Ghislaine's mouth to lift at the corners. "Aye. I fear that I have inherited much of his temper, too. It is an affliction that caused him much sorrow."

The laughter that they shared for a moment or two was halted by a sudden gust of wind that buffeted them mercilessly. Standing closer together for protection and warmth, Ghislaine found herself beginning to warm to this woman, despite having known her for a short while. At least she did not criticise nor did she condemn. She also displayed a sense of humour that was sadly lacking in most worthy and pious ladies of the court.

Ghislaine appraised the woman once again. Tall and thin, Helene du Beauregard still retained much of what must have been a great beauty. Her dark eyes were fringed with thick, black lashes whilst her abundant hair had turned grey. Fine lines creased her eyes and her soft pink skin. Ghislaine judged her to be in her forties, a great age for a woman of the court. Her speech and manners were both gentle and confident, not at all what one would have expected from one of Hugh d'Avranches's court followers.

"Do you live in Chester?" The question was direct and pointed.

A glimmer of a smile touched Helene's lips at the younger girl's lack of guile. "Nay. My manor lies half a day's ride to the south-east of Chester. I am come to settle a dispute over boundaries."

A common enough problem for anyone. Ghislaine visibly relaxed a little. "Then you do not live far from Chapmonswiche?"

Helene shook her head. "I live at Omberleigh. It is only a small manor with a few fields and a village, but it is well enough for my needs. A small company of guards protects us from any possible attack, and these days I am glad of the security."

"And your husband?" Ghislaine spoke without thinking, but wished she had said nothing at all as a look of pain crossed Helene's face.

"My husband is dead," came her toneless reply.

"I am sorry," she replied quietly. When would she learn not to open her mouth without thinking?

Helene reached out for her hand and patted it gently. "Do not concern yourself, Ghislaine. I am content now."

Her heartfelt sigh caused Helene to turn her head up to Ghislaine, for the girl was a good head taller than she. "I cannot believe that Margaret is dead."

"Did you know her well?" Helene asked solicitously, her eyes watching Ghislaine carefully.

She nodded slowly, pushing back some loose strands of hair. "Margaret was the only friend I had, really. She was married briefly to my brother, and when he died, she married my father's friend, Peter. How could someone as sweet and gentle as Margaret deserve such a fate?" she asked angrily. "She never did aught but good and look what happened. Both husbands die and she is murdered. There is no justice." She turned to blink away the tears.

Helene looked at Ghislaine's stiff back with sympathy and set her arm around her shoulder for comfort. "How old are you, Ghislaine?" she asked after a minute.

"Nineteen summers," came the muffled reply.

"Whatever Hugh decides," Helene began gently, "you must obey him, for his anger can be ruthless." Her dark eyes scanned Ghislaine's worried countenance. "It will go badly for your people if you do not."

Ghislaine's shoulders drooped at the mention of her villagers. "Aye, I know it. But the thought of spending the rest of my days either shut up in a convent or married off to some loathsome brute does not offer much hope."

Helene shrugged her shoulders. "Few of us have more choice than that. And," she paused to choose her words carefully, "not all men are so hard to bear." The light teasing of her words made Ghislaine's lips reluctantly turn upwards. "Or is there some other reason?"

"What do you mean?" Ghislaine's cheeks blushed suddenly. The question was clear, but she did not know how far she could trust this woman. "If you mean my manservant, Edwin, I have known him these past ten summers,'' she began slowly. ''He taught me how to shoot an arrow, to fish, to ride. He even showed me how to use a knife.'' Her eyes glanced up at Helene, their innocence shining. ''Edwin has saved me from death a thousand times and I have mended his wounds, revived him from the effects of too much ale and consoled the women he has cast aside. There is no more to it than that.'' Ghislaine could have said that there was, in fact, a great deal more to their friendship, but she was not so sure that Helene would have viewed their other activities with that humorous gleam in her eye. Not every Norman lady would consider the feeding of starving English folk a suitable activity for one of her own class.

Helene regarded her a little sceptically, for stories of her scrapes with the Englishman abounded the county. The man was reputedly handsome. And yet the girl seemed to be telling the truth. ''Nay, I did not mean Edwin. I had thought you interested in another. Perhaps I was mistaken.''

Ghislaine's cheeks coloured even more. ''There is no other,'' she denied with such vehemence that Helene knew she had hit on the truth.

Warming to the idea of discovering just who it was that Ghislaine favoured, Helene began to list the candidates she knew. ''Most are loud-mouthed, vulgar louts, as you intimated,'' she began. ''And of the rest, most are married. Robert of Montalt is probably too old and ugly; Gerard de Rospernaise shows more interest in his squires; Cadimane de Soubeyron might possibly turn the head of a girl like you, although his lack of height might be a problem.'' Helene eyed

Ghislaine slyly to see if she was getting close. "Walter de Belleme is handsome, tall and personable. He is a distinct possibility."

Ghislaine turned almost puce with embarrassment. "I hardly know him. He has been most kind to me, but beyond that, he has been very…circumspect."

Helene du Beauregard frowned. "Walter keeps some strange company, and I think it unlikely that any knight will counter the Earl's wishes," she said gently. "I fear that you will have to face your future alone. It might not be so bad." Her beautiful face saddened a little. "Women must submit to the will of their father or their lord, but you might be able to find some solace in your home or your children. Sometimes an affection can grow in time…" The expression on her face became distant again. Intrigued, Ghislaine could not stop the questions that crowded her mind. "Did you have a choice?"

The question caused Helene to pause for a moment, as if thinking back to that time so many years ago. "Aye. I had a choice. Marriage or the convent. For me it was no choice at all, though. The knight my father had chosen was handsome and young. I was glad to accept him."

"And were you happy?" Ghislaine watched the older woman as she pulled the cloak closer to her thin body. Time seemed to have been kind to her, although there was an aura of loneliness about her that did not leave.

Again her shoulders shrugged casually. "Of a fashion. I had children, a home. My husband…provided well." Despite the brightness of her words, Ghislaine detected a note of sadness. "The convent would not have suited me.'' Her lips smiled at these words as if she had said something that amused her privately. ''Do you like children?'' she asked suddenly, her dark eyes intent on Ghislaine.

''A-aye,'' stammered Ghislaine, somewhat taken aback by so direct a question. ''I would like children of my own, God willing.''

Her answer seemed to satisfy the woman, so Ghislaine took a chance. Moving over to the edge of the keep wall, Ghislaine's eyes turned to the busy port a little way up the river. Ships from all parts of the world came to dock at Chester, bringing spices, cloth, wine, livestock, furs and many other goods that rich people would pay dearly for. She watched the bustle of activity as a large ship was unloading its cargo.

''My father often used to say that I should have been born a boy, and sometimes I think he was right.'' She breathed in the soft, salty air slowly, as if savouring this moment of freedom. ''Sometimes I used to wish I could fight in the wars or sail across the water.'' Her eyes remained wistfully on the port. She was sure that even the understanding Helene de Beauregard would be shocked at such an admission. ''I wanted to be free to do whatever I wanted, like Richard. And yet, sometimes, I wonder what it would be like to have a child…'' Ghislaine's voice trailed off into embarrassed silence.

There was no censure in Helene's voice. ''You think no differently from many others, my dear. Unfortunately we cannot do what we like, but sometimes we can try to make the best of what we have.''

Helene had come to stand by her side and had placed a hand on Ghislaine's cold arm. ''Come. I think that the Earl has probably had time enough with de Courcy, and we are in great need of the fire.''

Ghislaine nodded, a vision of de Courcy's harsh, dark, scowling face rushing oddly before her. "I can only hope that he has rid himself of that murdering barbarian, but I fear that will prove to be a vain hope.'' A thought struck her. "Do you know of him?''

Helene sighed. "De Courcy is well known for his skills on the battlefield and I believe his tactics have outwitted many of William's more persistent opponents. I suspect that Hugh would be more than happy to hire his services.'' She looked at Ghislaine speculatively. "He is also rumoured to be handsome underneath all that hair.'' The words were spoken with a certain confidence.

Ghislaine gave a most unladylike snort. "He is a devil. Death would be too good a price for Margaret's murder.'' Her anger spilled from her as she stalked towards the steps.

As Ghislaine descended the steep stone stairway, she was thinking about her future. The convent would at least offer a form of peace and perhaps she could adjust to such a life. A deep shudder went through her body, for the cold and fear had taken its toll. If this barbarian had not decided he wanted her manor, her life would not have had to change. Life was just not fair.

Suddenly she stopped. Walter! She had forgotten about Walter! She conjured up his handsome face in her mind and the thought made her smile. His blond hair was the envy of many of the Norman ladies, but she liked his smile and the way his grey eyes made her feel special. He had been the only one who did not make her feel like a clumsy carthorse. Together they had laughed and talked about a million things, and the feelings she felt for him had grown with the months.

She remembered how her father had disapproved of their friendship to begin with, but Walter had somehow brought him round and became a frequent visitor to the estate. Since the death of his first wife, Walter had become lonely and had often expressed his appreciation of friendship with a woman who did not simper and giggle. Ghislaine had been impressed by his modest courage, for he had continued to hunt there at great personal risk despite the knowledge that the murderous outlaw, Thomas Bollyngton, had made the forest his domain.

Although nothing had been said, she could tell by the way he looked at her that his feelings were engaged. It was only a matter of time before Walter declared himself. Since her father's death, though, the impropriety of him visiting an unmarried girl had prevented him from seeing her much. She had missed him.

When Walter found out what had happened he would be sure to speak out. And yet, despite her belief in the depth of his feelings, Helene du Beauregard's words rang in her ears. Few would ever dispute the wishes of the Earl of Chester. Would Walter? A vague feeling of doubt began to float around her mind as she slowed her steps. He had always been quick to do his bidding, it was true. And yet, he would not abandon her. Nay, he would not.

Fortified by her own conviction, Ghislaine reached the foot of the steps in a more buoyant mood and awaited the slower arrival of Helene du Beauregard with a cheerful smile.

As soon as they entered the hall Ghislaine was aware of the highly charged atmosphere. Something had happened to increase the tension. All eyes were on her as she made her way to the dais.

The mercenary was no longer sitting at the table but was pacing before the fire, his expression even more thunderous than before. He was the very epitome of evil, she thought. He tosssed back another goblet of wine before suddenly hurling it across the floor in a violet temper. Ghislaine gulped. Hugh was still reclining regally in his chair, a raised eyebrow the only outward sign that he had heard de Courcy's outburst. D'Everard just stared at her.

"Ah, Ghislaine," drawled Hugh. "I am pleased you have returned." Ghislaine doubted that, but his words had a dramatic impact on de Courcy. He whirled round to face her, advancing towards the dais in huge strides. Had she not been so afeared, she would have stepped back, but Ghislaine found herself rooted to the spot.

"So you would trade this wench for my services?" De Courcy spat his words out in disgust, his blue eyes staring at her dishevelled, wind-blown appearance with barely concealed scorn.

Ghislaine stiffened in shock. "What do you mean 'trade'?" Her voice was no more than a whisper.

"I have decided that you cannot live at Chapmonswiche with an army of men, and I do not think the convent is the place for you, my lady." The Earl eyed her with an indifferent stare. "Your interests would be better served elsewhere. You will marry de Courcy."

The words penetrated her mind and Ghislaine was

left speechless for a moment. De Courcy looked as if he wished to kill her.

"I choose the convent," she began, her voice trembling. It was very hard to swallow the terror that seemed to be leaping from her throat. De Courcy stilled for a brief second, staring at her with cold blue eyes. Did she detect relief there?

"Perhaps I did not make myself clear," Hugh began slowly. "You will marry de Courcy on the morrow. Your servants are to serve your husband. I have no doubt you will see the advantage of such an alliance." The threat behind his words were apparent to all.

Summoning every ounce of courage, Ghislaine lifted her head in defiance. "You cannot marry me to a murderer. 'Tis not right in the eyes of God. I demand to go to the convent."

Hugh stared back at her, a heavy sigh lifting his chest. "On the morrow, my lady. Or your people will be put to death. Should you and de Courcy find your interests, shall we say, at odds, then I feel certain that you will manage to come to some suitable arrangement." There was a cold gleam in his eyes.

The candles swam about her as Ghislaine tried to focus on the one unchanging thing in the hall. The anger shining from the eyes of Guy de Courcy. At least they were agreed on one thing. A heavy fist smashed down onto the table, causing her to jump from her bemused state.

"She is not willing and neither am I."

"Neither of you has a choice. You need my protection and the lady needs a husband. I am sure you will both see the advantages of such a match by the morning." Hugh d'Avranches was pleased with his decision. He waved to the servant and a goblet of wine was placed in her cold hand.

''A toast to your future.''

Ghislaine's goblet fell to the floor and the red wine ebbed unnoticed into the midden round her feet.

Chapter Three

The cold morning light that stole through the cracks in the meagre shutters broke Ghislaine's fitful sleep. Neither the heap of fur skins nor the poor fire in the corner of her tiny dormitory could dispel the blistering chill of the priory from seeping through her bones. The corridors beyond her wooden door echoed with the chanting of the monks at matins. She felt empty. Cold and empty.

She rose quickly and pulled a heavy skin over her thin shift, hastily remembering to sketch the outline of a cross before the crucifix on the wall. Her bare feet were freezing as she opened the shutters which looked out over the courtyard. It too was empty in the half-gloom of the winter morning. What had she expected to find, she wondered? That Walter would be waiting for her? Or that Edwin had escaped his chains from Chester castle and come to rescue her?

She absently rubbed her hands over her arms as she looked up at the grey, cheerless sky. No doubt a fitting start to this marriage, she thought bitterly. Slamming the shutters in frustration, Ghislaine whirled round and proceeded to pace the short length of her cell. With her mind searching for the most sensible course of action, Ghislaine failed to notice how cold she had grown. It was not until a bitter gust of wind blew open the unsecured shutters and all but put out the poor fire that an idea formed.

Her feet and ankles had turned an ugly, mottled blue, whereas her long fingers were almost white. She remembered then that the priory had the rather unenviable reputation of having to accommodate one or two unsuspecting guests in the graveyard rather than in its spartan cells during the harsher months. Aye, she grinned. Death would be a very expedient remedy for this marriage. Or at least the appearance of her imminent demise. It was possible that the Earl would not insist on the marriage if he thought she was too ill.

The thought of ruining the plans of her murderous bridegroom spurred Ghislaine into action. The fire was doused down, the shutters pulled wide open and the skins heaped in a pile on the floor by the bed. All she had to do now was wait until she was discovered. Hopefully she would be a good shade of blue all over by then.

Easing her body under the thin blanket, Ghislaine soon began to shiver quite uncontrollably. A harsh, dark, unbarbered face made its unwelcome appearance in her mind, the blue eyes staring at her knowingly. She swallowed hard. Marriage to such a monster was sickening. He had murdered Margaret. And yet unbidden she remembered, too, the anger in his eyes when she had asked him why he had killed Margaret.

When their betrothal had been announced, all but the couple concerned drank to the forthcoming mar-

riage. In fact, she reminded herself, they had both ignored each other completely, their dislike of each other
plain for all to see. De Courcy had not bothered to
feign interest in her, and that, at least, was honest. He
had drunk himself into a sotted heap with his blond
companion, and as far as she was aware, he would
have remained on the stinking rushes all night. She
wrinkled her nose in disgust. The man was worse than
an animal.

Sweet Lord, the cold was truly freezing her to death.
It had been Helene's suggestion to bed in the priory
and she had agreed readily. Nothing would have induced her to spend the night on the Earl of Chester's
rushes. The old priory of St Werburgh had been built
in the north western corner of the city, offering respite
to travellers, merchants and visitors alike. The accom-
modation was spartan but clean, each tiny cell boasting no more than a pallet and a fire. The peace of the
place had finally allowed her some sleep, despite her
tortured dreams.

Walter had not appeared and yet as one of the Earl's
close confidants it was a distinct possibility that he
would arrive in time. She pulled the icy blanket
tighter. If she could at least delay the marriage until
Walter could devise a better plan, that would be
enough. He was very adept at shrewd thinking, and at
times she had admonished herself for considering him
a little too clever. Well, he would need all his skill
now.

Ghislaine's breath was icy white in the freezing dormitory before Helene came to find her.

''Ghislaine! What ails you?'' Helene took one look

at her before turning to slam the shutters to and hurriedly calling for her maid.

Ghislaine was now so cold that in truth she feared that she might die after all. It would be a poor joke, she thought ruefully. Her body had ceased to feel anything and her chest felt heavy and sore. Speech was nigh on impossible with her mouth frozen.

Helene and her maid worked swiftly. The fire was rekindled and coaxed into giving off some heat whilst more skins were ordered to put on the pallet. Helene chaffed her numb feet, whilst the maid went in search of hot water.

"Can you talk now?" Helene whispered urgently, peering anxiously over Ghislaine's blue-tinged face. "Do you feel any warmer?"

The woman's concern was so obviously genuine that Ghislaine felt a pang of remorse for her dissembling. She would make it up to her later, she vowed. "Nay," came the croaked reply. "I cannot move." That at least was true.

"Then I must send a message to the Earl. The marriage cannot take place today," Helene responded briskly and called one of the monks who was hovering outside the door. He was despatched with all haste and Ghislaine knew a profound sense of relief as the door closed.

Helene du Beauregard's dark eyes studied her for a few minutes. Ghislaine's heart contracted. Did she suspect her?

"If I were your mother, I would put you in a hot tub. 'Tis the only remedy other than a man in your bed that I can think of."

Ghislaine's eyes snapped open at such plain speaking. "I...I think I would prefer a bath," she stammered.

"Very wise," came the dry retort.

The hot water was a welcome remedy that returned Ghislaine to a more normal colour. It was so pleasant just wallowing in a herb-scented tub, so relaxing, that Ghislaine almost forgot her perfidy. Once she was pronounced warm enough, she was dried and reclothed in a thick monk's robe and returned to her warmed bed. The spiced wine heated her gently from within, and Ghislaine began to float away in a haze of drowsiness for a moment or two.

Her peace was interrupted by a loud rap at the door. Stifling her irritation, Helene opened the door and disappeared outside for a moment. The urgent whispering caused Ghislaine to prick up her ears for it was clear that something was amiss.

"Ghislaine," came Helene's entreaty. "You must awake." A stiff hand shook her gently until her eyes opened warily.

"It would seem that your bridegroom is more eager than he appeared last night. His men surround the priory and he is demanding to see you. He fears a trick, no doubt." The older woman's face looked pinched and tired as she smoothed back the wayward curls from Ghislaine's face. "I have sent a message that you are too ill to see him, but I doubt that will delay him for long."

The fear of having to face de Courcy caused her heart to beat more rapidly. Her throat constricted and her chest began to heave. Such a murderous barbarian would not enter these holy walls, she told herself rapidly in an attempt to calm down. He was but a man and she was safe here, wasn't she? The answer to her question was brought by the sound of heavy steps thudding along the stone corridor and doors being thrust open. A loud curse made her heart slam against her ribs. Sweet Lord, he had actually come for her.

"Don't let him in," she croaked to the scandalised Helene. "I cannot see him yet. Tell him…tell him I will see him on the morrow…" The words died in her throat as the door to her cell was slammed open and de Courcy pushed through the doorway. He seemed almost to fill the room, his filthy, dark appearance in stark contrast with the plain white of her chaste cell. His face was still scowling as his eyes rested on the huddled figure in the narrow bed.

"What trickery is this, lady?" His cold eyes stared at the outraged Helene who had pushed herself between him and the object of his anger. Ghislaine was almost certain, however, that the animosity in de Courcy's eyes was fixed more on Helene than herself and wondered what lay at the root of it. As far as she knew, they were strangers to each other. Yet there was something in the air between them.

"There is no trickery, my lord, save what goes on in your mind." Helene's tone was sharp but controlled. "The girl is half-frozen to death and I doubt that the marriage will be completed this day. She has taken a healing draught that will speed her recovery but rest and quiet are necessary."

Guy de Courcy ignored her pointed glance at the open door and walked over to Ghislaine's pallet. His very presence filled her with fear and she had the notion that without a lot of encouragement, she could vomit. At his next words, she almost did.

"You will be in the chapel directly, lady, or I shall see the priory burned and your people exiled at the very least."

To Ghislaine's ears, his threat sounded very ready but she could not forget Margaret.

"I have one question to ask you before I agree," she managed. "If you deny murdering Margaret Staveley, then why is your name linked with hers?"

He had not taken those piercing blue eyes from her pale face and they bore into her silently.

"I wished to marry her, but the lady was not…willing."

Ghislaine stared at him totally at a loss for words. How could such a wretch as this think of marrying a woman as delicate and lovely as Margaret? It made no sense, but looking at him, she doubted whether that was necessary. Somewhere, deep in her mind, she wondered if anyone did not obey him. Her hopes of Walter rescuing her faded in the face of his odious threats. Her head nodded almost imperceptibly as she forced back the anger and the tears of frustration.

"It pleases me to see you can be so biddable, lady. I will await you in the chapel directly." The weary tone in his voice was almost her undoing, but Helene stepped in front of him as he turned to leave.

"So an innocent girl is to be dragged from her sick bed to stand at the altar with an outlaw who stinks of the midden. I had not realised the de Courcys' honour was sunk so low."

Her stinging retort caused de Courcy to whirl round to face her. "And what do you know of the de Courcys' honour, madam?"

"Enough to know that you bring shame to the very

name.'' Helene du Beauregard fairly bristled with anger as she eyed him haughtily, her thin hands placed aggressively on her hips.

Her reply caused him to still fleetingly. ''Then it is as well that my parents are dead.'' He turned swiftly on his heels and left the cell, leaving Helene staring after him. After a moment she turned slowly to Ghislaine who was unmoving on the bed.

''Your bridegroom is eager indeed, my Lady de Launay. It would appear that Hugh Lupus must have been giving him a glowing account of your accomplishments.''

Ghislaine groaned into the hard bolster. ''He was probably exaggerating the extent of my wealth.'' Her voice was low and husky ''No doubt he is glad to be rid of me.'' Burying her face in the bolster, Ghislaine prayed hard that when she lifted her head, she would be back at her own manor and that this was naught but a terrible dream. Opening her eyes she found nothing changed except for the expression on Helene's face. Gone was the light-hearted amusement, and instead Ghislaine could only see sympathy and concern.

''I will do it,'' she whispered quietly. ''I have no wish for anyone to die on my account.''

Helene nodded her head and helped her out of her pallet.

The small, white-washed chapel was empty save for the priest who had obviously been commandeered into performing the wedding service. When Ghislaine entered the chapel, supported by a monk and Lady Helene, the priest moved forward but was prevented from progressing beyond the first pew by a large hand.

Ghislaine caught her breath as Guy de Courcy rose from his knees and turned to watch her approach. From the damp tendrils of his dark hair that clung to his forehead, Ghislaine realised that he had at least heeded some of what Helene had said. However, a quick douse of cold water was not likely to change his manners or his character.

The fact that she had chosen to remain in the monk's habit told him much about her opinion of this marriage, but his eyes were drawn to the cascade of bright copper curls that hung to her waist. Unadorned, her hair shone with dancing lights picking up the rays from the windows and moving softly in the breeze. His lips tightened. Perhaps he should not have treated her quite so harshly.

As she reached his side, she stopped to look up at him, a mixture of fear, anger and innocence. Guy scowled.

"The Earl took it upon himself to have his scribe lay out the marriage contract," he began, passing her a white scroll with a thick red seal. Ghislaine took it, her hands shaking a little. The marks made no real sense to her, but she did not wish to inform de Courcy of her lack.

When she spoke, her voice was under control. "Would you care to enlighten me?" She would not make this easy for him. After all, he was getting the bargain.

Guy found the parchment casually waved, unread, before his eyes and glared at her. He had no idea whether the woman could read or just couldn't be bothered. Previous experience of ladies and their whims had taught him to expect the worst. Hell's teeth, the woman was difficult. And yet not for the first time did he note her attempt at courage. It would give him a great deal of satisfaction in taming this wild cat. He stopped the thought. Taming—or anything else—did not form part of his plans. Nor did he have the inclination, he reminded himself.

"The terms are the usual ones," he began irritably, "save the parts to do with the payment for advowry."

"I have not married before," she interrupted quickly. "Pray, do explain the 'usual terms'."

His vexed expression afforded Ghislaine some satisfaction but it did not last for long.

"If you try my patience much longer lady, I will be forced to practise my husbandly duties before the marriage is complete. I am no fool and I am done with waiting. There will be no more delays."

So he had seen her ruses for what they were. Ghislaine tightened her lips, knowing that if she said more he would surely carry out his threats. Wife-beating was a common pastime amongst knights of his station. She lifted her head in haughty indignation as he gripped her arm, but despite her best efforts she could not free herself from his hold.

"But know this, lady. When I have cleared my name, I shall put you in the convent as you request and have done with this charade." So saying he turned to the priest and nodded impatiently. D'Everard hurried through the wooden door, accompanied by a lanky youth of indeterminate age, merely nodding at the assembled company and taking his place at de Courcy's side.

The marriage was solemnised quickly and without further interruption. Neither Walter nor Edwin came to rescue her, and Ghislaine had found herself repeating her vows in toneless resignation. Her life was now in the protection of this murdering barbarian, but she vowed that she would find a way to avenge the death of her friend.

In deference to her supposed indisposition, de Courcy had ordered a cart to take her back to the manor at Chapmonswiche. Inwardly, Ghislaine grimaced at the thought of spending so many uncomfortable hours in that contraption, but pride would not let her back down. Biting her lip, she climbed into the cart as gracefully as she could but cursed roundly when her cloak ripped on a nail. The look of amusement that de Courcy bestowed upon her made it plain that he did not for one moment believe her ailment was fact.

Helene gripped her arm tightly. ''I shall come to visit as soon as I am able.'' She paused as if about to say something further, but then shook her head. ''Do not push him too far, Ghislaine.'' Her anxious face smiled gently at her. ''If you need me, send word.''

Ghislaine nodded wordlessly, too overwhelmed by her sense of impending doom and loneliness to be able to say anything.

As the heavy cart trundled noisily across the wooden bridge that spanned the River Dee, Ghislaine looked back at the walls of the ancient city and tried to stifle her tears. She was married to a murderous mercenary who wished to put her in the convent. Her future looked very bleak.

Chapter Four

As the cart forged along the stony path leading to
the manor of Chapmonswiche, Ghislaine's spirits began to rise a little. At least she would be living in her
own home. The aches and pains in her jarred bones
melted at the sight of the familiar palisade and the
stagnant moat that had needed draining for years. If
only the ache in her heart would disappear so easily.

Her bridegroom had inexplicably remained with the
cart for the entire length of the dreary ride from Chester, his huge black destrier champing to push on. Ghislaine had stared at his stiff, straight back for some of
the time, wishing for some awful fate to befall him.
They were accompanied by some ten of his uncouth
soldiers, the rest having ridden on ahead with
d'Everard and Edwin. Escape was impossible, but
even so Ghislaine reminded herself of his threat to her
people.

As she watched him, the enormity of what had happened struck her anew. She had married the murderer
of her friend, knew nothing about him save his oafish
manners and surly disposition and could be sharing

her bed with him this night. Everything she possessed
and held dear was in his hands, and she was greatly
afeared.

Never in her life had she truly been afraid, least-
ways not of any one man. Her father's temper had
been explosive but short-lived, and like as not her
clever tongue had aided her to escape the palm of his
hand. She had been protected from the rest by dint of
her position, although Ghislaine was aware of the
harsher realities of married life. Her mother had often
treated women for the results of marital disputes, wife-
beating being in no way a respecter of rank.

The closer to the drawbridge they moved, the more
fearful and nervous she became. Of course she had
expected to marry, although her father had never taken
any pains to find another partner for her since her betrothed from the cradle, Robert of Warmundesley, had
unfortunately died of a fever some six years before.
Since the death of his wife, however, John de Launay
had found it more convenient to have Ghislaine look
after the manor and see to his needs and comforts, with
little thought for her own. Money had been hard come
by of late and there had been few suitors for so small
an estate. Her reputation as a wild and unbiddable girl
who consorted with the villeins and serfs had done
little to enhance her bridal worth, even though it was
in many ways unjustified.

De Courcy looked back at her over his shoulder and
treated her to one of his blacker scowls. At least, she
decided, he was predictable. And the thought struck
her then, that as he disliked her so much, he was unlikely to spend much time in her company. Were she

to give him such a disgust of her, he might spend no time at all with her. That thought was most pleasing.

"Do you need help, lady?"

Ghislaine started as the words pierced her thoughts. Her husband had already dismounted and was standing before her, an impatient frown informing her that he had been waiting for her to get down. As she looked up at his tall figure, a vision of Margaret stood by his side. He had wanted small, delicate, pretty Margaret as his wife. A sweet, god-fearing, clean, well-mannered girl with the experience of two husbands behind her, and, if she was truthful, not a lot of natural intelligence. She would have smiled had she not caught his cold, blue eyes raking her with disgust. A good start.

Without a word, Ghislaine rose awkwardly and attempted to trip out of the cart. She was thwarted by a pair of strong arms which pulled her to his chest.

"I am to ensure that no ill befalls you, lady, for your liege-lord is keen to see you survive the marriage." The words were uttered with a certain twisted amusement that caused Ghislaine's eyes to fly to his face. "Do you succumb in any way, then he has assured me of a place in his dungeon."

Ghislaine gulped. She had never been so close to any man before, let alone a barbarian, and she was unprepared for the strange feelings it stirred in her. He was younger than she had at first supposed, maybe twenty-five or so, but years of fighting in all elements had given him a worn appearance. In fact, Helene du Beauregard was right when she said he was reputed to be handsome. Were it not for those thick, black bristles on his face, he would be very handsome.

She realised that she must have been staring at him as his lips began to curl in irritation.

"If I am too heavy for you, husband, put me down. I am not noted for my delicate size." Her heart was still thudding wildly as those eyes of his bore into hers and it took all her will-power to control the trembling that had inexplicably set about her limbs.

His scornful stare was nearly the undoing of her, for he looked as if he would ignore the Earl's wishes and murder her right there. She found herself sprawling in the mud. His ways with ladies were most appealing!

"Do you wish to die, it can be arranged lady," he growled, the familiar scowl returning. "I am not of the opinion that you are the Earl's favourite ward."

"My wishes count for little in this arrangement," she retorted angrily from the ground. "What I wish to do is to enter the convent." Ghislaine stood up, momentarily forgetting her plan as she brushed the dirt from her cloak.

"That, too, can be arranged," he murmured as he turned his back on her to survey the manor. His only comment was a grunt, before he set about ordering his escorts to dismount.

Further conversation between them was brought to a halt by the arrival of Arnaud d'Everard in the company of Sir Brian de Ferrars, her household steward. Sir Brian had been with the family a good ten years and, although approaching middle years and a little unreliable as a result of his fondness for ale, was loyal and good natured. In truth, the manor was too small to require his services, but Sir Brian had been a close friend of her father's and even the normally hard-hearted Sir John had not been able to turn him off.

"A relief to see you returned in one piece, Lady Ghislaine." Sir Brian's bleary blue eyes surveyed his mistress closely, but seeing nothing amiss, turned to the tall stranger at her side with a look of suspicion on his face. Being only of medium height, Sir Brian had to look up to the newcomer, a fact which clearly annoyed him.

"I bid you greet Sir Guy de Courcy, my husband, Sir Guy, the head of my household, Sir Brian de Ferrars." Ghislaine's voice sounded far more controlled than she felt. Her relief, however, was short lived for she could see from his expression that Sir Brian had already made up his mind about the new lord of the manor.

"I believe in plain speaking Sir Guy," stated the older man baldly. "Your reputation is not an enviable one, and you are not the choice I would have made for Lady Ghislaine."

Ghislaine held her breath, waiting for the sword to fall at such a pompous greeting. Sir Brian was apt to take a paternal attitude when he deemed it necessary. Her eyes widened when they saw de Courcy nod his head in agreement.

"In your place I would feel the same, but the match was arranged by the Earl of Chester. He felt that Lady Ghislaine and I would be...well suited." The last statement was made with more than a touch of irony.

Sir Brian raised his eyebrow in question.

"I have wealth enough to bring to the property and a loyal army of twenty men. Lady Ghislaine has seen the wisdom of the alliance," he added with a faint smile in her direction.

Ghislaine's face suffused with pink at such familiar

talk, but although Sir Brian clearly remained suspicious of Sir Guy, she decided this was not the time to create a fuss.

"I see you have met Sir Arnaud d'Everard. He will have given you forewarning of our arrival, no doubt?"

"Aye, Lady Ghislaine. We have done what we could under the circumstances." The gloomy look that the hapless Sir Brian gave her told Ghislaine all she needed to know. The kitchens were run by a domineering woman whose swings of mood were as notorious as her morals. Elfrieda had turned up at their gates one freezing, wet day last winter. She had been heavily with child. The mercenary who had dumped her there had muttered that her only talent was cooking. He didn't return, but Elfrieda's skills in the kitchen had more than repaid her debt of gratitude.

Sir Brian had always found Elfrieda most intimidating and Ghislaine suspected that if they were to eat that night, then she had best sort it out herself.

"In that case, I shall see you in the hall when you have made the necessary arrangements with the men." And with those parting words, Ghislaine escaped through the gate house and disappeared into the bailed, leaving the three men staring after her.

"Edwin!" Ghislaine stared in horror at the sight of his handsome, battered face. "Did de Courcy do this?" she demanded, delicately probing his angry swollen bruises for any serious injury. Finding none, she took a step back to survey his scowling countenance. Sweet Lord, did all the men she knew scowl?

"Nay," he replied calmly, picking up a small cup of usquebaugh from the table before him. Clearly Effie had provided him with this from her father's stock. "This was the work of the Earl's men." His grey eyes continued to stare at her as he drained the cup quickly, and Ghislaine began to feel uncomfortable. They had grown up together and she recognised anger in him.

"You were right," she grudgingly admitted, finally able to take no more of his accusing looks. "Had I heeded your advice we would not be in this position. However, I did not and that's an end to it. At least you're not the one married to him."

Edwin uncurled himself from his spot on the bench and stood before his mistress, his long braids matted and filthy, his tunic badly torn. "This man is no fool, Ghislaine. Do not attempt to trick him or it will not go well for us." This speech was delivered gravely and Ghislaine knew that he was worried. He had been her sole protector for years. No one else save Richard had ever bothered overmuch for her safety.

She sighed heavily and turned to the fire. "I know that, but there must be some way to get rid of this oaf. Mayhap an accident?" Her hopeful tone caused Edwin to take a step closer and grip her shoulders in his hands. Gently he turned her back to face him.

Edwin had been the one constant person in her life. There had been a time when Ghislaine had thought of him as more than a friend, but that had passed years ago. They had settled into a relationship based on trust and respect. It didn't blind them to each other's faults, however. For some months, Ghislaine had sensed a change in Edwin. A restlessness seemed to have taken a grip on his soul and she had often caught him staring into the distant hills.

His anxiety was mirrored in his fathomless grey

eyes. "You would be dead before you finished the thought." His grim expression softened a little as he saw the fear that lay behind her suspiciously bright eyes. "Do not anger him, lady. He is a knight with rough ways and a bad temper. If you value your life, look to his needs quickly."

"Good advice, lady. I hope that you heed him this time."

Ghislaine whirled round to face her husband smiling down at her benignly. "You were listening," she accused, glaring at him.

"Did you have something to hide? There will be no secrets between us, wife." His gaze travelled to Edwin. "And this, I take it, is your partner in crime?"

Ghislaine did not even deign to reply, but watched in fascination as the two men assessed each other thoroughly. They were matched in size, although as Edwin was younger his body did not have the same strength as de Courcy's. Her husband did not scowl, but seemed to have come to some decision.

"The Earl informed me you were a skilled marksman. Does he have the right of it?"

Edwin crossed his arms over his chest and nodded.

"He was also under the impression that you had some…er…difficulty with our language."

Edwin sniffed derisively. "There was never anything I could say that would have changed his view of me," he said finally. "His men had no problem communicating with me."

His pride was shining from his swollen eyes, but he did not seem much like a man in love with his wife, concluded Guy. In fact, he appeared to treat her much like a brother would. With this thought in mind, he voiced his decision. "You would swear fealty to me this night?" he demanded. "I would ask no more of you than Lady Ghislaine does, except that you would ride with my men when I need you."

"And his alternative?" Ghislaine demanded angrily.

Guy shrugged carelessly. "I would send him to the Earl for trial for crimes of the venison. I am sure that evidence could be produced."

Edwin rubbed his hand over his beard and looked at him speculatively. "Would I be paid?"

Ghislaine gasped. He was going to accept the outlaw for a few coins.

"Aye. The same as my men. A silver mark a month, with food and a share of any treasure taken." Guy smiled slowly. So he had his price after all. Ghislaine, he had to admit, looked more thunderstruck than heartsore.

"I accept." Their eyes locked for a moment until Ghislaine, incensed by what she saw as Edwin's defection, interrupted.

"Excuse me whilst I go to organise the servants. No doubt there are still some who wish to do my bidding." With her eyes full of anger and her cheeks pink, Ghislaine whirled around. Her flourish was marred somewhat by her tripping on the long monk's robe she still wore, but she cared not.

Edwin watched Ghislaine's stiff and clumsy retreat before turning back to his new liege-lord.

"If you harm her, I will kill you myself." So saying, he picked up his bow and quit the hall.

"It would seem that your bride has made a full recovery,'' stated Arnaud with an impish grin. He was lounging idly against the wall, watching Guy's face.

Guy half turned towards him and grunted in response, pondering a little more on the curious relationship between his wife and her man-servant. He had a feeling that the Englishman was going to be less trouble than his wife.

"She inspires much loyalty, this wife of yours. If two grown men are so keen to defend her, it may be wise to treat her with perhaps a touch more…ah… courtesy.''

"Do you think I am afeared of them?'' Guy asked impatiently.

"Nay,'' came the guarded reply. "But it would not harm you to scowl at her less.''

"She does not appear afraid,'' Guy pointed out gruffly. He did not like his shortcomings being emphasised quite so obviously.

Arnaud's silence was most eloquent.

"I had no choice,'' he continued, his growl returning. "Were her behaviour and tongue more ladylike, she would not be in this position either.''

"Aye, true enough,'' agreed Arnaud amicably. Clearly he would win no ground with that approach. He decided to change tack. "It would do no harm to keep the lady sweet, though. We do not want to sniff the ale every time we have a thirst.'' That found its mark, and Guy sighed wearily.

"I did not want to be married to her. She was not my choice.''

So that was what irked him. He had gained a good estate but the bride was not to his taste.

"She is not that sore on the eyes,'' he pointed out

pleasantly. "The girl is perhaps not young but seems healthy enough."

"She has red hair," growled Guy, pushing his black hair back off his face in frustration, "and a tongue like a viper."

"Ah." Arnaud smiled to himself. It looked like things were going to be interesting. If his memory served him aright, Guy had never hesitated to choose a willing wench with red hair to warm his bed before. But perhaps the root of the problem lay in a slightly different direction. Lady Ghislaine was, after all, no camp follower and Guy was not used to dealing with ladies. It was possible that his friend felt very much at a disadvantage. No doubt the rejection from Lady Margaret had played some part in all this. "Then maybe we should search out some of that ale before she fills it with her venom," he grinned, pushing himself away from the wall.

Guy grinned back before slapping him on the back in good humour. "Maybe she would prefer your silver tongue. The Earl mentioned she prefers blonds."

Guy held his tongue throughout the ordeal of being presented to all the servants and vassals that inhabited the manor. His wife appeared reasonable, although he could tell from the noises her stomach was making that the girl was starving.

When they finally sat down at the lord's table in the plain, square hall, Guy knew relief, although he did remember to sniff the ale before he tasted it. As he did so, his eyes locked with those of Arnaud's. Each raised a cup in toast before tossing the spicy liquid back.

Amazed that he still lived, Guy tasted the venison and boar at his wife's bidding, as well as the fine white bread and nuts that she had brought to him specially. Grudgingly he admitted that the food was most acceptable, and with Arnaud's warning still ringing in his ears, Guy complimented his wife on the banquet.

"I am most impressed with the fare, lady. It is some time since we have eaten so well." He managed a nervous smile.

His words were received with little more than a raised eyebrow. "Most gracious, my lord."

As his wife was clearly not going to continue the conversation, Guy racked his brains to think of something else to engage her interest. He was pleased to see her drink freely of the ale.

"A fine brew, lady."

"I made it myself, sir. I am most pleased you find it to your liking."

He did not miss the sarcasm behind her expression, but was surprised to see her toss back another skinful of ale.

"What other accomplishments do you possess, lady?"

His question caused a deep flush to steal upwards from her neck. "I...I had thought the Earl would have given you a complete inventory of my...accomplishments, Sir Guy." Her eyes remained fixed on the table before them and it irritated him that she would not look him in the eye.

"Aye," came his grave response. "But I do not always set much store by what Hugh d'Avranches says."

Such treasonable words caused her dark eyes to fly

to his face. And they were very expressive eyes, Guy noted. At the moment they were trying to suppress what appeared to be amusement.

''I will confess, sir, that most of what he says is true. You have, I fear, landed yourself with a most unladylike wife.'' To his complete surprise Ghislaine rounded off her words by drinking more ale.

Guy looked at her flushed cheeks. Arnaud was right. She was quite comely, and he remembered thinking when he had held her earlier that she had felt good. He turned his attention to his food to divert the train of his thoughts. This was one woman he would not be bedding. He wanted no wife and she wanted to be in the convent. Well, so be it. Once this charade was over, the marriage could be annulled and they could all return to normal.

Despite his best efforts to entertain his wife, the girl proceeded to drink greater quantities of the ale. Somewhat deflated by being so ignored by a woman, Guy turned his attention to Sir Brian, who regaled him with tales of Ghislaine's father.

From the corner of his eye, he watched Ghislaine sink into a most unladylike stupor, and if he guessed aright, she would soon be collapsing into oblivion. Arnaud was right again, it seemed. The girl was so afeared of him, she would drink herself to sleep on her wedding night. He ought to have put her fears to rest on that point before now. Well, that would have to wait till the morrow.

He rose quickly and picked up his wife in what seemed to the assembled company to be a lover-like gesture of consideration. Sir Brian tottered to his feet, clearly unsure of his move.

''Rest easy, Sir Brian. My wife has had a long day. I will see to her comfort.'' Guy tried hard not to scowl and after a moment, the knight nodded curtly and sat down.

Guy reached the steps that led to the lord's room in three strides but was prevented from mounting them by Edwin. From his expression, the Englishman was not to be so easily dismissed. Guy sighed heavily.

''Your loyalty does you credit, but I can assure you that she will have no hurt from me.'' They both looked at the sleeping Ghislaines and Guy could have sworn that he saw a glimmer of regret cross the cold grey eyes of the Englishman. Silently, Edwin stood back to let them pass.

Chapter Five

A loud groan brought Ghislaine unwillingly from her strange dreams. It was a moment or two before she realised that the noise had come from her own lips, and that the terrible throbbing in her head and sick feeling in her stomach made her want to retch. Had she truly done this to herself?

A sound beyond the bed caused Ghislaine to lever the upper part of her body gingerly into a sitting position. She wished she hadn't.

"Awake at last, my lady?" Effie's normally soft tones grated violently against her aching head. Ghislaine raised her hands to her head and thought she was going to be sick.

"Sir Guy said to give you this when you woke. He thought it would help." That her maid sounded dubious was an understatement, but at that moment, Ghislaine would not have cared had the girl said it contained lethal poison. She took the goblet and swallowed the contents. It tasted disgusting.

"He said you would most likely be sick, but that you would feel better for it."

"Sir Guy is not here?" Ghislaine's bleary eyes slid around the bare room suspiciouly, noting a heavy dent in the mattress by her side.

"Oh, no, my lady. He was up some time ago." Effie tossed back her thick blonde braids and her blue eyes regarded her in a thinly veiled rebuke. "He went to the kitchen himself to make the potion." Admiration was shining from her eyes and had Ghislaine felt less like death, she would have done more than give her a sickly moan. She refused to contemplate how he had managed the volatile cook, Elfrieda.

Guy's prediction about her condition was sadly accurate, and when she was finally able to quit the privy, Ghislaine could do no more than sink back into a few hours more of dreamless relief.

When next she awoke, the sun was much higher and from the sounds outside, Ghislaine could tell that she had stayed abed far longer than usual. Dappled light shone through the rickety shutters, penetrating the thick gloom of the lord's room. She was alone.

The violent nausea and throbbing headache had been replaced by symptoms that were easier to cope with. Stretching back on the hard bolster, Ghislaine pondered her state. She had absolutely no recollection of how she had arrived here, and, far worse, what had happened to her when she had. The large dip in the bed by her side informed her that Guy had slept there too. There was an aura about the place that even smelled of his black soul. Hesitantly, Ghislaine drew back the blankets, and it was with some relief that the white sheets proclaimed her innocence. At least he had spoken true about his intention to keep her for the abbey. It seemed, for now at any rate, her innocence was safe, but how long that would endure she could not guess.

Slowly she slipped from the sheets of the large bed and pulled a threadbare blanket about her shoulders. Her eyes were drawn back to the bed. She knew what happened between a man and a woman, and judging by the whispered giggles of her servants, it was a pleasurable experience. But the thought of experiencing pleasure in the arms of that murderer drew a shudder from her cold body.

A shout outside made her venture to the window and pull back the shutters a little. Judging by the sun, it would be close to midday and she should be about her duties. Consumed by curiosity Ghislaine leaned forward to watch the activities below without being observed.

Small groups of unfamiliar men were setting to the repairs of the palisade, clearing rubbish and rethatching the stable roof. All of these were vital jobs that her father had refused to take in hand, and Sir Brian's indifferent health had allowed the state of the manor to deteriorate over the course of several years. Despite her pleas for many improvements and repairs, little had been done. Ghislaine watched with open-mouthed amazement at the scene below her. It was hard to believe that the instructions had come from her husband, for she was certain that he had little personal experience of running a manor. No, she decided finally. The orders were most likely to have come from Sir Arnaud, but Ghislaine found it intriguing to think that Guy de Courcy would allow his trained mercenaries to expend their energies on such lowly tasks.

A sudden glimpse of Arnaud d'Everard caused

Ghislaine to step back quickly and retreat into the safety of the bedchamber, reminding herself that she would have to face them all soon. No doubt she looked and smelled as if she had spent the night in the byre.

Despite her plan to give Guy de Courcy a disgust of her, Ghislaine could not deny herself the comfort of a bath. When she sank back into the tub, a sense of well-being and comfort stole through her. This was a luxury she had not often been permitted by her father, but for once Ghislaine had been determined to choose something for herself. If Guy de Courcy did not approve, he would have to tell her himself. Sighing, Ghislaine attempted to put all thoughts of her husband to one side. It was not to be.

"You are recovered, I see."

Ghislaine turned rapidly, causing water to splash over the edge of the tub and her cheeks to flush. The object of her thoughts had materialised silently at the door of the bedchamber, an expression of cool indifference on his dark face.

Ghislaine's lips tightened and her brain desperately tried to work convincingly. "Your concern is most gratifying, Sir Guy, but not at all necessary. My partiality for ale is well known and my body used to the effects." She then proceeded to affect complete indifference to his presence and smeared dollops of the sweet-scented soap onto her arms before sinking as low as she could into the tub.

Guy's lack of interest wavered somewhat on hearing those words. His wife's voice was attractive when she wasn't shooting venom at him. Low and husky. But why she should tell him a blatant lie about her drinking habits had him foxed. The girl could be most vexing. He closed the stiff door behind him and took a few more paces into the semi-dark room. The two candles flickering in the prickets offered little light. Her frugality, at least, was a welcome sight.

"I had not realised that drinking ale was one of your vices, lady." His eyes fixed on the soft white curves of her shoulders. "Have you any others?"

Unwilling to look up at him, Ghislaine missed the glint in his eyes and the underlying meaning of his question. "Oh, many," she replied airily as she splashed the water over her shoulders. "I am known to be a...glutton, too."

Guy raised an eyebrow. "There was not much evidence of that last night." He tried to picture his wife's figure but could only recall her telling him she was not noted for her delicate size. She had not felt a great weight in his arms either, but even as he puzzled over her words, he took another step or so forward.

"I was hoping that you would be...er...rested enough to show me the estate." His eyes followed the hand that was busy soaping her shoulders in gentle, almost caressing movements. As her hand moved lower, so did his eyes. Just below the water-line he could see the swell of her rounded breasts. His throat went dry as he recalled that it had been some time since he had tumbled a woman. His black scowl returned. He was acting like a young boy.

"I am sure that Sir Brian would be most happy to show you Chapmonswiche," she said coolly, still refusing to look at him.

His scowl deepened. He was not going to be dismissed like a lackey in his own home by this arrogant wench.

"Given the sudden nature of our marriage and my reputation, I had thought you would prefer your people to see you unharmed at my side. No doubt you know them better than I."

His words caused her to still and finally to look up at him. "Are you afeared that they will balk against the Earl's choice of husband for me?"

His lips tightened in anger at her superior tone. He should have known she would parry words with him and it was irritating beyond belief. "I have naught to fear," he snapped, "but should you do aught to incur my wrath, then you will have my hand to fear, lady."

So that was how it was to be. The cool way her eyes regarded him and her quick tongue had riled him so much he had let his temper take over. Were he to stay in the chamber a minute more, he would surely put his threat into practice. No doubt even the befuddled Sir Brian would have a better understanding of the estate anyway.

Ghislaine heard rather than saw Sir Guy's angry exit and she released the breath that she had been holding. For a few moments in his presence she had forgotten that he was a murderer of women, and his threats had sounded no more serious than those of her father. But if she valued her life, she must be more wary of him.

The rain had started to fall not long after she had slipped away from the manor and ridden into the village. There were the ploughing arrangements for the coming months to be discussed with the head villager and Ghislaine had also convinced herself that she wanted advice on herbal remedies from the old Angle crone, Hulda. She had thought Sir Guy unlikely to interfere with the general running of the estate immediately, and had seized on the excuse to escape the manor for an hour or so. She doubted that her presence would be missed for some time, everyone believing that she was closeted in the bedchamber.

She had donned her oldest tunic and braided her hair deftly in a style more practical than becoming. Briefly, Ghislaine wondered if she should take more care over her appearance in deference to her newly married status, but finally decided against it. All her gowns were old and worn and she was certain that her husband was indifferent to her looks in any case. He had married her for her value as ward of the Earl and for her estate after all.

Pulling on her leather shoes, Ghislaine noticed a new hole in the seam and sighed. Well, it could not be helped. Her father had believed any spare money better spent elsewhere. She had no reason to suppose that Guy de Courcy would think differently.

It had been easy enough to slip unnoticed from the hall, and as few of de Courcy's men had cast barely a glance in her direction, Ghislaine was able to lead her grey palfrey from the stable to the gatehouse unquestioned. To her own guard she only needed a smile and a nod and she had been given her usual free passage. Her husband had not forbidden her to leave exactly, but she knew that he would not be pleased by her absence. Still, as he would never know, it would do no real harm.

The village was sited no more than a short ride due south from the manor, close by a stream of sweet water. Boasting no more than about twenty families, the inhabitants provided little revenue for the manor, but were peaceful and friendly. Survival was based largely on a mixture of crops, cattle and pigs. Last year her father had bought some sheep and Ghislaine was hopeful that they would breed successfully and bring in some money for the woolclip.

The village huts were clustered around the muddy track that led directly to the old Roman road linking Chester with the North. The villagers muttered their congratulations to her but were plainly at a loss as to why her husband was not at her side. Offering a few hasty excuses about Sir Guy being detained on personal matters, Ghislaine hurried about her business.

Hulda lived at the far end of the village, a little apart from the rest. Respected by the others for her knowledge of cures and herbals, she was also a little feared. Some believed her to practise the old pagan rites of the Angles who had settled here before the Normans came, but Ghislaine dismissed such views as foolish. She had harmed no one and saved many. She had saved Edwin.

According to her brother, it had been Hulda who had saved the ten-year-old Edwin from the swords of the Norman soldiers whilst they hunted down any land-owning Englishmen who opposed the Conqueror. They had attacked the village ten years ago, killing the Angle thegn and his two elder sons. The youngest, Edwin, was left writhing in agony from his vicious wounds. When the soldiers had finished burning and looting, they took turns in raping his mother and sister. Both died from their injuries. Were it not for Hulda's skills, Edwin would have also succumbed.

When John de Launay had been made lord of the manor two years later, Edwin had already grown into a strong, surly lad who had been brought up by Hulda as if he were her own. No one in the manor knew of his aristocratic parentage, nor of his vow to kill the Norman dogs who had violated his mother and sister. No one except Ghislaine and her brother, Richard, and they had come by that knowledge painfully.

What had started off as a childish game had ended in unexpected violence. Ghislaine and Richard had often roamed the forest beyond the village, exploring, trapping and indulging in youthful fantasies of adventure. One day, Richard had discovered a thin youth tampering with their traps and immediately challenged him. Instead of turning tail and running, the boy had launched himself at Richard. All the venom and hatred Edwin had bottled within him had poured out, and Ghislaine had been certain that he truly would kill Richard. But when Richard's arm had snapped Edwin had turned pale. He had carried Richard to Hulda's hut where she had done what she could for the arm. It was there that they had learned of Edwin's past and his vow. It was there the three of them had forged a bond that would endure.

Ghislaine still remembered that first afternoon inside the dark hut. The smell of the herbs was overwhelming, pungent and yet wholesome. Everywhere there were bunches of the different plants drying, boiling, steeping. Strange pots crowded the table and floor, and it was hard to know where to stand.

As she looked through the open doorway, it was as if she were once again that tearful maid of eleven. Little had changed except that Ghislaine was older and, of course, married to a stranger.

"So. You've come, then?" A thin voice floated out from the gloom. "I wasn't expecting you so soon."

Hulda's grey, lined face peered up at her, the dark eyes missing nothing. She had few teeth left and rarely smiled, so a curt nod was an affectionate enough greeting. "You'd best come inside afore the rain sets in."

"Elfrieda thinks she's with child again, so she'll be needing some of your potion." Ghislaine idly picked up a bunch of herbs and sniffed them appreciatively. It was a comforting, homely sort of a smell that reminded her of her mother.

Hulda grunted, shuffling to the back of the hut. "What she needs is a husband."

Ghislaine shrugged her shoulders. "Aye, but none will have her now. Besides, she's a good cook." She replaced the herbs carefully on the table.

A deep sniff was the only answer Ghislaine received as the old woman sorted through her jars. "She cannot use it again, tell her. She may not carry her full time else."

"Aye. I'll tell her," said Ghislaine dubiously, taking the potion offered.

Hulda said no more, but carried on with her chopping and steeping, her face cloaked in the darkness of the hut.

"Have you spoken to Edwin since yestereve?" The question seemed innocent enough, but Hulda smiled to herself.

"Aye. He was here not long afore you came."

"So you know?" The disappointment was genuine.

"That you married a Norman and that Edwin takes a silver coin each month to buy his freedom? Aye."

"Why should he want his freedom? He has all he

needs with us.'' Ghislaine frowned, knowing the answer and knowing she sounded like a petulant child.

''His destiny is not with you, girl. He has always known that and it has not gone easy with him. Let him be now.''

Pushing her braids back over her shoulders Ghislaine turned to stare at the chickens squawking outside the hut. Edwin had always been there, watched over her, aye, and had always loved her. Her feelings for him, however, were those of a sister for a brother, and Edwin had never tried to change her mind. Sometimes though, she had caught him watching her. There had been such longing and passion burning in his eyes and she had been so lonely that once or twice Ghislaine had been sorely tempted to find out about passion in his arms. Yielding to the temptation, however, would surely have signed his death warrant, since the Earl would brook no such liaisons and marriage would have been out of the question.

Catching her bottom lip between her teeth, Ghislaine turned back to Hulda. ''I will miss him sorely. He is my only friend.'' Her voice was full of hurt and misery and Hulda was not proof against the young girl's anguish.

''He has to go, girl. It is time for him to start his journey, but he will return when he is at peace. You must be strong for him.'' Hulda's dark eyes burned into her and Ghislaine knew the woman was right. ''There is much for you to do here.''

Grimacing, Ghislaine looked across at the old woman. ''You have the right of it. Sir Guy's men are little more than a pack of wild animals and I have no doubt that trouble will come soon.''

Hulda paused for a moment and looked across at her. "It seems to me they've done more in a day than your father did in years. The blacksmith says his roof has already been rethatched and there's plans afoot to take a look at that stinking moat. Don't be too quick to condemn, my lady."

Managing a wan smile, Ghislaine picked up the potion for Elfrieda and left the hut. She was heartsore and in need of a friend. Knowing that Edwin was planning to buy his own freedom made her feel even more trapped. The only freedom she would find was in the convent.

The effects of the previous night's indulgence were beginning to take their toll on her once more, and Ghislaine found herself loathe to return to the manor just yet. The rain had stopped and the cool silence of the forest beckoned. According to Hulda, Edwin had taken the path in that direction and, if he was not going too fast, she could probably catch him. Ghislaine knew all his secret hiding places and she wanted to talk to him without her husband's eyes on her.

She had reached the first line of trees when the rain came suddenly in thick gusts of wind that soaked her cloak and her tunic within moments. The bitter cold froze her skin, and Ghislaine knew that she would have to find shelter or she would catch the fever that often killed travellers in this area.

The large, bare trees overhead offered little protection from the rain but did prevent the light from penetrating the darkness of the undergrowth. Ghislaine could see only a few feet in front of her with the rain driving into her eyes. Cursing herself for her foolishness, she made her way towards the stream where there was a woodcutter's bothy nearby.

Gratefully she took refuge in the meagre hut but was disappointed not to find Edwin there. Despite the holes in the thatch and broken shutters, Ghislaine was able to keep out most of the wet.

It was nigh on an hour later when the rain finally abated, and the light was failing. She felt so cold that all she could hear was the chattering of her teeth.

Her horse, Morwenna, greeted her with a friendly snicker as she patted her gently on the neck. For a brief moment, Ghislaine listened to the sounds of the forest, but all she could hear was the stream and the dripping of the raindrops on the sodden earth. The fresh smell of wet vegetation was everywhere. She was impatient to get back and worried that Guy de Courcy would discover her absence. He had threatened physical punishment if his commands were disobeyed and she was certain he would carry them out.

The mud prevented her from pushing on at speed, and as the dark gathered in, Ghislaine became increasingly concerned. Her impetuosity had once more landed her in a potentially dangerous situation, although she did not really imagine herself to be at risk.

Her position had always been a form of protection, for most knew of their lack of money. Few robbers would risk their lives on her. Yet, as the wife of a mercenary, Ghislaine realised belatedly that she now had much greater ransom value. Fear began to creep into her mind. It would also be one way of eliminating an unwanted wife without troubling the Earl's conscience. Would Guy de Courcy stoop so low?

Ghislaine did not know but a tiny voice inside her

said he was not to be trusted. He had murdered Margaret. At least, he had not denied it as vehemently as she would have expected an innocent man to do. She shivered, for suddenly she was very cold.

Behind her a twig snapped and Ghislaine froze. She could see nothing but she sensed she was being watched. Her heart was thudding as she drew her horse to a standstill, afraid of plunging headlong into an ambush. To her right, a bird fluttered suddenly from the undergrowth and she almost jumped out of the saddle. Icy fear crept along her spine. No one knew she was here and she would not be missed if she were attacked. Was this how her father had been killed?

Turning her head nervously to the place the bird had flown from, Ghislaine was sure she had picked up the furtive movements of her hidden enemy. Dismounting carefully, she peered into the undergrowth. The indistinct outline of two shadowy figures darted from place to place. Dressed in green and brown, they blended in well with their surroundings, and Ghislaine felt the cold hand of terror squeeze at her pounding heart. Should she risk riding on or try to slip silently from their grasp by playing them at their own game?

The decision was wrenched cruelly from her hands by a sudden whinny from her horse. Clearly unsettled by the tense atmosphere enveloping them, Morwenna stamped skittishly amongst the leaves and mud, her head rearing anxiously. Even as Ghislaine turned back to calm the horse, she could hear the men advancing quickly upon them. She had no choice but to mount and ride, despite her lack of time. Trying to haul herself clumsily over Morwenna's back, Ghislaine looked over her shoulder to see the first man emerging from the undergrowth, his arrow already poised for flight. She knew she was doomed but still reached desperately to pull herself up.

Quicker than she had expected, the low hum of an arrow in flight reached her ears and Ghislaine braced herself for the inevitable pain. But it never came. Instead, a piercing shriek broke the eerie silence of the forest, followed by a heavy thud. Risking a glance, Ghislaine saw her attacker felled by an arrow in his back. There was no sign of his companion, but she did not wait to find out what had happened to him.

Her palfrey bolted from her hiding place as if the devil himself were behind her. Twigs and branches tore at Ghislaine's hair and cloak. Behind she could hear shouts and then the steady thud of a horse in pursuit. As she looked over her shoulder, she saw them. A dark cloak atop a dark horse. There was naught else to see, but she would not stop to look further for the distance between them was closing.

She did not see the low-hanging branch that knocked her from the saddle, but she felt the pain in her arm and shoulder as she hit the ground with a heavy thud. For a moment she heard and saw nothing save a soft whirring before her eyes and a light-headed feeling that lifted slowly.

Two blue eyes bore into her, a mixture of relief and anger apparent.

"This is not so easily remedied, lady," came a low threat.

Ghislaine raised an eyebrow. She was most surprised to find her head propped up on her husband's lap, his strong arm under her neck. She did not immediately feel the need to move away for his huge hands had started to move along the length of her arms and legs, presumably to locate any serious injuries. She could not prevent her cheeks from burning; no man had ever done such a thing before.

"I am not hurt," she assured him, unable to look him in the eyes. When Ghislaine attempted to sit up, however, she saw stars before her eyes and the buzzing in her ears grew louder.

"You will be," he muttered as he picked her up, far more gently than she had thought possible for such an oaf. Her weight seemed no great thing to him as he strode towards his warhorse. There were eight of his men in the clearing, their eyes taking a good look at her this time. Edwin stood by the destrier, the expression on his face implacable. She was dumped less gently into the Englishman's arms whilst her champion eased himself into the saddle. Edwin regarded her steadily without a word, and his rebuking silence was worse than his bite.

Ghislaine began to shiver, whether in fear or as a result of the cold it did not seem to matter. Her desire to have some time to herself now seemed so childish and pointless, but she was sure that she was going to pay for her foolishness nonetheless.

"I would thank you for your timely arrival my lord. Had you not killed the brigand, I am sure I would now be dead."

Guy's eyes narrowed. "I killed no one, lady. Where was this?"

Ghislaine frowned in confusion. "Back down the path. I thought…"

Her words were interrupted by de Courcy's swift orders to five of his men. They charged off in search of her attackers. If the mercenaries had not saved her, then who had? She was passed back to Guy as if she were no more than a sack of grain. Her husband's arms gripped her like wet leather straps as they rode swiftly back to the manor. Dark was setting in as they crossed the drawbridge. Guy had said nothing to her on the journey back and she surmised that he was going to say it all on their return.

When her husband had dismounted, he pulled Ghislaine once more into his arms and stormed into the hall. She saw nothing save the lights of the wall sconces and concerned faces. The smell of cooking food permeated the entire building but she guessed aright when she thought she was not to savour any this night. Guy crossed the hall to the steps leading to the lord's bedchamber, but Sir Brian was there before him. Whatever he had been about to say, he did not say it; the look in Guy's eyes told him all. A look flashed between them and Sir Brian stepped aside.

As they mounted the stairs, Ghislaine's heart began to thud. He had threatened her with a beating if she did not behave and it looked as if he were going to show her the mettle of his words. Daring to look up at his grim face, Ghislaine's fears grew.

She was dumped on the bed as Guy paced the room. A good fire burned in the stone grate and yet another tub of hot water steamed in the corner. Three baths in two days!

"Why did you leave?" The question was spat out as her husband stared down at her, hands on his hips.

Ghislaine gulped. Her throat had constricted and her brain seemed to have ceased functioning "I…I had thought to spend a little time on my own." His black frown was not encouraging. She sighed nervously and began to push her wet hair from her face. "If you want the truth," she began, deciding he at least deserved the truth, "I was afeared and I had gone in search of Edwin."

He looked huge, looming above her, his dark hair wet and curling at the edges, his unshaven face rough and threatening. "Afeared? I had not thought it, lady."

Did she detect a hint of irritation at these words? He was glaring at her, his anger barely kept at bay, watching as she pulled herself to her feet. At least she was on a level with the man and could face him as an equal.

"If I did wrong, then tell me now, for I am unused to dealing with men such as you." Such plain-spoken words had an instant effect on her husband.

"I mean to do more than tell you, lady. You had fair warning earlier this day." He advanced towards the bed, his mouth set in a hard line. Ghislaine backed away, her heart racing.

"I had not thought to anger you," she replied with less confidence.

"It would seem you did not think at all. There are all manner of men searching for me, including Margaret Staveley's family. Dettingham is baying for revenge and as my wife you would make a good substitute. Nowhere is safe, girl. Were you hacked to pieces in the woods, no one would know."

His concern took her by surprise. "I did not think I would be missed," she whispered miserably.

That earned a derisive snort. "My protection depends on your well-being, lady, and I do not intend to lose what I have due to your whims and carelessness."

That put her in her place. Ghislaine gave him a fulminating stare but the effect was marred somewhat by her bedraggled appearance. She would take her punishment with grace and dignity and in no way would she give him any satisfaction.

"Now, do you set yourself on my knee or do I force you?" From the look on his face, her husband was perfectly serious. The choice was hers, and much as she did not like giving in to him without a fight, it would go ill for her otherwise. Ignoring his hand, Ghislaine stomped to stand before him, her chin high in indignation.

He sat on the edge of the bed and pulled her over his thighs. Distress and shame burned through her whole body. He would regret this, she vowed with heartfelt anger.

Suddenly she felt his hand lifting her skirt. "Nay," she gasped as she realised his intention. "Do not do this." Her voice told him of her misery and her complete distress. Her hand tried to pull her skirts back down, but he held her still. It was not until he had pulled her skirts up to her waist that he realised why she had suddenly begun to struggle.

The sight of her uncovered bottom stilled him as nothing else would. The girl wore no undergarments and he had not expected it. Aye, he had seen how poorly she was clothed, but he had not thought she would be as naked as a servant under her dress.

His eyes were drawn to the sight of her soft, rounded hips and shapely legs, and he held his breath. How could he have known that under those ugly garments, the woman hid such a body? He gave into the desire to touch that soft, white skin and felt her shudder. His reaction was instant.

Ghislaine found herself sprawling in the rushes at the foot of the bed, completely confused by her husband's actions. He had done nothing other than stroke her so gently she could hardly feel it, and then he had pushed her roughly to the ground. In that, at least, he was consistent.

"If you leave the manor once more without an escort, lady, you will surely feel pain the next time." His threat was issued as he strode towards the door, and without a backwards glance, stormed down the stairs. Ghislaine was left on the floor to contemplate her husband's strange behaviour

Chapter Six

Effie's gentle hand roused her from her sleep, and as the mists cleared from her mind, Ghislaine's eyes flew to the other side of the bed. The fact that it was empty told her much.

"Sir Guy bade me bring you this, my lady." Effie handed her the posset with a tight smile. No doubt she knew everything that had transpired the night before. "He was afeared you had taken a chill and says you are to rest in bed until he gets back."

"He ordered me to stay in bed?" Ghislaine stared at her maid incredulously. The man's arrogance knew no bounds. "There is naught wrong with me, Effie," she said briskly, attempting to rise from the bed.

Effie stared at her as if she were mad. "But he bade you stay there, my lady," she began.

Ghislaine gave her a look that told the girl what she thought of that particular piece of information. "Would you bring my clothes, Effie, and stop prating on about what Sir Guy said?"

Effie's eyes did not look up, and the girl looked

embarrassed. Ghislaine stared at such odd behaviour, and then narrowed her eyes in suspicion.

"My clothes, Effie. Where are they?"

"He took them, my lady. He took them all."

Ghislaine looked at Effie, aghast, It was clear from her expression that her husband had done just that, but the reason behind such behaviour was a mystery. She sat back in a huff, her arms folded across her chest, and sighed heavily. She would have to stay there until he decided otherwise, and it was most vexing.

"Did he say when he would be back?" Ghislaine demanded with as much authority as she could muster, for in truth she did not feel as if she carried much weight now. She remembered he had wanted a compliant, obedient wife.

Effie shook her head as she busied herself about the bedchamber, but did not volunteer any more information about her husband. That, too, was most odd. Seemingly loyal servants appeared to have traded their allegiances with little hesitation. She yielded to an unladylike outburst which earned her a reproving look from Effie.

Her empty stomach reminded Ghislaine that she had not eaten since early the day before. Her supposition that she would be allowed none of the evening meal turned out to be correct. She had bathed and then fallen asleep the minute her head nestled into the bolster.

"Am I allowed to break my fast?" Her tone was most haughty. Prisoner or no, she refused to act like one.

Effie's round cheeks coloured just a little. "He said

something about you weighing so heavy that missing a bit of food would do you no harm, my lady.''

Ghislaine received this piece of information with wide-eyed disbelief. And then her lips twitched a little. Guy de Courcy had thrown her words back into her face. So, he liked playing games. She nursed this thought for a while, deciding that it seemed most at odds with her perception of him so far. That a cold-hearted, oafish mercenary with a growl like a bear could have a sense of humour seemed very unlikely. And yet she could not prevent the smile from tugging at her lips every so often.

The next few hours were spent in mending and re-pairing the stockings and shoes that had been left, but as sewing had never held much interest for her, Ghislaine found it hard to concentrate. Effie and several of the women servants came to complain about the un-tidiness and the lascivious behaviour of her husband's men and she promised to broach the matter with Sir Guy when she had the time. It was not a conversation she would look forward to since her husband did not appear to take criticism well. It would be best to choose the right time.

Idly, she looked in her mother's carved wooden chest, which contained her own meagre possessions. There was not much to look at since her father had never bestowed gifts upon her and somehow the gath-ering of pretty objects seemed unimportant.

Carefully she laid each thing out on the bed before looking at them in turn. Her mother's comb was made of a delicately carved ivory, chased with gold. It was so fine that it would never survive combing her thick curls. She had also inherited a set of fine needles and thread, but these remained wrapped in their leather case. Amid the muslin parcels of sweet-smelling lavender, Ghislaine found the leather case that had contained her mother's jewels, all long since taken by her father.

Next came her mementoes of Richard. His thick blue tunic that had made him look so handsome and the bow and arrows he had used as a young boy. As she stared at these reminders of her family, memories flooded through her mind and her eyes began to prick with tears.

So absorbed was she by this task that Ghislaine did not hear the door open and she jumped a foot off the bed in surprise.

"So, lady. I take it you are restored and suffer no ill effects?"

Ghislaine whirled round, her anger mounting. "I am like to be lighter without food or clothes. You have kept me prisoner in my own home and I would like to know the reason." Her eyes glinted with fury as they rested on the object of her dislike.

She stood before him, hands on hips, dressed in a thin, well-patched chemise that had been clearly made for a smaller girl. Looking for all the world like a woman possessed, Ghislaine's thick red-gold curls tumbled over her shoulders in abandon and her eyes, dark and accusing, bore into him. Guy was rendered silent as he looked at the angry figure of his wife. His eyes were drawn to the chemise and he was certain that she could have no idea how worn the material was. It hid nothing from him, for he could see the clear outlines of her generous curves. His mouth dried at the sight.

"The reason? I had no desire to waste another day in the forest searching for you." He watched as she saw the direction of his eyes and the sudden rosy flush that stained her cheeks. Hastily she bent to snatch a blanket and all but disappeared under it. Her eyes narrowed accusingly as a lazy grin broke his scowl.

"I did not ask it of you," she replied bitterly her embarrassment diminishing. "I had merely gone to the forest to talk to Edwin." She paused. "Did you find the men?"

He shook his head. "Only a body, but that could tell us naught." He slumped down on the bed and eased his boots from his feet. "The forest is dangerous. Was your father not murdered there last year?"

"Aye, but we had never felt in danger before. My father would often go hunting and never come to any trouble."

Guy looked up then, alert, watching her fiddle with the edge of the blankets. "You doubt something?"

Ghislaine shook her head slightly. "It's nothing much, except that fewer attacks had happened here of late. We had thought the outlaws had moved further north for the richer pickings. There are never many travellers round here."

What she said made sense with the information he had managed to gather so far. Perhaps the girl's wits were not so addled as he had thought. "How many men were with him?"

"Three men-at-arms and Peter Staveley." The accusing tone in her voice made him frown. "They were all killed."

"Peter Staveley? Kinsman to Margaret?" His eyes held hers.

Ghislaine just nodded. It had been no more than an unfortunate coincidence, she was certain.

"And no one was ever caught?" Guy's voice had taken on a speculative tone.

"Nay. The Earl did not seem much concerned, although Walter spent many days investigating."

"Walter?" He sensed a softening of her voice when she mentioned the name.

"De Belleme," she finished. "He was a...friend of the family."

His eyes bore into her as she stammered out the last sentence. It was clear that he was more than a family friend. "He found nothing?"

She shook her head. "He believed the outlaw was Thomas Bollyngton and his men, but there has been no sight of them these many months."

"I have heard that name before, but who is this Walter de Belleme?" His dark face was now harsh and the dark scowl had returned. Whoever the man was, he would not be bothering his wife again.

"I told you. He was...is a family friend. He is close to the Earl and has an estate some ten miles to the north of here. He visited frequently after his wife died."

Guy digested this information in silence. So far the man had made no attempt to contact Ghislaine, unless she had lied and had ridden out to meet him in the forest yesterday. It would be interesting to see the man that had seemingly captured his wife's heart.

His eyes strayed around the gloomy chamber. In truth, there was not much to see. The tapestries on the walls were darkened and frayed, and the two seats before the fire were old and wobbly. There were no rugs nor floor coverings save the rushes, but these were sweet-smelling. Noticing the chest was open and that some fripperies lay on the bed, Guy stood up and sauntered closer.

"Is this yours?" He picked up the box.

Ghislaine looked at his unshod feet with contempt. "Nay. Richard used that before he went to foster."

"Richard? Another friend of the family?"

She shook her head before snatching the bow from his hands. "My brother."

The pain in her voice was there for all to hear, and Guy was not impervious to it. He watched her jerky movements as she stuffed her pathetic belongings back into the chest.

"How did he die?"

"Against the Welsh. He was caught in an ambush nigh on a year now." The words she uttered sounded like a sharp rebuke, but Guy had heard too many bereaved mothers and widows to be fooled.

"You miss him?"

Ghislaine looked at him then, before nodding her reply. The dark face was not scowling, but was softer than she had ever seen it before. "He was the only one who ever talked to me." The words were said simply but with such feeling that Guy almost gave into his instinct to soften a little towards her. But comfort was not what his wife needed.

"Was he a better shot than you?" Guy indicated the bow.

Ghislaine struggled for a moment about the impropriety of admitting she could use one more than adequately. "Absolutely not."

Guy's lips twisted in an attempt to repress a smile. "Maybe I should be enlisting you to my army."

Ghislaine could not help a tiny smile from breaking her resistance, for she was not proof against the most dazzling smile she had ever seen in a man. The blue eyes were alight and his teeth were perfect. Helene had been right, for underneath all that hair her husband was very handsome.

For a moment their eyes locked and Ghislaine found that her heart began to beat faster. She also found that her stomach began to protest loudly.

To her profound consternation, Guy just laughed. "I think your punishment has lasted long enough, lady. I bid you come to the hall to break your fast."

Mortified by her stomach and by his humiliating reaction, Ghislaine glared at him, her cheeks pink.

"Do you wish me to parade myself as I am?" she hissed. "Or will you return my clothes?"

Guy pulled her drabbest tunic from under his cloak and threw it at her, his expression blank once again. He was most changeable in his mood this husband of hers. "I will give you this one…gown, the others when I see fit."

Ghislaine stared at him open-mouthed. "So I am still a prisoner?" She did not think she could contain her anger.

He looked at her and raked his hands through his black hair. "You have been more trouble these last few days than my entire army. I doubt that either of us will survive."

He looked so perplexed that Ghislaine felt immense satisfaction, but it lasted only seconds.

"You will not leave the manor walls without my

permission first and only then accompanied by two of my men-at-arms. And do not think you will be able to smile your way out, for your men have been warned that should you ever slip out again the guard responsible will be hanged.'' He returned her defiant stare with a tight-lipped observation. ''You will obey me in this.''

''I do not understand,'' she began. ''Why must I leave with your men? If it is a question of safety, my men have always protected me.'' Ghislaine raised her chin a little, defying him to challenge her words.

''Precisely because they are your men,'' he retorted, taking a step closer to her. ''I need to be sure of your safety and your...loyalty.''

His meaning was not lost on her. ''Loyalty!'' she spat. ''I am not at all sure what I am supposed to be loyal to as your treatment of me hardly deserves my unquestioned obedience either.''

Why those words had slipped out, Ghislaine had no idea, but they propelled her husband into action. She suddenly found her wrist gripped by an iron fist and pulled into a solid chest. He smelled of the forest and horses, and it was not as awful as she had thought. His free hand came to rest under her chin and her head pushed back as he looked deep into her eyes.

''I had thought that you preferred the convent to the pleasures of the flesh, lady, but if you wish me to make you truly my wife, it can be arranged.'' His shadowed face lowered menacingly as he pulled her body flat against his. There was nothing between them now save a few layers of cloth. Breathing seemed to have ceased for both of them, and it was with great difficulty that Ghislaine managed to draw back a little.

"Take your hands off me, you great brute. I do not deserve this treatment."

"Do not deserve this? Lady, you push your luck." As he looked down at her, his eyes caught hers again and he could feel her soft curves pressing into his body. His body responded as if it had been lit on fire, but this time Guy de Courcy could not fight it, nor did he want to.

His lips touched hers with a softness she did not expect. They brushed her mouth again and then, without warning, his hand slid up to the back of her neck and lifted her mouth to his. Ghislaine found her lips being stormed relentlessly, his lips moving possessively over hers, exploring, tasting. His other hand lowered to pull her hips tighter to his, and Ghislaine could hardly breathe, her pulse racing.

Dazed by such strange sensations shooting through her body, she was powerless to deny his tongue the access it was demanding. Somehow, instead of pushing him away, her hands had curled around the nape of his neck, her fingers entwined in the thick, black locks, allowing her body even greater intimacy with his. Her mind was sent spiralling off into a world of darkness and sweet pleasure whilst his tongue danced with hers. Leaning even closer into him, Ghislaine felt his hand slide lower, caressing and squeezing, pulling her even tighter to him.

With a silent groan, Guy pushed her roughly away. He had been carried away by the sweetness of her response, and by the soft invitation offered unwittingly by her body. He closed his eyes remembering the feel of her, remembering her racing heartbeat, the shy touch of her fingers on his neck. Lust. Pure, simple lust. It was no more than that, he reminded himself as he put his confused wife at arm's length.

"Truly it would be easy to take you right now, lady, but unfortunately I have more pressing engagements elsewhere."

Ghislaine's cheeks fired with humiliation and confusion, for he spoke true. Had he carried on with this magic she would have surrendered with no real struggle. That he should dismiss her so lightly was very cruel.

"You are nothing but a scheming, stinking brute with no regard for anything but your own ambitions." Her true feelings were written on her face as she turned her back to him and attempted to get some control over her shaking body.

"Were you so perfect, lady, you would not have been…ah…available." His cruel response brought a sudden desire to fight back.

"Had you not captured me for your own evil ends, I might have married elsewhere. Despite what you think, my lord, I am not totally without attraction."

"And who was this paragon that so timed his absence to coincide with your wedding?"

The jibe came very close to the mark and Ghislaine tried hard to ward off the tears.

"His name is unimportant, for I will never be able to marry him. He is all that is good and kind, and is able to make me laugh. He listens to me," she finished in anger. "And he is barbered regularly," she added for good measure.

"Let me warn you, lady. If I find you alone with this man, or any other man, then I will surely kill you before you ever reach the convent."

Ghislaine stared at his retreating back as he left the bedchamber. The man was not destined for a long life.

The midday meal was a silent affair, enlivened only by d'Everard's light-hearted flirtation with Effie. Guy sat in sullen silence and Ghislaine followed suit, determined not to engage in conversation with her husband unless absolutely necessary. Their mood was visited on the rest of the men and servants who took their meal there, and conversation between them was unusually quiet.

Ghislaine took little interest in the spicy pottage or meats that were served, preferring the simple bread and cheese that was her usual fare.

"You do not drink the ale today, Lady Ghislaine?" Sir Arnaud's blue eyes twinkled at her in amusement.

Ghislaine gave him a withering look and proceeded to sip at the water. "Do not let my preference inhibit your own, Sir Arnaud. Our ale has a good reputation for its flavour. Sir Brian can vouch for it, at any rate."

"Aye, I have noticed." He glanced briefly at the worthy Sir Brian. "My compliments to your brewer, my lady. And the food is more than acceptable." Arnaud's blond head turned to Guy. "As your husband has done naught but fill his mouth since our arrival, you must regard it as total approbation. It is not often he is so silent over his food."

That dig earned Arnaud a black scowl which caused him to laugh. "Do not mind his lack of manners, Lady Ghislaine. It is not meant personally."

"I am most gratified to hear it, Sir Arnaud. I had been losing sleep over the matter, you can be sure."

Her words were delivered with such a haughty tone, that even Sir Brian blinked hard.

Arnaud noticed his friend's lips tighten at that retort and watched him thoughtfully for a moment or two as Guy sank his teeth into the sweet curd tartlets. He recalled that it had been a long time since Guy had relaxed enough to eat such food, and though his mood was rather sour at the moment, Arnaud had observed a general lightening of his usually sober spirit. Perhaps it had something to do with this new wife, since the man was constantly watching her when she was not looking and irritable when she was not in sight. He had been ready to kill the guards ere he found out she had left the manor yesterday.

"I am sure we would welcome the chance to visit your kitchen and buttery so that we could thank your people ourselves." Arnaud smiled at her with such sincerity that Ghislaine could not turn him down.

"Of course. Should you wish to make your preferences known, then please tell me. I will do all I can to make you feel comfortable." Ghislaine addressed her sarcasm to her husband, but he appeared not to hear her. The oaf was biting into his third tartlet. An oaf with a sweet tooth, then.

When the meal was ended Ghislaine did as she was commanded and led the way to the buttery. It was a small, dark room off the great hall filled with wooden barrels and the sour smell of brewing ale.

"We brew twice a month," she began, "depending upon our stocks. There are not often visitors or travellers here, but there is not much else for the men to do."

"And your wine, lady? Do you make your own?"

Guy glanced around the room but could see no evidence of the wine. "Or perhaps you have drunk it all?" His grin was positively childlike and Ghislaine swept past him with her nose in the air and a disdainful sniff.

The tour of the kitchen and the gardens passed without incident, with Guy relieved that his wife did not choose to display her venom before her people. At least she could be reasonable, although he did not trust her. Ghislaine was probably the same as all the other women he had known, but as yet had not shown her true colours. She was, in fact, most knowledgeable about the running of the manor and the estate, answering his questions quietly and thoughtfully, and he was impressed with her quick understanding.

As they approached the blacksmith's hut in the bailey, Arnaud was summoned to settle a dispute between two of the men. Ghislaine watched the heated fight with barely concealed dismay.

"There is something I have been meaning to discuss, Sir Guy. Since your men have had several days to adjust to living at Chapmonswiche," she began uneasily, "I would like to point out that their behaviour within the manor leaves much to be desired." She lifted her chin more firmly. "They are noisy and untidy and my servants have had cause to complain on several occasions. I would be grateful if you could perhaps discuss the matter with Sir Arnaud."

Guy stared at her. "My men are trained soldiers. I have noticed no deterioration in their behaviour. Besides," he added stiffly, "as far as I am concerned, it is my men who seem to be plagued by your women. You would be better advised to discuss the matter with

Sir Brian, I think, although the poor man appears to be overly stretched.''

''Poor man!'' Her temper exploded. ''He is lucky to have lived so long, for I have often been tempted to add to the ale he is so fond of.''

At those meaningful words Guy burst out laughing, the anger between them dissipating. It was a deep, attractive sound that had many of the men turning to look at them. ''And what prevented you?''

''Father Thomas did not think it would aid my case with God.'' Her lips had formed a tight line.

Her indignant reaction brought another burst of laughter from him and this time it was impossible to ignore such an infectious sound without grinning ever so slightly.

''I take it that Father Thomas lives close by to ensure that men continue to survive your ale?''

''He does. If you wish to avail yourself of his services, he will come on Friday to hold mass.''

''I fear my soul is beyond redemption,'' he sighed.

''You are not alone in that supposition, my lord.'' The words were delivered with such arch haughtiness that Guy was rendered speechless once again.

Deciding that retreat was her best policy, Ghislaine flounced off towards the hall, leaving her husband pondering her last sentence.

As he watched her leave, Guy's mouth curved into a broad smile. The woman was spirited, there was no doubt about it. Nor did she mince words and that pleased him too. What else caught his attention was the way her hair glinted in the sun and, despite what he had told Arnaud, he found it most attractive. In fact, Guy was beginning to find himself increasingly looking out for her whenever he was near the keep. Memories of her fragrant white skin and soft lips crowded his thoughts far more often than he would have thought possible. He raked his hair back from his forehead. No matter that his mind insisted he did not want this woman, his body told him otherwise. And that was a problem.

Chapter Seven

"I see him, Lady Ghislaine," squealed Effie in delight as she leaned from the window of the hall. Her plumply pretty body was wedged into the narrow opening as she strained to watch the men training in the bailey.

"He would not thank you for embarrassing him before Sir Guy's men," replied Ghislaine tartly as she laboriously stitched new blankets for the men. The completed heap did not seem so large and they had been sewing for days. A heavy sigh from the window caused Ghislaine to look up.

"Perhaps you are right. He has taken a hit. Do you think he noticed me?" The hopeful note in her voice caused Ghislaine to smile to herself.

"Edwin could not fail to notice you since you have been hanging out of that window and making enough noise to attract the attention of the whole manor." The reprimand was received with a pout as Effie flounced to her seat.

Guy had spent the past few days training the men hard, with daily sword practice, body fighting and mock jousting. Ghislaine had seen little of him save at meals; even then he was too tired to communicate more than the bare minimum.

She supposed he was sleeping with his men in the keep for he had not returned to her bedchamber. It should have pleased her since he was keeping to his word, but Ghislaine knew that his lack of attention irritated her and she could not for the life of her think why. The fact that she thought of him at all was annoying for the man was no more than a common outlaw.

Taking pity on Effie and determined to escape the confines of the walls, Ghislaine decided to brave her husband's wrath. Elfrieda needed some herbs, and the first shoots were already looking strong. The weather was cold but fine and it would be an ideal morning to go to the forest. Putting down her sewing in relief, Ghislaine went to put on her cloak.

"I doubt it will last another winter," she said, staring at it ruefully, her fingers searching the material for other holes. Had she not said the same last spring?

"That's what Sir Guy said about it, too." Effie's mumbled statement took Ghislaine completely by surprise.

"He said that? When?"

"The other day when he was looking at your things."

"Why was he doing that?"

Effie looked up from her sewing, a frown on her face. "He didn't say."

Ghislaine shrugged her shoulders as she slipped the cloak around her. It did not matter that the cold would seep through the thin layers of wool for she was desperate to walk in the fresh forest and breathe the pure air. At least there she could be herself.

"Come. With all this training, maybe Sir Guy will look favourably on a request to go to the forest?" Ghislaine raised her eyebrows in a question, and Effie, after a moment or two's hesitation, smiled her acceptance.

The bailey was awash with men and their war paraphernalia, and the two women had to dodge between swords and lances to reach Guy de Courcy. Ghislaine found her eyes drawn to the tall, dark-haired figure in the centre of the yard. Her husband was fighting in hand-to-hand combat with a massive blond warrior.

Dressed only in his braies, Guy de Courcy was a magnificent sight. His skin, Ghislaine noticed in embarrassment, shone nut-brown under the weak March sun. Taut muscles rippled in his arms and shoulders as he drove the stick up and down with agile determination. Long strands of his thick black hair trailed down his back as he lunged forward into attack, and she wondered what it would feel like to touch his bare skin. Her cheeks blushed with the sin of such thoughts and Ghislaine sternly reminded herself that she was bound for the convent.

As she approached the men somewhat apprehensively, Ghislaine sensed their eyes on her. Arnaud d'Everard, courteous as ever, was the only friendly face in the crowd. He, at least, managed a passable smile although, from the blush on Effie's cheeks, Ghislaine was not absolutely certain that it was meant for her.

At her bidding, the lanky youth she now knew as Raoul ran to inform Guy that Ghislaine wished to see him. From the grim expression on his face as he strode towards her, Ghislaine half wished that she had waited until he had finished his fight. Steeling herself against his irritation, she decided to try a different tack.

"A lovely day, Sir Guy," she began brightly. His expression remained implacable as the blue eyes stared at her with polite disdain. In one hand he carried his crumpled tunic but had clearly dismissed the idea of putting it on to save her blushes. Embarrassed to look at him, Ghislaine turned to look at the men who continued to practise. "You have been training them hard. Are you preparing for any particular target?"

"Should Margaret Staveley's relatives decide to pay me a visit to settle the score, there seems good reason for being well prepared. I am sure that the Earl also has plans which will require my services sooner or later," he replied stiffly. "Gratifying though it is," he continued, "I am sure that concern for my men was not the reason you asked to see me."

The expression on his face was not encouraging, but Ghislaine was determined to get her way this time.

"You are right, my lord. The truth is that the kitchens require some vital herbs and that I am in sore need of some fresh air in the forest." She looked at him then. "You said I could not leave the manor save with an escort of your choice." Ghislaine eyed him with a defiant toss of her braids.

Despite his irritation at having his practice curtailed, Guy could not deny the truth in her words.

"Herbs at this time of the year?" he queried suspiciously.

"Aye. There are a few near the stream." She did not like the scowl that was deepening on his face.

"Where I found you last time you made a foray beyond the manor?"

Realising the track of his thoughts, Ghislaine's spirits plummeted. She nodded her head with grudging resignation, knowing that she would be returning to the growing pile of sewing.

"I will take you myself."

Ghislaine was so surprised at his words that she was rendered speechless for a moment.

"You do not trust me." Her cheeks coloured in indignation.

"Nay, but then I find few women trustworthy," he replied flatly, wiping his brow with his tunic. "However, I am still prepared to accompany you."

Ghislaine gave him a withering look as she swept towards the stables. She would have to be content with his company then. Strangely she did not find that thought as distasteful as she had imagined, but it did make her feel rather nervous. Anyone, she decided, would be foolish indeed not to feel apprehensive in such company.

The ride to the forest was a pleasant one, despite Ghislaine's misgivings about her husband and the fact that he would not let Effie accompany them. When he joined her at the stables, the man had at least had the grace to put on his tunic and cloak so that her heart did not thump so fast as before. He rode before her on his destrier and thankfully made no attempt at conversation. The two men-at-arms who accompanied them rode behind her.

The sun had reached its high point by the time the party reached the forest and to Ghislaine's consternation her stomach began to protest at having been denied food for so long.

"I hear that you are in need of sustenance, lady."

Ghislaine glared at him, her chin high. How could he mention such things? The man was really an ignorant oaf.

"Perhaps we should sit and eat. I persuaded Elfrieda to pack some bread and cheese. An interesting woman, that." He signalled to his men to draw to a halt.

The demands of her stomach got the better of her and Ghislaine agreed with a curt nod. Elfrieda's acquiescence to packing any food was most strange. Not for the first time did she wonder at her husband's powers of persuasion. He had very little difficulty with other women, it seemed. They dismounted at a clearing by the stream and much to her surprise, her husband placed his cloak on the ground for her to sit on.

"There is no need to spoil your fine cloak to protect mine," she pointed out prosaically.

Guy straightened up and smiled at her lazily. "I was thinking more of your health than your gowns."

Such a nicety of manners wrongfooted her completely and Ghislaine could feel the blush stealing over her cheeks. Again! Was she never to remain normal before the man! Mumbling her thanks she sat down at his command and took the food he offered.

"Your wardrobe is not extensive, lady. Have you a dislike of gowns or do you prefer running around like a village hoyden?"

His softly spoken words caused her to cough violently and Ghislaine was glad that Guy had had the foresight to send his men-at-arms on guard out of earshot.

"There is not much call for finery hereabouts. Practicality is of far greater importance." Even to her ears she sounded very righteous, but nevertheless she was not going to admit her father's meanness to one such as this.

"A very commendable attitude which gladdens my heart, lady, as well as my purse. I do not relish spending on feminine fripperies unnecessarily."

Ghislaine peered at him, uncertain whether she had detected a note of sarcasm in his voice. He had stretched himself out at her side, his head propped by his hand, his eyes watching her carefully. His eyes, she noticed, were a wonderful blue, a summer-sky blue.

"I had not realised that my wardrobe held any interest for you." The words came out a little muffled as she had just bitten into a small loaf of grey bread.

He looked at her with interest as she gazed into the depths of the forest, long red wisps of hair escaping from the repressive braids she favoured. She was not pretty exactly, but there was something there that made him want to watch her. And he liked the way she chewed with such obvious relish. Remembering then those soft curves of her body caused a warmth to flood through his veins that had naught to do with the sun.

"Anything that is mine interests me," he replied finally with such an arrogant tone that her cheeks flushed in indignation.

"I may have been part of your agreement with the Earl," she retorted tartly, "but I do not consider myself to be yours." Her eyes were suddenly alive with contempt. "You promised to send me to the convent."

Guy paused in surprise at such a bitter outburst. It would seem that his wife had still not accustomed herself to her status. Yet with one look at her flushed cheeks and dark, glowering eyes he realised, rather belatedly, that she probably did not deserve such treatment as she had received at his hands.

"I always keep my promises," he replied somewhat gruffily.

"That is so reassuring."

"You still have not answered my question," he prompted mildly, his blue eyes holding her gaze. Ghislaine almost felt that she was being held by force and then gently freed as he turned his attention to the handful of nuts at the bottom of his pouch.

"Oh." It was suddenly hard to concentrate as her pulse began to quicken.

"Your gowns," Guy reminded her with a perplexed smile.

"Aye," she stuttered. "Well, I dare say your knowledge of appearance is far greater than mine." The contemptuous look she offered him as she looked over his attire caused his lips to twist into a grin.

"Most women seem to spend a great deal of their time and men's money on clothes," he remarked rather cynically.

"I have no need of them for there is rarely anyone to see me in them," she shot back suddenly. Her irritated silence and tightly drawn lips told him not to press the point.

As Ghislaine brushed the crumbs from her lap, Guy rose to fill his water bag from the stream. His stride was long and easy and she found her eyes drawn to his retreating figure. He was tall, much taller than her father or even Walter, and she admitted to liking the way his dark hair trailed down over his shoulders in a thick, black mane. Somehow it gave him an aura of pagan strength that made her shiver.

"How long have you been living here?" The question was so unexpected that Ghislaine had to pull her thoughts back to reality.

"About eight summers. My father was given the village by Hugh d'Avranches for his services in Normandy. We were sent for shortly after."

Guy passed her the water pouch and Ghislaine gratefully accepted. The cold water trickled down her throat.

"Do you desire to return to Normandy?" he prodded, his eyes roving over her face. He found the freckles rather endearing.

Ghislaine shook her head. "I remember little about it. This is my home." A gleam of pride lit up her eyes and Guy felt oddly touched by it. There was precious little wealth here and the girl barely had enough rags to cover her back, and yet she wished to stay.

"Have you other family?" Guy remembered that Hugh d'Avranches had been her guardian, so it was unlikely.

"Not that I know of," she dismissed lightly. "And if I had, I doubt if they would be much interested in having an extra burden placed on them."

"Ah," he began, the light clearly dawning in his mind. "Hence the convent."

She shrugged her shoulders dismissively, unable to look him fully in the eye. The man was sitting so close to her that she could feel the warmth of him, smell him even. It was decidedly uncomfortable as she was unable to think straight and would have risen to leave had a large, tanned hand not clamped down on her arm to prevent her.

"Is my company so awful?" He paused for a moment to clear his throat. "I am not used to speaking with ladies and I had not meant to cause you upset. My words are perhaps too blunt."

Expecting to see amusement glittering in those blue eyes, Ghislaine looked directly into them, a sharp retort on her lips. But what she saw there made her hesitate. It was a genuine admission of weakness without any hint of sarcasm. Guy was so close that she could see the tiny scars of battle on his face and the way his newly shaven chin was already growing dark. Lines of fatigue were etched lightly round his mouth and darker circles below his eyes.

"Awful?" she repeated with difficulty. Her throat seemed to have constricted. "Nay. I…I…am not used to you," Ghislaine blurted out quickly. "As for the rest, I think I prefer the truth."

Guy looked up to watch the darkening clouds gather above. He suddenly turned his face towards her and placed a forefinger below her chin, forcing Ghislaine to look at him.

"If I have treated you badly," he began gruffly, "I apologise, for you deserved none of it." He drew in a deep breath, as if drawing courage from it. "I would not send you from your home unless you truly wish it. Will you think about it?"

The unexpected question hung in the air between them as their eyes locked together. Ghislaine could feel her heart pounding faster beneath her cloak as his finger moved to push back some of the wisps of hair that floated across her face. Warmth from an unknown source crept through her body as his finger traced a gentle path along her chin. Had he tried to kiss her, she would have pushed him away and stormed off, but he did no such thing and she was not proof against that deep, gruff voice asking so simple a question.

"Why?" Her voice was almost a whisper as she looked into the fathomless blue of his eyes.

Guy ignored the question as he did not rightly know the answer himself. Because she was an innocent? Because he had changed the course of her life? He had known what he was doing when he started this and it had not bothered him then. Somehow this girl with the sharp tongue and her red hair had gotten under his skin. He had no desire to hurt her further and if he could repair some of the damage, then he would.

"I do not believe that you have a vocation." His eyebrow was raised in question, a grin lurking about his lips.

Ghislaine returned his grin with a reproving sniff.

"You do not know me at all, Sir Guy."

His laughter at such a proud response drew a twitch from Ghislaine's lips.

"I can see why the Earl was keen to rid himself of such responsibility, for you and your tongue are more trouble than a besieged keep." Guy watched as she laughed at that. It was a husky, most attractive sound that pleased him greatly.

Ghislaine smiled at the thought of proud Hugh d'Avranches being bedevilled by herself. "My father was of the same opinion. He would, no doubt, have approved of you."

There was not a trace of vanity in her, no coy looks

nor angling for pretty words. Guy felt the tension slide
from him as he stretched out on his back, his hands
behind his head and closed his eyes. "I doubt that,"
he said soberly. "According to Hugh d'Avranches,
John de Launay was an honourable knight of great
courage and honesty."

Ghislaine stared down at the body lying at her side.
In repose he looked younger, less…threatening. Aye,
that was the word. She drew her legs up against her
chest and wrapped her arms around them as she
thought then of her father. Well? Would he have approved of this outlaw and mercenary?

"Did you do all those things you are supposed to
have done?" She was suddenly curious about this
murderer who could laugh and tease her like any
brother.

"Some." His answer was delivered with complete
indifference and Ghislaine realised that she was heading for difficult waters. She could not stop now.

"Did you kill Margaret?"

He sat up at that, his eyes upon her. After a moment
or two, Guy shook his head slowly. "No." It was such
a simple word, uttered with complete finality. And she
wanted to believe him.

"Will you tell me?"

Guy sighed and shrugged his shoulders, his fingers
busy picking twigs off his cloak. "After I left her
keep, I received a false message to finish a siege near
Stafford. In the mood I was in, it was a very welcome
distraction. As it happened, it provided the perfect
cover for the real criminals."

Behind the seemingly indifferent words, Ghislaine
could sense the anger and resentment that had taken

hold of him, that threatened to eat him from the inside. She found herself wanting to believe him.

"But why did you not leave England and go back to your home in Normandy?" Guy's shoulders were stiff and unrelenting as he tossed the twigs away to the side of him.

"My living, and that of my men, depends on the strength of my reputation. People are quick to condemn without hearing all the facts," he added on a bitter note. "Besides, there is nothing in Normandy for me. This is as good a place as any."

Ghislaine wondered at that. For a man of his worth and skill there would always be someone willing to open their arms to him. And yet Margaret had not. Margaret. Sweet, gentle Margaret.

"Why did you choose Margaret as a wife?" As soon as she had spoken the words, Ghislaine regretted them but could not unsay them. She returned his gaze with steady eyes. For a moment she thought he would not answer, but then she remembered his habit of thinking carefully.

"I needed a wife," he said simply. "I was tired of bad food, cold pallets and stinking clothes." A wry grimace fleetingly touched his lips. "Margaret Staveley seemed to fulfil my requirements." His lips tightened into a straight line. "Unfortunately it would seem that I did not fulfil hers."

It was the words he did not say that tugged at her heart. Despite his gruff, cool exterior, the man was capable of feelings and desires just as the next. There was something about the way he stared sightlessly into the distance that made her want to put her hand on his arm. For comfort.

"And now?" She stole a look at his hardened face which once more sported his scowl.

"Now?" Guy turned slowly to look at her, his eyes colder than the winter sea. "Now I must fight to protect my name and to win back what is rightfully mine. I paid more than one thousand marks for a manor which now resides in the hands of Henry Dettingham with the blessing of the King's men."

For a moment, Ghislaine was uncertain whether Guy was upset more because of the loss of his one thousand silver marks than the loss of his reputation. And yet such admissions had shown her a different side to him. A side that she found vulnerable and human, and had wanted to trust.

"My father would have said exactly the same," she sighed as she stood to shake the crumbs from her lap. "I am sure you would have understood each other well."

"And why do I feel that was not altogether a compliment?" he responded mildly, gathering up his cloak.

"You fire the same black looks at anyone who displeases you," she ventured, a delicate brow raised in disdain.

"We have both been plagued by the same wench," came his instant retort.

Ghislaine smiled at him then, encouraged by his lightening mood. "That," she pointed out, "does not sound like a compliment either, my lord."

The forest was cool and smelled of the fresh mixture of decaying earth and budding greenery and Ghislaine found herself smiling as they made their way to the herbs that grew near the stream. Guy asked her many questions about the estate and the land about, showing her another side to his character. His manners might be lacking most of the time but his wits were not. The man knew much more about running a manor than she had imagined. She was curious about him.

"Do you have family, Sir Guy?" Ghislaine stooped to pick at the herbs carefully.

"Aye. Three brothers in Normandy."

Encouraged by his lack of aggression, Ghislaine looked up. "You must miss them."

A veil seemed to draw down over his face at that and she knew she was stepping on stony ground. Ghislaine knew the answer before his lips formed it.

"I never think of them."

As she tugged at the difficult stem, Guy handed her his knife. It was a handsome hunter's knife with an ivory handle chased in gold. She took it with a grateful smile.

"Never?"

Guy looked at the knife in her hands. "Keep the knife. You may have need of it."

She nodded silently. This was certainly a different side to her husband.

"Do you ever think of your brother?" He had side-stepped her question with an irritating lack of conscience, but Ghislaine wondered why. She stored the information for another time.

"A lot of the time I talk to him. As if he were still here," she added. That was something she had never admitted to anyone. Not even Margaret. "We were close."

Guy nodded at that, his dark hair glinting in the shafts of green-flecked light that filtered through the trees. He was watching the depths of the forest with half-closed eyes. Ghislaine considered the stern set of his mouth as she put the herbs in her pouch.

"So you have no one left?" His eyes had switched to her face and for some reason Ghislaine could not bring herself to look at him.

"Not now that Margaret is dead."

The words seemed to echo on the still air between them. She had not meant to say them, but something deep within her forced them out.

"Margaret? You knew her?" Guy's face was very still, his eyes boring deep into her.

"Of course. She was married to my brother before Peter Staveley. They had been wed only a few months before his death. Peter was a friend of my father's. That was how he met her." The words trailed off as Guy stood squarely before her.

"You did not know?" The words came out almost as a whisper. Then a thought struck her. "You are not in the least concerned about who you marry?"

His grim face lightened a little at the scandalised tone in her voice. "It was not quite that bad. Arnaud had looked into her background and found nothing amiss. I had planned to find out more from the lady herself."

His words were a little defensive and Ghislaine was intrigued. "Are you always so careless when you woo a lady?"

"It's not something I do every day," he admitted, a smile lurking on his lips. Her raised eyebrow told him what she thought of his methods.

"My lord, has anyone told you that offering your worldly goods to an unknown, or abducting an innocent and forcing them into marriage is not the usual way to go about these things?''

''Oh? Do you recommend a better method?'' Ghislaine saw the humour glinting in his eyes.

''Well I have not had much personal experience in these matters, of course, but ladies like to think that they have a certain attraction, of course.''

''Of course,'' came the grave response. ''I can see how badly I have erred.'' He smiled down at her, and Ghislaine held her breath. When he looked at her like that the man truly had no need for words. ''Have you any other advice?''

''Aye,'' she said tartly. ''Attempting to beat a woman is no way to curry their favour.''

As she bent down to pick up more herbs, his hand pulled her up again. His eyes roved over her face and she detected a gentleness that she had not seen before.

''I did not mean to hurt you, girl.''

She did not want his sympathy or his pity.

''My name is Ghislaine. That would be a start.''

Guy watched her flounce off, and he smiled to himself. Maybe he had been too hasty in his assessment of his wife.

By the time the party had reached the manor gates, they had been soaked in a sudden downpour. Despite her bedraggled appearance, Ghislaine's mood had lightened and the tension she had been feeling seemed to be slipping a little. Guy had ridden by her side and although he had not said much she sensed a thawing between them. At least he had not scowled. In fact, when he looked at her, Guy had this rather strange smile on his lips.

Looking down at her costume, Ghislaine realised rather belatedly that she did not appear in her best light. Her hair hung in sodden rats tails over her back and her cloak and gown resembled little more that dripping rags. A very feminine desire to look her best beset her. Preferring not to examine the cause of this desire, Ghislaine mentally went through the choice of gowns available to her. It was an exercise doomed from the start as Ghislaine knew deep down that there was nothing suitable.

"Ghislaine."

Shocked at hearing her own name from his lips, Ghislaine started. Her palfrey reacted in similar fashion and did not settle until Guy steadied her.

"I had no desire to startle you, lady." Back to normal, she thought wryly, but nothing could douse that small flame of cheer that began to burn when he spoke her name.

"Just deep in thought, Sir Guy."

Guy smiled at her use of his title. "I hope that you will join me this evening, lady. We have not supped together these past few nights and I believe that your company has been sorely missed."

He had not said that he had missed her company, but it was the next best thing. His eyes looked almost shyly into hers and what she saw there made her heart beat faster.

Warmth flooded through her as their horses drew to a halt alongside each other. Guy waved their escort through the manor gates and they were left alone. He picked up her wet hand and brought it to his lips. He pressed a gentle kiss on her frozen fingers and smiled at her. It was a smile that made her resistance to him weaken and her heart pound. It was a smile that promised much.

"My lord." One of Guy's men came running from within the gates. "We have visitors. They request your presence."

Ghislaine bit back the words of disappointment and turned her eyes to the gate. Whoever was there had very poor timing. She followed her husband across the moat.

"Walter!" He was the last person she had expected to see, although she had been willing him to come. And now he was here, she was suddenly very confused about her feelings. Ghislaine eyed her husband in a new light. She had witnessed a softer, more gentle man with humour and intelligence, but he was still her enemy. How could she have forgotten that? Divided feelings warred within her, for she belatedly realised that she had willingly let herself be won over by this enigmatic mercenary. What a fool she was.

Guy had dismounted at the same time as Ghislaine and had come to stand at her side. His cold expression told her that he knew the visitor's identity. Remembering his earlier threat, Ghislaine introduced the two men in as dutiful a voice as she could muster.

They eyed each other with dislike. Guy was a good head taller than Walter, his stormy blue eyes taking in every detail about the man his wife had confessed to loving. For a moment she saw him through Guy's eyes. Arrogant, disdainful and dressed like a peacock. But just for a moment. Those mutinous thoughts disappeared the minute Walter's gentle, friendly smile told her how relieved he was to find her still alive.

She felt contrition, for he was not to blame. Walter

de Belleme was as bound by convention as she. Defying the Earl could have been far worse for him than her marriage to Guy de Courcy. And she was pleased to see him. His short blond hair ruffled in the wind and his grey eyes told her what she wanted to know.

"I believe good wishes are due, Lady Ghislaine. Your marriage was most sudden. I came as soon as I was able."

Ghislaine ignored the snort that came from Guy's direction. She would have to be careful if Walter was to continue living. Despite his expertise with a sword, she did not doubt that her husband could overcome him should he put his mind to it.

"Greetings, Sir Walter. Your visit was most timely."

Walter's raised eyebrow and his rather pointed look at her sodden clothes told her what he thought of that. Flustered that she should be caught so out of looks, Ghislaine nervously suggested that he wait in the hall whilst Sir Guy and herself changed into more fitting attire.

She could feel Guy's eyes follow Walter's back as he made his way across the bailey. He had brought an escort of five men-at-arms and two knights she vaguely remembered seeing at the court. Had she been expecting a rescue party, Ghislaine thought wryly, she would have been sorely disappointed.

"I hope you remember my promise, lady." Guy's deep voice penetrated her thoughts. The charm and gentleness that he had displayed earlier were once again hidden beneath a black scowl, but Ghislaine was no longer fearful.

"I remember everything, my lord." Casting a disdainful look in his direction, Ghislaine lifted her chin and crossed the bailey, her dripping gown thrashing against her legs. She would not be gulled like a foolish child and at that moment she did not care what his reaction would be. That mercenary oaf had lumbered into her life and ruined her dreams. She had been the victim, not the other way round.

With such thoughts racing through her mind, Ghislaine flounced up the staircase to her chamber. It was not until she had peeled off the sopping gown that she belatedly remembered that Guy still had possession of her clothes. Her first reaction was to storm from the chamber and find him, to pour her anger over his shoulders. Her second was to remember to stay calm. It would benefit no one, least of all Walter, were she to stir her husband's temper. Irritated beyond all measure, Ghislaine threw herself onto the bed. She would have to ask Guy for suitable clothes.

Effie returned with her oldest, most threadbare gown of brown wool over her arm, her cheeks tinged pink with the humiliation her mistress would know. Ghislaine had spent her temper by rubbing her hair dry. As soon as she saw what Guy was giving her to wear, Ghislaine smiled to herself. Was he jealous? Was her oafish, scowling husband jealous of Walter? For a moment she wallowed in the delicious feeling of having two men fight for her attentions, before reality washed over her. Neither of them were interested in her for she had neither looks nor charm to recommend her. Hadn't she always known that?

Changed and coiffed, Ghislaine felt no less nervous than before, but her courage had returned. She would face her fate with bravery and she would save Walter.

A soft tapping at the door of her chamber did not cause her any concern. Thinking it was one of the servants, she bade them enter whilst she continued to adjust her braids.

"You are in better looks, Lady Ghislaine."

Ghislaine whirled round to see Walter standing before her, admiration beaming from his eyes. Or was it something else? The flicker of uncertainty must have registered, for Walter stepped forward in concern.

"Do not worry, lady. Your husband is in the stables still. I would not willingly cause you grief but I had to see you alone."

"Your concern does you much credit, my lord, but it is unfortunately a little tardy."

"You are upset," he began soothingly. "But I have come to rescue you, Ghislaine." Walter had closed the gap between them and his hands had risen to her arms. Gently he pulled her towards him.

Ghislaine stiffened. "And what makes you think I wish to be rescued, Sir Walter? I was married to Sir Guy before God. Naught can change that now."

There was no mistaking the accusing emphasis that Ghislaine had laid on that last word and Walter released her quickly. A look of acute distress flooded across his face.

"Aye. You are right to be angry, Ghislaine." His hand reached out to move a tendril of hair from her eyes, but she moved back to avoid his touch. Walter smiled wanly and pushed back his own perfect curls with a sigh. Why, she thought, did that movement look so contrived?

"I tried to stop the marriage," he murmured miserably, "but the Earl would not allow it."

Ghislaine eyed him uncertainly. She wanted to believe him, but so much had happened that she no longer knew whom to trust. At least Guy was open with his scorn and his anger.

"Why would you wish to anger the Earl with my rescue now?" Ghislaine almost held her breath as she waited for his reply.

Walter hesitated for a fraction of a second. "You would not need to be rescued," he began. "De Courcy is very likely to meet his end sooner rather than later. It is, after all, the price a mercenary pays. Dettingham and his men are sniffing round all the time. It won't be long before they catch up with him."

His words echoed in her head. She did not wish to be married to de Courcy, but nor did she wish him to die. "No."

Walter stared at her and for a moment, Ghislaine was sure she detected irritation in those soft grey eyes.

"Are you sure?" His hands covered her shoulders and began a gentle, rhythmic rubbing with his thumbs.

"Aye. He was not my choice, but I do not willingly wish his death, if I had understood you aright." She shook off his hands, her pleasure in seeing him again somewhat marred. "I thank you for your concern, Sir Walter, but I think it best you leave my chamber."

Tight-lipped, Walter nodded and left her without a sound. It was not until she heard his voice below that Ghislaine let out a sigh of relief. At least he was safe. But what of Guy? Was he safe? Somehow she did not think Walter would give up quite so easily, although she was sure that he was not interested in her any more. And if it was not her, then what was it?

Puzzled, Ghislaine left the chamber.

Chapter Eight

Ghislaine glared at the spindle and the mangled heap of raw wool in her lap with a malevolent eye and stood up. The distaff and wool swept to the floor as she retreated to the fire in the hall. Her patience and her temper had been much tried this past week since Walter's disastrous visit and Ghislaine was in no mood this morning for practising her limited skills in the art of spinning. Her ineptitude in such matters was widely lamented.

Several of Guy's churlish men were lounging noisily in the hall, gaming with dice or arm-wrestling and generally disturbing the peace and order that had always reigned in her home. Treating a particularly loud and discordant trio to one of her glacial stares, Ghislaine determined to tackle her husband about his men's general behaviour. She had continued to receive complaints from her women about their coarse language and lewd suggestions. Sighing with frustration, she turned back to the fire.

Talking to Guy de Courcy was another problem. Since Walter's mistimed appearance, she and her husband had barely exchanged more than a few words. Any rapprochement that might have existed between them had been well and truly shattered.

The meal that dreadful night had been a quiet, strained affair, with Walter and his knights attempting polite conversation whilst her husband had just scowled at them. Eventually his black mood had descended on the whole company and it had come as a relief when Walter had announced their immediate departure.

Ghislaine had retired to her chamber in silence, leaving her husband to pour his wrath on his own men. She had lain awake for hours, contemplating Walter's belief that Guy might be killed, and had finally come to the conclusion that as the de Courcy widow she would be richer than as John de Launay's heiress. Had that been the key to Walter's renewed interest in her? Ghislaine had grown stiff with cold and misery, torturing herself over her own naïvety. She had not wanted to believe it, but she had had to admit that Walter had not tried very hard to prevent her marriage to the mercenary.

And now? She was married to a man who was using her to clear his name, who scowled at the world, who was a murdering mercenary. But honest, voiced her inner conscience. He had always been truthful with her. He had never hidden his feelings or his reasoning in his dealings with her. No, she could not honestly wish for his death

"Lady Ghislaine?" Effie tapped her mistress gently on the shoulder.

"My pardon, Effie. I was woolgathering."

Effie cast a baleful eye in the direction of the spindle and the wool. "Aye," she said doubtfully. "And most of it on the rushes."

A loud guffaw from the direction of the noisy trio caused Effie's cheeks to flush a becoming shade of pink.

"There's a pedlar at the gates asking if we need aught. Can we allow him in?" Her eyes shone with eager anticipation.

They could do with the diversion and Ghislaine knew that many of the women would welcome the chance to purchase ribbon, needles and several other items so essential to the female mind. As Guy was out hunting, the responsibility lay on her shoulders. "Aye," she said finally. "Have him come to the hall."

The pedlar was unknown to them but not unwelcome for that. A small, thin man with straggly brown hair and one blind eye, he welcomed the bowl of pottage offered and drank a skin of ale with relish. Ghislaine noticed that as he ate and drank, his good eye was carefully observing the men and the surroundings.

"Have you come far?" she enquired. His observation was making her feel uneasy.

The man shook his head. "Not far," he responded pleasantly enough. "Spring is always a good time of year. You ladies is always keen to buy things to attract the eyes of the men."

His words were well meaning if a little crude. "Then we would not wish to delay you on your travels. Perhaps you would show us your wares?"

Correctly interpreting her desire for him to conclude his sales speedily, the pedlar quickly arranged his goods to advantage. Ghislaine had to admit that the array was enticing and soon found herself caught up in the excitement. She had need of a new comb and several new laces and took great pleasure in making her final choices. Her eye was also caught by the perfumed phials and trinkets which elicited such sighs of pleasure from the others. The hall was buzzing with the animated chatter of the women and their exclamations of delight over their purchases when in walked Guy de Courcy.

At first, Ghislaine did not notice his entry but a loud thumping on the table soon brought her attention to him.

"A word with you, lady," came his voice, loud and cold, across the hall. It seemed as if the entire crowd was holding its collective breath as Ghislaine headed towards the door. Flushed to her toes with the humiliation, Ghislaine faced her husband with tight lips.

"You wished to speak with me, my lord?"

Guy stood before her, his hands on his hips. It was not an encouraging posture, she decided.

"You are right, lady." His eyes had turned a dark blue and his skin was still pink from the chase. "I demand to know who gave permission to let the wretch in?"

Ghislaine stiffened. "I did. There seemed no harm…"

"No harm!" came the interruption. "Do you know him? Have you proof of his occupation?"

Ghislaine had to shake her head, and the suspicions she had initially harboured returned. The man had seemed unusually observant. "Perhaps you wish to share your concerns with me?" she suggested with as much dignity as she could muster.

"I had thought there would be little need to explain things to you, lady. But it seems I must. All Henry Dettingham needs is proof of my existence here and information about the number of men under my roof. The Earl's men have not yet materialised and we remain vulnerable to attack. Your lack of vigilance endangers every life within these walls. No stranger is to enter the gates of the manor without my express permission. Have I made myself clear?"

Had he spoken quietly, then Ghislaine might have been able to swallow her pride for what he said made sense. However, Guy de Courcy seemed unable to speak quietly and she was certain that everyone in the hall must have heard him, including the pedlar. Her humiliation was complete.

"You have made yourself perfectly clear, my lord. However, I would like to point out that the women, myself included, had need of several items offered by the pedlar and were glad of his presence. I take it we will be allowed to complete our purchases?" She eyed him with a mixture of humiliation and irritation.

"The other women may do so, but I am not aware that you have enough money to pay for your own items."

Ghislaine's cheeks burned at such treatment. "Sir Brian will…"

"Sir Brian will no longer be providing you with funds just to indulge your fancy whims, lady. I thought I had made it clear that I do not fritter hard-earned money on women's nonsense." His words left her speechless. Had she ever harboured any softer feelings towards the man, they were certainly destroyed now. Ghislaine lowered her eyes, determined not to let him see how much he had hurt her. Aye, the things were no more than indulgent fripperies, but he had deliberately made her look foolish.

"Very well, my lord. Sir Brian will send him on his way."

"See that he is gone by the time I return from the stables. I trust him not." So saying Guy stalked off towards the bailey leaving Ghislaine uncertain whether to cry or to attempt murder.

The pedlar left within the candle notch and Ghislaine retired to her room to lick her wounds. Her husband had been right; she had made a foolish error of judgement and it would not happen again. There had been no good reason why he should have upbraided her in such a high-handed manner, though, and the incident had upset her deeply. It would seem that she received less consideration than his squire. So much for his soft, gentle words of the week before.

A curt knock at the door caused her to stand quickly and wipe her eyes with her sleeve. So her husband had relented already! Well, if he thought her willing to take such treatment meekly, she was going to disabuse him right quickly.

When she yanked open the door to find Sir Arnaud d'Everard, however, her face must have betrayed her thoughts.

"I am sorry to disappoint you, my lady, but I have come to bring you some wine and company. I had thought you may have need of both." His smile was gentle and Ghislaine was not proof against it. She stood back to allow him entry. There would be no need of a chaperon with Sir Arnaud.

"Your charm is difficult to resist, Sir Arnaud," she returned. "'Tis more than a shame that so little seems to have rubbed off on Sir Guy."

He looked up at her sharply as he poured the wine into two goblets. "He has not had much charm in his life, lady. It is not surprising that he may seem harsh at times. He has much on his mind."

"He is often like a bear with a sore head," she retorted as she turned to look out of the window embrasure. "It is not at all easy to deal with him. My servants are terrified of him."

Sir Arnaud was silent as he handed her the wine.

"His temper can be sour, but he is a good man. It would be hard to find a more trustworthy friend."

"Aye. I'm sure that may be true for you, Sir Arnaud, but he does not view me in the same light," she replied doubtfully, turning back to look at him.

Arnaud laughed. "Now that, lady, seems most promising to me."

Ghislaine gave him a withering look. "He prefers not to view me at all," she continued. "Most of the time he avoids my company. When he does attempt conversation, more often than not it is to upbraid me in a most harsh manner."

The amusement had died from Sir Arnaud's eyes as he watched Ghislaine's spirit sink.

"Do not take it so badly, lady. It is just his way with ladies."

Ghislaine snorted her disgust before taking a soothing draught of sweet red wine. "He is naught but an oaf. It matters not to me that he lumps me with the rest of womankind, but I wish to be treated with more respect. He has control over my home, my servants, any money…everything. For the time that I have left here, I want…I want to be treated as if I mattered.'' She turned her back towards Sir Arnaud so that he would not notice the brightness of her eyes, nor the trembling of her chin.

''Lady, I am sorry for your distress, but mayhap I can relieve some of your troubles by way of explanation.'' He looked warily about but the room was empty.

Ghislaine turned to look at him, her mouth set in a hard line. ''I will listen, Sir Arnaud, but I doubt you will change my mind.''

Arnaud inclined his head and shrugged his shoulders. ''Nay. But it might go some way to help you understand him better.''

''Very well, but do not expect too much.''

''He has never liked ladies much,'' he began hesitantly, and frowned at Ghislaine's responding sigh.

''His own mother left him at the age of three to run off with her lover. His father had some maggot in his head that the fault lay at Guy's feet and practically ignored him from then on.''

''Guy?'' she questioned. ''How can a three-year-old be responsible for that?''

Arnaud shook his head. ''Guy was a difficult child whose boisterous behaviour had caused disagreements between his parents. His mother was a gentle creature apparently who resisted her husband's attempts to discipline the child. It would seem his father was a harsh man who beat Guy and his three brothers frequently. When he was seven, Guy was sent to be fostered as squire under the wings of Lord Marigny, whose reputation as a brutal taskmaster was well deserved.''

"And that was where you met him?" Ghislaine asked.

"Aye. We became friends. He had the brawn and I the art of diplomacy. Between us we managed to survive those early days."

"Most interesting, Sir Arnaud, but I fail to see how his treatment as a child is different to that of many other men. He has had time to get over a few beatings surely?"

"Perhaps a little more patience, lady? I am not yet done." Sir Arnaud paused to sip the wine. "Marigny always seemed to single him out for punishment if there was trouble of any kind. Guy didn't complain since he was determined to make his father proud of him. He was convinced that once knighted, his father would show him some respect and their differences buried. He finally won his spurs at eighteen and I swear that was the first time I had ever seen him smile."

"Well, that perhaps goes some way to explain his bad temper, but not his attitude towards myself?"

"Despite his scowls, Guy's looks drew much attention from women. He was ever a shy one, but felt most at ease with the simpler, serving wenches who demanded nothing more from him than an hour or two of his time." Even Sir Arnaud flushed a little at that! "The ladies of the keep wanted much the same, but would also mock him for his plain speaking and lack of pretty words. In the end he found that surliness answered the problem best. Until he went back home."

"Home?" she enquired, her curiosity piqued. "Where is that? Guy has never talked of it."

"His father owned a good-sized estate near Avranches, but that meant little to Guy since he was the fourth son. Still, a home is a home and Guy had hoped that in eleven years his father would have become more approachable." Arnaud paused to swirl the wine round in his cup.

"So he went back to the estate in the end?" she prompted.

"Aye. But it was not much of a home-coming. After having his first marriage annulled, his father had hopes of remarrying a younger, very pretty daughter of a neighbouring landowner. Guy welcomed the match but it would seem his new step-mother-to-be found it impossible to keep her hands off him. She followed him everywhere and finally, when she could not get him to bed her, she went to his father accusing Guy of trying to do exactly that."

Ghislaine frowned. "He must have denied it?"

"Of course. It did no good, though. His father wished to hang him on the spot, but his elder brother, well aware of the lady's predilections, helped him escape."

"So he became a mercenary," she surmised.

"Aye, and never had anything to do with women of rank since then."

"Until Margaret Staveley, thinking she would be a good wife?"

Arnaud sighed. "Luck was not with him there either."

"Margaret would have made a good wife." Ghislaine pointed out sadly. "She was good, kind and loyal. And very pretty," she added.

"Perhaps," said Arnaud distractedly, sniffing the wine.

"You do not think she would have made a good wife?" Ghislaine was fascinated by the very idea.

He hesitated. "I am not sure Margaret Staveley would have made Guy a good wife."

"Margaret would have made any man a good wife. Except she would not have liked his black scowls."

"You do not seem to mind them so much," he replied flatly.

Ghislaine shrugged her shoulders. "They are rarely based on substance of any sort. Besides, I have noticed that he shouts and threatens a lot, but rarely acts."

"Do not let the men know that, lady, or his reputation will be worth naught."

They laughed together at that unlikely thought.

"Are you suggesting that the next time he shouts at me I cover myself in bruises?" Ghislaine smiled at him.

"Lady, the fact that he shouts at you at all is what interests me."

"How so?" Ghislaine demanded, fascinated at this line of thought.

"He has never shown so much interest in any other woman."

Ghislaine frowned. "I can assure you the experience is one most women would gladly avoid."

"I meant that he finds it hard to stay away from you."

Ghislaine shook her head. "You are wrong, Sir Arnaud. He avoids me at all costs. I would even go so far as to say that he plans it like a military campaign."

Arnaud laughed. "You might find a little gentle persuasion works wonders."

Ghislaine received this suggestion with a contemptuous expression. "I am not at all convinced of the wisdom of encouraging his attentions, Sir Arnaud. My husband has made it clear on several occasions that he will be pleased to rid himself of me and my accursed tongue."

Arnaud d'Everard regarded Ghislaine with a thoughtful expression on his face. "He is a proud man who has had to fight for everything. There has been no kindness in his life, no warmth and no love. Were he to be shown a different way, lady, he might learn to change." He paused to place his goblet on the floor. "I believe you to be a good woman, lady. Be patient with him and you may find Guy a worthy husband."

"You ask much, Sir Arnaud. He has caused me hurt and humiliation." Her dark eyes challenged him. "Give me one good reason why I should. The convent seems a more acceptable solution."

Sir Arnaud pushed his blond locks back from his face in frustration. "I cannot believe you have a vocation," he offered hopefully. "Nor would your life ever be dull."

"A most unoriginal thought, Sir Arnaud," she replied waspishly. "But if it makes you feel better, I shall consider what you said." Inwardly Ghislaine chided herself for such weakness. She had absolutely no intention whatsoever of considering a proper marriage to such a man. None at all.

Elfrieda stood in the middle of her warm kitchen with her arms across her ample chest and glared with intense dislike at the huge man stood before her.

"This brute thinks that just because he catches most of the meat, it entitles him to take liberties." The woman's voice was indignant and somewhat too self-righteous for one well-known to enjoy the pleasures of the flesh. Ghislaine stood between the warring pair in an attempt to prevent mayhem from destroying the evening meal.

Whatever Elfrieda's morals, the woman had proved herself an excellent cook since the previous incumbent had died suddenly from a lung fever last Yuletide. Although most head cooks were men, Ghislaine had seen no point in replacing her. Her quick temper, however, was legendary.

Despite being no more than twenty-four summers in age, Elfrieda ruled the kitchen with strict authority and had no time for idle loafers and scroungers. Anyone found to be overstepping the mark was subjected to a tongue lashing of great volume and thrown from the kitchen under a hail of pans and bones. Mindful of her husband's admitted parsimony, Ghislaine felt it was an extra expense they could do without.

Tall for a woman, and plump as a well-fed chicken, Elfrieda's size and stubborn expression would have been more than offputting for most men. Her clear blue eyes flashed mutinously and her generous mouth compressed in a tight line as she prepared to do battle with Guy de Courcy's giant sergeant.

Joachim, however, seemed not one whit dismayed by Elfrieda's aggression. A Frank with a sullen disposition and thick, greasy blond braids, he ruled the de Courcy mercenaries with little more than a few growls and snarls. None of those louts had ever shown any desire to pit their strength against Joachim's huge bulk. Elfrieda knew no such apprehension, and Ghislaine was almost certain she saw a responding glint in the sergeant's dull blue eyes.

Feeling somewhat like an insect caught between two huge rocks, Ghislaine held up her hands. "I will not have any disruption in my kitchens," she began in a firm tone. "Go to the bailey and get about your duties. If you have any complaints, address them to Sir Arnaud and we shall deal with them in a civilised fashion."

"Oh, aye," responded Elfrieda with a sly glance at Ghislaine. "Like you and Sir Guy, you mean?"

"Hush, woman." Joachim's two words practically boomed around the kitchen and even Elfrieda seemed a bit taken aback. "Show respect to your mistress or I will beat you." He stared intently at Elfrieda, his sullen face almost carved in granite. After a moment or two of silence, he nodded curtly at Ghislaine and turned to leave.

Ghislaine exhaled in relief as he thudded down the stone-flagged corridor to the bailey. Elfrieda appeared to be rooted to the spot, completely taken aback at having been spoken to so roughly. It was certainly a novel experience.

Just as she was about to upbraid Elfrieda, a sudden outburst of frantic shouting in the bailey distracted their attention. Hurrying outside, Ghislaine found her bailey swarming with Guy's mercenaries and her own soldiers charging to their posts. Joachim stood in the middle of it all, like an immovable tree, dispensing orders in his slow, gruff voice. There was no sign of her husband or Sir Arnaud.

Catching sight of Edwin, relief flooded through her. At last, a friendly face! Her pleasure was to be short lived. "Get inside the keep, my lady, and stay there. That's an order!"

"I will not move until I know what's happening," she retorted defiantly. Edwin had certainly changed over the last few weeks. Gone was the gentleness and the familiar resignation, replaced by a light in his eyes which she fancied was a sort of excitement. Her husband had taken her childhood friend and brought him to manhood. Edwin had left her behind. Maybe it was time for her to take the same path.

Crossing her arms over her chest, Ghislaine faced Edwin in much the same way Elfrieda had faced Joachim. Edwin pulled an iron helm over his head as he spoke. "Dettingham has arrived with his men and he is likely to cause trouble. Now go inside and deal with the women and servants." His narrowed eyes were watching the men beyond her shoulder.

"Where is my husband?" That brought Edwin's eyes to hers.

"Putting on his hauberk and expecting obedience from you." He reached to touch an auburn braid in a familiar gesture, his expression softened. "Do as he says, Ghislaine. I need to know you are safe."

A pang of fear shot through her. Edwin was genuinely worried. "Aye," she grinned at him reluctantly. "I'll go, but if you get yourself hurt because of Guy de Courcy's quarrel, I shall be most vexed. Take care."

Reluctantly, she returned to the keep. Was Dettingham's presence a result of her foolishness? Chastened by the very thought, Ghislaine set to sorting out the supplies in case of battle. Much as she wanted to put him from her mind, Guy de Courcy was at the forefront of her thoughts. Had she signed his death warrant by her actions?

When the water was boiling in the huge cauldrons and enough cloth had been gathered to make binding for wounds, Ghislaine made her way to the top of the keep.

"What do you think you are doing here, lady?"

Guy de Courcy's angry voice boomed across the battlements. He was standing at the south side with Sir Arnaud and three of his men. Flushed with the effort of climbing the steep staircase, Ghislaine had to wait a few moments to catch her breath. Biting back a scathing retort, she advanced on the group of men.

The view from the battlements was most informative. Beyond the palisade gathered a large group of mounted soldiers headed by a smaller group of more elaborately attired knights. Swords, rivets and helms glinted in the last rays of the late afternoon sun.

"I wondered if I might be of help, my lord." Ghislaine stood before her husband, her eyes drinking in the sight of his sword and helm.

"You would be of more use within than up here," he barked irritably. "Obey me in this."

Ghislaine schooled her temper. "I have met with Henry Dettingham, my lord. He came to my brother's wedding and is…was a kinsman in a way. I thought perhaps if I could talk with him…"

Her voice trailed off as her husband's scowl grew

even blacker, if that was possible. "You have done more than enough…"

"Wait, Guy," interrupted d'Everard quickly. "The lady has a good point. If he trusts her, he may agree to talk. It's worth a try, don't you think?"

Ghislaine offered Sir Arnaud a grateful smile. Her husband continued to frown, but rubbed his chin in thought. "Aye," he conceded eventually, "but I am not sure that I trust her."

Ghislaine flushed to the roots of her hair. "You are most insulting my lord. My concern lies more with the safety of my people than your own skin, I admit. However, I am not so foolish to think that, by delivering you to Henry Dettingham, my people will be spared. You have threatened their lives often enough and I am sure that Sir Arnaud will not hesitate to carry out your orders in such an event."

Both men gaped at her for the space of several minutes. Guy de Courcy was the first to find his tongue. "Honesty was always your strong point, lady," he ground out. "But you are right. In the event of your treachery, your manor would be wasted and your people killed."

Ghislaine noted the look exchanged between the three-men-at-arms behind them. She was beginning to realise that those orders were merely a threat to keep her in check. She had no wish to put it to the test, though. "I give you my word that I shall commit no treachery."

Guy sighed heavily, his eyes distracted by a movement in the formation of soldiers below. Ghislaine recognised the small, rotund figure of Henry Dettingham detach himself from the main body and position himself before the manor gates. His grey destrier pawed at the ground restlessly as if he sensed the tension in the air.

"Come out, de Courcy. You cannot hide forever and the Earl's men are not here to protect you. I have no wish to destroy the manor so I offer you a duel. A fight to the death and that will be an end to it."

Henry Dettingham's bluff voice carried to the battlements.

Guy shook his head resolutely. "You know what to say, Arnaud. Take my wife. He may harbour some liking for her, at least."

Arnaud d'Everard inclined his head. "As you say." His lips had twitched slightly at his friend's last words.

As the huge gates were opened, Ghislaine felt a frisson of fear shoot through her. Perhaps Henry Dettingham had changed and he would not listen to her? He had been a mild-mannered, rather diffident man who had a penchant for pompous speeches and ale. Not even Henry could allow his sister's murder to go unchallenged, though. Her heart went out to him.

"Courage, Lady Ghislaine." Arnaud smiled at her as they urged their horses forward. Ghislaine could do naught but swallow as they came to a halt before their doughty foe.

Henry wore a bright red tunic over his hauberk which made his pale, round face look sallow and washed out. Small green eyes stared out below bushy brown brows. His body, ever broad and thick, was now portly and his plain, kindly face flabby. The man did not cut an imposing figure.

"Sir Henry," she began rather nervously, "I bid you greetings."

"My Lady de Launay," he exclaimed with sincere pleasure. "It is some years since I have seen you."

"De Courcy now, my lord. I am recently married to Sir Guy." Ghislaine gazed at him with steady eyes. No, she doubted if Henry had changed.

"Aye, I had heard rumours of that monstrous agreement." His gaze transferred to the man beside her. "You are not de Courcy, I take it?"

Ghislaine shook her head. "Sir Arnaud d'Everard is come to speak on my husband's behalf."

Henry Dettingham drew his small figure to his most imposing height and stared pointedly at the handsome d'Everard.

"The man is as great a coward as ever. He takes refuge within, I see."

Sir Arnaud's grey eyes glittered and Ghislaine knew he was reining in his anger. "My Lord de Courcy bids you greetings, Sir Henry, and begs you to reconsider your position."

"The man's a coward," came the pompous reply and Henry turned to his band of knights and shook his head.

"Guy de Courcy is innocent of the crime of murder. He is hopeful of clearing his name and in doing so may discover the true criminal. He regrets your loss deeply, Dettingham, and was heartsore when your sister was killed. You must have heard he offered her marriage."

Henry snorted rudely. "If he was keen to marry Margaret, then he should have come to me first before skulking around her skirts like the brigand he is."

"Sir Henry, I beg you to think again," broke in Ghislaine. Raking over old insults would get them nowhere. "My husband swears he committed no crime against Margaret and over the past few weeks I have come to believe he speaks the truth." Sir Henry's expression was not encouraging, but she decided to continue. "He has never denied his rough ways nor his ability to kill adeptly, but I have come to know him as an honest man. Guy de Courcy would gain so little from her death that it would make no sense."

"We waste time, Lady de Courcy. Your husband is a mercenary with a liking for money. Margaret's keep was sacked of its wealth. There is reason enough." Dettingham brushed aside her reasoning with a wave of his gauntleted hand. "It grieves me to see you so trapped, but I offer you my protection. Come with me to safety." Henry's green eyes watched her carefully.

"You mistake the matter, sir. I gave my husband my word that I would remain loyal to him for all the right reasons. I stay here with my people and my husband." Ghislaine lifted her chin proudly.

Sir Arnaud inclined his head in her direction. "My lady speaks well. Guy de Courcy refuses to come out because he will not waste blood needlessly. Go home, Sir Henry. The man responsible will be found sooner or later and then we can all live in peace. You do yourself no favours with the Earl here."

"Think you to gull me so simply?" Dettingham hissed sharply. "The Earl cares not whether a crime has been committed. His only concern is to keep de Courcy alive so that he can receive his silver marks. I'll wager that no one is brought to justice under such a system."

Ghislaine stared at him, a thought striking her. "How did you know where to find my husband?"

Henry Dettingham shrugged his shoulders. "Walter de Belleme sent word."

So Walter had tried to engineer this fight after all. Shocked at such underhand manipulation, Ghislaine searched the ranks of his men. "He is not here, though?" she enquired carefully.

"No. This is between me and de Courcy."

It was clear to Ghislaine that Henry was not going to go away. He wanted a fight. Just as she was about to signal to Arnaud, there was a shout from Dettingham's camp. "The Earl's men!"

All eyes turned south, scouring the line of the forest. Ghislaine counted at least thirty soldiers standing amongst the trees. She breathed a sigh of relief. They had been saved.

Henry Dettingham jerked his horse's head round and turned back to his knights. Following several minutes of heated discussion, he returned to Ghislaine and Sir Arnaud. "Do not think for one moment that this is the end. You may have the Earl's men to help you now, but I shall kill de Courcy for what he has done." He nodded briefly at Ghislaine. "My compliments, Lady de Courcy."

So saying, he wheeled round and joined his army. Wordlessly they departed, leaving Ghislaine to stare at the reinforcements. "They do not wear the Earl's colours." She squinted her eyes to peer more carefully.

"They are not the Earl's men. They belong to Lady du Beauregard from Omberleigh," came the curt reply.

Ghislaine looked at Arnaud in surprise. The man seemed not at all grateful for Lady Helene's timely intervention. Confused, she turned back to the palisade. She, for one, would welcome the lady with pleasure.

Chapter Nine

"Why did my husband not meet with Henry Dettingham himself?" she asked Sir Arnaud. "It would have been much simpler."

"Aye," allowed her companion as he helped her dismount. "But Guy de Courcy places little trust in a man demanding vengeance at any price. Nor," he added grimly, "has he any wish to kill him. Sir Henry is no swordsman."

Once more on firm ground, Ghislaine turned to face her husband's friend. "True, but I had no idea that Sir Guy would be willing to sacrifice his reputation to compassion."

"Make no mistake, lady," warned Sir Arnaud. "If his life was in danger, Guy would not hesitate to fight. However, he believes that Dettingham's death would neither clear his name nor allow him the return of his old manor." He flickered her a look of reproach. "His name is all he has and the manor he lost was the first step to making a real home for himself. He will not rest until they are restored."

Their attention was claimed by a rider approaching

the gates. He bore a request from Lady du Beauregard for permission to enter the manor gates and Ghislaine gave her assent.

"Do you not stay to bid Lady du Beauregard welcome?" she chided, as Arnaud turned towards the keep.

Arnaud's grey eyes bore into her before smiling lightly. "No doubt you ladies have much to discuss without my interference."

Ghislaine drew in her breath sharply at the inferred insult. "I had thought you might wish to thank her for her timely appearance."

His grey eyes turned steely and seemed about to say something, but thought better of it. "I have no doubt that the lady will be more than satisfied with your gratitude," he murmured finally, tossing the reins to the stable boy.

Lifting her chin, Ghislaine regarded him coldly. "I had not thought you the sort of man to continue a petty disagreement. Surely you can forgive the Lady du Beauregard for her concerns over my health before the marriage."

A frown marred his brow. "You are too trusting, Lady Ghislaine. People are not always as they seem." With those enigmatic words, Sir Arnaud turned on his heels and picked his way across the mud-churned bailey.

His words were most confusing, but Ghislaine had no time to ponder them as Helene du Beauregard passed beneath the manor gates atop a magnificent bay gelding.

"Greetings, Lady du Beauregard, and welcome." Ghislaine smiled as she rushed towards the older woman. The stable lad aided Helene to dismount and she brushed the dust from her riding cloak.

"I am pleased my appearance was timely," Helene remarked, her cheeks flushed with the fresh air. "I had feared I might be too late."

"You knew?" Ghislaine slipped her arm through Helene's and guided her towards the hall. She was glad to see her friend appeared in better health.

"Aye," came the guarded reply. "I admit to being concerned for you and had some men watch over the manor." She stopped and turned towards Ghislaine, taking the girl's hands in hers. "I hope you will forgive me for such an intrusion, but there was every possibility of a reprisal against your husband. I believe my men saved your life with a good shot in the forest."

At last an explanation for the mystery. It was a relief to know that the other men had been friendly. Ghislaine still remained somewhat surprised by Helene's unexpected intervention, though, and thought back to Arnaud's odd words of parting. Clearly he knew more about Lady du Beauregard than she had at first thought. Smiling, Ghislaine placed her arm around the woman's shoulders and led her inside the keep. "I can only be grateful for your vigilance since we remain safe."

When the du Beauregard troops were organised with ale, Ghislaine returned to Helene. She was sitting comfortably by the fire in the hall with her head tilted back and her eyes closed.

"You are tired, Helene? Perhaps you would prefer to lie on my bed for a while?" Ghislaine regarded her anxiously.

Helene smiled and opened her eyes. "Not at all, my dear. I have simply learnt to take advantage of every opportunity to rest. A short nap can be most restorative." She sat up and leaned closer to Ghislaine, gesturing her to sit by her side.

"And how have you fared, Lady de Courcy? Has marriage to the mercenary been as bad as you feared?" Her expression showed concern rather than a desire for gossip and Ghislaine did not take offence at the question.

Shrugging her shoulders, she smiled wanly. "He is not an easy man to live with. Sometimes I think I have made some progress and then he does something which causes me much vexation." Placing her head on her hand, Ghislaine sighed heavily. "He will be pleased to put me in the convent, I believe."

Effie bustled up with some wine and a bowl of nuts. Helene smiled her thanks and remained silent until she had moved out of earshot. "Do you still think him guilty of the murder?" Helene regarded her with searching eyes.

Something in her expression struck a familiar chord in Ghislaine, but the memory remained just out of touch. She lowered her eyes and plucked absently at a loose thread on her mantle. "No, and for all his brutish ways he has always been straightforward in his dealings with me."

Pursing her lips thoughtfully, she edged a little closer to Helene. "I do not think him all bad," she admitted reluctantly. "And once he was even quite…gentle." Her cheeks heated, but somehow she did not mind talking to Helene. It had been a long time since she had confided in another woman.

Helene folded her hands in her lap and stared into the fire as if deep in thought. "Would you perhaps reconsider your decision to retire to the convent if your husband was more…amenable towards you?"

It was a question Ghislaine had pondered several times over the past week. Today she had learnt quite a lot more about her husband thanks to Sir Arnaud and, despite her protestations to the contrary, his words had given her pause for thought.

That day in the forest, Guy had admitted he found it hard to speak gently. In truth, pretty words were not what she wanted. She liked his honesty and straightforward speech. Over the weeks he had proved hardworking, responsible and astute. His authority over his men was absolute and in return they offered him their loyalty—aye, he had even won over Edwin. He lacked manners, but of late these had shown some improvement in her company. His temper, of course, left much to be desired and yet that was really so much hot air.

Nor had he ever forced himself upon her, she reminded herself. Many women of her station would no doubt welcome such a paragon! "I think I find it hard knowing what he expects of me," she murmured softly. "Sometimes he glares at me as if he hates me."

Helene shot her a sideways glance. "Would you really prefer the convent?"

"I am not what he wants in a wife." Ghislaine's voice had taken on a weary tone. "He frequently tells me how much trouble I am."

At that, Helene laughed. "And what sort of a wife would you think a man like Guy de Courcy needs? A sweet, meek creature such as Margaret Staveley?" She raised her dark brows in question.

"W-well…" stammered Ghislaine, searching for the right words. Suddenly she stopped and looked at Helene. "How do you know what sort of wife he needs?"

"I know far more than you about Guy de Gourcy, my dear." She reached down to smooth her gown over her knees. "More to the point, I think you would make him a good wife." Her face was expressionless as she watched her words sink in. "Don't you?"

Ghislaine eyed her warily, confused by the way Helene had managed to twist things round. She was reminded of Arnaud's parting words. "I'm not sure."

"Well, perhaps you should find out."

Raising her hands in confusion, Ghislaine shook her head. "I understand none of this. Why are you so concerned about this marriage? Neither of us wanted it and we have agreed to go our own ways once Guy's name is cleared."

Helene smiled, her eyes resting on Ghislaine. "I made mistakes in my marriage that I now regret and I do not wish you to tread the same path."

It was quiet in the hall for a change with just the crackle and hiss of the wood in the fire to disturb the peace. The shutters at the windows had been closed and the only light within came from the torches on the walls. Now that the danger from Henry Dettingham had gone, temporarily at least, the tension that had been building up had suddenly eased.

"I still don't see how…"

Helene held up her hands. "Enough talking, young lady. Since your mother is not here, I think I knew her well enough to know she would approve of me giving you some maternal advice. Come. Let us go to your room. I believe it is time you were taken in hand.''

Submitting herself reluctantly at first to Helene's lamentations over her gowns, her hair and her freckles, Ghislaine eventually began to relax. Effie's presence was requested, and between them they experimented with several suitable styles for her hair. Privately Ghislaine doubted whether Guy would notice any difference in her appearance, but it was an enjoyable experience nevertheless. She had never spent time on such feminine frivolity, lacking both an attentive audience and a teacher, but it was certainly a change from hunting down the Earl's game!

Once Effie was dispatched to concoct a salve for roughened hands, Helene turned her attention to Ghislaine's clothes.

Casting a baleful eye over the contents of her wooden chest, she shook her head. ''I cannot believe you manage with such rags. Has your husband said nothing?'' Helene picked up the tattered hem of Ghislaine's current gown and let it fall in disgust.

''No. He seems to regard my gowns more as a method of restricting my activities.'' Ghislaine hesitated and then added more quietly, ''Nor is he overly keen to spend his money. He does not seem to rate gowns very highly.'' Feeling somewhat guilty for being disloyal, Ghislaine continued, ''But then, if I'm to enter the convent, there really seems little point.''

Treating that remark to a dismissive gesture, Helene stared thoughtfully at Ghislaine who was perched on the edge of her pallet. ''I have one or two gowns that might be suitable.'' She rubbed a long finger over her chin. ''They might answer for now.''

Neither of them had heard the door open. "I'll thank you to leave the question of my wife's attire to me." Guy de Courcy stood in the doorway, his hands placed somewhat aggressively on his hips. Although he had at least removed his helm, Guy still wore his battered leather hauberk and looked every inch the mercenary of his ill repute.

Helene jerked her head in his direction. As the silence lengthened, the tension between them increased. "Then the blame for such rags can be placed at your feet, my lord." The lines around her mouth deepened in disapproval. "Does it give you pleasure to see your wife shamed like this?"

Colouring furiously, Ghislaine jumped to her feet. "Please, Lady du Beauregard. This is a matter between my husband and myself."

Her words were ignored as Guy and Helene faced each other. "I thought I had made it clear in Chester, lady. Your presence is not welcome in my home." Guy's handsome face was bloodless as he eyed the woman with contempt.

Ghislaine felt as if she was a spectator in a scene she had only half understood. She was certain now they knew each other. "Guy! After Lady du Beauregard gave us aid against Henry Dettingham, the least we can offer is our hospitality."

Her rebuke earned Ghislaine nothing more than a scornful glance before he advanced menacingly on Helene. "Lady du Beauregard has sampled enough of our hospitality. I am sure she has pressing business in her own manor."

Ghislaine's cheeks burned with embarrassment at such a pointed remark. "Lady du Beauregard is welcome to remain here as long as she wishes," she hissed, glaring at her husband. "This is also my home, Guy de Courcy, and I have greatly enjoyed Lady du Beauregard's company. I have had little opportunity to indulge in feminine company over the past few years, and I confess to having missed it greatly."

Boosted by the warm smile she received from Helene, Ghislaine watched him cross the room. Carefully he placed his gleaming sword on the rushes and then unfurled his great length on the bed. She was reminded very much of a disgruntled child.

"It sorrows me to tell you this, wife, but I cannot permit your acquaintance with...Lady...du Beauregard to continue." He stared at her boldly, almost daring her to gainsay him.

"Give me one good reason for such an order," Ghislaine answered, her hands almost shaking in anger. How dared he presume so much? They were not man and wife in fact, after all.

His eyes glinted dangerously. "Because she is a brazen whore." Guy raised Ghislaine's goblet of unfinished wine to his lips and drained it in one movement.

Wheeling round to face Helene, Ghislaine was confronted with a raised hand. Helene was more than ready to deal with such lies.

"I have paid for my mistakes, in many different ways," she replied wearily. Her dark eyes were centred on the man laid out so nonchalantly on the bed. "And I see in Ghislaine and you much of myself and my husband. I have no wish for you both to end up the same way."

Guy's frown deepened. "I have no fear that you and Ghislaine are made of the same cloth, my lady."

Helene stooped to pick up her cloak and threw it about her shoulders with a proud flourish. "Then you must tread warily, my lord, for your wife does not seem very content to me."

"No," she assured Ghislaine, turning to her quickly. "This quarrel has naught to do with you, it is between me and Guy alone. I have no wish to come between you and so I shall leave without further ado." She squeezed Ghislaine's shoulders and headed for the door. "If you need me, please send word."

With a quick nod towards them both, Helene left silently, Ghislaine felt almost bereft. "How could you say such things to her?"

"They were true." He looked up in surprise "I do not expect you to further your acquaintance with the woman, or the consequences will be dire."

Chapter Ten

"If I am to dress, I need something to put on." Ghislaine's voice rose in frustration. Her husband had sent Effie to wake her at dawn and her mistress had not appreciated the early call. Sleep had been long in coming the night before, with visions of Guy and Helene walking in her dreams.

"He said you could wear this, my lady." Effie held up an old blue gown that had been well-mended and that was definitely on the small side. She looked at it dubiously. "I did tell him that it didn't fit now, but he didn't seem to hear."

Ghislaine stared at the dress. "So be it." She was too tired to argue and her head was aching.

Sighing heavily, Ghislaine donned the dress and allowed Effie to pull her hair into a more becoming braid than usual.

"It doesn't seem as tight as it was," offered Effie as she surveyed the fruits of her work.

Ghislaine smiled wanly. "Aye. Sir Guy seems to have kept me hungry of late. Perhaps he had this gown in mind?"

Seeing naught to smile at, Effie shot Ghislaine a look of exasperation. "Well, not all of you has succumbed to his methods, it seems."

Ghislaine followed the direction of her eyes and admitted that the gown was strained across her chest. She shrugged her shoulders. "It would appear not."

The hall was quiet when she descended. Torches spluttered on the walls for the morning light was not yet advanced enough, but in the gloom she could make out the lone figure of Guy de Courcy. He was standing with his back to her, watching the bailey from one of the side windows. At a sound he turned, his hand on his sword. It was not his instinctive reaction that caused Ghislaine to draw her breath so suddenly.

Her eyes widened as they took in the magnificent sight before her. Never could she have imagined how handsome he could be. His long hair had been trimmed and washed and his tunic of midnight blue gave Guy a most elegant appearance. Yet it was his face that was transformed. The weeks of thick, stubbly growth had been barbered to reveal a face that was strong, masculine and devastatingly attractive.

Realising that she was gaping at him, Ghislaine gathered her wits.

"I see you took my advice," she began tersely. "But I do not consider your first bath as cause enough to rouse me from my bed."

If he had expected a humble and contrite wife, he was sadly mistaken. Ghislaine's tongue was as sharp as ever. A wry smile formed on his lips.

"No?" he countered. "I had thought you most eager to share the moment with me."

In an effort to dispel the effect of this vision of

masculine beauty before her, Ghislaine retreated to a facial expression of complete disdain.

"Why am I here?"

Guy offered her a seat at the table. A servant emerged from the gloom to provide her with a dollop of grey porridge. If he noticed her gown was tight, he made no mention of it, although Ghislaine was aware of his eyes on her.

"I have to leave for a few days." The statement was short and to the point.

Ghislaine felt herself go cold. Already he could not bear her company. "I still do not see why it necessitates my presence at this hour. Sir Brian is perfectly capable of protecting the manor in your absence." Her tone was cool and stiff, belying the turmoil within her.

His dark brows raised at this evident inaccuracy but he shrugged his shoulders rather than voice his thoughts. "Sir Brian could not tell me whether you wished to accompany me."

Her eyes flew to his. This was no jest.

"Where do you go?" The words were almost a whisper.

"Chester. On business with the Earl."

Ghislaine stared at him a moment, trying desperately to stop herself from flinging her arms around him.

"And he wishes to see me?" Ghislaine certainly had no desire to see him.

Guy shook his head. "I thought you might wish to purchase more spices and cloth. You have spent the past few weeks pointing out how needy the kitchens are and I have seen for myself that you are lacking in gowns."

"Aye," she replied as dutifully as she could. "The kitchens are in sore need of stocks." Her eyes remained fixed to the porridge, not risking a glance in his direction. Did the man think this was some sort of chore?

"Then we leave in five minutes. I leave d'Everard to aid the worthy Sir Brian." Guy strode from the hall before she could utter a word. Ghislaine sat there another full minute savouring the elation before finishing the porridge and hurrying for her cloak. Life was certainly not dull these days.

The sun was at its highest before the walls of Chester came into view. The turquoise banner of Hugh d'Avranches could be seen fluttering in the March wind from the keep of the castle. Halting on a ridge some distance to the south of the city, the party was able to view the comings and goings at leisure.

Ghislaine watched the great River Dee flow and curve around the city walls and then off north towards the sea. A large trading galley was moored in the port on the west side amid a hubbub of activity. Below them, to the south of the Bridge gate, the wheels of the flour mills paddled steadily through the water. Beyond them stood the outline of the Lupus's castle. Proud and impenetrable, its walls were heavily fortified against any Welsh attack.

Pulling her cloak close to, Ghislaine could not conceal a shiver against the cold wind that blew in from the coast. Morwenna stomped and whinnied, keen to find a warm shelter and bag of oats. Ghislaine had other reasons for wishing the journey ended. Her nerves had been stretched to the limits by her endless

expectation of an attack, either from Walter de Belleme, Henry Dettingham or outlaws. Each noise had
caused her to jump and to look about carefully, her
eyes locking on to anything that moved. She had ridden alongside her husband, too nervous to offer more
than desultory conversation.

Guy, sensing her reluctance to talk to him, honoured
her silence and was pleased to sink into his own
thoughts. He needed all his wits about him to deal with
the wily Earl of Chester.

It was with great relief that the party was allowed
entrance to the city. The de Courcy colours had been
identified long before they had reached the bridge and
the guards allowed them passage with little attention.
Quite carelessly, Ghislaine decided. Had her men done
as much, she would have had them whipped.

Inside the walls, the noise was almost deafening.
The sounds of people and animals echoed through the
narrow, muddy streets that led off the main way to the
Cross. Ghislaine stared about her at the cramped,
wooden buildings that crowded inside the walls. The
smell of human life washed around her and Ghislaine
thought she was like to choke with the stench. Her
mother had been right about the place. It would be
easy to die here.

Her palfrey picked the way carefully through a
filthy passage, her ears twitching nervously when a
screaming child came too close. Ghislaine's eyes
drank in the scenes as if seeing them for the first time.
When she had visited with her father, he had insisted
on taking her directly to the castle, and she had barely
a glimpse of the colour and the life that existed within
the city walls. The streets were teeming with noisy

people who paid scant attention to the danger of Guy's huge horse. Pedlars idled against the walls of the narrow dwellings, their eyes darting hither and thither, hoping to catch the attention of a passing maid. Street-sellers mixed with bewildered farmers, journey-men with tavern wenches. Ghislaine stared wordlessly at the stalls that sold fine silks and linens, furs, cheese, soaps and pots.

As the cross came into view, Guy turned to the left, and Ghislaine was able to see another gate at the end of the street. Beyond the top of the gate fluttered the flags of the large galley they had seen earlier in the harbour. Hardly able to contain her excitement, Ghislaine could not help her gasp of delight.

"We head for the harbour?"

Guy turned at her words, and watched her unguarded face for a moment.

"Aye. I have business with the captain of the *Isabella*. You will wish to view the wares in the storehouses along the quayside. Joachim will accompany you."

Ghislaine nodded. Joachim was Guy's second-in-command when Arnaud d'Everard was elsewhere. Few men were willing to gainsay him; for those that were, his menacing war-axe proved a mighty deterrent.

The party halted in the shadows of the old wooden gate whilst Joachim dealt with the guards. A steady stream of merchants and purchasers made their way in and out of the gate, but it was a sorry line of dark-haired men shuffling towards the harbour that caught Ghislaine's eye. They were dressed in tattered leather and wool, chained at the ankle to the man in front and behind. None looked anywhere except the ground before them, their lips tight, backs straight.

"Where do they go?" Her eyes followed the men until they had passed between the gates.

"They are slaves for trading." Guy's voice was toneless in reply. "They will board the *Isabella* and be sold en route."

Ghislaine stared at his harsh profile. "But they are Welshmen."

"And are a valuable commodity to Hugh Lupus."

Sickened by the knowledge that these warriors would leave their homelands, families, friends, to be sold to the highest bidder in a foreign port, Ghislaine closed her eyes. "Where is the *Isabella* bound?"

"She heads south to Normandy and then on east through the Mediterranean to Genoa and Venice."

The day had suddenly turned sour. The dealings of men were sordid indeed. Ghislaine turned to look at her husband. "You have business with the captain, you said?"

Guy nodded, his blue eyes following the silent line of warriors. "Personal business." The flat tone of his voice and the set of his lips brooked no further discussion, but Ghislaine could not help herself.

"Do you trade in slaves?" She regarded him steadily, her mouth equally set. Whether she realised it or no, her breath held until he gave his reply.

"Nay. I trade information only." His black frown dissuaded any further discussion.

Ghislaine followed as Guy progressed slowly amongst the throng, her mind busy with the latest piece of information he had given her. Why would Guy de Courcy wish to buy information from a pedlar of human flesh? He had denied trading, and she knew him so far to be honest. Mayhap it had to do with the murder. She would have to keep her ears open.

The ship was a truly breathtaking sight. From a distance it was beautiful, but from close to she was magnificent. She bobbed gently with the lapping waves, gulls flapping near her masts. The giant sail was furled carefully away, leaving the rich wooden skeleton to rise and fall majestically. Unable to tear her eyes from the *Isabella*, Ghislaine watched the cargo being loaded by strangely garbed men of indeterminate origins.

Guy de Courcy stood at her side, an eyebrow lifted in question.

''I'm sorry?'' she said. ''Did you say aught?''

Guy viewed her distracted gaze with irritation. ''I said that I would join you in the warehouse later. This purse contains more than you need for your purchases.'' He had her full attention now, he noted wryly. ''Joachim knows what to do.''

The leather pouch felt surprisingly heavy at her waist as she dismounted outside a large wooden trading house. Guarding her money as best she could, Ghislaine took grateful refuge behind Joachim as he cut a swathe through the crowds. Ignoring the urgent requests of the traders to sample their goods, he made his way silently to the far end of the building. The noise and the colours were beginning to press painfully in her head and Ghislaine longed to be out in the fresh air once more.

At the far end of the warehouse Joachim gestured Ghislaine to stop whilst he disappeared behind a heavy arras. A moment later he emerged once more and beckoned her to follow him. The arras hid another

world from the hubbub of the warehouse. Ghislaine's
head echoed with the noise and the colours, but gratefully entered into a small, low chamber that at first
seemed empty save Joachim and herself. A cool breeze
gently breathed air into her throbbing head and Ghislaine closed her eyes momentarily with relief.

"Would you sit, lady? I will bring refreshments for
you."

A small pair of faded blue eyes blinked up at her
before uttering words in a strange tongue into the
gloom at the far end of the chamber. Gratefully Ghislaine sank into the comfortable seat offered her. It was
like nothing she had ever encountered in her sheltered
life. It was more like a small, narrow bed but draped
with cloth and padding that allowed her to lie back
and rest her weary shoulders.

"My thanks, sir. I would be most grateful for a little
wine for we have travelled far today."

The tiny man nodded his grey head and gestured
towards the shadows. He was dressed most oddly in a
voluminous surcoat of blue and grey stripes, his thin
hair pulled into a braid at the back of his large head.

"I would suggest, my lady, that you may wish to
try a tisane? A hot drink that is both reviving and
refreshing."

The merchant, for Ghislaine was now convinced
that was his business, stood before her, his hands
clasped before him in the manner of a willing trader.
And yet there was nothing humble about him. The
man was of indeterminate age, tiny but well-formed,
and stood assessing her with eyes that spoke volumes.
Intelligence, shrewdness and compassion were visible

in their pale blue depths. Despite his lack of humility and his proud air, Ghislaine felt at ease.

"That would be most welcome, sir." She smiled at him, a little unsure for all the boldness of her words. "I am sure that Joachim would also wish to try this…tisane."

The merchant smiled faintly. "Joachim's tastes will be catered for. As you wish." A gnarled hand snapped in the air and a bronze flagon was placed before the Frankish warrior by a small boy that Ghislaine would have sworn came from thin air. At her nod, Joachim grabbed the flagon and retreated to a gloomy corner where he proceeded to down its contents with obvious relish.

The same boy brought another seat for his master and a small wooden table. Upon the latter he placed a steaming bronze vessel and two tiny blue and white bowls. Quite the most exquisite Ghislaine had ever seen. Her fingers reached out to touch them. They were smooth and very delicate. The merchant proceeded to pour a light brown liquid into each bowl, the pungent aroma that met Ghislaine's senses quite unlike anything she had encountered before. He then picked up one of the bowls and sipped lightly from the rim. Not wishing to seem ill-mannered, Ghislaine followed suit. The tisane was strong and so hot that it burnt her lips. She replaced the bowl firmly on the table.

The merchant's eyebrows raised in question. "And what may the house of Kalim offer you, lady?" He sat perfectly still as he awaited her reply.

"My husband sent me in your direction for I have need of cloth and spices." For some reason she could not fathom, Ghislaine was aware of an undercurrent between them, as if he were expecting her to say more.

After a brief pause, Kalim smiled slowly to reveal perfectly white teeth. "When you have finished your tisane, lady, I shall be glad to show you my wares."

Ghislaine sipped at the drink again more slowly, but found after a short while that the taste was becoming less unpleasant. In fact, she certainly felt less tired and dusty.

"You know my husband?"

"Guy de Courcy has been known to me for many years, lady. I have always found him to be a fair man. And an honest one."

Had the merchant added those last words for her benefit? She took another sip of the tisane, allowing the strange flavour to fill her senses before swallowing. The man was right, for she was beginning to revive a little.

"You are not from this land?"

The merchant shook his head, causing his silver earrings to jingle. "I am a merchant, lady, travelling from land to land. My home is where I choose it to be." Ghislaine watched in fascination as his long, beringed fingers raised the bowl to his lips. As he did so, their eyes collided and held. Kalim put the bowl down slowly.

"May I ask you a question, lady?"

Ghislaine flushed at her implied gaucheness and inclined her head in assent.

"Do you trust Guy de Courcy?" Those faded blue eyes bore into her, compelling her to answer truthfully. After no more than a few seconds, the words came.

"I, too, believe him to be an honest, proud man who

does not give his word lightly. Although we have not dealt long together, I find myself increasingly willing to trust him.'' Where had those words come from? Ghislaine flushed at her garrulous tongue. How could she be so bold with such a stranger?

''Then he chose well.''

Ghislaine felt the blood rush to her cheeks, but her innate honesty compelled her to explain. ''He did not choose me, I was forced upon him.''

All her shame and misery were expressed in those few words. The merchant watched her for a moment as if deep in thought. ''It is often so that the burdens we find the hardest to bear may bring us the richest rewards.'' Kalim sighed before rising gracefully to his feet. ''I will show you some of my wares now, lady. Maybe you will find something that takes your eye?''

His gentle smile chased away some of the gloom she was feeling at being reminded of her predicament. Ghislaine rose, her limbs stiff from the long ride, but grateful to avoid further conversation of such a personal nature. It was indeed painful to be reminded of her shortcomings.

Kalim's chamber was filled with beautiful cloth which Ghislaine eyed longingly. Bolts of gorgeous materials were paraded before her and Ghislaine found the choice almost impossible. Practicality, however, reasserted itself and she decided finally on soft grey and blue wool for herself, and serviceable browns and greens for the servants. Two bolts of linen were added to her list. A rich red brocade, chased with gold caught her eye, and in a fit of extravagance, Ghislaine decided that Guy would look particularly fine in a tunic of such attractive hue. Realising that her husband was also probably in need of further garments, she purchased some green and blue wool which could always be used for others if need be.

The food spices were more easily purchased. Ginger, cinnamon, nutmeg, mace, cloves and cardomoms were placed in a small chest, together with galingale, cubebs and grains of paradise to flavour the salted-down winter meats. Kalim also persuaded her to try currants, figs and dates as well as a generous portion of almonds to use on fast days and Lenten stews. Reminded that her husband had a sweet tooth, Ghislaine added some dried fruits to try in the custard confections he seemed partial to.

As she was deliberating over the wines, the arras was pulled back and Guy de Courcy stalked into the chamber. One look at his grim countenance told Ghislaine that she had probably purchased far more than she had licence to do and his disapproval told its own story. With a curt nod to Kalim, who bowed quietly and retreated to the shadows, Guy stopped before Ghislaine.

"I see you have nigh on exhausted my funds, lady." As the expression on his face did not change, Ghislaine gulped quietly before mentally discarding those items not absolutely essential. She cursed her own greed and childlike excitement in having such great choices. Pulling at her fingers, she murmured that she had indeed gone beyond her limits.

There was a momentary pause before Guy spoke in a more gentle tone. "Perhaps you would show me what you intended to take." Ghislaine nodded and commenced an item by item account of her purchases, but it was not long before Guy interrupted with amusement in his voice.

"Wife, your choices are most creditable. But," he added softly, "I had hoped that you would buy yourself some more…ah…some finer cloth."

Ghislaine looked up at him sharply. Gone was the grim frown that he had entered the chamber with. Mayhap she had misinterpreted his look.

"I thought only to dress appropriately, in the circumstances, my lord." Her tone had returned to its usual waspishness and that brought a faint smile to his lips.

"Aye. And your choice of cloth is most…worthy." His large hand raked his black locks as he surveyed the assortment of cloths. "Kalim. It would seem I have need of your excellent advice." The merchant stepped forward. "My wife requires some finery. Have you aught that would do?"

Seizing his opportunity, Kalim smiled broadly and pulled down bolt after bolt of jewel-bright emeralds and blues, golds and creams, chased and plain.

"With your lady's unusual hair colour, perhaps some brighter hues that would enhance and complement?"

Ghislaine held her breath as her husband and the merchant selected three. Ghislaine could hardly believe that she needed anything near so fine and yet found her protests sounded weak even to her own ears. The idea of her possessing such beautiful gowns was an exhilarating one. Together the merchant and Guy had decided upon the emerald-green and the peacock-blue with little difficulty. It was the final choice that had Ghislaine feeling no more than a fine object.

When they had finally plumped for a gold brocade chased with midnight-blue, Ghislaine had retreated to a dark corner in high dudgeon. No one had consulted her about the choice, and much as she approved of the material, she remained inexplicably angry nevertheless.

Ignoring her protests, Guy then went on to examine the brooches and belts. His largesse was making her feel most uncomfortable and she had no idea how to stem the tide of such uncalled-for generosity. At no time in her life had anyone bestowed such gifts upon her and, in truth, it was hard to accept them so. She was used to very little, and realised how vulnerable that made her.

"Are you purchasing my goodwill, sir?" she demanded finally.

Her rudeness took him by surprise for he had genuinely not realised how offended his wife was becoming.

"I did not know you offered it for sale. Had I done so, I feel certain it would have cost me less dear."

His bantering tone only aggravated Ghislaine more and he knew it. "You are most insulting. If you wish something of me, you have only to ask, although that is not within your nature since you took the rest of my possessions without my leave." So saying, Ghislaine flounced towards the arras and would have pulled it aside had Joachim not forestalled her with his huge bulk. Not relishing the prospect of an undignified scuffle that she would undoubtedly lose, Ghislaine sat on the comfortable seat.

"Perhaps my lady would now like to take some wine whilst Sir Guy completes his purchases?" Kalim stood before her, his cool eyes informing her of his disapproval.

Aye, her behaviour had been less than ladylike and she flushed with shame that she could have let her feelings show. Since Guy de Gourcy had entered her quiet life, Ghislaine had found her emotions difficult to contain. And there was no good explanation for her bad temper. She would enter the convent as soon as he cleared his name. That was what she had demanded and he had agreed. Why she found it so difficult to behave normally when she was with the man, Ghislaine was at a loss to explain. Mayhap her wits had gone begging after all.

"I do not deserve such consideration, Kalim, but you may be right. The wine might help to restore my temper, if not my wits."

Kalim bowed gracefully before the repentant Ghislaine before summoning the boy once more. "Your husband is not a man used to sharing, lady. But he acts with no ill will."

"I know it," Ghislaine murmured. "I, too, have much to learn."

Kalim smiled. "It is not my place to suggest it, but perhaps he has much on his mind."

The merchant retreated to a gloomy corner and involved himself in searching amongst his wares for something that was no doubt vital. Joachim, apparently satisfied that she was not about to escape the clutches of her husband, sidled rather self-consciously towards Kalim and muttered a few words under his breath. Ghislaine picked up the two goblets of fruity red wine that the boy offered and made her way towards Guy. Her husband was frowning at the pile of cloth and did not change his expression when he saw her approach.

She gritted her teeth. "It is not usually my way to be so ill-mannered." Ghislaine ignored the raising of his eyebrow. "Well, perhaps it is. But you did not deserve such treatment."

Guy took the wine stiffly, not in the least mollified by his wife's words. "If the cloth was not to your liking, you only had to say," he said finally.

Ghislaine's cheeks flushed. "I like your choice well enough. It's just…" her sentence trailed off as his blue eyes pinned her mercilessly. She tried again. "It is pointless to waste such finery when I am bound for the convent." The words were spoken but still she held her breath.

Guy knocked back the wine before slamming the goblet down on the table. "Maybe so. But I have no need to be laughed at further by having a wife who looks like a serf. Until you take your vows, lady, you will dress with more care and not besport yourself in gowns that do little to hide your ample…charms."

Her face burned with the indignity and the implication. "You chose this gown yourself," she hissed in fury.

"It was the only one that hid your ankles," he retorted heatedly.

"No one else seems to have noticed that before.

"Walter de Belleme's eyes were hot on you last week?" he growled. His hand raked back his black hair as his temper rose.

"So that's it!" Ghislaine's outburst was one of complete disbelief. "You do not want me, but you will not allow anyone else to have me either. There is no dealing with you, Guy de Courcy.''

So saying, Ghislaine would have pushed her way past him, but her husband was quick to react. Her arm was caught in a hard grip that brought tears to her eyes. Looking up at him with fury, Ghislaine got a perverse pleasure from seeing that he was equally as wroth.

''I am no uncouth soldier to be ordered around as you see fit, my lord. I will not be treated as less than a member of your family.''

Those words earned a humourless laugh. ''If you wish to be treated like a lady, then you needs act more like one. If you do not, then I give you fair warning that your people will suffer harder than you.''

Chapter Eleven

Ghislaine glared at Guy as she waited for him. He had taken his time over the final transactions knowing that the delay would irritate her. The chamber seemed much smaller since his arrival and she longed to be in the fresh air and sunlight—or what remained of it. She had no idea how long she had spent with the merchant, but she was certain that it was longer than Guy had intended. And more expensive.

The thought that she had spent more than was absolutely necessary did not give her any pleasure and Ghislaine felt irritated with herself that she had allowed Guy to purchase the extra cloth. And yet his jealousy had given her a warm glow that had not died in their clash. It was completely unexpected and all the more surprising since he had given her no indication that he took any notice of her or how people treated her.

As she watched him now, Ghislaine no longer knew what to think. His countenance remained as grim and dour as ever, but from the way he stood and talked with the merchant, it was clear they had dealt with each other oftimes before, as the merchant had said. The purses of silver marks that Guy handed over were far in excess of the amount due, as Ghislaine was aware. What possible reason would he have for giving Kalim so much? The answer was not likely to come easily. It could be an old debt, but knowing her husband's insistence on paying for goods with silver in the hand, Ghislaine doubted that was the reason. More likely it had more to do with the murmured words than aught else.

When he joined her, Guy was frowning darkly. "'Tis time we left. I have business with the Earl." His voice reflected his irritation.

"I…I wish to apologise for my behaviour," Ghislaine began. "It was uncalled for." She peeped at his face shyly, but her heart plummeted when she saw his expression unchanged. "My father…I…" Why were the words so difficult? She tried again.

"I am not used to receiving gifts and have not learned to be graceful in my thanks." Her eyes held his steadily. "If it makes you happy to bestow such finery upon so unworthy a recipient, then I will gladly accept."

"'Tis lucky that I did not return the cloth then," came his curt reply. Despite the coolness of his words, Ghislaine was sure she detected a slight thawing in his manner. Well, at least the man was predictable in his grouchiness and she would have to be content with that. Except that those moments in the forest when he showed such gentleness kept intruding in her dark thoughts. Aye, the man had a softer side to him, and perhaps it was best hidden.

*   *   *

It was the smell of roasting pig that set her mouth watering as they walked up the wooden steps of the castle bailey. The castle guests had been called to dinner almost as soon as they entered the gates, and Ghislaine had been sore pressed to wash, brush her hair and shake the dust from her gown. Aware of how dowdy she appeared, especially as her husband looked so fine, Ghislaine quaked inwardly at having to face the court of Hugh d'Avranches. Unable to quell the trembling of her hands she hoped that Guy would not notice it through his thick surcoat.

"I had not thought you feared me, lady." They drew to a halt beneath a flickering torch. The dark frown was ominous but not threatening for all his great size. It was on the tip of her tongue to tell him that, aye, she feared him, to hurt him just a little for his grudging acceptance of her apology, but the words would not come. Anger and frustration played far more on her emotions than fear, and she doubted that lying would help much.

"I do not fear you, my lord."

"Then why does your hand shake so?"

Ghislaine glared at her husband. Did the man really not know how she must feel about entering a room full of spiteful tongues, especially dressed as she was? Truly the man was lacking in wits.

"Have you really no idea?"

He shook his head in confusion. "I would not have asked if I did, but as you have pointed out before, my wits are clearly lacking."

Mercy! Could the man read her mind now? Ghislaine's cheeks burned a little at his perception. After a glance about the bailey to ensure that they were alone, her eyes returned to his. "I have no wish to make a fool of myself before the Earl's court."

Guy just stopped himself from raising his eyebrows. This was probably not the moment to remind her that she had made a fool of herself there before without any help from him. "How so?"

Ghislaine gave him a withering look that was rewarded with a quizzical shrug. Sighing irritably, she decided that she would have to tell him.

"I look like a serving wench in this gown," she hissed. "And you look so fine. They will laugh at me and pity you." Folding her arms firmly across her chest, Ghislaine turned away from Guy, embarrassment stamped across her burning cheeks.

Guy cursed his own stupidity. Were women not well-known for their foolishness over their gowns? And there was also that tiny feeling of relief to know that the woman did not fear him. Where had that come from? And those other words?

"Fine? You think I look fine?"

"Have I not already said so?" came the disgruntled reply.

"My finery is an improvement, then?"

Ghislaine shrugged her shoulders, reluctant to commit any more words and knowing that her actions were childish but unable to react any other way.

"Mayhap this will help? I had thought to give it to you later…"

Ghislaine turned round slowly to face her husband. The man was really infuriatingly unpredictable in this strange mood, and she was not at all sure that she preferred it. At least when he was frowning she knew where she stood.

In his outstretched hand was a small bundle wrapped in blue cloth which she took with a rather bemused smile. What on earth had come over him? Carefully she undid the thin cord and unwrapped the gift.

"'Tis beautiful, my lord." Never had she seen a more magnificent belt. Three fine strands of gold were interwoven with a delicate pattern of filigree. An opal gleamed prettily from the clasp. Guy took it from her shaking fingers and placed it around her waist. His closeness had an immediate effect on her heart which suddenly began to pound. If he noticed, Guy gave no sign of it.

"It would please me were you to wear it this night." He was standing so close to her that she was forced to look up directly into his eyes.

"I have never seen so pretty a belt—" she began, but her words were halted by a finger on her lips.

Whatever he was about to say was interrupted by a loud gurgling. Guy grinned down at her burning cheeks. "Perhaps the clinking of the belt will disguise the noise from your stomach, lady. But unless you eat soon, I will be accused of your starvation."

The great hall was alive with light and music when they arrived. Scented beeswax candles lit up the rich colours of the tapestry hangings on the walls and the huge fire at the top end of the hall was stoked with the more pungent wood from the orchards. New rushes had been recently laid on the floor, although the hounds that fouled them were still in residence, Ghislaine noted with a sniff.

Drawing a long, steadying breath, Ghislaine stepped into the light. For a few heartbeats she was plunged into dazed confusion by the sight that greeted her. There must have been close on fifty people sitting at the long table, ranged on either side of the hall. Others remained standing, talking or watching a dazzling performance of acrobats and jugglers. Above the noise and hilarity Ghislaine could hear the music of the troubadours.

Hugh d'Avranches surveyed his court from the raised dais in front of the fire. Lounging back in his chair with his thick arms stretched across the back of his neighbour's, his eyes surveyed the scene with regal satisfaction. Feeling his eyes on them, Ghislaine was almost tempted to retreat to the shadows of the ladies' bower, but she knew that she would have to face these people sometime and she would not be called a coward.

A large hand covered hers and placed it gently on his sleeve, reminding her of his presence. Ghislaine darted a look of grateful relief into Guy's glittering blue eyes and then lifted her chin as she tried to walk gracefully to their places on one of the lower tables.

It was as if they were walking through a sea of eyes. With her stomach churning, Ghislaine tried to shut out the scorn directed towards her and concentrate on each step at a time. If only she had taken more notice of her mother's strictures on dress and behaviour, she would not be feeling so gauche.

The open admiration she witnessed as the women caught sight of her handsome husband only made her misery greater. That Guy de Gourcy was feeling as uncomfortable as she only served to fuel her frustration. Had he not kidnapped her, none of this would be happening. As they took their seats, her stiff, tight-lipped expression caused Guy to frown in confusion.

That Hugh d'Avranches always provided an excellent feast was the only reason for which Ghislaine had to be grateful. Roast pork, venison and lamb were served to the lower tables, either plain or cooked with garlic and honey. The emergence from the pantry of an elaborately stuffed peacock earned a buzz of excitement amongst the guests, although Ghislaine found the flavour not at all to her taste. Fortified at last by strong wine, well-spiced food and de Launay courage, Ghislaine scanned the crowd for a glimpse of a familiar face.

She spotted Walter easily as he stood near the fire talking to a tiny woman with thick blonde tresses and an older man, presumably her father. Walter had a silver goblet in his hand and his head was bent low as he listened attentively to the smiling girl. He laughed at something she said and Ghislaine flushed as she remembered only too well the way he had laughed with her.

Oblivious to the din around her, Ghislaine watched him and realised how little she really knew of the man. Here, in the great castle, Walter de Belleme was in his element. He revelled in the power and the glamour, the hubbub and the excitement. All the things she hated and would have despised him for in time. Part of her girlish dreams dissipated with the laughter and the noise and a veil came down over her heart. Never again, she vowed silently, would she be so naïve.

Abruptly, Ghislaine forced her wandering wits back to reality as she realised belatedly that she had continued to stare at Walter, and that he had suddenly looked up to catch her in the act. Flushed with embarrassment over being caught staring, Ghislaine hurriedly reached out for the goblet of wine before her, knocking it over.

"I suppose you think that was my fault as well?" The words sounded harsh but Ghislaine was sure that she detected teasing. She turned sharply to look at Guy.

About to open her mouth in retort, the meaning of his words suddenly sank in. It was impossible to stop her lips from forming into a quirky smile. "Whatever made you think that?" she replied airily.

"Hah! It is any immense fortune that your eyes are not weapons, else I would be long dead, lady." Guy tossed another goblet of the wine down.

"Most fortunate indeed, my lord. However, I do have other weapons at my disposal that could achieve the same end." Was this really Guy de Gourcy she was talking to? Nay, flirting with? He was surely not the same man?

That seemed to strike a chord within and Guy burst out laughing. Ghislaine looked on amazed. Without the grim frown, the man was positively beautiful. She did not doubt it for almost every woman in the vicinity had turned to look at him.

"Ah, yes. The ale."

"Ale?" She looked at him quizzically. Perhaps his wits had gone a-begging after all. "Nay, I was talking about my arrows." A quick glance round at the rest of the hall told her that they were no longer the focus of attention. "I have a good aim." The pride in her voice shone through.

Guy turned the full force of his blue eyes upon her. "There are times, lady, when you miss the target."

His eyes strayed momentarily towards Walter and Ghislaine flushed as she realised that he had witnessed her humiliation. Had he been watching her then? Her eyes searched his face but she detected no sign of pity. And she did not wish to see that from him, she realised. His teasing, however, was most unsettling. To cover her discomfort, Ghislaine took another sip of the wine. It burnt a path to her stomach and boosted her courage.

"I thought you had business with the Earl?" she enquired coolly.

"Aye, but I had not reckoned with this." His large hand gestured to the gathering before them. In doing so, he clipped his goblet and the red wine seeped across the table.

A mortified sigh from the page behind them caused the two of them to twitch their lips conspiratorially.

"It would seem that we have a problem, the two of us."

Ghislaine could not prevent an involuntary chuckle over his double meaning and she looked at him with a warm sparkle in her eyes.

"Just the one, my lord?" she enquired conversationally.

Guy gave her a withering look and raked his hair back. The familiar gesture sent a smile fluttering across Ghislaine's face, but the frown on de Courcy's deepened.

"Do not waste your pretty smiles on me, lady. I am not de Belleme."

The icy tone of his voice doused the warmth of her feelings most effectively and Ghislaine was left wondering why on earth she had ever thought the man was human. Her thoughts were interrupted by a large hand grasping Guy's shoulder.

"So, de Gourcy. It pleases me that you came with such speed. I was mightily concerned that you might have fallen foul of Dettingham after all."

Hugh d'Avranches' blue eyes bored into Guy with piercing shrewdness. Ghislaine noticed that her husband's black frown had turned into one of icy politeness and for some inexplicable reason, it pleased her. At least she had not been subject to his cool distance.

"I was given to believe that you desired my presence immediately."

The Earl's fat jowls quivered as he nodded, the hooded eyes not leaving Guy de Courcy for a moment. A slow smile crept over the fleshy lips but it did not reach his eyes. "Your directness is most commendable, de Courcy, as one would expect from a mercenary."

The intentional sneer in the Earl's voice caused Ghislaine to hold her breath: but her husband surveyed him with an expression devoid of feeling. "I take it that you are in need of my skills, sire?" His voice was as cold as ice.

Hugh d'Avranches returned the cool stare and then transferred his gaze to Ghislaine who had remained silently seated, praying to God that he would forget about her. Unfortunately, God was not listening this night.

"My lady. A pleasant surprise."

Ghislaine inclined her head stiffly, murmuring her words of acknowledgement.

"Marriage seems to suit you, my lady."

Ghislaine shot him a quizzical look. "I had not noticed any appreciable difference, my lord."

"My foresters have reported no lack of game near your manor since your wedding and for that I must extend my thanks to your husband." The Earl smiled lazily at her and Ghislaine could feel the heat rush to her cheeks. She noticed that several of the couples seated near them were watching avidly and seemed to be enjoying her discomfort.

Before she could reply in kind, Guy interrupted. "I can take no credit for the increase in your game, sire, but it may be that the poachers have stayed away since the arrival of my men." Ghislaine shot him a grateful smile.

The Earl briefly inclined his head. "Then I may be doubly in your debt, de Courcy. Not only have you curtailed your wife's less endearing habits but you seem to have the manpower I need at the moment."

Guy's expression did not alter. "The men I have, sire, but I cannot admit to aught else. In truth, I have found my wife's behaviour most…refreshing. Marriage is far more diverting than I had imagined."

Ghislaine could hardly believe her ears. Guy de Courcy was defending her before half the court. No doubt he had a reason, came the voice of conscience. Aye, but it felt good to hear none the less.

"Most gratifying, de Courcy. Then mayhap we can examine the extent of your gratitude privately." This was not a question. Hugh d'Avranches nodded to his two nearest companions. One she recognised as William FitzNigel, whose lands stretched far beyond the rest in the county. The other was a smaller, younger man who had a look of the Earl. Ghislaine decided he was probably one of the Earl's bastards.

Guy rose to follow the three men without even a glance at her, but his words had been enough. She did not trust the Earl and whatever business he had with her husband would no doubt be dangerous. Ghislaine's eyes searched once more for Walter. She had to find out whether Walter was still entertaining hopes to kill Guy and the only way she could do that was to talk to him. Fortifying herself with another goblet of the soft wine, Ghislaine determined to find him.

She did not have to search far. A gentle hand grabbed her wrist as she made her way towards the acrobats.

"Well met, my lady!" Walter's soft grey eyes roved over Ghislaine's face. Whatever his feelings, they were well hidden. Did he trust her still?

"I had not thought to see you here, Sir Walter." Her voice was deliberately prim and cool since their last parting had been less than cordial.

"Nay?" His blond hair curled perfectly around his handsome face and Ghislaine suddenly wondered why she had found him so trustworthy. Everything about him, from his delicate hands to his handsome boots, seemed so perfect. She noticed his lips twitch as he took in her drab attire. Had he always been so? "Then a happy coincidence, my lady."

Ghislaine smiled at him wanly. "It would appear that this is not your only happy coincidence, Sir Walter. You seem to make a habit of talking to ladies."

She hoped fervently that his vanity would take control and think her suffering no more than jealousy. His grey eyes brightened considerably at her words.

"Blanche?" His eyes surveyed her speculatively. "She was a close friend of my wife. I had not seen her since Anne-Marie's death." His demeanour suddenly took on a much more sombre appearance. It was strange that she had not noticed that chameleon-like ability before.

A rather cheerful conversation under the circumstances, thought Ghislaine suspiciously. And if the name rang true, Blanche Cholmondston was one of the wealthiest widows in the county. How simple he must think her. And yet, if he thought her so gullible, it might not be too difficult to allay any suspicions he might have about her.

"Forgive me, Sir Walter, but I have not been myself of late." She peered up at him shyly, her mouth making a brave attempt at a cheerful smile. "My marriage was not of my making and I fear that I need some time to...adjust." Her fingers twisted nervously at the gold belt draped low over her hips. "My husband is not...the man I would have chosen."

Ghislaine took a chance and turned her eyes back to her companion. "I hope you will not think ill of my manners, Sir Walter?"

Sympathetic grey eyes pierced into her and Ghislaine wondered, just for a second, whether she had truly misunderstood him and Walter was still the man she had dreamed he was. Ruthlessly Ghislaine quashed the thought. She had not dreamed up his plan to kill Guy de Courcy.

"I think I have already told you how I feel, Ghislaine." The words were murmured softly so that only she could hear. "Mayhap I expressed myself too strongly at the time."

"I had not expected it," she replied quietly.

"Had you not?" His voice inflected a little so that she would hear the amusement in his words. "For all your simple appearance, I have never underestimated you."

Was that a warning? Ghislaine raised an eyebrow. She would have to brave it out. Around them the acrobats flared into action, encouraged by the appreciative shouts of their audience. They watched a tiny woman draped in green and gold fly through the air to be caught by her burly companion. Ghislaine looked towards the dais but was denied sight of Guy by the crowd that had gathered around the acrobats.

Ghislaine turned back towards Walter and watched him as he laughed at the players before him. His skin was soft and lightly tanned. Strange that she had never noticed that about him. "You spoke of a plan. Have you thought any more of it?"

Walter's eyes remained glued on the shapely form of the woman. "Nay. Not as yet." His eyes darted quickly in Ghislaine's direction.

For a sick moment, Ghislaine wondered if Walter de Belleme had seen through her after all, but judging by his slight smile, she decided he hadn't. Across from them the woman acrobat smiled invitingly at Walter. Slowly he turned his head towards Ghislaine. "I was waiting for your assent."

Ghislaine's heart froze as she heard the soft words. "My assent?" she whispered hoarsely. "What had you in mind?"

"Oh, nothing terrible. A simple riding accident in the forest. Or an ambush." The words seemed to Ghislaine to have been plucked out of thin air, but they had not. She knew that deep within her. Walter de Belleme wanted her husband dead.

"When?" came her quiet reply. She had to know. Her heart was racing as she waited.

"Not yet." Walter turned the full blast of his soft eyes upon her as he gently pulled her fingers to his lips. "Not yet, sweet Ghislaine." The feel of his lips made her jump back in surprise. Walter smiled. "I will come for you soon."

They parted before crowds of people as if they had done no more that speak of the weather or of hunting. His bow was perfect even if hers was rather clumsy. Ghislaine made her way back to her seat in a whirl of thoughts.

The gentle flickering of the torch in the ladies' bower drew Ghislaine's eyes. Sleep had eluded her for some time and she could tell from the lightening shadows that dawn was well underway. And yet it had not been the coughs nor the snores from the other ladies that had kept her awake, even though the noise from them would have been loud enough to waken deaf Leowulf, the village smith. Nay. It had been Guy de Courcy that had caused her puzzlement.

The moment Ghislaine had left Walter to resume her seat, Guy had swooped down on her. Without a word, her husband had led her from the hall, smiling coolly at passing courtiers and their ladies, until they had reached the other side of the heavy doors. He had gripped her arm so tightly that she could feel the bruise even now. Tight-lipped, he had propelled her without a word to the door of the ladies' bower. His face was dark and angry, and instinct warned her not to say a word. Whatever the cause of his anger, she was sure she would find out.

"If you take an assignation with de Belleme," he had whispered in her ear with such disgust, "then I promise you, lady, your people will find out the truth of my reputation. Do you understand me?" He underlined the question by shaking her.

"Yes!" As the answer had been wrenched from her, Guy had pushed her roughly from him and stalked away into the shadows, leaving Ghislaine to recover her breath and her senses.

That had been hours past and Ghislaine was no nearer the answer than she had been then. Seeking respite from her jumbled thoughts, she finally closed her eyes and sank into a wild turmoil of shattered pictures and voices.

Chapter Twelve

Ghislaine stared gloomily at the hunched shoulders of Guy de Courcy, his whole body radiating anger and irritation. Light rain was blowing in gusts from the north-west and dusk was already sweeping across the darkening sky as the band moved steadily onwards. Relief began to seep through her bones as Ghislaine recognised familiar landmarks. Home was not far now.

The journey back to Chapmonswiche had been a long one. Guy had hardly addressed one civil word to her and had treated her like a leper. Indignantly she had remained behind Guy's destrier, resenting her petulant reaction but wishing to provoke a reaction all the same.

As they headed towards the forest, Ghislaine's preoccupation with their safety grew. The outlaws operated almost with impunity in the area, especially in the darkening half-light. It would, she decided, be very easy for Walter to do the same. A cold shudder ran through her.

Ghislaine eyed the forbidding back of her husband with increasing uncertainty. Guy de Courcy had been acting like a jealous lover ever since he had seen her talk with Walter. He had asked her no questions nor, more oddly, had he offered any opinions on her behaviour. He had just taken her away without a word. If she told him why she had been talking to Walter, she doubted very much that he would even listen.

A rustling of the leaves to the side of the track made her jerk her head round, but nothing was there. Ghislaine's heart slowed down and she wiped her palms on her dusty cloak. Guy had barely spared a glance in the direction of the noise and she silently cursed his ignorance. Of all the people she knew, he was the only one who was capable of resisting any attack of force. It was his living and he would be defending his own property. Resolving at least to try to talk to him, Ghislaine gently spurred her horse on to catch up with her husband.

''Why have you left Joachim in Chester?'' she asked as pleasantly as the gusting wind would allow. Guy's cold silence echoed about them whilst the guards stared doggedly on ahead. Ghislaine shot him a dark look that fell on very stony ground.

Angered by his continued refusal to talk to her, Ghislaine tried another tack. ''Surely you did not forget Joachim, my lord?'' Her mocking exclamation earned her at least a hardening of the jaw, a sure sign that he was listening. ''Poor Joachim,'' she continued unabashed. ''But yes, you have the right of it, Sir Guy. Joachim is not really a man you would notice, and although his skills are certainly…''

''Cease this prattle, girl. Joachim remains in Chester to oversee the supplies. To my mind 'tis your wits that have gone awandering.''

Guy settled back into disgruntled silence, his eyes fixed on the path ahead. Ghislaine sighed. At least she had earned his attention if nothing else.

"My wits?" she continued in shock horror. Cocking her head to one side as if contemplating the thought, Ghislaine then smiled broadly. "You are right, of course. It was my foolish wits that allowed me to be taken hostage by a desperate mercenary, to be married off as part of some deal and then treated as if I didn't exist. And," she continued with inspiration, "if that weren't enough, as a reward I have been allowed to spend the rest of my days in a convent, to forgo children and all those other domestic chores that seem to give the rest of womankind such pleasure."

Ghislaine slid her eyes over Guy's face and decided she was about to get a reaction.

"Your mindless chatter is doing naught but testing my temper, girl. If you had any wits about you, you would be contemplating how best to avoid my hand on your backside when we reach home." Guy spurred his horse a little faster as if to place himself beyond her reach.

Ghislaine was momentarily diverted by his use of the word "home" to think about what else he had said. It seemed strange to hear anyone other than her family call the manor home. When she finally realised what the man had said, her irritation with his pig-headed, obstinate truculence provoked her into more drastic action.

Kicking her horse forward, Ghislaine suddenly galloped ahead. With the wind and the rain pelting into her face it was hard to see where she was going, but she ploughed on. Behind her, Ghislaine could hear the shouts of men and on another level a heavy thud that could only be her husband's horse. Determined to put as much distance between them as she could, Ghislaine pushed on.

The track they were following to the side of the forest was awash with mud and rainwater, and Ghislaine's horse was finding a steady pace increasingly difficult. Slowing a little to negotiate a hanging branch was her undoing, for Ghislaine found her reins ripped from her frozen fingers and pulled hard towards the black destrier. There was no sign of the other men.

Remembering her provocative attitude just moments before, Ghislaine paled. Guy had clearly taken exception to it and was planning to chastise her here and now. She had not honestly believed he would lay a hand to her, for he had often made that threat without ever following it up. But he had seemed to be far angrier than normal. Leaning forward, Ghislaine tried to grab the reins back, but Guy's grip was too firm. As the horses came to a halt, she held her breath, watching her husband dismount. Running did not seem to be a sensible option.

As his strong hands gripped her waist, she finally found her voice.

"What do you plan to do?"

"You were warned, lady." The fierce look in his eyes was not something she could ignore. When her feet finally sank into the mud, Ghislaine's eyes searched for the safety of his men. In vain.

"Now? Here?" For some reason she seemed unable to utter any more and watched in disbelief as he tied the horses to a nearby branch and then yanked her towards the undergrowth. They stopped behind a large hawthorn clump.

Ghislaine was roughly turned towards him and slammed into his hard chest. It was difficult breathing but she was determined that he would not see how alarmed she was.

"Do not forget that I am your wife, Guy de Courcy," she uttered with a defiant gleam in her eye.

"I do not forget it for a moment, lady," Guy cut in sharply. "But it would seem that you do."

Her mouth opened and then abruptly shut. Mayhap defiance was not the answer either. "Nay, I do not forget it," she replied quietly. Her head was level with the middle of his chest and she closed her eyes as his hand slid under her chin and forced her to look upwards.

"So you have no longing for the convent after all?" Guy's voice was harsh and uncompromising.

"I did not say that exactly." Surprised at the question, her eyes snapped open.

"I distinctly recall you regretting the pleasures of domestic life. Was I wrong?" He shook her slightly and caused her to gasp. Her continued silence wrought another shake.

"This marriage was not of our choosing and I have no wish to remain a burden on anyone." Her decision to remain calm forgotten, Ghislaine's eyes spat fire at him.

Guy watched her with narrowed eyes as the cold wind blustered about them. "You have no vocation, that much I do know," he countered.

"You know no such thing," she retorted her lips tight. "In fact, you know very little about me at all."

Guy continued to stare at her for a moment before the merest hint of a smile broke his icy expression. ''Then I shall put it to the test.''

Before Ghislaine realised what was happening, Guy's lips had taken possession of hers in a kiss that seemed to go on forever. The more she resisted, the more insistent he became until finally her lips parted. As his tongue explored the softness of her mouth, Ghislaine felt all thoughts of resistance flutter away. As the kiss deepened, Ghislaine's hands slid up his arms to tangle her fingers in his thick hair.

Guy's mouth became more demanding whilst his hand slid from her waist to caress the full curves of her hips. Ghislaine gave herself up to such unfamiliar, erotic sensations as his tongue began to move in a forbidden rhythm that set her nerves dancing.

Startled by the strength of her response, Guy lifted his mouth from hers and gazed down at her flushed face. Slowly he put her from him and drew a steadying breath as Ghislaine's scattered senses returned.

In a daze of confusion, Ghislaine forced herself to focus her thoughts. Shame roared through her as she realised just how willingly she had yielded to him. Frantically she tried to think of something witty or defiant to say, or anything at all, but no words formed in her mind. Her cheeks burned hotly and she felt like a child who had just been taught a lesson.

''Take your reins, Ghislaine. The men are waiting back up the track.''

Her eyes shot to his, but whatever her husband was thinking was masked by a cool veneer of apparent indifference. It had meant nothing to him, this kiss, after all.

Wordlessly Ghislaine turned to mount her horse.

The dark was swirling about them as the group finally entered the manor gates. Guards scattered in all directions as Guy slid wearily from the saddle and Ghislaine noted that there were more men in evidence than usual. Guy helped her from her palfrey and she warily placed her hands on his shoulders. She need not have worried for Guy did not linger. He turned on his heels and strode towards the hall issuing orders as he went.

"Sir Guy! Lady Ghislaine!" Sir Brian's loud voice carried across the bailey, halting both mid-step. This was not his usual method of greeting and the tone of his voice did not bode well.

"Is aught amiss, Sir Brian?" Ghislaine was pleased to hear her voice sound confident.

The hapless knight looked drawn and pale in the flickering torchlight as he stammered another greeting and bowed low before them. "Grave news," he began. "D'Everard is badly wounded and I fear for his life."

Guy stared at him for a moment in disbelief before he turned back to where Sir Brian was hovering. "How did it happen?" His voice was toneless but Ghislaine was beginning to realise that he always spoke this way when he wished to hide his feelings.

"Only a short time ago, in the forest. D'Everard was searching for the outlaws as you ordered when they were set upon. He has a bad wound in the thigh."

"Was there any other damage?"

"One dead and two minor wounds. Three of the horses have cuts." Sir Brian's hand gripped and ungripped his sword as he spoke.

"How many of them?"

The older man raked back his grey hair in imitation of the new lord. "About twelve to our eight, Sir Guy. It was a surprise ambush, although the guards say they were not soldiers. Like as not it was the outlaws."

There was not a sound in the bailey as Guy rubbed his chin with his gauntlet. "Where is d'Everard?"

"In the hall."

Without a word, Guy turned quickly and headed towards the hall. Ghislaine put her hand on Sir Brian's arm. "Could you send Effie with my medicaments and get Edwin to fetch Hulda from the village?"

Sir Brian nodded curtly and rushed off, grateful no doubt to be out of Sir Guy's way.

Even before she had reached the hall, Ghislaine could hear Guy blasting the men and she quickened her pace. They had no need of further injuries as a result of his anger.

The two wounded men possessed bad sword gashes on their arms and legs but Ghislaine quickly assessed their condition as curable. D'Everard was a different matter. His tunic and chausses were soaked in blood and he was very pale from loss of blood and exhaustion.

"How long has he been bleeding like this?" She addressed the question to the man hovering about Sir Arnaud.

"Since he was hit, my lady." The soldier frowned as he attempted to guess the time. "Nigh on two notches of the candle. We brought him home as gently as we could, but there was not much else we could do aside from removing his chain mail. Your maid did what she could." Silently he handed her an iron-tipped arrow. "He pulled it out himself. The tip's missing, my lady." Casting a pitying glance at Arnaud, the soldier shuffled to the far side of the hall.

It was far worse than she thought. Quickly Ghislaine directed a torch to above Sir Arnaud's leg and eased away the blood-soaked pad. In his muscular left thigh was a large, jagged hole that oozed blood.

Ghislaine had treated many such wounds before and was used to the sight of blood, but it was the sight of her husband that moved her most. Their eyes met as she assessed the extent of the damage. The arrow had torn the flesh badly but she was not certain whether a piece of his chain mail as well as the arrow tip was still within. If that was the case, then infection would set in quickly and Sir Arnaud would not linger long. Guy's face was white.

"Tell me the worst, lady."

Her eyes dropped to the wan face of his friend and decided honesty was the best she could do.

"I do not yet know how bad he will be. If the fever sets in, there is no telling whether he will pull through or not. I must clean the wound properly first but it will be a day or two before we know." She stared at her husband steadily. It would be no use promising life if she could not save him. It was in the hands of the Lord.

"Whatever you need, lady, just ask. The man is like a brother to me." The gruffness in his voice was heart-rending but Ghislaine put all tender feelings aside. Sympathy was not what he needed.

"I have sent for Hulda. She will save him if she can."

Guy opened his mouth as if to protest, but Sir Arnaud groaned most eloquently and he took two steps back. Nodding gravely, he retreated to the back of the hall, ushering out the rest of the men and sending for servants to provide whatever she deemed necessary.

The arrow had indeed caused much damage and d'Everard had lost a great deal of blood. The man was weak and in poor shape to fight for his life; Ghislaine decided he had best take a sleeping draught to gain some strength. First she set about forcing some poppy juice down his throat, and then, when satisfied it had taken effect, she had him moved to a smaller chamber where Ghislaine could examine the wound more carefully.

Her fears were justified. The tip of the arrow was lodged deep within although there was no sign of any chain mail. It was some time before she was satisfied that the wound was clean and could heal safely. Hulda, arriving soon after, was not hopeful of success. Every so often the old woman would stare at Arnaud's face and shake her head gravely, before examining the colour of the blood still seeping from the wound. Finally she placed a vile concoction of mallow, holly bark and elder over the clean hole to reduce the swelling.

At last she sat back and looked at Ghislaine. "The Norman is in God's hands now. There is no more I can do."

Ghislaine nodded as she took the pot of herbs from Hulda and searched the man's face for any sign of improvement. D'Everard looked very grey and ill.

Hours later, the fever took hold of him and Ghislaine truly feared for his life.

Through the night and all the next day she changed his bandages and forced various of Hulda's concoc-

tions down his throat, but the heat from his body
would not abate. As his thrashing continued and de-
lirium took hold of his tongue, Ghislaine sent to the
Abbey for a priest. No matter how ungodly the man,
she would not let him die unshriven.

As the last rites were being said over his friend, Guy
stared impassively at the group but made no attempt
to join them. He had remained in the chamber the
whole time but had not approached the pallet, carefully heeding Ghislaine's warning about not disturbing
Arnaud. He had ordered fires, wallhangings and clean
bedlinen as required. When the priest had finished,
Guy quit the room.

Ghislaine watched him leave with a heavy heart.
There was naught she could do to ease his suffering
but maybe capturing the men responsible would go
some way to help. She wished him luck.

"Lady Ghislaine, I have a message for you." The
priest's reedy voice was close in her ear and Ghislaine
whirled round, somewhat flustered at being caught
watching her husband.

"Aye. There is a purse for the abbey, Father. I will
send Effie for it."

Father Gregory was a small, thin man with a thin,
foxy face that missed nothing. "My thanks, good sister. That would be most appreciated." He hesitated a
moment and Ghislaine watched him dart a quick look
around the room to see if anyone was listening. She
drew closer. "I have a message. Father John wishes
to speak to you concerning Margaret Staveley. He…is
most anxious to see you."

Arnaud's groan captured Ghislaine's attention.

"Aye," she replied distractedly. "I'll come when I can." It was an odd request, but then priests were not of the same world. "Please take food and drink, Father."

She had the impression that the priest would have said more, but finally nodded his thanks and disappeared into the kitchens. Dismissing her fancies, Ghislaine hurried to Arnaud's side.

The fever finally broke the next morning, much to her relief. Had the man died, there was no knowing how her husband would have taken the news. She sent silent thanks up to heaven and a messenger to Guy. It was late in the afternoon when he finally returned and d'Everard had improved greatly.

His search for the bandits had proved fruitless so far, but he burst through the chamber doors with a hopeful smile on his face.

The smile wavered when he witnessed how pale and ill his friend looked, but he sat down at his side none the less. D'Everard blinked up at him, his eyes dull and sullen. He offered Guy a clammy hand to clasp.

"So, d'Everard. You go far to find a way to stay in bed." His blue eyes looked suspiciously bright.

Arnaud managed a faint grimace and plucked at Guy's arm. "If you need my services, best get me some food. Your lady would starve me on gruel."

Guy grinned up at Ghislaine as d'Everard sank back into exhausted silence. "My thanks, Ghislaine. Arnaud sounds almost himself again."

The smile he turned on her was dazzling and she was quite flustered by the sincerity she saw there.

"Thank me not, Sir Guy. It is merely my duty as lady of the house."

"None the less, you have watched over him tirelessly. Name whatever you wish, lady."

Her smile began to fade. He had called her Ghislaine before, and she had no wish to be paid for her services.

"There is no debt, husband," she replied stiffly. As she turned, her arm was gripped tightly.

"I did not mean to offend you, girl. My thanks are most heartfelt."

Ghislaine looked up into grave, blue eyes and her huffiness melted. She nodded, disturbed somewhat by his closeness. "Have you caught the outlaws?" They needed a distraction.

Guy sighed heavily. He looked very tired. "Nay, not yet. But I will."

Ghislaine had no doubt that he meant it and that cold gleam in his eye did not bode well for the men he finally caught. "Go eat and sleep, my lord, or else I'll have two patients on my hands." She watched her husband glance at d'Everard. "If there is any change, I'll wake you myself," she assured calmly. As she spoke, Ghislaine had placed one hand on his arm to add reassurance.

Guy placed his callused hand over hers and patted it gently, almost as if they had been married for years. "You are right," he grimaced. "I'm bone tired and stink like the devil. We'll speak on the morrow, Ghislaine." With a parting glance at d'Everard, Guy left the room.

A good night's sleep had worked wonders for her patient and Guy had left the manor with a much lighter heart that morning.

"So, my lady. Am I well enough now to eat like a man or must I persevere with this…slop?" Sir Arnaud's querulous tone brought a smile to Ghislaine's lips.

Rising quietly from the embrasure where she had been watching the forest, Ghislaine made her way to her patient's pallet. "If you are well enough to grumble, I am sure that you are well enough to eat something more substantial, Sir Arnaud." Bending over him, she placed her hand on his forehead. It felt cool to touch, although she did not like the grey tinge that lingered around his mouth.

Noticing her frown, Sir Arnaud sighed heavily, expecting Ghislaine to change her mind. "Hulda's gruel would be enough to make even your husband ill, lady. Perhaps we ought to try a little meat, as an experiment?" His voice was so plaintive and desperate that Ghislaine was not proof against it.

Raising her hands in defeat, Ghislaine smiled. "So be it, my lord. I'll send for a little chicken and bread."

Sir Arnaud tossed a surly look at her. "Chicken and bread! I think you and that hard task-master of a husband of yours have more in common than you think."

Ghislaine smiled broadly at the petulant tone. "You may be sure that I am not about to waste days of care by allowing you to eat yourself into death. Sir Guy would no doubt agree, were he but here." Her expression was implacable.

Sir Arnaud flushed somewhat guiltily. "Aye, that was most churlish of me. I am grateful for your care, lady."

"Think nothing of it, Sir Arnaud." Ghislaine rose to add some more fragrant wood to the fire. "I am well aware that my husband would be most disappointed were he to find you dead. Since you have managed to consume a goodly part of his wealth over the years, I am certain Guy de Courcy would view you as a poor bargain."

A reluctant smile played on his lips. "In truth, lady, it is not just myself who finds your domestic comforts attractive." He raised his hands in mock defence as Ghislaine shot him a withering glance. "Guy has lost a little of that bad-tempered surliness you complained of. See, lady! I warned you that with patience and a little comfort the man could be changed."

Staring into the flames as she raked over the embers, Ghislaine thought more of the man she had married. He had been a loyal friend to Arnaud and he had shown her how much he cared about him. Were he to feel the same about her some day! "Maybe," she replied distractedly.

"I have seen him watch you as you tended me; he looked much like a jealous man, lady." Arnaud slid her a covert glance as he settled himself comfortably against the bolster. "Perhaps if you lavished more care on him he might respond more…er…amicably?"

Ghislaine frowned, not at all certain that Guy wanted her attentions. "Why do you tell me all this? I would have thought it would suit you far better to have me sent to the convent so that you could return to the old life." She jabbed the stick deep into the fire.

"He is lonely and I think you do him good, Lady Ghislaine. Our friendship runs in both directions." He looked over at her, his smile gone. "Try it, lady. You have nothing to lose."

The light was fading fast by the time that Guy returned from his outlaw hunting. The cold, blustery wind of the day had turned bone-perishing and Ghislaine had made sure that extra wood was burning in the grate. She had also taken the trouble of ordering roast beef and Guy's favourite sweet tartlets. Whatever she had said to Arnaud d'Everard, Guy's story had played on her mind and touched a soft spot deep within. For some unfathomable reason she felt sympathy. It was her duty to try to give him some comfort, she told herself.

Guy's face was etched with lines of tiredness and the sullen expression he wore told its own story. Ghislaine rose to greet him as he entered the hall. Self-conscious that she had changed her gown and brushed her hair, her hands twisted the edge of her cuff as he approached. He was not only tired but very wet.

"Come, take off your cloak and rest by the fire to warm whilst I get you some wine."

Guy looked as if he would say something but obviously changed his mind. An expressive grunt was the most he could manage before he threw himself gratefully into the chair. Ghislaine carried away the discarded cloak and brought him a goblet of spiced wine.

"To what do I owe this?" he enquired with eyes closed as he stretched his long legs before him.

"I had thought you might appreciate it. If I was wrong, you have only to say," she replied stiffly. Had she really felt sympathy for this oaf?

Guy let out a low groan. "I did not mean to offend you, Ghislaine. This is…most welcome."

Thawing a little, she nodded. "I did not mean to be irritable either. There is a bath in…our room if you want it."

She stood up only to be stopped by his hand on her wrist. "Is aught wrong with Arnaud?" His eyes were grave and anxious.

"Nay. He is full of complaints. At this moment he is resting, but I am sure that he will be giving you a complete list of my crimes first thing in the morning."

His answering grin was one of relief, but he did not let go of her wrist. Instead he stood up.

"You have earned my deepest thanks, Ghislaine. I repeat that whatever you wish will be yours."

He raised her hand to his lips and gently placed a kiss on her fingers.

"Well, there is one thing," she remembered hesitantly. "Father John has asked to see me at the abbey and I would like to go."

Guy looked down at her, his eyes holding hers. For once his closeness did not distress her nor make her uncomfortable. "You have my word, if you promise to return the same day. My men will accompany you to ensure your safety."

A soft glow lit deep within her as Ghislaine nodded her agreement. Maybe Sir Arnaud had spoken some sense.

Chapter Thirteen

From the dark recesses of the bedchamber Ghislaine sat watching the sleeping form of her husband. The weak light of the dawn filtered through the shutters but did not reach the bed. He had not moved since he had collapsed on the bed the night before and she had not had the heart to wake him. There was always room amongst the women servants and Ghislaine had found a quiet pallet where she would not be disturbed by the gossiping and snoring. Normally she fell asleep immediately, but last night her mind had continued to think about her husband.

Eventually she must have dozed for she was awakened by the clattering of the women around her who were rising to begin the chores. So that the servants would not wake him, Ghislaine had laid the fire in the bedchamber herself to ensure that the room would be less chilly when he awoke. She had also placed a pitcher of the ale he liked and a small, freshly baked loaf of bread near the bed.

Pulling her knees to her chest, Ghislaine continued to stare at him. The man did not even snore, she realised suddenly and decided that he would be far easier to sleep with than the women. A deep flush stole across her cheeks at that daring thought and she was grateful that Guy was not awake to witness it.

His dark hair was tousled in a boyish way and made the harsh planes of Guy's face much softer. Long, dark lashes fanned his cheeks and his lips looked very gentle in the firelight. She wondered what he would have looked like as a boy and decided he would probably have been rather endearing. Maybe, as Arnaud had suggested, it was the harsh treatment he had received that had made him the man he was. Yet he did have a softer side and he had shown it to her on occasions. Guiltily, Ghislaine remembered how badly she had behaved towards him when he did try to show some consideration towards her. Resolving to act with more grace, Ghislaine uncurled her cold, stiff limbs and moved closer to the fire.

Mesmerised by the dancing flames, she sat back in the seat and let the warmth seep through her body. At length her mind began to slow down until sleep finally claimed her.

A sharp crack from a log on the fire made Ghislaine shoot up in surprise. The shock had numbed her brain for it took a minute to realise where she was or what she was doing there. The light was much brighter and Ghislaine surmised that she had been asleep for at least a candle notch. Looking quickly over in the direction of her husband, she was taken aback to see him sitting up and staring at her, a frown creasing his forehead.

"Good morning," she offered.

"Did you sleep there all night?" he demanded, the frown deepening to a scowl.

Ghislaine rose as gracefully as her stiff legs would allow. He was always grouchy in the morning. Smiling pleasantly, she shook her head. "I slept with the other women. You were so tired that I would not wake you."

"Most thoughtful, lady." If anything the scowl had grown blacker.

Growing uncomfortable with the increasing tension, Ghislaine decided perhaps honesty would clear the air. "Have I done aught to displease you? If that is the case, please tell me so that I can rectify the problem. I do not wish to worry about your scowls all day."

"I did not think you worried about my scowls," Guy countered.

"At times they have been justified," she allowed, "but I can think of no reason this morning."

"You have a clear conscience then?" His eyes regarded her suspiciously.

Ghislaine stared at him, her mouth agape. His arrogance knew no bounds. Resolutions forgotten, she advanced on him with a fierce gleam in her eyes. "If I were a man, Guy de Courcy, I would run you through. As I am not, I shall have to resort to other means. It grieves me to think that I laid the fire and brought you some ale and bread. My wits must certainly have gone awandering if I thought you might be grateful for a little care."

Angrily, she turned on her heels and stormed towards the door, but just as her hand touched the latch his voice reached across the room.

"I am grateful for your care."

Her fingers stilled mid-air. "You do not sound very grateful," she responded dryly.

"Then come back here and let me try again." His voice was no longer harsh, but soft and compelling.

Sir Arnaud's words echoed in her mind and Ghislaine sighed heavily. Why did she want to believe what he said? She turned slowly. "If you shout at me once more or give me another black look, I will leave," she muttered.

Guy nodded curtly. "Perhaps you could warn me when my looks start to get too offensive?"

That little play on words caused the barest twitch of her lips as she sat down gingerly at the foot of the bed. "Rest assured, Sir Guy, I will inform you."

"I prefer it when you call me Guy."

Ghislaine inclined her head. "Very well."

There was a momentary pause when neither of them seemed to know what to say, and Ghislaine was finding her proximity to the man rather nerve-racking. She was determined to sound as casual as she could. "Perhaps you would explain why you were so angry with me."

Guy looked at her with a wry smile on his lips. "I remembered nothing after I fell on the bed last night other than you had been insisting I ate and bathed. It…er…bothered me that had you stayed here, I knew naught about it." Guy shifted uncomfortably. "I…er…wondered why you had looked after me so well." He had the grace to blush under her curious gaze.

"But I did little."

"Aye. Well, that is the reason," he replied gruffly. "My apologies if I upset you."

"You are very easy to please," she teased gently.

Reaching for the ale, Ghislaine poured a small amount into the silver goblet and handed it to him.

Guy eyed the goblet with an odd expression on his face. "Did you brew this yourself, lady?"

Ghislaine could have sworn that his voice was laden with suspicion, but that was too far-fetched. "Aye. A good batch, I am given to believe."

"You have not tried it yourself?"

What was wrong with the man? "If you do not want the ale, Sir Guy, you have only to say."

Guy frowned at the stiff tone of her voice. "Nay. 'Tis not that," he added quickly. "I have a definite preference for ale brewed by you." So saying, he closed his eyes and tossed back the ale in one.

"My thanks for the compliment, Sir...er...Guy." Why did she feel so tongue-tied and awkward? "I shall remember it."

Guy was still staring at the goblet, sniffing tentatively at the residual aroma.

"Do you wish for more?"

Finally he looked up at her and smiled his boyish smile. "Not at the moment, but I admit that a man could set used to this personal attention."

That brought a flush to her cheeks. "If you continue to be so charming, I might be persuaded to try more often."

Guy leaned forward so that she could smell the lavender he had used in the bath. The sheets slipped and she realised that he was naked beneath it. The squire must have undressed him after she had left. His finger touched her cheek lightly and he smiled into her eyes.

"And what sort of persuasion would it take, lady, to stop you from going to the abbey?"

It was not just the question that caused the heat to flood through her body. His face was close to hers and she could see the stubble on his chin and the softness of his lips. The other hand had wandered to her braid and was gently pulling it towards him.

Ghislaine knew he was going to kiss her but she could think of no good reason to stop him. Slowly, so slowly he lowered his mouth to hers, but she did not pull away. His lips were soft and sensuous, caressing hers gently and without demands. It was over before she could respond.

"Why should I not go to the abbey?" she breathed, her eyes watching his lips.

His fingers slipped down to her arms and pulled her towards him once more. The blue eyes were turning darker as he kissed her with more force.

"I told you. You have no vocation," came the rasping reply.

Ghislaine tried to make sense of his words whilst her wits were scattered far and wide by the sensations swirling within her. Whatever his kisses contained, they had a seriously debilitating effect on her.

"What? Nay," she murmured breathlessly. "You misunderstand. I received a message to visit one of the priests there, no more." Watching the look of relief on his face, her mind began to act. Placing her hands on his chest, she pushed him back and gave him a look of much displeasure. So this was just a ruse to keep her here.

His hands snaked back around her arms again and

he looked at her almost fiercely. "So you do not stay there, then? This was no plan to escape?"

"Nay, it was not. I would not do anything so faint-hearted, When I leave for the convent, I will tell you."

His fingers relaxed their tight grip on her a little but did not let her go. "What message did you receive?" His voice was suspicious.

Ghislaine shrugged. "It was from Father John. He wished to talk to me about Margaret Staveley. There is naught odd about it," she continued as she saw his frown. "He would often stay with her. Margaret was most devout."

Guy thought for a few minutes and then sighed heavily. "It seems I must apologise once again, lady. I admit to thinking it merely a cover for an assignment with your lover."

Ghislaine stared at him aghast. "My lover?" she repeated. "Who is my lover?"

Guy gave her a withering look. "Walter de Belleme, lady. Do not play games with me."

Ghislaine folded her hands across her chest. "So that was why you behaved so jealously in Chester?" she demanded crossly. "You thought he was my lover."

"You deny it?"

"Aye."

"Then why were you talking to him for so long, looking at him just so, smiling?" His lips were set tight in an angry line and he imitated Ghislaine by folding his arms across his chest.

Ghislaine hesitated and lowered her eyes. Now was the time to tell him. "When he was here last," she began slowly, her fingers pulling at the sheet nervously, "he told me he had a plan to—"

"What plan?" Guy broke in. "Why did you not tell me afore this?"

"If you interrupt me again, I will not explain." Two bright spots of red burned on her cheeks and Ghislaine closed her lips tightly.

Guy gave a snort of disgust and fell back onto the bolster in frustration. "Go on," he murmured through gritted teeth. "I shall endeavour to keep my tongue and my hands in check."

Ghislaine raised an eyebrow at the threat, but she trusted him to keep it. "He planned for you to have an accident."

"So he would marry you and inherit not only your land but mine too. The Earl has not been slow to tell his knights of the details in our marriage contract," he finished bitterly.

She frowned at this further interruption but nodded. "Aye, I believed that his plan stemmed more from greed than for a desire to marry me." She gave a rueful, self-deprecating smile. "I could not agree to it, but I had to find out what the plan was so that I could warn you."

"And were you successful?" There was a disbelieving tone in his voice that Ghislaine did not like.

She shrugged her shoulders and shook her head. "He only said that he would arrange for a riding accident or an ambush, but not yet."

"Why did you wait until now to tell me?" Guy's eyes had turned flinty blue and she found it hard to look at him. Shamed by her lack of courage, Ghislaine turned her head away.

"You were so angry, you would not listen. I did try, but then Sir Arnaud…" Her voice trailed off. "I am sorry," she whispered.

"And why were you not tempted to be rid of me? It would seem that de Belleme was offering you a simple escape."

Ghislaine looked at him sharply. "I have no wish to see you dead. You may be a bad-tempered, ignorant oaf at times, but that is not deserving of death."

"And why should I believe that?" His voice was gruff and the expression on his face unreadable.

"It seemed sensible at the time," she retorted waspishly. "My wits must have left me."

Guy smiled at her huffy expression. He reached a hand out to gently brush back an errant curl and Ghislaine did not move back. "And how might you prove to me that you mean what you say?"

"I…I have no idea."

The soft smile returned to his lips and Ghislaine found her eyes drawn to them once again. His fingers had trailed gently down her arm and were tracing circles on the sensitive part of her palm. Confused by his actions, she looked up into his darkening eyes.

"Come here, wife."

A curious lethargy had taken hold of her body and Ghislaine knew she should move right away from Guy de Courcy. But she did what he had commanded without even realising it.

Hesitantly, she placed her hand in his and found the warmth there oddly reassuring. His fingers pulled her gently down to him so that she lay alongside his body, her lips practically touching his. There was nothing gentle about his kisses this time.

His hard body rolled half across her so that their legs became tangled amongst the sheets. For a brief moment Guy hesitated, drinking in her flushed cheeks and huge brown eyes that seemed suddenly so child-like. And then she raised her fingers to his face, gently tracing the outline of his lips. That was his undoing. With a soft groan Guy closed his eyes and pulled her tight against him so that she could feel every inch of his body. How much he desired her. The knowledge filled her with a feeling of elation, of power, and something else she was not sure of.

When his mouth covered hers, Ghislaine responded instinctively. Her lips parted and her tongue tentatively touched his. As their kiss deepened, his hands glided over her body possessively. His touch felt so good, so deliciously exciting that she no longer wanted to think at all. She felt herself falling slowly into a whirling sensation of sensuality and awakening passion that she was powerless to stop. Did not want to stop.

In some distant part of her mind, she felt his hands fumble with the front of her gown and then the shock of his lips on the delicate skin. His hands rose to gently cup her breasts and Ghislaine gave a gasp of delight. When at last Guy lifted his mouth from hers, his breathing was harsh and rapid and he looked as if he wanted to devour her.

As he gazed down at her white skin and soft, rounded breasts, Guy placed a finger under her chin and lifted her face to look at him. His eyes were smouldering with desire.

"I want you, Ghislaine," he whispered.

Her fingers gently touched his face and pushed back the locks of black hairs. Slowly her hand crept around the back of his neck and pulled him back to her again. It was all the answer he needed.

The urgent banging at the door shocked them into a tense stillness. Guy lifted himself, his body alert.

When the banging came again, Guy was already on his feet, pulling on his braies.

"News of the outlaws, Sir Guy. Edwin is outside and would have words with you."

"A moment," he answered as the tunic went over his head. Turning back to the bed, Guy bent over Ghislaine who was still dazed and confused. His features were no longer soft and lover-like but harsh and implacable.

"We will speak when I get back, Ghislaine."

She watched him stride through the door without a backward glance, her mind in a whirl and her body still yearning for his touch.

Chapter Fourteen

The abbey lay but a short ride to the south of the forest and Ghislaine was heartily glad of the fresh air and the chance to think. Arnaud was recovering well and she had left him to Effie's enthusiastic care.

Surrounded by six guards, Ghislaine felt embarrassingly overprotected but Sir Guy had insisted. She had no wish to argue with him. As they made their way through the valley, she kept thinking about her husband. Nay, that was not right. She wanted to put him from her mind completely, but memories of his face, his voice, his frown kept crowding in. Finally, she simply gave up trying.

It was most odd that he had thought her likely to escape to the abbey. Stranger still that he had not wanted her to go. There was no good reason for that either—at least, none that he had given. Her lack of vocation would not normally be a barrier for a husband wishing to rid himself of his wife.

Other, more erotic memories kept dancing through her mind causing her to blush suddenly. None of the guards seemed to have noticed this unfortunate affliction, however, but none the less she kept darting covert glances at the men nearest her.

Perhaps, she decided restlessly, time spent with the priest would douse the fire that seemed to burn within her still.

She ought to have been grateful for the timely interruption, but what she had felt was cheated. It was so good lying with him, touching him, kissing his soft skin, being caressed. Her control had long gone and he knew it. She would have done whatever he had wanted her to, willingly. He had made a wanton of her and it hadn't mattered.

But what then? He had always insisted he did not want marriage to her. It was his freedom he wanted. A gawky wanton was not part of his plans. Would she then have gone to the convent willingly? And if there were a child? A wry smile played around her lips at that thought. What a monster they would produce between them! No, she could never give up his child.

As the abbey gates came into view, Ghislaine resolved to put all thoughts of Guy de Courcy from her mind and concentrate on pure love. But it was hard.

The guards remained outside as the young nun at the gate led her across the muddy courtyard. The abbess's rooms were located beneath the low stone arches at the far side, next to the heavy oak doors of the chapel. Ghislaine waited outside, as bidden, watching the peaceful lives of the nuns trickle by. It was curious that the faces of those women seemed remarkably smooth and unlined, as if, by missing the great joys and sorrows of womanhood, time did not leave its mark. Was that what she wanted? To be untouched by life?

"Lady Ghislaine, please enter." The abbess's stern face was full of foreboding, and Ghislaine followed the tiny, thin figure into her room. The cold seemed to echo around the stone floor and walls and then seep into her very bones. There was but a meagre fire in the large grate that seemed to Ghislaine to have no effect at all. She shivered.

Ghislaine sat on the simple wooden stool offered by the abbess. Declining a goblet of wine, Ghislaine pulled her cloak closer.

"Father John sent a message to you. Is that the reason for your visit?" Her voice was surprisingly low, but Ghislaine detected the tension in it.

"Aye," she replied. "He wished to speak to me of Margaret Staveley, I believe."

"That is so, but I must ask first if your husband is close by?" The round, grey eyes of the older woman watched her steadily.

It was an odd question. "Nay. He is searching for the outlaws in the forest."

"Good. You will understand in a minute, Lady Ghislaine." For the first time, a thin smile banished her joyless expression. "Father John." Her voice was raised no more than a fraction, but a heavy curtain to the right of the fire stirred. "Come, come," she urged the tall, nervous figure who emerged to step closer towards Ghislaine.

Father John gave the abbess a quick nod which was the signal for her to leave the room. Once alone, he turned to Ghislaine. He was not so old as she had at first thought. Thin brown hair blossomed out from his tonsure and covered a broad forehead. He had a boyish air, although she reckoned him to be in his late thirties. Myopic brown eyes peered down at her.

"I am most anxious to restore the peace to my soul, Lady Ghislaine, but the information I must give you to do so could be dangerous for us both. Margaret Staveley always spoke highly of you, of her regard for your friendship, so I place my trust in you." His voice was high, nervous, and the words delivered in a staccato fashion that was at odds with the normally quiet, slow pace of the priests.

Ghislaine inclined her head, not quite understanding what he meant. He must have sensed her confusion.

"I was present when she was murdered."

Ghislaine paled at his words, a wave of ice cold flooding through her body. "Why are you telling me?" she demanded in a fierce whisper. "You must know the name of my husband and why he demands protection from the Earl."

"I do, but I also know that the marriage was forced upon you. You did not choose to do so. Your first loyalty is to God. Am I right?" He watched her with nervous eyes.

"Aye. But I must first tell you that I believe him to be innocent of the crime." Ghislaine rubbed her freezing hands together to warm them a little, her eyes not leaving the man pacing backwards and forwards before her. She took a shallow breath at his continued silence. "Do you know who killed Margaret?" Her wavering voice betrayed the tension that was building deep within.

"Yes…and no." The priest's eyes darted about the room as if he feared attack at any moment.

"I do not understand," she replied. "Did you not recognize who murdered her?"

"I did not see him, Lady Ghislaine. I was hidden behind an arras in an alcove. It was his voice I heard."

"You heard what happened? You survived?" she breathed.

"Aye," came the bitter reply. "And I never wish to hear such sounds again. My faith…has been sorely tried these last few weeks." He stopped before the fire to watch the tiny flames. "In the end, God prevailed over my fear." He turned to face her, a weary, haggard expression on his face. "But I need your help."

"My help? How?" Ghislaine stared at him.

Father John looked at her unblinkingly. "Your husband is accused of the murder. If I heard his voice, I would be able to recognise it."

A cold hand seemed to squeeze her heart. She had wanted to believe his protests of innocence and now she was being given the chance to put it to the test and clear his name. Or prove him guilty.

"I will do what I can, Father. My husband wishes to clear his name and I am certain, despite his…violent profession, he would not kill an innocent woman for refusing him marriage." And if he was found innocent, he would have no further use for her. She lifted her chin. "I am certain you will have no cause for alarm."

The man looked rather doubtful but smiled hesitantly. "Your husband is not known for his gentle nature, Lady Ghislaine, and after what I…heard, you must understand my hesitation."

Ghislaine returned his smile, but it did not reach her eyes. "Aye. I understand. Surely, though, it would be better if Sir Guy did not know the reason for your presence. There are some amongst us who would be grateful for your advice, although I doubt my husband is one of them.''

Father John nodded his head. ''As you wish, Lady Ghislaine.''

He lapsed into silence, his thoughts elsewhere.

''What did you hear?'' She had to know what had taken place, to know what Guy was accused of.

Closing his eyes as if picturing what had happened, the priest sighed wearily. ''I had been preparing to pray with Lady Margaret in a small chamber off the hall. It is hidden from view by a heavy curtain to ensure privacy. She preferred to pray without an audience,'' he added softly. ''As a truly good woman would.''

''Strange, loud noises caught my attention as I prayed, and I went to the curtain. Lady Margaret was shouting. She was very angry.''

''What did she shout?'' demanded Ghislaine.

The priest raised his hands in a despairing gesture. ''I could not hear everything, you understand, but she told him he was a despicable man, a murderer, a betrayer whose life depended on the misfortunes of others.''

Ghislaine blenched at the words and her fingers rose to her throat. Could Guy have lied to her? Aye, he could. Very easily, came the voice in her head. The man killed for his living. Lying well must be a bonus in his profession.

''Was there aught else?'' she asked quietly. Surely this could not be the man who had threatened her loudly on several occasions with a beating but had never carried any out, despite severe provocation? She could not believe it was, no matter how damning the evidence.

"When Lady Margaret repeatedly refused his offers, he threatened to kill her. Even then…" His voice trailed off. The priest turned to the window and stared up at the sky as if exhorting God to give him strength. "Even then…I did not go to her aid. I cannot forgive myself for being such a coward. She needed me and I stayed behind the curtain."

Ghislaine stared at his shuddering back, hearing his agony but unable to help him. "She would not have wanted your death, Father John. Margaret would have called for you had she thought you might have been able to help." The words sounded empty and trite to her own ears.

He raised his hand to stop her words. "This is between me and God now, Lady Ghislaine. The only way I can help her now is to name her murderer. Although…it was not at his hands that she died."

Ghislaine raised her head to look at him. "How did she die?" She waited as the man gained control of his voice, dreading his words.

"She jumped from the window to her own death," he whispered. "The others were killed by the knife," he added with a shudder. "They knew what they were doing. None survived. When they had gone, all I found was blood, bodies and a mess. They had taken the silver, her jewels…even the gold and pearl cross from around Margaret's neck had gone."

The priest turned towards her, his face white and old in the light. "I could not tell them she died by her own hand. She did not deserve that. I wished her to be buried like a good, honest woman, in the church-yard next to Sir Peter.''

Ghislaine rose from the stool and stood before him. ''Thank you, Father John. You are a kind man.''

Their eyes held for a moment before he looked away and Ghislaine saw there the torment and the agony that the man was suffering.

''If you are ready, we should go now.''

When they eventually rode back across the moat, they were greeted by confusion. Carts and unknown men littered the bailey. A wild profusion of colours, provisions and tongues assaulted their eyes and ears. Kalim and Joachim had arrived.

The priest's nerves had increased with every step that took them closer to Chapmonswiche and now that they had arrived, the man jumped at the slightest noise. The fact that Guy had not yet returned did little to relieve the escalating tension in his mind. Seeing his trembling hands and the anxiety in his face, Ghislaine dismounted and showed him the way to the private chapel. As far as she knew, she had been the only visitor there for some time. Father John retired grate-fully to his gloomy seclusion. Food and drink would be sent to him as soon as she saw the kitchen staff.

When Ghislaine entered the hall, she found Kalim and Arnaud sitting comfortably before the fire, sipping some of the wine that had just arrived. A small chest lay next to Kalim's feet.

''My lady.'' He rose gracefully and took her hand. ''I am most pleased to see you in good health.''

Ghislaine smiled warmly. ''My thanks, Kalim. I

was not aware that you would be bringing our supplies personally.''

The old man held her questioning eyes for a moment and then looked around the hall. ''I have much to discuss with your husband.'' His cold hand squeezed hers gently. ''Perhaps you would sit with me awhile, if you have the time?''

Something in his eyes warned her that this was not going to be as casual as it sounded. ''Gladly,'' she responded quietly. Kalim pulled a chair for her next to his and handed her the wine when she had made herself comfortable.

''I shall make myself useful in the bailey,'' Sir Arnaud began tactfully as he pulled himself to his feet. ''But before you say aught, Lady Ghislaine, I am not about to undo your good care. Rest easy.'' The merry grey eyes twinkled down at her.

As Sir Arnaud was not noted for his love of hard work, Ghislaine smiled her agreement. ''Be sure to return to the fire the moment you are fatigued,'' she replied sternly. Her eyes followed him as he limped heavily from the hall.

''Sir Arnaud has been most impressed by your healing skills, Lady Ghislaine. I am interested in how you acquired them.'' That was not what he was here to discuss at all, but he wished to do so and Ghislaine complied. Her mind was racing on ahead to the moment when Father John heard Guy's voice. To the moment when Guy realised he had no need of her.

''If you twist the belt much more, Lady Ghislaine, it will fall to pieces.''

Ghislaine looked up at him, startled and then down at her own fingers. She had not been listening. Flushing with shame at her lack of manners, she began to apologise.

Kalim held up his hands. "You have many concerns at the moment and have no need to explain." The old man's nut brown face creased into a smile. "I have a gift for you." Bending down to open the chest, Kalim gently took out a small pot. "My tisane?" he announced gravely. "It will help your nerves."

"I think I will need more than a tisane, Kalim. But your gift is very kind."

Kalim nodded slowly. "Then perhaps the information I have will assist in some small way."

"What information?" Ghislaine's interest was piqued.

"About Walter de Belleme." He took a long draught of the wine before taking a sidelong glance at her. "He has been frequenting the harbour more and more of late, recruiting the scum of the waterfront to his employment."

Ghislaine did not really know why that was so important, but hesitated to say so.

"It is also well-known that he has been borrowing money in the expectation of receiving a large sum shortly."

That caught her attention. "How do you know all this?" she asked, a frown creasing her smooth brow.

Kalim shrugged. "I have my sources and they are always reliable."

A welter of thoughts collided around her mind at once. Walter must be planning the attack soon, but why should he be expecting money? If he was going to marry her, then he would not receive any large dowry. That was well-known. Unless... A thought

suddenly struck her. Guy had said something odd
about the Earl not being slow to tell all his knights
about their marriage contract. At the time she had ignored it, but perhaps there was something most sig-
nificant in it.

"I know he plans to ambush my husband," she began slowly, "and I have warned Guy. But as for the
money, I know nothing about that."

Kalim continued to stare at the fire. "He is a man
who loves only himself," he said eventually. "The
greed in his heart shines in his eyes."

"Whereas it is the anger in my husband's heart that
shines in his eyes," she added quietly. Ghislaine
looked up at Kalim, her eyes mirroring her worry.
"Arnaud told me much of Guy's life and how wary
he is of women." For a moment she watched her fingers fiddle with her belt. "I have found that I have
grown to care for him, despite his temper and his oafish ways," she admitted. "But it is very hard to show
him when I doubt he is concerned at all."

Kalim watched her clenched jaw and tightened lips,
knowing how hard it had been for her to admit to such
feelings. "Perhaps it would interest you to know that
Guy is not completely lost to feeling," he said
thoughtfully. "I have heard him say he knows nothing
of his family, but he still gets information about his
brothers in Normandy."

"He does?" she questioned.

Kalim nodded his head. "He usually buys it from
one of the captains on the trading ships at the harbour.
At a price, of course."

For some reason, that piece of information cheered
her up. So he had been trading information with the

captain of the *Isabella* about his brothers. The thought of him paying for the information made her smile. "He said he never thought of them," she murmured.

"It is hard for Guy de Courcy to admit to caring for anyone, but he is just a man."

Ghislaine raised her eyebrows in wry disbelief at that statement. "'Just a man'," she repeated in a voice loaded with sarcasm, "does not apply to my husband."

Kalim laughed, his white teeth flashing in the firelight. "You are wrong, Lady Ghislaine. I have no doubt that should you wish to put it to the test, he will not be proof against your pretty smile and a warm welcome."

Ghislaine felt the blush steal over her cheeks. Did she wish to put it to the test?

The pale sun was low in the sky before Guy's arrival home was announced in a flurry of movement and excited calls. The trestle tables were already laid in preparation for the feast Ghislaine had ordered.

A cow had been killed in honour of their guest and a fat pig was roasting on the spit. Several mouthwatering pies and pasties, chicken boiled in wine and mushrooms and pike served with galentyne sauce were being enthusiastically prepared in the kitchens. Sweet cheese tarts and coloured custards were kept for dessert. Elfrieda had excelled herself and Ghislaine wondered greatly at her cooperation. Whenever a feast had been ordered in the past, Elfrieda's temper was predictably explosive. Now, not even Joachim's inexplicable presence in the kitchen appeared to upset her. She decided to think on the matter later.

Effie had brushed Ghislaine's long hair until it shone like coppered blonde. Despite her drab green gown, Ghislaine's eyes told her that she looked much better than usual. Perhaps she was growing up?

Guy strode through the door of the hall, a broad grin on his face.

"My lady. Good news indeed." His smile was infectious.

"You have found them?" she guessed excitedly, his good humour lightening her heart.

"Aye, we did. No small thanks to your man, Edwin."

As all eyes turned to the tall figure behind Guy, Ghislaine watched as a slow smile began to form on the Englishman's face. Guy clapped his large hand on Edwin's shoulder and shouted for ale.

"A good day's work. It pleases me greatly to see you anticipated our success," he noted with an amused smile on his face. The grin broadened as Ghislaine blushed in embarrassment.

"I...er...Kalim has arrived with the supplies and the cloth, my lord. We...thought you would appreciate a...celebration."

Guy gave her another crooked grin and then, to her complete shock, he pulled her close and kissed her full on the lips.

"My lord," she gasped, as soon as he let her go, "what are you thinking of?"

"What I have been thinking of all day," he whispered into her ear, before giving her a playful peck on her burning cheeks. Ghislaine looked around quickly, relieved to see that no one else seemed to have heard. The fire within was ignited.

The night was spent celebrating the capture of Thomas Bollyngton and four of his men, with each knight giving their own competing account of their bravado and skill. There was much laughter and good-natured pulling of legs as each tried to outdo the other.

Guy was like a different man. The frown was banished for the moment and Ghislaine was able to see him for what he was. Young, handsome, strong and brave. He was also astute and the men respected him. Not perhaps very god-fearing…her thoughts suddenly flew to Father John. She had not seen him since she had slipped into the chapel earlier to tell him that Guy had arrived. He had declined her invitation to eat with them, saying that his presence might not be too welcome this evening.

Deciding to see him in the morning, Ghislaine slipped away from the feast. Guy was deep in conversation with Kalim and the rest of the men were doing their best to exhaust their new supplies. She had ordered Effie to pack the beautiful material away in a lined chest, since she was sure that Guy would send it back when his wits returned.

The fire was burning brightly when she entered the bedchamber. Below, she could hear the shouts and raucous laughter of the men. Guy had not spared her a glance as she left, and her heart was heavy with disappointment. Slumping down on the stool before the fire, Ghislaine slowly unbraided her hair and began to comb it carefully, her thoughts lost with the flames.

The door latch clicked back firmly into place and Ghislaine whirled round.

"Escaping, lady?" Guy leaned back against the

door, his eyebrows raised in question. His hands remained behind his back.

"Not at all, my lord."

"Guy," he supplied gently.

Her heart began racing. His voice was soft and compelling.

"Guy," she repeated nervously as he sauntered towards her stool. "I thought you wished to celebrate with your men."

"I had other plans for this night, Ghislaine."

She gulped hard as his hand reached to take the comb from her hand. Gently he pulled her to her feet.

"Kalim's arrival was most timely, though."

"It was?" Her voice was almost inaudible.

"He bought me a special order. For you." He held out a small parcel.

Ghislaine looked at him as if he were mad and then nervously set about unwrapping the gift.

"They are beautiful," she whispered, as she held up the delicate linen for inspection. Two of the loveliest chemises she had ever seen. They were made of the softest linen and embroidered with exquisite patterns. A deep blush flooded her from top to toe. He had paid someone to make them for her.

"I had thought," he whispered back huskily, "that you would wish to express your gratitude more fully."

Her eyes raised slowly to his and saw the leap of desire there. Her finger pushed back an errant lock of his hair. She smiled.

"What had you in mind?" Ghislaine peeped up at him coyly.

"A kiss, perhaps?"

Standing on tiptoes, Ghislaine gave him a gentle peck on the cheek. "Like this?"

"That would be most…worthy, had I given you a…horse comb," came the dry retort.

"I see," she replied, catching her lower lip between her teeth. A frown completed her puzzled expression. "Perhaps you could give me a hint as to the worth of these chemises then, Sir Guy?"

His lips twitched with amusement before claiming hers in a soft kiss that completely took her breath away. Ghislaine stepped back, her chest still rising quickly.

"That was most clear." She smiled up at him, drowning in the desire she saw there. "But I really believe that I would find it…easier to express my thanks…if there was perhaps less light."

The spots of red on her cheeks were proof enough of her shyness and they tempered Guy's growing impatience a little. With a heavy sigh, he doused the wall sconces so that the only light came from the fire. Standing before him, watching his face glow in the flickering light, Ghislaine gave him the answer she knew he was waiting for.

Slowly her fingers pulled at the ties at the neck of her gown until they came free.

Unable to tear her gaze from his, Ghislaine watched as Guy's fingers reached out to touch her unbraided hair. "Have I told you how lovely you are, Ghislaine?" he whispered fiercely, pulling her gently towards him.

She shook her head, denying the thought as well as the words. "You have called me many things over the last few weeks, most of them less than flattering," she teased gently.

This time it was Guy's cheeks that flushed. "Each one well deserved, no doubt," he countered grimly. "Have I also told you that you are a most troublesome baggage?"

Ghislaine laughed at the ominous frown. "I think I feel less nervous when you scowl at me."

The frown deepened as his fingers lifted her chin so that her eyes looked into his.

"You are nervous?" he asked uncertainly. He could feel her trembling and did not need the slight nod she gave to tell him she was very nervous. His finger slid over her cheek in the briefest of caresses before lowering to catch her hand and place it palm down on his chest.

Ghislaine could feel his heart hammering beneath his touch. He had shown her what he found so hard to tell her. Did she really have that effect on him? Sliding her hands slowly around his neck, she pulled his lips down to hers and kissed him as gently as he had done to her.

As she watched him breathlessly, her cheeks flushed, Guy stood back to remove his tunic and chemise. At the sight of his sun-darkened chest, Ghislaine's throat contracted. He was so beautiful, she just wanted to reach out and run her fingers over his soft skin. Hesitantly, Ghislaine placed her palm over his heart once again and she felt it race at her touch. Had she made him do that? At her look of surprise, Guy took her other hand and placed that one on his chest too. When his arms encircled her, pulling her body flat against his, and his lips touched hers, Ghislaine stopped thinking.

His mouth did not stop at hers. It trailed gently over a soft cheek to just below her ear, nuzzling wickedly at the tender skin beyond. Strange feelings she had never known shot through her body, causing it to arch against his. Her skin prickled with the velvet roughness of his tongue as it circled upwards towards the nape of her neck. Unable to bear the sensuality, her head fell back, thrusting her breasts into his chest. His lips moved to the creamy skin exposed just above her breasts. A gasp of delight escaped from Ghislaine at such sinful behaviour.

Just as she thought her knees would give way under this assault, his mouth returned to hers for a scorching kiss that ignited the fire within her. This kiss was completely different from any others. It was full of passion and longing, but there was tenderness and reassurance there too. He wanted her tonight. And she wanted him.

Guy's hands moved up and down her body possessively, sliding over her hips, pulling her deeper into him, showing her how much he desired her. Ghislaine felt herself slipping into the unknown world of passion, surrendering her aching body to the touch of his hands.

It was not until she felt the cool air on her breasts that Ghislaine realised that her gown no longer covered her, but as his hands gently cupped her swelling flesh she no longer cared. Her back arched into his erotic caress, her hips pressing into his. Softly his thumbs circled her hardened nipples as his mouth nibbled its way down her neck.

Weak with pleasure, Ghislaine was no longer able to support herself and wound her arms around Guy's neck. Her fingers tangled in his thick hair as his strong arms pulled her upwards until her breasts were within reach of his mouth. Her body exploded with sensation as each nipple was gently licked and then sucked until Ghislaine thought she would die with the pleasure. Slowly, she felt herself being lowered the full length of his hardened body until her feet touched the floor. Her gown and chemise fell at the same time.

She felt no shame standing before him naked. His eyes were dark with passion and told her that she was beautiful. His hands told her how much he desired her. Without taking his eyes from her, Guy removed the rest of his clothes. There were no more barriers between them and Ghislaine made no protest when he swept her up and carried her effortlessly to the bed.

They sank down together, Guy stretching out at her side. The firelight was not so bright on this side of the room, but she was able to see his eyes glittering with passion as he gazed down at her.

''Touch me,'' he commanded gently.

It was all the encouragement she needed. Hesitantly her fingers trailed a path across his chest, exploring the deep cuts of war and swordplay, the muscles of his arms. His soft groans of pleasure made her bolder still as her hands lowered to caress his back and his hips. She revelled in the soft feel of his beautiful body, of his hard muscles, of the dark hair that grew where hers did not.

Unable to endure her exploration any longer, Guy's hands cupped her face gently. ''Kiss me,'' he ordered huskily before pushing her onto her back. His fingers tangled with her hair as his tongue parted her lips and kissed her with an intensity which left both of them gasping for breath.

Shudders of delight raced through her as Guy pushed his naked body hard against her. It was a raw, primitive act which served only to enflame her. A throbbing began somewhere deep within her with a rhythm that matched the thrusting of his tongue in her mouth.

Ghislaine responded instinctively by lifting her knees and winding her legs around his hips. His tongue plunged deeper into her mouth as his fingers explored her slender thighs. As they reached higher, Ghislaine tensed, uncertain suddenly.

"Don't," he whispered hotly. "It will make it better for you, Ghislaine." His voice was deep and husky with desire. She could not stop now. With a conscious effort, Ghislaine forced herself to relax as his fingers touched her in her secret place. His mouth trailed hot, wet kisses over her face, her eyes, her neck as his finger slipped inside her, exploring, rubbing, pleasuring.

Her eyes opened wide at the sensations he was creating in her, her breathing jerky and strained. Suddenly, a feeling so exciting, so erotic, fluttered deep within her and she pushed against him harder, knowing that he would be able to help her find it again. Raising her body, she buried her face in his neck, flattening her breasts against him.

"Show me," she whispered "Show me what to do."

Guy paused, his handsome face dark with passion. "It will hurt for a moment," he groaned, desperately wishing he could lessen the pain he would cause her. "Only for a moment."

Ghislaine wrapped her arms around his neck, her eyes full of trust. Guy placed his hands beneath her, lifting her hips. As he pushed gently towards her, his mouth covered hers in a tender kiss.

At first there was no pain, just the unfamiliar sensation of feeling him inside her. But as he pushed again, each time going deeper, Ghislaine realised he was just easing himself in as gently as he could. He waited until she was used to him before he started to move again.

Suddenly he plunged deep within her, deep into the tight, hot core of her, hating the pain she would feel. He waited a moment for her pain to subside and then slowly, as slowly as his aching body would allow him, Guy rocked backwards and forwards until he felt her push against him. As her body began moving with his, he thrust deeper and deeper, trying to give her the pleasure she was instinctively chasing.

Ghislaine felt the thrusts quicken as she pushed against him. The pleasure she was feeling was indescribable. Nothing had prepared her for this. Nothing. Desire leapt within her as the throbbing increased. Suddenly she stilled as his thrusts took her right to the brink of a sensation she could not name. Sensing she was almost there, Guy drove full length into her, again and again until he heard her gasps of pleasure as the spasms racked her body. When she stilled, floating dreamily in the aftermath, Guy surged to his own release, spilling his seed deep within her.

As sleep claimed her, Ghislaine snuggled up against her husband's warm body. There could be no sin in such pleasure. But how could she ever live in the convent now?

Chapter Fifteen

Dawn was spilling into the bedchamber as Ghislaine's eyes flickered open. Slowly, she turned to look at Guy sleeping soundly at her side, his arm possessively draped over her shoulders. A sense of well-being filled every inch of her body and she stretched languorously, revelling in the unfamiliar sensation.

Disturbed by her movements, Guy shifted position in his sleep. His hand slipped from her shoulder to cover her breast and his mouth began to nuzzle the delicate skin of her neck.

Ghislaine shivered with the sheer ecstasy of having his body touch hers. Sighing softly to herself, she snuggled closer. His smell pervaded her senses and she breathed deeply, drinking in his male essence.

She could not have known how it would feel to be made a wife, not in a million years. She was certain that she would look very different, that everyone would somehow be able to tell. Her cheeks flushed at the thought of having to face them at breakfast.

Her eyes swept over her sleeping husband and she

knew without a doubt that she wanted to be with him, to find out about love with this man, to bear his child.

Gently she moved a lock of his hair that had fallen over his eyes. He was so beautiful, this scowling husband of hers, but he had not been deterred by her plain looks last night. He had even called her lovely. There had been no trace of a frown then. The desire in his eyes had made her feel delicate and pretty, and he had urged her to touch him and love him with warm, encouraging whispers. Remembering the things he had done to her sent hot and cold arrows shooting through her body. The pleasure he had given her so generously had seemed to last for hours, and she wondered if he had found as much pleasure in her touch.

A deep, contented sigh reached her ears and a gentle squeeze from the large hand at her breast brought a smile to her lips. He looked so innocent.

Innocent? Her thoughts halted. A chill enveloped her as she remembered Father John's story of Margaret's terrible death. Could the Guy de Courcy she knew really have caused Margaret to take her own life? She looked at his hand, the hand that had given her such pleasure, the hand that had never carried out his loud threats.

Nay, Ghislaine was certain he could not. He may have been a cool mercenary with a reputation for excelling in that vile profession but he had never displayed any violence towards innocent people. But if he were innocent, and it could be proven, he had wanted to return to his old life. A life without her. He had only married her as part of his deal with the Earl. It had been one of the few things that they had agreed on that she was to go to the convent and their marriage was to be annulled. He would then be free to look for someone more suitable. She grimaced. If Margaret Staveley was his first choice, then she didn't even come close. His desire for her was all the more inexplicable.

A frown creased her brow. Was it really so odd? She was not so innocent as to the nature of young men and Guy was young and lusty with the same desires as any other. Lust, she decided. It was simply lust.

The germ of hope that had flickered into life died then. All he had felt for her was lust, and if that was all it was, it would haunt them both for a lifetime if she let it. Watching his desire wither and die, seeing the indifference in his eyes would be a living death.

Idly she began to stroke the sun-coloured skin on his back as she tried to imagine how it would be between them. Cold, perfunctory and joyless. Nay, she could never want that.

Ghislaine gazed at him with loving eyes. Did she love him enough to let him go? A cold band squeezed her heart. How could she not? A strange calm descended as she came to a decision. She would make it easy for him, she resolved firmly. The convent would provide peace of sorts for her. A vision of the smooth-skinned nuns danced before her and Ghislaine suddenly felt a rush of tears.

Sensing a change in her breathing pattern, Guy opened one drowsy eye. Her tears were the first thing he noticed about the passionate wife who had loved him so joyfully the night before, and the smile in his heart faded.

So she regretted it? Had he really been so mistaken about her? He felt her long fingers slide up and down his back in an unconsciously seductive movement that stirred his pulse and his body. Covertly, he watched the expression of pain on her face as she touched his hair. Nay, he did not think he was mistaken, despite his mistrust of women. She was an innocent who was playing no game. He had known that instinctively last night.

Hot blood fired through his body as memories of the night before flooded him. She had been so sweet and unexpectedly passionate. Whatever the problem, he wanted her to trust him. Ruefully he reminded himself of all the criticisms she had launched at him. Oafish, brutish, scowling, stinking. Aye, he had been all of those things in his dealings with her, and she had not hesitated to let him know it. He had learned to expect the truth from her lips. Ghislaine was always prepared to tell him what she expected of him, and he recalled that he had made several attempts of late to do what she had asked. It was quite amazing that he should even consider it, but her lovely smile had somehow made him feel very pleased with himself. He liked to please her, and he certainly enjoyed her attempts at pleasing him!

His hand brushed gently down over her hips and thighs and he could feel the tremors it evoked in that wonderful body. He had not realised just how beautiful she was beneath those hideous gowns. Her skin was white and smooth, covering curves which were deliciously soft and generous. She was not an obvious temptress and that pleased him greatly, although not nearly as much as her wanton behaviour in private. He should have known as soon as he saw her flashing eyes and that first seductive toss of her fiery hair. No convent would take her in, he smiled confidently.

Experimentally his thumb flicked over a pink tipped nipple that puckered instantly and he ached to take it in his mouth.

"What are you doing?" Ghislaine gasped, heat flooding through her body.

"Taking advantage of your body," he murmured softly as his tongue trailed around one hardening nipple.

"You want to do this again?" she whispered faintly, not daring to believe it. As passion ignited at his touch, Ghislaine told herself that this would be the last time. She would love him once more. Just once more. As his mouth tugged gently at her breast, Ghislaine captured his head in her hands and pulled him closer.

"Again and again," came the muffled reply, before his hands gently caressed and explored the rest of her body.

They were both wordlessly caught in the mounting passion between them and surrendered without resistance. This time there was no pain, just sweet, almost unbearable sensation as Guy thrust slowly and languorously. Ghislaine was swept away by a wave of throbbing pleasure, and as she floated back, Guy followed her into blissful oblivion, groaning loudly as he reached his own release.

Bright sunshine was filtering into the bedchamber when Ghislaine woke again. Judging by the noises without, it was close to midday and it was the latest she had ever slept in her life.

Her mouth was suddenly caught in a soft kiss that made her heart shudder.

"How do you feel?" Guy asked quietly, pulling himself up onto his elbow.

Smiling up into his concerned eyes, Ghislaine pushed back the ever-drooping lock of his hair. "Like a wife," she replied firmly, before realising what she had said.

Guy looked at her, his eyes shining a deep blue. "Is that good?" he asked doubtfully, his interest kindling nevertheless.

"I feel very…peaceful," Ghislaine amended. Desired. Cherished. Those had been the words she had wanted to say.

"Peaceful," he repeated with a lazy smile. "You have never accused me of having that effect on you before." Idly, his finger began to trace patterns on her arm.

"No-o-o…" she allowed, distracted by the feelings the finger was creating within her. "But then you have never called me lovely before either."

Guy flushed. "I said that?" he questioned in mock disbelief.

Ghislaine sighed and gazed at him steadily. "You do not have to say those things."

Guy's eyes snapped open at the serious tone in her voice. "What do you mean by that?" His voice had lost its gentle teasing and his brows began to wrinkle into the beginning of a frown.

Ghislaine shifted uncomfortably. If she was going to save them both, she would have to be strong. Stronger than she felt. Her fingers twisted the sheet into convoluted knots, unconsciously baring her breasts.

"I mean," she began hesitantly, "that you should not make more of this than it is."

Guy continued to stare at his wife, watching her fingers and finding it very hard to take his eyes off the luscious curves exposed before him.

"You think I am making too much of it?" He questioned slowly, his mind trying to work out what she was leading to.

"A-aye," she stammered. "And I am not pretty at all, as you were pleased to remind me on several occasions." She held up her hand as Guy opened his mouth to reply. "But that is not really what I meant."

"Then perhaps you would explain exactly what you are getting at."

Ghislaine looked up at his darkening frown and almost smiled. Schooling her expression carefully, she hauled herself to a sitting position. "Last night has changed nothing," she explained carefully. "It was simply the result of a surfeit of drink and lust."

Nonplussed, Guy continued to stare at her. Perhaps he had best hear her reasoning. It was well-known that women had strange ideas about men. "Drink and lust," he murmured. She could not seriously believe that.

"It should not have happened," she continued. "But I have decided that the convent is where I still intend to go."

Guy eyed her in disbelief. "The convent," he said flatly, "would not have you."

"Oh?" she enquired, her eyes narrowing. "And why not?"

"Because you are an unruly wanton with a shrewish tongue, a huge appetite and a penchant for drink." The words were delivered with total resignation as he folded his arms across his chest. His disgruntled tone almost made her laugh. He was not making this easy for her.

"Since when have those particular traits barred entry to the convent?" she retorted haughtily.

"When they are accompanied by an angry bloodthirsty mercenary with twenty armed men threatening to attack if they did not," came the instant reply.

Ghislaine glared at him, irritation welling up inside her. "You," she accused angrily, "are naught but an oafish tyrant. We agreed I was to go to the convent."

"Things have changed," he snapped, his patience beginning to fray. "You are now my wife in body as well as in name and there may be a child."

Ghislaine stared at him open-mouthed. "You have frequently stated your desire to be rid of me. If I go to the convent, I will take the child with me."

"The child stays with me," he stated without hesitation. "Or is this part of some bizarre plot to deprive me of heirs?"

"What? What nonsense is this?"

His statement was as idiotic as her words, but it was the only thing he could think of in the heat of the moment. He forged on with the argument. "It is clear that you seduced me so that you became my true wife. If you disappear to the convent I would be unable to marry again and so produce no more legitimate de Courcy heirs." Guy had rounded on her, placing his arms either side of hers, his mouth just inches from hers.

Ghislaine pushed herself back as far as she could. "Why should I want to do that?" she asked weakly. "It makes no sense."

"Why indeed, lady? But rest assured I intend to discover the truth," he growled, trapping her legs within his.

A hot flush shot through her body as Ghislaine reacted to his nearness. "You would torture me?" she asked faintly.

"Whatever I need to do," came the soft reply. His lips moved over hers, gently seducing a response from her.

"Do not," she gasped, dismayed at her own weakness. "This is not fair."

"I fight for what is mine by any means I can." His lips moved to the tender spot at the base of her throat.

Ghislaine knew her will-power was slipping and that if she was to succeed, this would be her last chance.

"Do you wish me to hate you for it? Could you live like that?" she demanded with enough emotion to halt Guy's lips.

He stared at her, not believing she meant a word of it, but angry that she could not trust him with the truth.

"So be it," he growled and pushed himself away from her. "You would choose the convent. But you go on one condition. You remain here to ensure there is no possibility of a child."

"And if there is?" Ghislaine demanded.

"Then you stay until the child is born."

"That is too cruel," she said hotly.

Guy stood up and walked naked across the room to retrieve his discarded clothes. Ghislaine found it hard to take her eyes from his body. "You have the choice, I am perfectly willing to accept you as wife."

Ghislaine glared at him. "You are a cold-hearted, oafish brute. The convent will be a welcome relief."

The door slammed with finality as Guy stormed out of the bedchamber. It was not until she heard him thudding down the stairs that she allowed her tears to fall.

Kalim had left the manor long before Ghislaine set foot in the hall and, much to her relief, few people seemed to notice anything different about her. She busied herself with the new supplies, deciding what was to be stored or used. The whole time, Ghislaine found it hard to concentrate on any task and her fingers seemed permanently beset with clumsiness. Finally, in exasperation, Ghislaine sought peace in the chapel.

The cool simplicity of the white-washed walls had a calming effect, as they always had at moments of crisis. It was almost as if the world did not exist beyond the walls of this small room. Ghislaine knelt in prayer before the altar, unsure still whether she had committed a true sin.

"You are troubled, Lady Ghislaine?" Father John's voice seemed calmer and more controlled.

She scrambled to her feet. "My mind is somewhat distracted today," she admitted. That was no lie at least.

Father John nodded. "If you wish to make your confession, I will be glad to perform the duty." His dark eyes regarded hers steadily, and Ghislaine knew that he would not be harsh on her.

"I am not sure that what I have to tell you will be welcome," she explained hesitantly.

"We shall have to put our trust in God," he replied kindly.

Her story was quickly told, and despite her lack of certainty about telling this man how much she loved her husband and how convinced she was of his innocence, Ghislaine finally told him all she could.

Father John looked at her with pity in his eyes. "We do not always have easy choices to make, Lady Ghislaine. I am sure that if you have made the right one, you will find comfort in the convent."

Ghislaine sighed. "I know it but my husband is not making it easy for me."

"Have you told him why you wish to go?" asked the priest suddenly.

Ghislaine nodded. "At least, part of why I wish to go. For the rest, I doubt whether that would be of interest to him." She could never tell him how much she loved him for he would never believe her.

"Then I will pray for us both, Lady Ghislaine." Father John knelt at her side.

It was late afternoon by the time Guy returned from his hunting. Ghislaine had delayed the meal until the guards announced his arrival and she was certain that the toughened meat would put him in an even blacker mood. Well, so be it.

She had spent hours dreading his return, worrying, thinking, and all to little avail, whilst he had been enjoying the fresh air. When he stormed through the doors, however, Guy did not look as if he had spent a pleasant afternoon.

''So, wife. I must be grateful that you have made no attempt to escape.'' His bitter sarcasm grated on her wrangled nerves.

''I have been happy to do your bidding, my lord,'' she replied as demurely as she could, knowing her tone would irritate him.

His snort of disbelief told her what he thought of that. Picking up a goblet of wine, Guy was about to toss it down when he caught sight of Father John. ''Plotting again, lady?'' he demanded quietly before drinking deeply.

Ghislaine flushed guiltily. ''Father John is here to offer help and advice to those who require it. Perhaps some could do with more than others?'' she added pointedly.

''When I need advice from a priest I will seek it out. My concern lies with what he has been offering you, lady.'' His blue eyes were glittering with anger as he looked at Ghislaine.

''Father John will be staying but a short time, my lord. I am sure that a few hours here will be enough to convince him that his efforts here are futile.''

Ghislaine knew that she was provoking him greatly, but was unable to stop. Guy glared at her and poured himself another goblet of wine in utter frustration. ''Enough, woman,'' he growled. ''But if the good father so much as utters a word in my presence, he will find out firsthand the price of staying in so brutish a household.''

Ghislaine gasped at such terrible threats and turned, red-faced, to the priest to apologise for her husband's outrageous remarks. Father John, however, on hearing Guy's tone and the marked antagonism between husband and wife, had removed himself quietly to the far end of the table out of harm's way.

Throughout the meal, Ghislaine kept glancing nervously at him, trying to assess his reaction to Guy's voice. He had certainly witnessed an angry situation that would have embarrassed most of the clergy, but he had kept his head down throughout the following ordeal of angry silence and not looked once in her direction.

The food was hardly touched by either Ghislaine or Guy and Ghislaine noticed that Guy kept staring at the ale in a most peculiar fashion. Only Sir Arnaud seemed able to carry on a lively banter with some of the other men, still discussing the fate of Thomas Bollyngton. The outlaw languished in the keep, awaiting instructions from the messenger Guy had sent to Earl Hugh. News was expected hourly.

By all accounts Bollyngton was a dead man. The dreaded court of Eyrie would deal harshly with so active an outlaw, even in a county as lost to law as Cheshire. Ghislaine wondered if she would have the chance to see him, thinking he might throw some light on the death of her father. She doubted if anyone else would remember.

"My lord," called a guard from the door. "A messenger comes."

Ghislaine breathed a small sigh of relief as Guy ended the meal by standing and throwing the finger cloth to the table.

"Send him in as soon as he comes." Guy moved to stand casually before the huge fire.

The messenger brought with him the smell of night

air as he handed Guy a roll of parchment bearing the seal of d'Avranches. Guy hastily broke it and cast his eyes over the message it contained. The man drank deeply of the ale he was given.

For a few moments Guy said nothing. He just looked at the parchment and then rolled it back carefully. His black scowl returned as he stared into the flames.

Unable to contain her curiosity, Ghislaine went to stand by his side.

"Is there aught wrong, my lord?" she asked quietly.

Guy did not turn to look at her, but handed her the message. She unrolled it quickly and saw the seal was indeed the Earl's. The words made no meaning since she could not read, but it was easy to guess what was wanted of him.

"He wants your services now? I thought you had agreed to go after the harvesting."

"The Earl of Chester is able to change his mind," he stated dryly. "I am to take my men to Chester this night."

"But what is so urgent that he requires you without delay?" she demanded. "And what of the outlaws?"

Guy did not answer immediately but went back to staring at the flames, deep in thought.

Ghislaine turned to the messenger. If Guy was not going to ask questions, she would do it for him. "Did you see the Earl before you left?"

"No, lady." The messenger wiped his mouth on his cloak. "I was given the message by one of his squires. He said it was most urgent and I was to get it here before nightfall. The squire told me that an escort will come on the morrow for Bollyngton and his men."

"Why can you not take the outlaws yourself?" she asked her husband. This turn of events was most vexing.

"It would hold us up," came the mumbled reply. "We would travel faster without them." Guy rubbed his stubbly chin with his hand and then turned towards her. "I suspect the Earl is using us as a decoy of sorts and it would seem I have little choice, lady. The Earl demands my services and my men. Much as I would rather stay here and see to Bollyngton, my continued protection from the shire reeves depends on Hugh d'Avranches."

His blue eyes pierced her as he placed his hands on her shoulders. "We also have unfinished business, Ghislaine. I would ask you to await my return before acting rashly."

Ghislaine smiled at him wanly and nodded. "I give you my word."

Content with that, Guy pulled her close and brushed her forehead with his lips. He then strode from the hall issuing commands to all and sundry. Ghislaine watched him disappear through the doors before picking up a goblet of wine.

Within the hour, Guy and his men had set off for Chester, although not without a great deal of noise and upheaval. He had left Sir Brian and Sir Arnaud in charge of the manor and the outlaws. Ghislaine could tell he was not content with the command, but he could do nothing. The Earl was his liegelord and his protector, and his life depended upon his mercy. Their farewell was cool.

Returning to the hall, Ghislaine sat in front of the fire, her thoughts scattered.

"May I join you, Lady Ghislaine?" Father John stood before her.

Ghislaine jumped up, suddenly remembering why he was here. The priest held up his hand, a smile on his lips.

"Fear not, Lady Ghislaine. Your husband is not the man, for all his anger. Your confidence in him was not misplaced."

Relief flooded through her and Ghislaine breathed again. "His temper leaves much to be desired, though."

The priest smiled again. "He is much tried, by the looks of him." The smile faded. "However, it means that the killer is still at liberty and I must continue my search. It would be too much of a risk to clear your husband's name and reveal my knowledge until he is discovered and brought to trial. The truth might never come to light otherwise."

Ghislaine's joy at the news was short-lived. Her husband's honour depended on the survival of this one priest. She could not let that happen.

"It would ease my mind greatly if you were to write down what happened as well as clear Guy's name," she appealed to him. "If aught were to happen to you, then he would never be free of suspicion."

Father John nodded slowly. "I would be pleased to do that, but it would be best to return to the abbey. At least there there is no chance of the information falling into the wrong hands."

Ghislaine gave him a dazzling smile. "I shall make arrangements for you to leave in the morning."

The manor seemed strangely quiet without Guy and his men. The noise and the mess that had caused her such aggravation over the past few weeks were gone, and Ghislaine found herself staring at her tidy hall in despair. Somehow, it just did not look right.

She laughed to herself. Guy would be much amused to hear the woman who had given him such earache over the less domestic attributes of his men say she missed them. But it was true.

The only remedy for such foolishness, she admonished sternly, was to keep busy. But for how long? The Earl's message had apparently given no indication as to how much time Guy would spend in his service this time. It could be days, weeks or even months. Dispirited, Ghislaine remembered the prisoner in the keep. If the Earl's men came on the morrow, this would be her only chance to find out if Bollyngton knew anything about her father's death.

The light from the one torch gave the small room a shadowy glow that looked most eerie. Ghislaine hesitated at the door, but firmly quashed all her fears. No one else would find out about her father. A small stocky man lay casually on the pallet at the far end of the room, his head resting on his hands, his pale eyes staring at the ceiling. Ghislaine was grateful that his hands and ankles were chained securely to a post in the wall.

At her entrance, Thomas Bollyngton merely raised his head briefly and then resumed his former position. A little piqued by his casual dismissal of her, Ghislaine advanced towards the bed.

"You are Thomas Bollyngton?"

A round, pale face with a small bulbous nose turned towards her. As his pale eyes roved over her with com-

plete indifference, the thin lips broke into a smile
which revealed a row of discoloured, sharp teeth. He
reminded Ghislaine of an arrogant pig.

"I assume you are here to feed me or pleasure me,
woman. In either case you have no need of my name."
His voice was as loathsome as his body. It had an odd
strangled quality that grated. As he shifted to sit up
and watch her, Ghislaine took a step back in alarm,
but not before his smell assailed her nose.

"I am here to do neither," she retorted haughtily.
"My interest in you is confined to your…activities in
the forest." Her voice sounded calmer and more confident than she felt. Knowing that there were two
guards outside the door was some comfort.

Disappointed, Bollyngton resumed his former position, his greasy thatch of sandy hair shadowing much
of his face. "I have no reason to discuss anything with
you, woman. Now leave me be." His voice had a hard,
irritated edge to it that did not inspire confidence.

Nevertheless, decided Ghislaine, she would keep
trying. "I suggest you make it your business or you
will find yourself without food or water for as long as
you are here."

Bollyngton continued to stare at the ceiling, completely unconcerned at her threat. It seemed most odd.

"Think you a lack of food or water will have any
great effect on me?" he eventually replied.

Ghislaine shrugged, fascinated by his calm, almost
relaxed behaviour.

"Would it not?" she enquired.

A slow smile spread over his ugly face as if he
found her words amusing. "Not for long," came the
quiet reply.

"We await the Earl's men in the morning. I have no doubt you will feel more co-operative then," she added with more than a tinge of satisfaction.

Bollyngton just continued his annoying little smile by way of reply.

Clearly she would get no information from him and Ghislaine glared at him in frustration. There was naught she could do. As she left the room with an angry swish of her skirts, she thought his attitude was most odd for a man facing certain death. He was calm, cool and very at ease. It was almost as if he did not think anything was going to happen to him at all.

Somehow, there was a nagging feeling that something was not right. Ghislaine left the keep with much on her mind.

Chapter Sixteen

"My lady?"

The guard's voice broke into her thoughts as Ghislaine sat before the fire in the great hall. In the few hours that Guy had been gone, she had been puzzling over Thomas Bollyngton. As night drew in, nothing made sense and the uneven stitches in the hem she was attempting to sew bore witness to her poor concentration. Even the patient priest had been driven by her lack of conversation to take refuge in an alcove off the hall for private reflection. And she felt very vulnerable at the manor. Guy had taken his best fighting men and had even had the gall to commandeer Edwin. A weakened Sir Arnaud and a nervous Sir Brian were not a great deal of comfort. She stabbed at the linen in frustration.

"Sir Walter de Belleme is here on the Earl's business and requests entry."

Ghislaine's hand froze at the mention of his name. Sweet mercy, the man was here. At least Guy was safely on his way to Chester.

"Is he alone?" she demanded, thankfully putting her sewing aside.

"There are five men with him bearing the arms of the Earl of Chester, my lady."

Ghislaine nodded. "Send him to me here and see that Sir Arnaud and Sir Brian are informed of his presence."

When Walter de Belleme strode through the hall doors, Ghislaine had managed to compose her thoughts. Her trembling fingers remained firmly behind her back.

Searching his handsome face for clues as to his thoughts or suspicions, Ghislaine saw nothing there to alarm her. His grey eyes shone warmly as he greeted her and his smile seemed truly genuine.

"Lady Ghislaine. I am pleased to find you at home."

The tone of his voice was friendly and confident.

"Sir Walter. You are always welcome here." She smiled back as sweetly as her fluttering stomach would allow. "But I believe you are here on behalf of Earl Hugh?"

Walter advanced to the fire, tossing his thick green cloak onto the table as he went. Ghislaine noticed the fur trim on his beautifully made tunic and the handsome leather boots he sported. Indeed, the man lavished large sums of money on himself, it seemed. He accepted the proffered goblet of wine with a smile.

"Indeed I am. We are to escort the captured outlaw to Chester whilst your husband forays north to settle a dispute with one of the Earl's more truculent vassals."

"North?" exclaimed Ghislaine. "Why, I had the

impression that Guy was destined for the Welsh hills.''
As soon as she spoke the words, she wished them
undone.

"You must have been misinformed, Lady Ghislaine,'' he replied smoothly. But she did not miss the
nervous glance he shot around the room nor the slight
faltering of his smile. She must tread carefully if she
was to find out what scheme he had concocted. Nor
must she underestimate him.

"Aye. Most likely I paid little enough attention. I
find all this talk of keeps and strategy somewhat te-
dious.'' She smiled self-consciously and even managed a faint blush.

Walter relaxed a little and moved closer to Ghislaine. "Indeed, my lady. It must be a sore trial to you,
having so bloodthirsty an oaf as de Courcy for husband.'' His eyes held hers for a fleeting second.

Ghislaine sighed and shrugged her shoulders de-
spairingly. "I confess my life has changed greatly
since my marriage, Sir Walter. I had never envisaged
it so.'' No one could accuse her of falsehoods there.
"My husband and I do not always see eye to eye. It
has led to…misunderstandings and disagreements.''
Ghislaine allowed her eyes to remain cast towards the
floor, giving the impression, she hoped, of trying to
hide something far more intolerable.

Walter took her hand. "My lady,'' he murmured.
"I have offered you help before. Are you minded to
accept it now?'' His eyes looked into hers with concern.

Ghislaine took a deep breath. "You risk much, Sir
Walter,'' she whispered, a blush staining her cheeks.
"I have no desire to see you in danger for my sake.''

Walter smiled seductively, his grey eyes warm with anticipation. "There is little danger for me, Ghislaine. But I would willingly take a risk to ensure your happiness."

Ghislaine widened her eyes in disbelief. "I could not ask it of you, Sir Walter. My husband is a jealous man who would stop at nothing to protect what is his, no matter whether he truly wants it or not."

"If your husband were to…disappear, Lady Ghislaine, what would you do?" Walter stepped closer so that she could smell the rosemary in his clothes.

Ghislaine turned to face the fire. "Why, I don't know for sure, Sir Walter." She hesitated in a coy gesture that she hoped would find its mark. "There is always the abbey for women such as I. It has long been my desire to do so."

Walter remained still for a few moments and did not speak until Ghislaine turned back to face him. His face betrayed nothing. "It can be arranged for now at least," he stated finally. "Aye, that's a good plan."

Ghislaine's whole body went rigid with fear. "How so?" she asked, her voice almost a whisper. "My husband has ordered me to remain here. I dare not disobey him for he can be so…brutal in his displeasure." She shuddered with great effect.

"Leave it to me," he replied, gazing at her worried face with an expression of studied calm. Had he always schooled his thoughts so, Ghislaine wondered? If he was going to be this cool, how on earth was she to find out his plan for Guy?

Her thoughts were interrupted by the arrival of Sir Arnaud.

"I apologise for the delay, Lady Ghislaine, but Sir Brian has just left to take care of a fire in the village."

"Is it serious?" she demanded, her voice full of alarm.

"We do not know. The guard reported seeing flames and the villagers do not appear to have put it out yet. Sir Brian rode out with some men to see what they can do."

Ghislaine nodded. "Keep me informed, Sir Arnaud. Have any homeless villagers housed in the keep for the night. We have plenty of food and blankets."

Sir Arnaud inclined his head in assent but continued to stare at Sir Walter with undisguised interest. "Sir Walter. Your presence here is most…reassuring." Did Ghislaine only imagine that second's hesitation? "You are here to escort the outlaws I assume? We did not expect you until the morrow."

Walter stiffened but when he replied, his voice was bland. "That is so, Sir Arnaud. The Earl decided we should arrive earlier in case of treachery." He paused a moment, as if suddenly struck by a suspicious thought. "If there is trouble, then I believe I must take them without delay."

Sir Arnaud pulled his brows together in a suspicious frown and glanced at the five men Walter had brought with him. They stood perfectly still at the far end of the hall, their hands at their sides, awaiting orders. He rubbed his hand over his chin thoughtfully before appearing to come to a decision. "You are right. I'll have the outlaws taken to the bailey and you will be escorted past the village."

So saying, Sir Arnaud turned on his heels and left

Ghislaine and Walter staring after him. The faint smile playing on his lips was most unnerving.

Ghislaine shot Walter an apprehensive look. "What now?" she asked quietly.

His gaze, which had rested on the worn tapestries adorning the hall, shifted back to Ghislaine. "I shall take you with me."

Ghislaine swallowed hard. "But I said I wished to go to the abbey, Sir Walter." Her voice sounded determined despite the seesawing of her stomach. "Is there a problem with that?"

His eyes flicked over her flushed face. "Not at all. I intend to return to Chester via the abbey. Your safety is paramount and I cannot leave you to such despicable treatment a moment longer." Walter's eyes roamed over her face almost tenderly. "You must know that I once entertained hope of your hand, Lady Ghislaine, and I would like to think that we could both be very happy, should your husband die." His gloved hand reached out and gently touched a red-gold braid. "You are different to most of the other women I know."

Ghislaine was so dazed by this unexpected confession that for a brief second she believed he was serious. "Is that good?" she asked, unconsciously echoing a question that Guy had put to her only hours before.

Walter's skin flushed a little as if he suddenly realised what he had been saying. "I wish to be more than a friend to you, if you would allow it." His hands started to delve into a leather pouch hanging from his belt. "Perhaps you would wear this as a testimony to our friendship? It would give me great pleasure to think of you wearing it.''

Ghislaine stared at the delicately pretty gold crucifix decorated with pearls. It shone with a red glow in the firelight and Ghislaine took it from him to examine it more closely. Something about the crucifix looked familiar, but she could not place where she had seen it before.

"It is beautiful," she murmured as she placed it round her neck. "But you had no need to give me so valuable a gift. My friendship is freely given."

Walter smiled in the warm glow of his generosity. "It has been in my family for some time. Keep it close, Lady Ghislaine."

"You have my word."

"Good. Then I suggest we leave now."

His tone of voice did not brook dissension, but Ghislaine still had no idea as to what his plans were nor how to alert Sir Arnaud. Suddenly, from the corner of her eye, Ghislaine noticed the tiniest of movements behind a curtain covering the alcove. For a second she deemed it most odd that whoever was behind there had not emerged before now, but before she could say aught, she realised who it was. Father John! He had been there all along.

A wave of cold fear washed over her. Perhaps the reason why Father John had not identified himself before was because he had heard what was going on. She looked down at the crucifix. Margaret had worn one just like this. Ghislaine closed her eyes, fear seeping through every bone. He had to know the killer. Walter had to know. He had given her a vital piece of evidence to wear around her neck and only she would be able to say who gave it to her. Unless, of course, she were dead.

Her stomach lurched as she took a few steps closer to the curtain. Maybe Father John could help her.

"What am I supposed to tell Sir Arnaud?" she babbled nervously to Walter. "I cannot just leave without a word." Her eyes pleaded with him.

Walter thought for a minute. "Tell him you believe that de Courcy murdered Margaret Staveley and that you can no longer bear living with him. You intend to make the abbey your refuge until the matter is resolved to your satisfaction. With me as an escort and so few men here, Sir Arnaud is not in any position to prevent you."

Ghislaine went quite still. It made sense, and it was well known that they had argued about her going to the convent. Guy had made no secret of it. "You are right, Sir Walter. I doubt if Sir Arnaud will prevent me from leaving. My cloak is in the bedchamber. I will just fetch it."

Somehow she had to let Sir Arnaud know the truth and warn Guy that he may be walking into a trap.

"No." Walter's voice sounded almost irritated. "I will fetch it." This was not an offer, it was a command. Not wishing to make him suspicious nor angry, Ghislaine acceded gracefully.

Sir Walter returned with her cloak within a few minutes, but she could not help but think it odd that he would wish to collect it himself. He had never shown the slightest inclination before to fetch and carry. Perhaps he was already suspicious of her.

The bailey was lit by several torches, but Ghislaine could see how few of Guy's men were left to guard the manor. Were she to cry out now, it would be to no avail. Walter would kill her and escape with little difficulty. Her best ploy would be to try to escape in the dark. Guy's hunting knife lay safely hidden under the folds of her skirt and she would use it if necessary.

"Do you leave too, Lady Ghislaine?" Sir Arnaud's voice sounded harsh and accusing.

Ghislalne turned to face him, the cold night air making her shiver. "Sir Walter has kindly agreed to escort me to the abbey. I have decided I can no longer continue to remain under the same roof as a murderer such as Guy de Courcy."

"I see. You would run like a coward, lady? I had not thought it of you." His contempt for her shone in his eyes.

Ghislaine gritted her teeth. He was not going to make this easy for her. "He would not let me go." Her eyes held his, trying desperately to convey the message. "I really have no choice."

"You do him an injustice, lady. Guy de Courcy is a fair man. I thought you gave him your word you would do nothing in his absence."

"A desperate woman will say or do anything if she has to, Sir Arnaud." She did not move, her whole body trying to tell him of the danger, but his face told her what he thought of her.

"I will have your horse saddled, lady." He whirled round and barked the order.

Surrounded by outlaws and the escort, Ghislaine felt most uncomfortable as the party skirted to the left of the village. Flames still licked at one thatch, and she could hear the shouts of the people as they tried to douse the fire. Walter urged the riders on and they soon left the noise and the acrid smell behind. Sir Arnaud's escort remained at the village boundary without any clear sign of suspicion.

The dark closed in on them as they headed south for the abbey. Strange noises emerged from the unfamiliar world of the night, and Ghislaine gritted her teeth to stop them from chattering in fear.

At one point, Ghislaine was certain she could hear the sound of horses and her heart lifted. There was a slim chance that Guy had turned back and was now on her trail. But it was soon clear that this was a false hope for the sounds died away.

Beyond the meagre light of the torches, she could see very little. It was difficult to tell where they were exactly, for she had been aware for some time that they had been taking odd turns in the road. Walter kept turning to look behind them to see if they had been followed, but so far he had spotted nothing.

"Do you fear attack, Sir Walter?" she asked. His agitation had not lessened.

Walter looked at her and then at Thomas Bollyngton. "There's no telling if his friends will try to rescue him. I doubt that they will have realised yet that he is gone from Chapmonswiche, but with the fire in the village, it is best to be wary."

Ghislaine looked over at the outlaw who was riding just ahead of her. His expression was still calm. It was almost as if he was out on a pleasant ride. His four companions, likewise, did not seem unduly perturbed by their nocturnal exercise. It did seem odd that there were only six men to escort five brutal outlaws.

Her alarm grew as they veered off the track and headed for the edges of the forest.

"Where are we going?" she demanded as Walter picked up her reins.

"We will have better cover in the forest, Lady Ghislaine." His voice was confident.

"But that would be the perfect place for an ambush," she exclaimed nervously. "And we are heading away from the abbey."

Walter did not reply, but kicked his horse on, pulling her behind him. Escape was impossible for she was surrounded by outlaws and escorts, and Walter had a tight grip on her reins. Were she to fall off her horse, she would be trampled underfoot by the others. A deathly fear washed over her. She was going to die.

They had not gone far when Walter drew to a halt in a small clearing. She could hear running water not far away. All around her loomed the tall, black shapes of the forest trees.

"Why have we stopped?" Panic finally hit Ghislaine as Walter strode purposefully towards her. "Is there a problem?" she asked, frantically thinking of anything that could give her a way out.

"No." He held his hands up to her. Wordlessly, she slid into his arms, her heart thundering.

"Will you explain why we are here?" she demanded defiantly. If she was going to die, she was going to do it as a de Launay should. And a de Courcy, she remembered belatedly.

Walter looked at her for a moment. "In good time, Ghislaine." He then turned and indicated that the others should dismount. Nervously Ghislaine glanced at them. The outlaws were rough men who looked as though they had spent a lifetime attacking innocent travellers. As she surveyed the escort they seemed little better.

Her mouth went dry. She had to find out from Walter what was going on. And whatever happened to her in the end, she suddenly found that she did not want Guy de Courcy to think that she had betrayed him. For the moment, silence was probably the best she could do.

Sitting on a fallen log, she was able to watch the others more carefully. Whilst his men were overseeing the outlaws, Walter had walked to the edge of the clearing, distancing himself from everyone else. Sensing the alertness in his still body, Ghislaine held her breath. Was he waiting for someone, or something to happen? After a minute or two, Walter seemed to relax and turned back towards the group. Breathing once more, Ghislaine shivered with the cold and fear. At that moment, she would have given anything to see her scowling husband and his band of marauding oafs. Ruefully reminding herself of the number of times she had wished them to the devil, Ghislaine quickly wiped the brightness from her eyes.

A heavy sigh caused her to look up suddenly. Walter was staring down at her, his face grave.

''You are going to kill me,'' she stated flatly. It was not really a question.

She could see him debating whether or not to tell her the truth. ''Honesty is best,'' he began quietly. ''And I have no wish to insult your intelligence. Believe me when I tell you how sorry I am, Ghislaine.''

Ghislaine stared up at him, every bone in her body

shaking with fear. Would he do it right away? "Why? At least tell me why?" Her eyes were round with fear.

Walter turned swiftly to cast a quick glance in the direction of Thomas Bollyngton before carefully arranging his cloak on the soft ground and sitting down.

"I doubt if I should tell you, but in all conscience, I find that I wish to."

"That is most…considerate, Sir Walter."

Her provoking words caused his mouth to twitch in irritation. "It is not necessary," he warned.

"I shall try to curb my tongue henceforth," she replied quietly. "Please explain."

Despite the first spots of rain, Walter did not move. "I am," he announced, "a man of taste. I desire fine clothes, a beautiful home, good food and wine. Such things require a great deal more money than I had, but after a while, I realised that there were other ways of earning the sort of money I needed."

Ghislaine stared at him unblinkingly, desperately trying to keep from throwing up all over him. "Such as?"

"Oh, at first it was only on a small scale. Working for the Earl brought me into contact with a great many undesirable people. I found ways of forcing them into giving me a share of their earnings. It wasn't until later that I realised how much more could be done."

At her questioning look, Walter stared at his hands. "I am not a man who enjoys physical violence, you understand, but I do have my wits. Teaming up with an outlaw, for instance, was the perfect solution." He glanced at Bollyngton, who lounged a little way off.

Ghislaine's mind whirled with this information. He had been very clever. No wonder Bollyngton had survived so long and so well. "What will you do with him now?"

Walter breathed in deeply and shrugged his shoulders. "I have not decided yet," he replied cautiously.

"So," Ghislaine thought aloud. "You visited Chapmonswiche so frequently because it offered you the perfect cover for clandestine meetings in the forest. How foolish and naïve I must have seemed." Ghislaine gave a self-conscious laugh.

"Actually, I quite enjoyed my visits with you. But, as you say, there was a purpose. Indeed, I had considered marriage with you."

"So that was not my imagination?"

"Not until your father became suspicious."

Ghislaine's head snapped up. "It was you!" she accused. "You killed him?"

Walter's face was just a pale blur in the darkness and she could not make out his expression. "He followed me. I was unusually careless, unfortunately, and your father was a quick man. When he saw me with Bollyngton and his men, he drew the correct conclusion. To my immense good luck, he decided to challenge me. That was his mistake."

"And you killed Peter Staveley," she added thoughtfully. Then her blood ran cold. "But Margaret? Why in God's name did you have to kill Margaret too?"

Walter was silent for a moment, considering his words. "She was a rich widow. Like you, she lived close to the forest, but unlike you, sweet Ghislaine, she did not ask so many questions."

"I still do not understand."

"I had not banked on her sense of honour," he

remarked slowly. "Apparently, she was aware that you were expecting an offer from me." He sighed. "There was every chance that she would tell you what had happened. Her death was…unfortunate."

"You are a monster," she whispered. "I trusted you, and you betrayed my trust to your own ends."

"In the beginning," he replied quietly. "But I admit to a fondness for you, Ghislaine. I had hoped that I might have been able to persuade you to help me. Unfortunately, you have a righteous streak like your father. Like him, it will be the cause of your own undoing."

Ghislaine remained paralysed with fear, anger and misery. "You will not escape this," she hissed vehemently.

Walter laughed softly. "Your naïvety astounds me, Ghislaine. The Earl may well have been aware of my…activities for some time. He chose, however, to ignore them. I am sure that he has other plans for me. Those for your husband, however, will be short-lived."

"What have you planned for him?" she asked, her heart thudding loudly.

"The message to go to Chester was false, of course. He will have been ambushed by Henry Dettingham along the way. Any minute now, I expect to have news of his capture."

"He will not be killed?"

Walter shook his head. "I need him to be proven guilty of the crime of murdering Margaret beyond a shadow of a doubt. Your contribution will be invaluable."

Ghislaine looked down at the crucifix. "I could not

live with him for murdering my friend, so I intended to retire to the abbey. Unfortunately, my untimely death on the way prevents me being able to corroborate any defence he may bring.''

The blond curls of her captor nodded. ''More or less. I also took the liberty of placing some of Margaret's jewels and valuables about your bedchamber.''

''And Guy will be unable to refute any of this,'' she added quietly.

''The Earl will not be able to ignore a direct order from the King. Henry Dettingham will bay for justice. I have no doubt that the Court of Eyrie will dispense the correct punishment.''

''And what do you get out of all this?'' she demanded in disgust.

He shrugged his shoulders. ''Dettingham will allow me your manor and a share of your husband's treasure in return for granting him his revenge.'' He smiled bleakly. ''Honest people are so depressingly naïve.''

''You will rot in hell for this, Walter,'' she spat.

At that moment, Walter stood up abruptly. He held his hand up to her, indicating that she should remain silent. Ghislaine could hear nothing odd but sensed, as Walter did, that something had changed.

''De Belleme,'' growled the coarse voice of Thomas Bollyngton. ''Cut me loose.''

Ghislaine swirled round to see the outlaw approach, an angry expression on his ugly face. Walter stared at him silently, weighing up his options. Suddenly, Ghislaine realised what he was planning. If he was expecting reinforcements then he would have no difficulty killing Bollyngton and blaming her death on him. On the other hand, the others had not yet arrived and Walter was simply biding his time. An idea formed from her desperate thoughts.

"Loose?" she repeated with a puzzled expression. "You told me you would kill him!" Ghislaine turned on Walter with an accusing look. "We don't need him now."

The look of shock and then anger on Walter's face would have given her a great deal of satisfaction at any other time, but she was petrified that he would kill her before she had a chance to do anything else.

"Hold your tongue, you lying bitch," he hissed. But the outlaw had clearly been harbouring enough doubts of his own to give her words some credence.

"Then cut me loose now," he demanded angrily.

Realising he was cornered, Walter fought back. "If they send the guards back to check on us, we'll never survive. Think, man. Wait until they arrive."

Bollyngton glared at him, clearly unconvinced by Walter's explanation but unable to do much about it. With a snort of defiance, he slumped down at Ghislaine's side.

Her eyes slid over the surly face of the outlaw and decided he had no real liking for Walter de Belleme. His anger was growing by the minute and Ghislaine could see the tension in his body. Did he hate him enough to kill him?

A steady thud of hoofbeats reached their ears and Walter jumped up. This would be her only chance, she realised. Once Dettingham arrived, she would die.

Whilst Walter was giving orders to the escort, she slid the hunting knife from under her skirts and edged towards Thomas Bollyngton. His face was no more than a pale smudge in the dark, but Ghislaine could see his eyes glittering with comprehension. It was but the work of a few seconds to cut the binding round his wrists, although it had felt like a thousand years. Her hands shook with fear until finally it sliced free. The outlaw's thick fingers curled around the knife.

As the sounds beyond the clearing grew louder, Bollyngton launched himself at Walter with the silent stealth of a practised killer. Her legs would not move as the two men rolled in the mud, fighting for their lives. Suddenly her mind cleared and Ghislaine pulled herself to her feet. She had to get to the shelter of the forest.

A piercing, animal-like scream rent the air. Turning to see what had happened, Ghislaine saw the outlaw fall to his knees, his fists clenched round his stomach. Walter was staggering to his feet, looking wildly for her. Dread surged through her body as she tried to scramble to the safety of the trees. A second more and she would have made it.

As his hands closed around her ankle, Ghislaine fell head first into the mud. Furiously kicking, Ghislaine twisted round and attempted to pull herself to her feet, but he pulled her back down.

"I had meant to do this in your sleep, you stupid wench," he ground out. Transferring her gaze from Walter's angry face to the knife he held at her breast, Ghislaine's hope for a reprieve died.

"Ghislaine!"

Both of them turned at the same time. It was not Dettingham. Walter threw her back to the ground and lurched to his feet, but Ghislaine, realising that he would escape, clung on to his belt.

"Let go of me, you stupid bitch," he shouted frantically. Ghislaine tried to protect herself from his kicks and blows as best she could, pain dulling her senses. Somehow she hung on until she felt the blade in the back of her shoulder. Amid shouts and the grating sounds of swords clashing, Ghislaine slipped into a world of pain and darkness.

Chapter Seventeen

Each time the bells rang her head threatened to explode. When the deep thudding did not abate, Ghislaine attempted to open her eyes. Bright, piercing light flooded her vision, and she blinked hard, raising her hand to allow herself some small respite.

"Ghislaine? Can you hear me?" A low, melodious voice spoke softly near her ear, and she felt a cool, gentle hand on her brow.

"I don't want to hear anything," she croaked crossly. "I want to go to sleep but the bells and my head refuse to allow it."

"Well, I for one am pleased to hear it." The voice sounded amused and Ghislaine forced herself to sit up to try to see more easily. It was, however, a big mistake.

"Am I dead?" she groaned. "I feel as if I am." She was apparently lying in a bed.

"Very nearly," came the more serious reply. "We did not think you would survive at all."

"Survive?" Ghislaine forced her eyes open, but be-

yond the blinding light there were only shadows.
"Where am I?"

"At the abbey."

A cup of cold water was placed at her lips and Ghislaine sipped it warily. It tasted sweet and refreshing.
Moving her hand from her eyes, Ghislaine gingerly
peered at her companion. Gradually, as her eyes adjusted to the light, she was able to make out the shape
of a grey-haired woman.

"Helene? I... What are you doing here?" Ghislaine
pushed herself further up the pallet.

"Looking after you," came the reply. "With the
help of Effie and Hulda."

Ghislaine shook her head slightly in confusion. Why
on earth was she lying in a bed in the abbey with Effie,
Hulda and Helene du Beauregard to care for her? None
of this made any sense at all. All she knew was that
her head was throbbing and her body almost unable
to move with exhaustion.

"What did I survive?" She could see the look of
tired concern etched clearly on Helene's beautiful face
as she pulled the sheets into some sort of order.

"Do you remember anything?" Helene reached
over and put her hand on Ghislaine's forehead.

The blank look on Ghislaine's face was answer
enough.

"You were wounded in the shoulder with a knife.
Unfortunately fever set in, and we had a battle to bring
you back. Hulda has created every concoction known
to man. And a few more that aren't," she added in a
wry tone. Helene's deliberately light-hearted chattering slowed into silence as Ghislaine swayed. "I think

it would be best if you tried to sleep a little more. Drink some of this. It will help.''

Ghislaine wanted to refuse it, whatever it was, but the pain and tiredness suddenly overwhelmed her again and it was all she could do to lay her head back on the bolster and drift into oblivion for a while. Strange, half-remembered scenes of forests, knives and tortured screams invaded her memory until a blissful peace slowly billowed through her.

It was the smell of the pottage that woke her. Strong and spicy, the aroma wafted gently in to her room and lingered close to her nose. Unable to resist, Ghislaine forced her eyes to open. Relieved that her sight seemed to have returned without ill effect, Ghislaine hauled herself up a little. The effort caused her to slump back against the wall in exhaustion. Every bone in her body ached and her flesh was bruised and tender.

The room was spotlessly clean and gleamed white from the rays of the midday sun. Her eyes rested on the small window opposite in the bare white-washed wall. The wonderful smell must have come from there.

Casting her eyes about the rest of the room, Ghislaine noticed how oddly comfortable it was. A good fire crackled in the grate on the far side with a small stock of chopped logs piled to the left. Before it stood a comfortable chair covered in a gaily coloured blanket and several plump cushions. Open-mouthed, Ghislaine stared at the tapestry covering the cold floor stones. It hardly resembled the spartan rooms at any abbey she had known.

Running her fingers over the exotic red and gold covering on the bed, Ghislaine wondered why, amid

all this finery, she felt so heartsore. Despite the warmth
and the colour in the room a bleak sadness drifted
around her that seemed inescapable.

The sound of quick footsteps outside her door
caused her to look up expectantly.

"My lady!" exclaimed Effie loudly as she hurried
to the bed. Her plump face was wreathed in smiles as
she felt Ghislaine's forehead. "The fever seems to
have gone right enough. I'll go fetch Lady Helene."
With a quick reassuring smile back at her charge, Effie
bustled out again, leaving Ghislaine bemused.

A few moments later, Helene appeared with a large
bowl of steaming pottage in her hands.

"You probably won't feel like eating much," she
announced as she sat down on the pallet, "but you
need to build up some of your strength."

The smell was even better than she had imagined
and Ghislaine's mouth watered. "Is there only one
bowl?" she asked as Helene held out a spoonful to
her lips.

"My son told me about your love of food," the
older woman replied dryly.

"Your son?" questioned Ghislaine as she savoured
the wonderful flavour of the pottage.

"Guy," came the reply.

Ghislaine stared at her. "Guy de Courcy is your
son?" As Helene merely nodded and held out another
spoonful, Ghislaine's mind cranked slowly into
thought. "Does he know?"

Helene retracted the uneaten spoonful and looked
back at Ghislaine. "He has always known but understandably refuses to admit it," she said simply, and
offered the food again.

Ghislaine gulped it down, remembering Sir Arnaud's tale of Guy's parents. "Why did you leave your husband?" she asked, wondering why anyone would leave four sons and a home for a life of exclusion and scorn.

Helene continued to feed pottage to Ghislaine slowly, her mind reliving the scenes and the thoughts that had propelled her into closing the door on her old life. "I was a foolish, young girl who yearned to be loved and needed by a cold, harsh man. My husband viewed me solely as a vessel for more heirs as well as a source of income," she said bitterly. "I was offered the chance of a different life by someone who showed me a world of love and need."

"Was it worth it?" Ghislaine demanded, feeling anger on Guy's behalf. And yet lurking behind the anger, Ghislaine knew that those were the very reasons she had not wanted to stay with Guy.

"I have many regrets of course," she paused. "My lover died and I was forced to survive as best I could. I found protection with a succession of knights, some worse than others. My sons would have suffered far more than I did, had I taken them," she said finally. For a brief moment, Helene's face reflected the pain and the torment she had endured, and then the expression vanished, replaced by the familiar concern she had shown to Ghislaine.

"But God has seen fit to punish me in his own way. There were no more children and I pined for those I had left. Especially Guy." Her fingers traced the intricate pattern on the bedcover. "I have not much time left on this earth and I choose to be near him now. Watching over your manor was but a small thing."

Glancing up at Ghislaine, Helene squeezed her hand gently. "The fact that he came himself to ask me to tend you has given me much joy."

"He did?" Ghislaine was suddenly struck by the importance of those words. "He is alive?"

Helene offered her more pottage. "He brought you here himself."

Despite the warmth of the room, a sudden chill descended on Ghislaine's leaping heart. He had survived the ambush after all, but her gladness was tempered by the fact that the first thing he had done was bring her to the abbey. As he said he always would.

"He was not injured?" she asked, wondering what had happened.

Helene shook her head and pushed the spoon closer to Ghislaine's mouth. "Not physically," she replied absently. "But in the last two weeks, his spirits have been very low. He blames himself for your injuries."

Ghislaine frowned. "I...I don't understand," she began. "How is he responsible? It was Walter..."

Helene eyed her patient with concern. Placing the unwanted pottage on the floor, she turned back to plump up the bolster and make her more comfortable.

"If I have the story right, it would seem that when he received the command from the Earl, Guy suspected that it was a trick. He made a show of leaving in force, but sent your Edwin with some men to hide along the track and return to your manor later. When Walter appeared, demanding the outlaws, Arnaud sent word to Edwin. He trailed Walter and then attacked when he heard screaming. Guy managed to outwit Dettingham and followed Edwin. Unfortunately, they arrived too late to save you from injury."

''I heard the horses coming,'' Ghislaine remembered.

''Guy blames himself for allowing you to be caught up in the attack. Apparently he did not believe you would go with Walter.'' Helene watched Ghislaine's stricken expression.

''I wanted to find out what he planned to do with Guy,'' she whispered. ''There was nothing else I could do.''

''It would seem that Guy greatly underestimated your courage.'' Helene smiled at her warmly and squeezed her hand. ''If it is any small comfort, he has been greatly distressed by your illness. In fact, when there seemed little hope, I actually saw him pray in the chapel.''

Ghislaine stilled at those words, remembering something else. ''Father John! He can prove Guy's innocence.'' She grabbed Helene's sleeve. ''You must find Father John.''

''Ah, yes. It was Father John who was able to tell Arnaud where Walter was taking you. Fortunately the men I had sent to watch your manor reported the activity and I despatched some soldiers to help. When Dettingham finally realised he had been duped, he came back to the manor in search of Guy. My men persuaded him to wait patiently. Guy's name has been cleared of guilt these past two weeks. Dettingham was allowed his revenge on de Belleme.''

Helene's soothing words were intended to calm Ghislaine but they heralded the end of Guy's need of her. He had placed her in the abbey because that was where he wanted her.

''Two weeks?''

"Aye," replied Helene. "You have been very ill and much has happened."

"Has…has my husband been to see me?" she asked wretchedly, knowing the reply, but wanting to hear the words. It would make it easier.

"Every day. I was much struck with the change in him," she added, watching Ghislaine's pale face speculatively.

"Change?" murmured Ghislaine. "What change?"

"He smelled so nice," Helene announced rather proudly. "He was also clean, well fed and handsome."

Ghislaine smiled shakily at that, but, to her horror, tears suddenly began to pour down her cheeks.

"Ghislaine, my dear! Whatever have I said?"

"Nothing. I'm being stupid," she replied tearfully, attempting to wipe them away with the back of her hand.

"Not as stupid as my son, I think," said Helene, handing her a rag.

"What do you mean?" Ghislaine dabbed at the tears.

"I have no idea why you are here and not at home in your own bed. His wits were clearly lacking for he said something about you preferring to be here."

That brought a fresh wave of tears to her eyes and it was several moments before Ghislaine was able to talk again.

"I did say that," she mumbled in between sniffs.

Helene stared at her in astonishment.

"But I didn't really mean it," Ghislaine continued miserably. "I thought it would make him happier."

Understanding suddenly dawned on Helene. "I

think you had better explain,'' she said kindly. ''You may be in need of further maternal advice.''

Ghislaine eyed her somewhat warily, but in truth she had sore need of telling someone how miserable she felt. After much prompting, she told Helene as much of the story as she could.

''Well. It seems that the pair of you have been a little foolish, but I am well aware how cold my son can be.''

Ghislaine's questioning look prompted Helene to sigh. ''He has much of his father in him.''

''That is so reassuring,'' came the muffled reply.

''The difference lies in the way he looks at you,'' Helene continued. ''If my husband had looked at me in the same way, I would not have left.''

''What way?'' This made no sense.

Helene just laughed. ''Rest now, Ghislaine. You are still very weak. Effie will stay with you since I have to leave for a little while.'' She gave her a reassuring smile. ''I want you looking your best for tomorrow, Ghislaine. Promise me?''

Ghislaine nodded wordlessly. She did feel better for talking, but it had not made the problem go away. Helene's suggestion of sleep suddenly seemed very attractive. ''I promise,'' she muttered, closing her eyes, but wondering what was so special about tomorrow.

The next morning, Ghislaine was badgered into breaking her fast with fresh bread and honey by a tyrannical Effie. When she had at last eaten to Effie's satisfaction, she was ordered into a tub of steaming water. Her body was scrubbed clean and her hair washed until Ghislaine wondered if there would be any left.

Sweet-smelling oil was rubbed into her tired and aching limbs and Ghislaine felt a sense of languorous well-being creep through her body. As she sat resting before the fire drying her hair, Effie cleaned and dressed the wound in her shoulder. To complete the transformation, she handed Ghislaine a new night-rail.

Ghislaine stared at the garment in wonder. The linen was the softest she had ever felt, and the sleeves and collar were trimmed with pretty lace and ribbon.

"It's lovely," she breathed, holding it to her. "And it fits!"

"Of course it fits," scoffed Effie. "Your husband had it made for you."

Ghislaine stilled. "He had it made for me," she repeated disbelievingly. "When?"

"Whilst you were ill." Effie smiled. "He was that concerned that you should have lots of gowns and pretty things," she confided. "He had five seamstresses come from Chester to make up all that cloth Kalim brought. He asked Lady Helene's advice."

Effie crossed the room to the chest at the side of the bed. "Look, my lady. He sent them as soon as they were ready."

Effie was right, realised a dumbfounded Ghislaine. One by one she took out the beautiful gowns, petticoats, surcoats, cloaks and underwear, taking care to spread them on the bed. The array was breathtaking, it was all so fine. The materials were gorgeous: embroidered silks, brocaded velvets, finest wools, and some she really had no idea about at all. The instant she saw them, she knew they would suit her colouring:

golds, emerald-greens, peacock-blues, pewter-grey. Ghislaine closed her eyes. He was making it very difficult for her.

"None of this is suitable for the abbey," she said as calmly as she could.

"I don't think so either," replied Effie doubtfully. "But then he was that upset, he wasn't thinking straight," she added quietly.

Ghislaine stared longingly at the gowns. They were beautiful, truly beautiful, and no one had ever given her anything so lovely. But she had no right to any of it.

She sighed heavily and then looked up at Effie who tried hard to quickly mask a very miserable expression. "You never know, Effie. With me in the abbey, you might have more time to persuade Edwin to take pity on you?"

Effie's eyes welled up. "He's gone. Sir Guy asked him what he wanted as a reward for saving you and he took his freedom. Said you didn't need him here any more."

Ghislaine felt numb. Edwin had always been there. "Where has he gone?" Her face was as stricken as Effie's.

"He went in search of his family's killers, he said." Effie subsided into muffled sobbing.

Memories of another lifetime flooded Ghislaine's mind. When they were young, he had always vowed he would search for them and take his revenge. Now Guy had given him that chance.

"He'll be back, Effie," she said quietly. All she could think of was that even Edwin had deserted her.

A knock at the door sent her quickly to her bed whilst Effie went to see who it was.

"Father John!" Ghislaine exclaimed, pleased to see him.

Effie bobbed a curtsey and took the opportunity to escape and find a quiet corner to nurse her sorrows in.

"I hear the fever has passed, Lady Ghislaine," he smiled, sitting at the end of the pallet.

Ghislaine returned his smile. "I believe I have you to thank for the fact that my injuries were as slight as they were."

"You are too kind," he stammered, blushing with pleasure. "I did what I thought was best."

"Aye, you did." Ghislaine's smile faded. "And is your soul at peace now?"

The briefest of smiles touched the friar's lips. "In a way." He lifted his hands in a despairing gesture that she understood. "I think it will take time for me to forgive myself."

"We are often our own harshest critics, Father, but I am most grateful for your intervention." Ghislaine reached out to touch his arm.

The priest placed his long, knotted fingers over hers in an act of friendship. "I am pleased to tell you that your husband has also shown the extent of his generosity."

When Ghislaine raised her eyebrows in enquiry, the friar's face fell. "I hope I have not betrayed a confidence," he frowned.

"Generous?" Ghislaine inclined her head in confusion. "Just how generous has he been?"

"He has donated enough to rebuild the kitchens. It is his belief, apparently, that those spending their lives following the path of goodness deserve a good meal at the end of the day. It was an odd thing to bestow, but we are grateful, of course.''

Ghislaine stared at him wildly for a moment before the amusement bubbled to the surface. ''My husband has a sense of humour, too,'' she laughed.

''Your husband is essentially a good man, Lady Ghislaine. He has, however, found your illness a sore trial, and, I believe, that there will be many at Chapmonswiche who will be singularly grateful for your early return.''

''I... That is, I am sure that my husband expects me to stay at the abbey, Father John.'' Her expression spoke volumes despite her attempted cheerfulness.

''If it helps,'' he began kindly, ''your husband was almost beside himself when he found out you were so badly injured. He insisted on carrying you himself and he spent the first two days here with you. He did not leave your side.''

Father John looked across at her tight-lipped expression speculatively. ''There is something else that I should not in my capacity as a priest divulge. But I am sure that God would perhaps understand. We spoke at length about your desire to go to the abbey. Your husband was under the impression that you wished to go there to escape him and several times stated—most convincingly—that you had no true vocation. He also showed a great interest in when exactly I told you he was not the man who murdered Margaret.''

Ghislaine must have looked perplexed, so he hastened to enlighten her. ''It was not until after...Kalim had left.''

Understanding dawned and Ghislaine blushed.

Whatever she was about to say was interrupted by the arrival of a very flustered Effie.

"It's him!" she shrieked. "He's come for you. The abbey is surrounded."

Closing her eyes, Ghislaine tried to blot out the lurching of her heart and the sudden excitement that was welling within her. She tried to tell herself to be calm, that he was just here to complete their "unfinished business' as he called it. When her eyes opened again, Effie was staring wildly at her, wringing her hands. Father John had rushed to the window and stood on a stool as he looked out.

"It's true," he confirmed quietly. Turning back to look at Ghislaine, he added, "And I think he's come to do more than talk to you."

Despite her outwardly calm appearance, Ghislaine's mind was frantically thinking of what she would say to him if she did see him. She loved him, but she could not stay with him if he did not want her. It would be far better to stay now. Far, far better.

The sound of heavy footsteps thudding along the corridor reminded Ghislaine of a similar occasion, just six weeks earlier. Only this time, she felt very different. Then she had been scared of a monster she did not know, who had been accused of murdering her friend, who had kidnapped her for his own ends and who scowled at the world. This time, she wanted to go with him.

As the wooden door banged open, Guy stormed in, filling the room with his presence.

"Out," he growled. Effie and Father John looked

towards Ghislaine in pity before scuttling from the tiny room.

"Helene du Beauregard said you wished to talk to me." His voice was almost a growl.

Cold blue eyes raked her with deliberate slowness as Ghislaine pulled the sheets closer to her chin. Determined not to show any sign of weakness, she lifted her head in defiance, tossing her hair back over her shoulder. The movement seemed to mesmerise him for a moment.

"Did she?" Ghislaine's voice was almost a whisper. What had the woman done?

"I am pleased to see that you are recovering," he said eventually.

It was hard to tear her eyes from him for he was looking so fine. The unruly, dark hair had been trimmed into order and the dark stubble normally thick on his chin had been barbered very carefully away. Somehow, he did not seem so very threatening.

"No small thanks to you, I believe." She was relieved to hear her voice sound almost cheerful.

Somewhat wrongfooted by the pleasant tone of voice he noted, Guy took a few steps forward. Casting his eyes about the room, his fingers flicked the cushions on the chair. "Have you been comfortable?"

Ghislaine smiled back a little self-consciously. "To be honest I have not really had much time to appreciate it. But I'm sure I will," she added quietly.

At those words, Guy immediately stiffened. "Not as much as you would wish, lady. You return with me this day or I will burn down the abbey."

All her good intentions dissipated at that threat. "You forgot to add that you'll have my people exiled," she railed, the sheet slipping in her anger. "Presumably you've had little opportunity for practising your threats since I've been ill."

His lips tightened to an angry line and his hand raked through his dark hair. "Your stay here has done little to improve your temper," he bit out between his teeth.

"I," she announced with icy superiority, "have been ill. What is your excuse?"

Guy glared at her with narrowed eyes before turning suddenly to stand before the fire. Ghislaine was left to stare at his back. "You betrayed my trust by leaving with Belleme."

"But I did not want to escape with him," she whispered. "He forced me to go and I demanded he take me to the abbey in the hope of finding out what he planned to do with you."

Guy stared at her, a look of disbelief on his face. "Will you return with me of your own free will, then," he asked suspiciously, "or do I drag you back?"

"Why?" she asked quietly. "Why do you want me back? I am pleased to hear that you are now a free man and can return to your old manor. What need have you of me?"

"I have no idea," he said crossly, turning to face her once more. "You eat huge amounts, you drink the cellars dry, you career across the county shooting the Earl's game and you have an abominable temper." He frowned darkly as Ghislaine stared at him, her mouth agape.

"Well, it seems to me that my particular accomplishments do not hold much appeal for you. I see little point in dragging me back for further abuse," she snapped.

She sounded so aggrieved by his description of her that Guy could not prevent a smile tugging at the corner of his lips. Walking over towards her, he sat down at her side. The harsh gaze was replaced by a softer, much warmer appraisal.

"Ghislaine, I have no desire to find another wife, I do assure you. My mother has been keen to extol your virtues to me, and in truth her arguments are sound. Nor," he added as an afterthought, "do I think I can persuade Joachim to leave with me. He is under the impression that he is the only one who can control Elfrieda's temper and she is adamant that her place is at Chapmonswiche. They have asked for permission to marry." He shook his head. "I think that finding another wife would be most troublesome to me."

"I thought you did not want a wife at all," she accused. The man was most vexing. "Your old way of life with Arnaud held more attraction. Now that your name is cleared, you are free to return to your old manor."

Guy's head lowered and he rubbed the back of his neck to ease the tension there. "Aye, well, I've become accustomed to you over the weeks," he allowed. He looked up at her. "Besides, my old manor no longer suits my purposes so well."

"It does not?" Ghislaine queried Her husband was a very changeable man.

Guy shook his head. "Dettingham petitioned the King so often that William was forced to make enquiries. Earl Hugh has suddenly shown himself right keen to reduce the number of outlaws in the area and felt I might be of help.'' He smiled briefly at his wife's perplexed expression. ''This will come as a shock to you, but your disreputable husband is now a very respectable shire reeve.''

He reached out and closed her mouth gently. ''Arnaud has gone to take charge of the other manor, and Sir Brian and I have come to a satisfactory working arrangement, but neither of us has proved up to managing the women very well. So you see, I have grave need of a wife.'' Pausing to take her hand, he added softly, ''There are other reasons, of course.''

He was sitting uncomfortably close, and Ghislaine was finding it increasingly difficult to remain calm with her hand in his.

''I know,'' she replied, desperately thinking of these other good reasons. ''You've had all those gowns made up at considerable expense and they are unlikely to suit anyone else.'' Ghislaine found it hard to look into those searching blue eyes.

''No. That's not the reason. Although,'' he added thoughtfully, ''I had not thought of that.''

Ghislaine noticed that his eyes kept straying to the top of her night gown. The sheet had slipped and she had forgotten how transparent her gown was. Glaring at him, she pulled the sheet back up. ''Lust will fade quickly,'' she replied confidently. ''And then you'll be left with a wife you no longer want.''

Guy was speechless for a moment. ''Is that what all this is about?'' he demanded, enlightenment spreading over his face.

Her chest heaving with indignation, Ghislaine turned on him. ''That may be all to you, Guy de

Courcy," she fired at him, "but I can assure you it is no small matter to me."

It took a minute for him to digest that information. "So," he said slowly, "you are confident that your own lust will not fade so quickly?" He raised an eyebrow in question.

Ghislaine blushed furiously at his words. "Nay," she said hoarsely. "I mean…yes… I…"

A finger gently lifted her chin and Ghislaine found herself looking into smiling blue eyes. "Perhaps you would care to tell me how long you think it might last." He was teasing her and she found his humour misplaced.

"I doubt, my lord, that it will last that long," she replied airily. "My duties at Chapmonswiche are so arduous now, with all those oafish men of yours forever creating work, that I am likely to drop dead within the year."

"Ah! But you are confident your desire will last a lifetime then?"

"Yes!" she snapped back, angry that he had forced such an admission from her. "But I fail…?"

Her words were stopped by Guy pulling her into his arms and kissing her with an intensity that fired her blood. Tearing his lips away, Guy placed his forehead on hers. "I swear to God, Ghislaine, that I never realised how much I loved you until I thought you would die. Marry me."

Ghislaine disentangled herself from his arms to face him. "You love me?" she whispered in disbelief. "Truly?"

"Aye. But don't ask me why, for it defeats me,"

he said curtly. He looked so disgruntled that she could not repress a chuckle.

"Well?" he prompted. "Will you marry me?"

"We're married already," she said, staring at him in confusion.

"I believe that I was somewhat despotic during the ceremony, and I have to admit thinking that you weren't putting your heart into your vows." The smile he gave her was almost boyish, and very convincing.

"I cannot fault your logic, Sir Guy," she said joyfully, not quite able to believe that this was true. "But I think I will accept your kind offer."

"Think? Perhaps you need some persuasion?" he offered, gathering her into his arms for another heart-warming kiss.

"And the terms of the marriage contract? Are they the usual ones?" Ghislaine turned dark, questioning eyes on him, whilst tracing the outline of his mouth with her fingers.

Guy merely nodded his head, distracted by her finger.

"Then I have an additional stipulation," she announced.

Guy stiffened slightly in her arms. "And what might that be?"

"That you practise your husbandly duties with greater frequency than you did during our last marriage."

Guy's smile was devastating. "You are naught but a saucy wanton sent to try my patience greatly, wench. And if I do not comply?"

"Then I shall have no choice but to send you to the

priory and search for a husband who possesses more natural charm.''

Guy laughed and pulled her back to him, proceeding to demonstrate thoroughly that he was keen to adhere to her demands.

* * * * *

Don't miss the next exciting volume in
MEDIEVAL LORDS & LADIES COLLECTION,
The War of the Roses.
Available in September 2007 from M&B™.